THE
VOYAGEUR

PAUL CARLUCCI

Swift

SWIFT PRESS

First published in Great Britain by Swift Press 2024

1 3 5 7 9 8 6 4 2

Copyright © Paul Carlucci 2024

The right of Paul Carlucci to be identified as the Author of this Work has been asserted in accordance with the Copyright, Designs and Patents Act 1988.

Text design and typesetting by Tetragon, London
Printed and bound in Great Britain by CPI Group (UK) Ltd, Croydon, CRO 4YY

A CIP catalogue record for this book is available from the British Library

ISBN: 9781800753150
eISBN: 9781800753167

To Jessica Murphy,
with infinite love.
Long may we coze.

CONTENTS

PART I
Dégagé

LATE SPRING, 1831

I

THE WHISPERING HAD STARTED A FEW DAYS BEFORE, BUT that morning, as the men clambered up the stony beach and blackflies besieged them, they spoke of him openly, and with anger. Serge had come down with consumption. He'd slept with dogs in the streets of Montréal and now the brigade would have to leave him behind before his condition spread, if it hadn't already, and tant pis, because the man was a dreamer and a sodomite and he was too old besides.

They'd left Lachine six weeks previous, about twenty men and an Algonquin woman who made their food and patched their boats and suffered their lechery. They brought their French into the wilderness and imagined it might cling to the rocks in the rivers and wash up on the banks as well. Their red toques were tattered, their sashes torn, and their canoes heavy with kegs of rum and barrels of gunpowder and many dozens of crates full of smaller items to trade for fur at Fort William. They carried as well a collection of axes and fiddles and blankets and rope. They'd already paddled four hours that morning and it was eight o'clock when they stopped for breakfast on the cliff-enclosed banks of the Rivière des Français.

There were rumours about Serge. He'd gained his spot on the brigade after beating an officer of the Hudson's Bay Company in poker, which seemed a plausible story because he'd brought two unsullied blankets with company stripes as well as several bottles of premium rum and he quietly refused to portage the heavy boats and the lighter ones too. He was slowing them down. They should've been at the fort by now, guzzling rum by the keg, but Serge carried only a dozen pounds of supplies at a time and never once did André l'avant take him to task for even the most outrageous lethargy or fatigue, and so upsetting was this double standard that soon there were angry rumours about André as well: he'd entered into a secret agreement with the company's senior officers, des angluches to the rotten last; he'd disavowed his Canadien heritage and would become a clerk once they returned to Montréal; he wasn't a leader at all, just another special case like Serge, and like Serge he'd bring them to a broken end.

Their third source of discontent was the boy. They were all sick of this boy, whose name was Alex. He'd come along with Serge like the older man's blistering cough and he'd been sullen and reluctant at La Pointe au Baptême, where all men new to the trade were soaked in the waters that flowed lazily past an enduring stone church, and since then he'd bothered them more and more. He was skinny and feeble and fragile, and they laughed at the little tufts of boyish beard that grew like windswept shrubs on his bony cheeks. They gave him only the worst servings of salt pork, pieces so tough and chewy he had to swallow them whole. They called him cul crevé right to his face and among themselves they agreed it was partly the boy's fault they'd let Serge's sickness settle so close, because the two had been sleeping together in a deerskin tent, not under les canots with the rest of the men, and so for a time it was easy to ignore Serge's wretched hacking, until gradually the situation became clear and they could abide mortal danger no longer.

It was the first day of June and the heat was rising despite the persisting rain and they longed for the cool of early May, when in some places there was still ice on the shores and snow in the forest. The men lit their pipes and handed out pemmican and Serge slung a deerskin bag over his shoulder and motioned for Alex to follow as he lumbered down the beach. They had affairs to discuss. The sand gave way quickly to stone and behind them was a forest of ragged pine and across the water a large cliff, the summit of which was bathed in a lone shaft of yellow sun. They found a spot with a wide view of the dark and glassy water, and Serge unfolded a bearskin and spread it over a rounded slab of grey rock. A loon hollered from mid-river and the forest behind them seemed somehow ill. Serge took from his bag a flask of rum and passed it to Alex, who drank and passed it back.

'Tu vois,' said Serge in his mumbled French, 'they won't let us travel with them anymore.' He issued a wet, snapping cough and a curl of red foam shot over his lips and clung to his beard before he wiped it away.

Alex looked from Serge's damp and shiny eyes to the wilderness surrounding the men and their canoes. What would they do out here? How close were they to Fort William? Days away, maybe more, ample time to die on the banks of the river or in the forests that crept away from either side.

Serge put his arm around Alex's shoulder and gave his tiny frame a squeeze. 'T'inquiète pas, Ali. First, we smoke my pipe. Then I'll challenge André to a fight and win some supplies, don't doubt it. I only need a few days' rest, and after that we can make our own canoe and continue to the nearest post. We're not far from Fort William now.'

Alex looked at Serge's wide and hairy knee emerging from torn trousers. He wanted to reach out and touch it but was worried the men would see this and become even further enraged, so he took up one of his own hands with the other and worried them in his lap. 'But what if you lose?'

The men up the beach had formed a mob around André. They shouted and spat and pointed at Serge and Alex and it was clear they'd had enough, what they wanted now was violence.

Serge watched this and dredged his throat and the sound of blood in his airway was evident. 'On va gagner, mon gars. On gagne t'jours.' He gave Alex's shoulder another squeeze and unfolded his pipe from his sash and a pouch of tobacco, and together they smoked and drank and watched as André l'avant conceded to the demands of his brigade.

They'd met in Montréal ten months previous. Stocky and bearded and dressed in buckskins, Serge was doubled over in the midday street with his hands on his knees vomiting in the gutter outside Plus Jamais Tavern. Next to it was the squat brick grocery store where Alex worked as a stockboy and a cleaner and a clerk. The street was quiet and the sun blazed on the cracked spruce shingles of nearby houses and a brothel and a spate of slumping taverns. They weren't far from the port, and when the wind was wrong the neighbourhood stank of fish.

Alex was picking rotten apples out of the display crates on the creaky wooden porch so they might be sold at a slight discount to an orphanage, and the sorting was a slow business, painful, because le patron had caned his knuckles only a few days before, this after a band of sooty delinquents stole a sack of potatoes and Alex cowered as they leapt off the porch and scattered in all directions.

Le patron was Lewis Anderson, the son of a Scottish railroad baron, and the grocery store was a gift from his father. M. Anderson was a thin man, barely twenty-five, and he wore suspenders and spectacles and smoked a pipe with an ivory handle. He'd hit Alex before, half a dozen times at least, and for any reason at all: dust on top of the cabinets, a jar shelved with the label facing inward, too many flies on the display tomatoes when the heat was high. Each time, Alex flinched and winced and felt his eyes sting with tears, but he didn't grieve until he was alone and curled up on the straw-stuffed mattress that M. Anderson allowed him in the back room.

When his papa returned from France, he'd have his revenge. Whereas Alex was soft and slight, his papa was a logger and a fisher and a Catholic with powerful arms and the hands of a giant. Alex imagined those massive fingers clamped around M. Anderson's throat, squeezing, and he imagined le patron's feet in their polished shoes kicking above the boards of the floor. He imagined how he'd snap the broom handle over his knee, the sound it would make as he threw it to the floor, and then he'd walk out of the store next to his papa and on the ground behind them le patron would lie weeping, the stem of his pipe broken neatly in two.

But it had been two years since his papa had boarded a sail-ship and Alex had yet to receive a letter from Paris or anywhere else. He was patient because his papa told him he'd have to be: it would take time to earn enough money to come back and buy them a plot of land in the countryside. Alex would have to work hard in honour of his maman's memory. She died a few months before his papa went to Europe, which was sad, even his papa agreed, but the family had known death before Alex was born – his brother, after whom he'd been named, died at just six months old. His maman never recovered from the loss, and it was precisely that weakness that left her open to infection, but Alex and his papa couldn't allow death to distract them, not if they didn't want to fall sick themselves, and this was a lesson he'd do well never to forget.

The day before his papa boarded the ship, the two of them walked to the Port of Montréal and his papa put his hand in Alex's hair and closed his fist and told him to take a good look around, not at the ships that were due for voyage or the well-heeled people who walked the gangplanks but at the teen-aged filth fighting one another for a chance to sell newspapers or fish or bread and the younger kids curled up on mouldy blankets in the shadows along the wharf. His papa said he'd made an arrangement to keep his son from such a terrible fate. Alex wouldn't be paid and he'd have to work for a man who was both a Protestant and an angluche, but he'd have a place to sleep and a bit of time to himself, and that was more than most people could expect in a British colony or anywhere else.

After his papa left for la mère-patrie, Alex spoke hardly at all. His hair grew long and thin and he hid behind the limp brown strands that hung in his face. He endured the abuse and was grateful for the mattress. He waited for his papa and didn't think life could happen any other way, not until the porch planks creaked under Serge's considerable bulk and the air filled with the stench of puke and sweat and shit.

'Donne-moi's'une pomme, mon gars,' said Serge in a plodding slur. 'Tout'suite.'

Alex had dealt with drunks before. He'd seen men pass out in the mud and piss themselves leaning against the walls of the grocery store and accost him for bread or fruit or whatever else they thought he might give out, and so he knew that the best thing to do was to ignore them, to look away, and if necessary he would go inside and bar the door, and he was about to do exactly that when he saw the glint of copper in Serge's outstretched palm, so in French he said, 'You can take your pick, sir.'

Serge's knuckles were plump and scabby. His nails were chipped and cracked and stuffed with dirt and blood. He chose a healthy apple and bit into it and wiped his lips with his sleeve. He was short, barely more than five feet tall, but wide in the shoulders, and his beard was long and matted and so was his hair and his nose stuck out of his face like the blade of an axe. Alex knew that men like this lived in the swamps and shanties along the St. Lawrence. They were thieves and worse and they came to town to drink and gamble. He knew he should be afraid, not just of Serge but also of M. Anderson, who would be furious if he came out and found them chatting. But there was something charming about Serge, a curious warmth, and maybe it was like approaching a wood stove on a frosty night: you got close because you didn't want to be cold, but too close and you'd smell your flesh when it burned.

Serge finished the apple and threw the core in the street and told Alex his name as if they were passengers in a carriage. He gave Alex a coin for the apple and then another coin, which he told Alex to keep for himself, and he said, 'You work hard, but you aren't paid much, am I right?'

Alex nodded and opened his mouth to speak but heard footsteps from inside the store and knew M. Anderson was coming to check on him, so quickly he turned his back on Serge and slid the coin into his pocket and pretended that he was ignoring this drunken brute from the tavern next door.

'You there,' declaimed M. Anderson in his unwieldy burr. He appeared in the doorway with one hand in his pocket and the other pinching a pipe in the corner of his mouth. 'You will remove your torn-down wreck of a self from this property lest the consequences be severe. Have I made myself clear?'

Serge swayed on the porch and licked his lips and dredged his throat and spat in the street, and a tiny cloud of dirt flew up where the gob hit the ground. Alex turned from this sight to the apples, the soft ones with brown craters and the crisp ones with shiny skins. He

8

felt tension coming off M. Anderson like wind blowing off the river, and he glanced at the man and saw his florid face and a vein bulging in his neck and his pipe at an upward angle because he was crushing the stem between his teeth.

'Crystal clear,' said Serge in English. The porch creaked as he stepped into the street. 'But I will be back, you know this, because I like your apples very much and I don't want to find you bruise them. I won't like it one bit. Have I made *my*self clear?'

Alex turned his focus to the apples once more. He heard Serge tromp away and M. Anderson hesitate in the doorway before clearing his throat and tapping the embers out of his pipe and wordlessly going back inside. Once le patron was gone Alex peered down the street to catch a final glimpse of Serge, who lingered in the door of the tavern. The two made eye contact and the latter waved before staggering back inside.

On the beach they fought for maybe five minutes and thrashed their way from the rough sand to the water. They looked tiny in the lee of the far-shore cliffs and a crow took flight from an emaciated pine and wheeled above them before croaking downriver. It was obvious to Alex and everyone else that André had been waiting for an excuse to make violence with Serge and obvious that he'd win from the first punch, which landed hard and loud in the pit of Serge's right eye, hard enough to pump a shot of blood from the older man's brow, and more blood streamed down his cheek and into his moustache and beard.

Alex took a step forward but had no real intention of interfering on Serge's behalf, he was too scared, but a few of the voyageurs found his movement excuse enough to push him to the sand and kick him in the ribs, and even though they were only wearing moccasins Alex felt the wind sail out of him and he spent the last minute of the fight gasping, unable to cry out as Serge fell to his knees in the water but remained stubbornly upright while André threw one fist after another into his face, knocking clear a bloody tooth and finishing his barrage with a punch to the throat. Serge's eyes bulged and he clamped his hands over his neck and fell back in the shallows, wheezing, defeated, and

9

with one last effort he crawled out of the water and onto the beach, where he brought his knees to his chest and clutched his crumpled throat.

It hurt to breathe and Alex held his ribs and felt the birdlike frailty of his frame beneath his palms. He crawled across the pebbly beach and kneeled over his fallen friend and tried to assess the wounds, but they were too hard to distinguish in the gruel of blood. He only knew that his friend's great blade of a nose had been broken and that this would cause pain as the consumption settled deeper.

Above and around him the men were laughing and quitting the beach. They loaded les canots and splashed into the shallows and pushed the boats into the deeps. It seemed to Alex that he and Serge would be left there to die with nothing, but then André loomed in his torn-open cotton shirt cascading water and the front all spattered with blood. The flesh of his chest was twisted into scars that looked like burns, and in each of his muscled hands he held a canvas sack, both of which he threw on the beach as he said, 'For you, I feel pity. I feel pity that this man has devoured your innocence and sorry you can never have it back, sorry that you are cul crevé and that you must die on this beach with an emissary of the Devil. So I give you these few supplies and in return I pray le seigneur spares me and my men your deadly disease.'

Serge muttered something unintelligible. His breathing was laboured and his eyes were glassy and blood streamed from his nostrils. He shifted in the sand, turning to watch the Algonquin woman hurry out of the forest, where she'd been gathering sap to patch les canots, and as she gave them a pitying look he clenched his fists and yelled, 'M'aide-nous, salope sauvage!'

André snorted and turned and walked down the beach and into the shallows, the woman sloshing after him as he sank to his waist. They mounted one of the long boats and André shouted for the men to dig deep their paddles and heave off into the morning. The brigade broke into song and was soon out of sight, and the water turned dark and calm once more.

*

M. Anderson didn't spend nights at the store. He lived in the suburbs in a large house with his father and mother and siblings, and
their neighbours were of the finer stock who continually arrived from
England: politicians, judges, aristocrats, barons, so many of these
people as well as their inferiors that les Canadiens were beginning to
lose their majority in cities like Montréal. Alex had nights to himself,
just as his papa had promised, and some of them he spent cross-legged
on his mattress drawing passable pictures of the St. Lawrence with a
piece of coal and scraps of wood he found in the alleys around the
neighbourhood, while during others he drew not much of anything at
all, just took a large lump of coal in each of his hands and moved them
rapidly and at random across his makeshift canvas as he looked up at
the shadowy rafters and closed his eyes, thinking of his papa clutching
his hair or his maman cradling his shoulders or M. Anderson striking
his face, and when he looked down again all the swirls and whorls
and smudges and smears seemed to say something about how he felt,
about how fast his hands had moved and for how long and why.

He seldom ventured outside, not even to Mass. He knew his
maman would've urged him to go to la Chapelle Notre-Dame-de-
Bon-Secours to take Communion before the fabled statue of the
Virgin Mary, for there was power in the flow of her robes and warmth
of her open hands, power that had lessened the plight of sailor and
beggar and whore, and when his maman was alive they took the
Sacrament and attended the grand Masses, most of which were delivered in English to cater to all the Irish and Scottish who'd been filling
the pews, and so it was doubly important for a young Canadien to
make himself present in the congregation – the church was a symbol
of New France, not Great Britain, they couldn't have everything even
as they thought they had it all. But Alex didn't like being alone in the
city. There was no one to protect him and the grey stone buildings
soared and the muddy streets sucked at his feet and he'd jump at the
sudden splash of a horse's hoof. He found the people tense and there
were smells that made him gag and unnaturally black shadows trailed
behind him like smoke from the chimneys. It was safest in the back
of the store, where sometimes he prayed, and whenever he did, he

apologized to his maman for not attending la Chapelle and once he thought she expressed forgiveness when he knocked a large jar of preserves from a top shelf; the glass didn't break and M. Anderson failed to notice the noise of it striking the floor, so Alex was spared a beating.

The room at the back of the store was small, barely big enough for the mattress and a few shelves, and there was a little window above a door in the back wall but no view because the hotel across the alley rose up too high. When he had to empty his bladder or bowels he went out the back door and used a bucket, which in the morning he poured into a gutter that ran past the tavern. The alley was where he cleaned his teeth with a rag and salt and also where he bathed, which he did once a week when M. Anderson gave him a small chunk of soap and allowed him to heat water on the wood stove. He'd recently begun using this soap and a dull razor to shave the sparse strands of hair on his neck and cheeks. He was grateful for the hot water but found in the winter it made no difference: his teeth still chattered from the cold.

His life wasn't as comfortable as when his maman was alive and his father was always away fishing in summer and logging in winter and they lived in a coach house in the suburbs where she worked as a maid. It wasn't nearly as comfortable, but it wasn't so bad. Each night M. Anderson left him a heel of bread, a couple boiled eggs, and an apple, and on special occasions like Christmas Alex was given cheese and a few pieces of sausage. He disliked le patron but recognized in his situation a charity he wouldn't have enjoyed if instead he'd wound up hawking fish or bread or newspapers down at the port, which was nevertheless his favourite thing to draw because of the smudgy ships sailing far away.

He didn't label his drawings because he couldn't read or write. When he was a boy his maman's patron offered to put him through school, but only in English because what use was education in a dying language? Alex had already learned crude expressions from this man and his wife and their three sons, and so it wasn't too late for him to grow into an adult unhampered by language or accent. But Alex's papa came home from the coast and his hands were thick and scarred and

12

he said Alex would be better off working around the property because he was too weak to work the bush and too frail to fish the river, and so he'd have to learn something practical if he was to have any hope of survival. Le patron acknowledged that every man had the right to shape a future for his son and though he'd pay no more for the service, he wouldn't prevent Alex from helping his maman with her cooking and cleaning, and anyway English would impress itself upon him as it did all it encountered.

Tonight, Alex placed one of the coins Serge had given him on a piece of quartered hardwood and scoured the area around it with a lump of coal. When he removed it, the space beneath recalled a full moon and around it he shaded a midnight sky and below that the rickety wharfs of the port. He worked on this until it was finished and then went outside to shit in his bucket. The alley between the grocery store and the hotel was dark and muddy and full of trash, and Alex squatted and peered into the darkness but saw nothing. It was windy and the sky was black as filth and Alex knew a storm was coming. He wiped himself with a few torn pages of newspaper and was about to go back inside when he saw movement in the shadows and froze.

'Bonsoir, mon gars, bonsoir.' There was first the powerful stench of rum and then Serge's face emerged from the gloom, but not entirely, rather just enough to see him smile through the wet tangle of his beard, and they stared at each other for a quiet moment.

'You shouldn't be here,' said Alex, gathering himself in the door frame.

Serge chuckled and his teeth seemed to float in the dark. 'Oh no? Says who? That Scotsman? M'en fous d'ce con. Don't worry about him, my friend, all right?' He stepped closer and Alex saw that his hand was outstretched and in his palm were several copper coins. 'I need a place to stay. Just for tonight. We should be friends, nous deux.'

Alex knew he should close the door and lock it and maybe even go out front in search of a watchman, but that knowledge was dim and unconvincing in the face of Serge's copper coins, and besides, this man had shown him kindness earlier that day and he felt he had to return the gesture, in particular because a storm was overtaking the area and what was the harm, there was no harm. M. Anderson wouldn't be back until after sun-up and by then Serge would be elsewhere and no one the wiser. He nodded and Serge grinned and Alex felt a swarm of giddiness all through his chest. He smiled and cleared the door frame and Serge stepped inside, pressing the coins into Alex's hand, more money than he'd seen in who knew how long, maybe ever. Alex felt he should sleep on the floor in return, but Serge shook his head when offered the mattress.

'The floor's fine for me, my friend.' He put down his bag and began to unlace the throat of his buckskin shirt. 'It's the storm I don't like. As for the ground, like you, it's an old friend.'

Alex sat on the bed and tried to hide his drawing under the prickly blanket. 'You'll have to leave before the sun comes up.'

'Ho-ho!' cried Serge, and it was suddenly obvious how drunk he was as he reached out and snatched the square of wood from Alex's fingers. 'What have we here? You're an artist! Mais 'garde ça, donc. It's very good, my friend. It's excellent.'

There was only a candle to light the room and Alex thought it was strange that Serge could see the drawing well enough to proclaim its merit, but he was happy as the first drops of rain tapped against the tiny window. He felt no embarrassment as Serge bent over and propped the wood against the wall by the door, where they could see the drawing in the staggering candlelight.

Serge lowered himself, arms wheeling, then fell backward, his skull thumping the floor next to a pile of scrap-wood canvases Alex kept by the head of the bed. He laughed and righted himself on his elbows, then picked up one of the drawings and angled it into the candlelight, squinting. Alex could see it was one of those drawings that wasn't much of a drawing at all, one of those that was all smudges and smears, and he felt a sudden rush of embarrassment, but then Serge shook his head mournfully and said, 'Ah, but you're hurting, my friend, you're sad.' That drawing he placed delicately next to the first, and as the rain picked up there were now two drawings to behold.

Serge took off his shirt and made a pillow of it and curled up on the narrow strip of floor between the bed and the door while Alex blew out the candle and lay back on his mattress. The straw poked his back and he shifted until the discomfort went away.

The rain fell harder and harder and Serge's voice croaked beneath it: 'Would you like a drink, my friend, before you sleep?'

'No, thank you.'

'All right, then, bonne nuit.'

'Yes, sir, bonne nuit.'

Alex had seen death when his mother fell sick and now with Serge beaten so bloody and at the same time so ill, he knew he was seeing it again. The morning had gotten old and a bank of clouds had arrived from somewhere beyond the looming cliff, smothering the sun and hanging heavy with rain. The beach was too exposed and they couldn't stay where they were. They'd have to go into the forest and make a plan, but any such plan would be pointless because Serge was going to die, that much was clear.

André had left them pemmican and beans and a few biscuits made of water and flour, and there were also three tattered furs and a bottle of rum and an axe and a kettle. In Serge's bag Alex found some dry touchwood and a chunk of flint and a piece of steel as well as a few portraits of Serge he'd made before they left Montréal. Serge coughed wetly from time to time but wasn't conscious and Alex left him on the beach. He took their supplies into the trees and was again struck by the sickly appearance of the forest, its skeletal branches and tufts of moss turned brown and the cool air it held in its darkness. He gathered wood and made a fire, but the wood was damp and the flames powerless against the chill.

Alex returned to Serge and took a shot of rum and tried to rouse him, first by lightly shaking his shoulders then by cupping the crotch of his trousers, but Serge only coughed and blood bubbled between his lips. It was as if he were both on the beach and somewhere else, but mostly somewhere else, and Alex recalled a similar feeling at his maman's deathbed.

Her patron had been generous enough to give her a room on the top floor of the house, and although it took effort to get her up the stairs, everyone knew they'd only have to strain once more when they took her body down, and this the doctor confirmed when he came to visit at le patron's request. The room was more comfortable than the coach house and after work Alex took his meals at her bedside, watching her chest rise and fall and dabbing a wet cloth on her forehead. His father was away working, and although they'd sent a message to his camp he'd not yet come home or sent one back.

Alex spoke to his maman at length but didn't tell her how her patron had taken him aside and put a hand on his shoulder and told him he wouldn't be able to continue in his role as houseboy after his maman passed, but not to worry, le patron would make suitable arrangements with Alex's father. Instead he told her menial details about his work around the house and about a little dead deer he'd seen while walking in the woods and all the insects crawling chaotically throughout its guts, which had been torn free of its body, probably by wolves. His maman was tiny and frail beneath a white sheet and she seldom acknowledged him with more than a moan, until one evening she was lucid and she sat up against the headboard and told him about his brother, his 'tit frère, who was born with a full head of black hair and never cried once because he was strong and powerful and brave, but quickly it was noticed that he struggled to breathe and frequently coughed up a pink foam, and after just a few days he died, perhaps from a buildup of fluid in his lungs. Alex was born a year later and they named him after his brother and this time the strength prevailed.

He'd told Serge that story back in Montréal and Serge had held him close and said he felt the power too. Now he'd have to use his puissance to haul Serge into the woods. First he'd roll him onto the bearskin and then he'd drag him over to the fire, and this he did despite a bark of pain from Serge, who came out of his stupor once Alex had moved their belongings into the trees.

Alex wrapped the bearskin around Serge's enormous shoulders and threw more wood on the fire and offered Serge a piece of pemmican, but Serge couldn't swallow because of the pain in his throat. He tried nevertheless, and the effort led to an explosive fit of coughing and both men heard the weak fire sizzle and silently they recognized this as the flames devouring whatever drops of blood had flown from Serge's lungs then mouth.

It began to rain, at first lightly but soon much harder, and neither the deerskin tent nor the company blankets had made it off the boats.

'Serre-moi fort,' said Serge, so Alex put his arms around him and held him in his lap as the rain quickly extinguished the fire, and although they had their rum, Serge couldn't imbibe but encouraged Alex, who drank despairingly as his friend began to sob.

The rain plastered Serge's hair to his face and his beard to his neck and he shook with the force of his tears. Alex wanted to stroke his cheek but both sides of his friend's face were scabby and swollen, so instead he just squeezed one of Serge's hands. 'T'inquiète pas, Serge. On gagne toujours, tu t'souviens-tu? Tout l'temps on gagne.'

Serge nodded but didn't otherwise respond, and it seemed as though they were the only living creatures in an endless forest of dead brown needles.

Serge left before M. Anderson returned to the grocery store in the morning, and all throughout the day Alex struggled to conceal an inner glow that must've been happiness and maybe even joy. Serge came back that night and this time sat on the mattress beside Alex and told stories about his life, and when he offered his rum, Alex took a sip and winced but continued to drink whenever the bottle was passed. In return he gave Serge a few pieces of his bread, though he'd already eaten the rest of his meal.

Serge grinned and said his great-grandmother had been one of les filles du roi sent to New France by the Sun King and therefore his blood was nearly royal but his life experience was not. He'd grown up in Montréal a generation after the British took control and had known nothing but hardship and labour. He'd watched his mother die of cholera and his father like his grandfather was a coureur de bois, one of the remaining few who set out for Athabasca not long after his mother's death, but the man never came home and there were no reports of his demise, only rumours that he'd chosen to live with the Cree or the Dene, no one knew which.

When Serge was twenty he decided to quit his job working the port and go find his father. He spoke of adventures both wonderful and wild, such as a bear that attacked his group and killed their leader and the men wandered off course in the wilderness and many died before they met a group of Indiens and traded their tin cups and tobacco pipes for guidance, but these men had never heard of his father and could speak very little French besides.

'Weren't you scared?' Alex felt himself crude and sheltered but was nevertheless filled with pride that Serge chose to spend time in the back of the store when clearly he was a man who could avail himself of other options.

Serge smiled and shook his head, non, non, but then he sighed and sipped his rum and said, 'Franchement, it was the storms that scared me from time to time, because the lightning once struck the trees and the whole forest turned to fire and in the flames I saw the Devil, but it seemed he didn't see me himself, or if he did he wasn't ready to take me, grâce à dieu.'

It was windy outside but not overcast and there was the faint light of the moon that found its way into the alley and through the dirty window. Alex shivered at the thought of the forest aflame and Serge stretched his arm around the boy's shoulders and held him close and continued his story.

He spoke fondly of les Indiens and said over the course of many years he learned to speak Cree and Dene and some of the northern Iroquois spoken by the Huron, and after a deep pull from his bottle Serge remarked on the strength of these last people in particular, because although greatly reduced by disease and war, like the beaver they still survived and would persist even thereafter, and who could not respect such focus and fortitude? Serge said Indian languages were crucial in his development as coureur and to prove it he issued a series of strange sounds that Alex had not previously known possible, and he tried not to laugh but failed.

'C't'amusant, j'l'sais,' slurred Serge, and he grinned and his teeth were yellow and one of his incisors completely brown. 'But I'm telling you, my good friend, these men and women of the land opened my eyes to the biggest secret of my life.'

'They helped you find your father?' Alex heard the squeal of excitement in his voice and realized the rum had taken hold, but Serge was quiet and only drank from his bottle and shook his head, then drank again and passed the rum to Alex.

'Non,' he said after a pause. 'I never found my father and to tell the truth I forgot what he looked like by the time I saw the Devil, and afterward I could never remember again.'

'I'm sorry,' said Alex and he took Serge's rough and hairy hand and held it but didn't tell him about his own father, not right then, it felt wrong to commandeer the conversation, and the two of them held hands while Serge collected himself and returned to the topic of the secret revealed to him by les Indiens.

'I stayed with them in their villages,' he said. 'We coureurs got on very well with them, better than most of these voyageurs you see now that things are organized. We respected them and they respected us and there was much trading not just of goods but also knowledge.'

Alex gave Serge's hand a squeeze. 'What did they teach you? What?'

Serge looked down at Alex and lifted the boy's hand to his chest, and he chuckled and said, 'They said I'm berdache, but slightly different, because I don't concern myself with the work of a woman and nor am I the youngest in my affairs of love.' He gave Alex an affirmative nod. 'I'm slightly different.'

Alex didn't understand and said so even as he began to feel tired and woozy, and Serge released his hand and patted his knee. 'I think we've talked enough for tonight, my friend, don't you? Let's go to sleep now and talk more tomorrow, yes?'

Alex nodded and lay on his side and Serge blew out the candle and stretched out on the little strip of mattress, and just before Alex fell asleep he felt Serge's arm encircle his chest and pull him close, and that was a feeling of warmth and safety.

Serge whispered in Alex's ear. 'You are very soft, Ali.'

Alex smiled in the dark.

Serge said, 'You know, in the trade, it's the soft beaver we like best.'

'Why?'

'It feels nice against the skin, very soft, and therefore people want it most.'

It rained all throughout the afternoon and into the evening, and for a while Alex sensed the presence of the sun behind the blackness of the clouds, but then it vanished and the two of them were lost in the wet and roaring darkness that was sometimes shattered by bolts of jagged blue lightning dancing across the summit of the cliff. In his right hand Alex clutched the rum and with chattering teeth he prayed to le seigneur that they'd be spared the flaming forest of Serge's past. When he felt around with his left hand he was dismayed because Serge was mostly still, just the occasional and almost imperceptible rise of his wide chest.

Alex cried out but was unable to hear himself over the howl of the wind and the fury of the rain, and he didn't want to but nevertheless and despite the treachery began to regret their ambition. Even if he'd been able to change the course of events he'd not have removed Serge from his life, non, jamais, but he would've steered them toward a different fate, and why not France, to find Alex's father instead? But he'd suggested this and Serge had promised they'd indeed board a sail-ship, or maybe even a steamship, who knew, and together they'd make the journey, but first they needed money. They had to take advantage of what was surely the final era of fur trading brought about by the forced merger of the Hudson's Bay Company and the North West Company after those two organizations had spilled each other's blood throughout the great eastern forest and all the way across the northern plains as well. When Alex said he didn't understand these details, Serge raised his finger and said he had only to understand that it was necessary for him to finally shed the old ways of the independent coureur, good and just for hundreds of years but no more, and they'd become not only licensed voyageurs but two among the hardiest hivernants who travelled from Lake Superior and into the rugged north, all the way to Lake Athabasca and the western height of Rupert's

Land, where the best furs could still be found in huge abundance and despite all the obscure machinations of business and the bloody friction between global powers, money could still be made, money they'd need if they were ever to travel to France to find Alex's father. It was necessary, said Serge, for a man to be controlled before he could be free. That was just the miserable way of a miserable world.

This wisdom rang true and Alex was filled with further confidence when he learned of Serge's prowess in the trade: the man could carry over two hundred pounds on his back with a tumpline cutting into the flesh of his forehead, he'd survived the musket blasts of rival trappers, he'd twice killed a bear with a single shot from a stolen firearm, and he'd beaten six men at once in a tavern fight in Grand Portage before the American border tariffs were enforced, after which he beat five more in Fort William. Serge said his reputation was fearsome and known throughout the trade, and within its culture and along its waterways he and Alex would be respected, not like in Montréal, where they were battered animals sneaking friendship in the shadows of maudit streets overrun by Protestants and Englishmen and all manner of pute and con and diable.

But now look at them, thought Alex, his eyes full of tears. Now look at their situation: ruined. What furs they had were too drenched for comfort and too tattered to trade, even if such an option were possible. As for food, the biscuits had probably dissolved in the deluge, but Alex thought he might find the pemmican and beans, even in the darkness, and he swigged from his rum and came across the axe instead. He held it in his left hand and like the rum wouldn't let go lest Serge's devils burst out of the storm and drag them away.

'Buggery!' bellowed M. Anderson, holding open the door to the back room with the palm of one hand and making a fist of the other. Alex wasn't quite awake when he heard this but knew he wasn't dreaming, just as he knew the pain in his head and the dryness in his bones were the work of the rum, though it had left behind an oily film of pleasure as well. He was still cupped against Serge's body, the stout giant's arm across his chest like a plate of armour, and he felt himself shielded by strength as Serge vaulted shirtless off the mattress and squared his hairy shoulders at le patron. This happened quickly and Alex hadn't yet sat up and it was clear M. Anderson also didn't expect resistance or outburst, not because he'd thought about the matter but because his instincts had always told him such things weren't his concern, and so his expression was almost comical in its nudity of first-born shock and fear. M. Anderson's knees gave out and his mouth hung open, so strange and feeble when not gathered and pressed around the tip of his pipe. Serge was too principled to harm a man so frightened, but Alex knew that if violence had come to pass, the question of the victor would've been no question at all, and afterward they would've burned down the store and felt no remorse, rather left M. Anderson to crawl back to his father's estate, battered and reduced. But it didn't come to that, for Serge merely slammed the door in le patron's face. Then he turned and with a smile he said, 'Emmène tes affaires.'

And so they spent the end of the summer and the whole of the winter living together in a hotel by the port, and these days and nights were unlike any Alex had known. Their room was simple and modest, comprised of a small bed and a night table, a candle and a chamber pot, and it had a window that looked down onto the street, which at first was muddy, and then, as the months passed, snowy. During the days, Serge toured the taverns playing cards and mostly winning and with the proceeds he paid for the room and fed them both. At night, he returned with rum and meat and cheese and sometimes even wine. They stayed up late, holding each other in bed, and in the safety of their candlelit cocoon Alex told Serge about his maman and his papa and the 'tit frère he'd never met. After the story of his maman's passing, Serge gathered Alex's face in his brutish hands and kissed the boy as tenderly as his coarse lips would allow, and he said, 'C'est trop dure, mon cher Ali, bien trop dure.'

Alex began to cry and Serge led him from the bed to the window. They surveyed the filthy snowdrifts below and the huddled people walking between them and a bright red sleigh pulled merrily by a team of horses, and he told Alex that in the spring they'd leave this city behind. He'd met an Englishman in the taverns who recruited people on behalf of the fur company, and it didn't matter that this man didn't like Serge, because he couldn't beat him in cards, no matter how often they played, and his pride led them to play often.

All of life, said Serge, was a sequence of random opportunities and it was the task of every man to await the arrival of his own, even if later he convinced himself and others he'd been the one to contrive the circumstances in a howling absence of luck and good fortune. In time Serge would be able to turn the recruiter's debt into a service, and that service would be two positions on one of the voyageur brigades that would set out from Lachine in spring, and although most men found the work both difficult and dangerous, for them it would be otherwise because the Englishman would guarantee special treatment for the few months it took to reach Fort William, whence they'd join up with another brigade and work their way north, and here Serge wouldn't have to rely on guile to be recruited because the northbound brigades suffered many losses due to hernias and drownings and starvation, so positions on les canots were always available.

'After that, the work will get harder,' said Serge, 'much harder. But you'll be stronger and more capable, and together we'll head north to make our fortune.'

'And then,' sniffed Alex, 'will we go back to Montréal and continue to France?'

Serge returned to the bed and plucked a hunk of meat from the nightstand. He popped it into his mouth and opened his arms and beckoned for Alex to join him, and when the boy was again in his arms Serge promised they'd set out for Paris as soon as they were ready, and by that time Alex would be a powerful man the likes of which would inspire pride in his papa and everyone else besides.

Giddy with this vision, Alex drew pictures during the day but not just with scraps of wood and lumps of coal; rather Serge through cards had won him three sheets of paper made from rags in Argenteuil, Québec, as well as pencils imported from France. On the sheets he sketched a rough portrait of Serge sleeping in bed with the covers bundled at his waist and another of Serge with his hair obscuring his face and another of Serge selecting an apple from the displays outside

M. Anderson's store. When he went back to the wood and coal and looked at the ceiling and closed his eyes and moved his hands rapidly and at random as he'd done so many times before, the results were different, the whorls and swirls were joyous, the smears and smudges ecstatic, and Serge had a carpenter attach a length of wire to the back of one of these efforts, and with a delighted smile he hung it from a nail in the wall over their bed.

In February, Alex was sitting beneath it and working on a portrait, and the sun had gone down and Serge had yet to return when there was a knock at the door. Alex imagined his friend on the other side, arms too full of rum and sausage to manage the handle himself, so he climbed out of bed and opened the door, but it wasn't Serge who stood there, rather a tall and clean-shaven man with a tiny mouth who spoke English in an accent too thick for Alex to comprehend, and this confusion turned to horror when the man threw his fist into Alex's face.

Alex fell to the ground and felt one of his elbows thump the floor and go numb. He'd been beaten before, not just by M. Anderson but also countless times by the sons of his maman's patron, and he knew that understanding why wasn't as important as protecting his head and ribs, so he curled fetal as the man set about kicking him across the floor and under the bed, after which he opened his eyes but only to see the bed lift off the ground and fly into the wall, this because his assailant had thrown it there and kicked him in the mouth and called him a sodomite and kicked him in both forearms as Alex once more managed to cover his face.

The kicking seemed as interminable as the winter until Alex heard the familiar sounds of Serge grunting and swearing, and when he lowered his arms he saw his friend toss the assailant into the wall and then grab him by the hair and slam his face into the wood panels until a bloodstain appeared and gradually expanded and droplets broke free and trickled to the floor.

After half a dozen of these blows or more, Serge released the man's hair and the man crumpled to his knees and fell backwards, his face a pool of furrowed flesh and shining blood. Serge took him by the wrists, spun him around, and dragged him into the hall, then closed the door and rushed over to Alex and collected him in his arms. Alex was nearly unconscious but terror kept his senses alive and so he heard the commotion in the hall and the pounding of fists on the door, but the noise broke off when Serge bellowed that it must, and Alex wouldn't remember what happened until a few days later when he awoke in bed and Serge was at his side and explained that a man he'd bested in cards had tracked them down but no one would ever be so foolish as to attempt such an assault again.

'There'll be people who see that we're strong and try to take it,' said Serge. 'But we'll never let them.'

Alex tried to smile but his face was swollen and the pain was intense and Serge reached below the sheets and coaxed from his body the special sensation he'd come to love.

'J'ai d'bonnes nouvelles,' said Serge after the sensation had subsided and the wet had been dried. 'We leave with a brigade as soon as the ice breaks on the rivers. It'll be exactly as I promised.'

Alex awoke beneath the trees still holding the axe but not the bottle because he'd drunk all the rum during the storm. It was morning and the sun was shining and his face and neck were coated with blackflies. Booze had scraped out his skull many times in the past ten months, but this time it hadn't left any lingering quality of joy, and he knew before turning over that Serge was dead, so he stayed as he was for a while, letting the tears stream out of his eyes. When he did roll over and look at his best friend slumped against a tree in front of the sodden firepit, he saw that hordes of flies were eating the smashed pulp of Serge's face and only the man's broken nose emerged from this melee, but crooked and sad. Alex crawled over and laid himself across Serge's stiff and wet and lifeless lap and tried again to sleep but couldn't and thought he might never manage anything like sleep again. He lay there until the sun crept across the sky and night fell once again over the river and its forests and cliffs, and in that inky darkness he sketched with his mind an outcome more like the one they'd intended: the two of them aboard a steamship as it left the St. Lawrence and entered the Atlantic, bound for Paris and the new life there promised.

2

SERGE'S BODY WAS TOO HEAVY TO CARRY OR DRAG, AND come the next morning Alex understood he'd have to abandon his friend to the insects and animals. The sky was cloudy and he went to the river and looked across at the stark grey face of the looming cliff and kneeled in the weeds and drank from the water until his belly sloshed. He set about gathering what supplies were left scattered about the beach and the edge of the forest. He'd been grief-stricken before and now he was again and this was surely the will of le seigneur, and perhaps like his papa he was too afraid to complain lest he summon from Heaven yet another bolt of anguish and loss.

He was careful not to look at Serge as he went about his task but couldn't ignore the frantic buzzing of a thousand flies. He had a kettle, but there was no wood dry enough to make a fire, so he swallowed a handful of raw beans that went down like pebbles. Then he found some pemmican and chewed it while rooting through Serge's deerskin bag, which he discovered half-buried in the mud. The portraits he'd made were rolled up inside, but the rain had ruined them and he'd have to work hard to never forget the way Serge had looked in Montréal.

After an hour he was ready to leave. He sobbed and swayed and slung Serge's bag over his shoulder and took up the axe in his right hand and walked in the direction the brigade had gone two days before. The shore was rocky and the river glassy and the forest still. He felt flushed with shame because he recognized in himself a longing not just for Serge but also the men of the brigade and even M.

Anderson, because truly he was lost and these men might've helped him no matter the coarseness of their hearts.

He walked for half a day and still felt strong and that worried him. It didn't make sense that the river was so calm after such a downpour, and why wasn't he sick after spending so much time so close to Serge? Maybe the Devil had crawled out of the storm and claimed his soul while he slept drunkenly in the mud. His unease worsened as time went on and the dull grey light of day lessened not at all.

Eventually the shoreline petered out and he had to walk waist deep in cold water at the base of tall cliffs and he worried that soon the riverbed would slope away and he'd have to swim, which he couldn't do because he'd never learned. At one point he heard the sound of splashing paddles, and in the middle of the river he saw an elaborately painted canoe containing four of les Indiens whose faces were gaunt and scarred, and behind them were more canoes and then still more, a fleet of hundreds crowding the river, all men, women, and children, their arms and necks and faces peppered with yellow pustules and all about them the bracing stench of death. Alex waved and hollered, but even though the people looked right at him they seemed not to hear or see, and then, like ghosts, they passed and were gone.

Soon the water rose above his waist to his chest and then to his neck, and he found that he couldn't motivate himself to continue because his fear of drowning was too great. He realized also that the axe was too cumbersome a burden and he let it sink to the bottom of the river. The water was clear enough for him to watch its descent and also to witness a thick black snake swim between his ankles.

He stood there with the river beneath his chin and after a time he heard a roar from somewhere behind. He turned but saw nothing at first, and then a moment later came a wall of water the face of which was teeming with the tormented souls of les Indiens who'd passed him earlier, and it was crashing down the river and in no time captured him and swept him away.

His limbs were pulled in every direction and with such force he worried they'd come unstuck from his body. He couldn't tell up from down and all was cold and black. He struggled to hold his breath but the pressure on his chest was overwhelming, and with his eyes bulging he sucked in water and coughed and sucked in water and coughed, and then he sucked in water and his lungs were full. He began to sink, and this was how he discovered the direction of the bottom. A thicker blackness than that of the river lurked down there and it rose up and overtook him and he saw nothing and felt nothing, not even the pull of the current, and so he knew he'd died in the flash of the flood, if indeed that had been what it was.

He floated for a time in darkness until far away he saw a twinkle of white light, very dim at first but then gradually brighter and moving toward him. He felt strength return to his limbs as well as the sudden knowledge of how to move them and he swam toward the light, which grew brighter and whiter and took on the shape of a human being: a pale boy floating before him with thick black hair spinning round his head in the chaos of currents, and this child with lips cracked and blue pressed his mouth against Alex's own and Alex felt the water drain from his lungs and fresh air replace it, after which he began to float, even as the river thrashed and strained to pull him back into the abyss from which it flowed, but still Alex kissed his 'tit frère and still the two floated upward and away from the endless black, and then he found himself sloshing out of the shallows of a lake and belching out mouthfuls of foul-tasting water. He collapsed in the mud of the beach with eyes stinging, and an incredible fatigue overtook him such that he fell into a deep and dreamless sleep.

3

WHEN HE AWOKE HE FOUND HIMSELF ALONE AND WRAPPED in blankets beneath a canoe. It was morning and very hot and he was sweating profusely, but his body didn't feel at all weak the way one might expect after undergoing whatever experience he'd undergone, only he was hungry and his heart was heavy and in his mind was a thickness much like he'd felt for months after the fever had devoured his maman.

He threw off the blankets and rolled out from under the boat and saw that he wasn't on a beach as expected but rather inside the apron of a forest with the beach maybe fifty metres away. It was small and rocky and farther down the shore, cliffs rose out of waters clear and blue. He could hear a river rushing from somewhere in the woods and all around him were the pale grey trunks of white pines and in between two of the trees stood a young deer with its brown legs long and thin and clumsy. It snorted and looked at him with soft eyes and he at it, and then part of its head exploded and Alex heard the blast of a musket. The trees around the deer were splattered with clots of brain and fragments of skull and it slumped against a trunk and slid lifelessly to the forest floor, and the sudden smell of blood reminded Alex of the blacksmith near M. Anderson's shop. His mouth watered as a hoot of triumph rang out from elsewhere in the woods, and Alex turned to see a man holding a smoking gun and wearing the red toque and sash of a voyageur.

Fearing this man might be from his old brigade, Alex's first instinct was to flee, but there was nowhere to run and anyway he saw other men emerging from the trees. They were armed and Alex realized he couldn't escape even if he were brave enough to try.

A man spoke English from somewhere behind him: 'You must be fixin' for a bit of game, am I right, lad? Because you're skin and bones and little of that besides.'

The man stood a few yards away with his foot on a stump and his elbow resting across his knee and next to him was a pool of sunlight, but he remained in the shadows cast by the pine. His face was grizzled and his thick brown hair was tied back and he wore a blue coat with brass buttons that had the stern quality of a military garment. A sabre hung from his hip and even from a distance the blade looked clean and sharp.

Alex found not a word of English in the sad sludge of his thoughts and could only say, 'On est où? Vous êtes qui?'

The man chuckled and stepped off the stump and rapidly closed the distance between them. 'Never been one for the French, I'm afraid.' He held out a hairy hand for Alex to shake. 'Just the language, mind. Not the folk. I'm partial to the folk, I am, and I'd like to thank you personally for what your motherland did mine when mine was going through all that bloody mess of gettin' born. Accordingly, men like us exist in natural friendship. That's no joke, lad, not at all.'

Alex took the man's hand, and it was warm and powerful but respectful in the shake it administered.

'You can call me Captain Charlie Jones. Captain for short.' He smiled and his teeth were yellow and some were missing and others chipped. He had red and bulging eyes with blue swirls spinning around their pupils like whirlpools. 'Unless of course some fur-swapper this here side of the border wants to know, in which case you say nothing but rather just follow as we go a-running to the shore and head back across that bay and right out into the lake on the other side of them westerly islands, and if as we go our muskets should find themselves both a-boomin' and a-smokin', well lad, keep your head low and that way you'll be sure to keep it on your shoulders. You follow me?'

Alex followed well enough and nodded and glanced at the shot deer, over which had gathered a group of voyageurs and already they had the animal partially skinned and a few fillets cut from its hind as well.

'Welcome to the American Fur Company,' said the Captain, clapping Alex on the shoulder. 'You're hereby invited to join us for breakfast. It'll be our first proper meal in days, and maybe you can tell us how it is you came to be washed up on that beach down there. If we believe your story, well, later on you can help check the traplines too.'

4

LES CANADIENS WERE NOT AS FRIENDLY AS THE AMERICAN. Some scowled behind the tangled mess of their beards and others averted their gaze. A few had stretched the deer's hide between trees and it hung like a bloody sail, flies buzzing across it like storm clouds devouring a tormented bay. The rest sat around the fire and each waited for the twisting column of smoke to chase the bugs away, and the light of the rising sun speared the tattered canopy of pine. The Captain was perched on a high stump covered in wet moss and he passed Alex a few pieces of meat and the taste was explosive and strong and the pieces juicy and tender. Alex tried at first to chew with dignity but couldn't restrain himself as the other men fell upon their portions like wolves. He was stung that Serge wasn't there to enjoy the meal and several times his eyes became watery and he hoped the other men would attribute this to the smoke.

'All right then,' said the Captain, wiping his lips with the sleeve of his coat. 'As I said previously, it's been days since we've had our bellies so full, but now that they are, it's time for all gathered to become properly acquainted. We'll be expecting the true tale of your arrival on this beach, and in return we'll give you some work on this here expedition, ain't that so, lads?'

There were about a dozen voyageurs of various ages and only a few of them nodded, while the others maintained faces cold and judicious. A few had dark, almost brown skin, and Alex remembered their sort from the streets of Montréal and he knew they were métissage because he remembered how his papa once yelled at one for bumping into him in the marché, and on the way home his papa explained that they were descended from people who'd come from France and settled in the cities of Lower Canada before drifting down the rivers in search of furs to trade. In so doing they were transformed and took Indian wives and made Indian children and some of these men would return to the cities, where their European wives and children awaited, and their métissage offspring would follow and be sent away and wind up working for companies like this one. One of these men had braids tied into his black-and-grey beard, and he stood up and with mouth full and accent thick he said, 'We don't have time to tell stories this morning, Charlie. We need to be checking our traplines before the catch is damaged, if even there's a catch to become damaged. We have finally eaten and now we must go back into the woods to work.'

A few of the other men nodded and grumbled but were silenced when the Captain held up a finger and shook it back and forth. In a tense voice he said, 'Rémi grows bolder by the day, gentlemen, see him as he grows. But see too how by the day he harms his reputation and affects both his coming pay and his future prospects in what's left of this trade.'

The nodding men became still and the grumblers fell silent and with a scowl Rémi sat on a rock and began furiously packing tobacco into the bowl of his pipe.

The Captain pointed at Alex. 'Please, lad. Go ahead. And I'm sorry for the interruption.'

Despite the advance warning, Alex hadn't yet managed to extract a believable story from the muck of his grief. He knew the true tale wouldn't inspire the trust of these men, and theirs was a trust he desperately needed, so he was silent, listening to them chew, and he saw the sweat shine on their brows and felt the cracks between his teeth grow larger to accommodate the threads of venison therein.

The Captain stared at Alex and blinked and chewed and stared some more, and Alex thought of Serge sitting on his bed in Montréal, unspooling stories with ease, and then he opened his mouth and started talking. His English was clumsy at first and his voice was low and feeble, but a few of the men leaned forward to take better note.

He told them he'd left Montréal roughly eight weeks previous as a member of a brigade bound for Fort William with supplies to trade for northern fur. The group was large and their boats were numerous and Alex had been contracted as un milieu. He was inexperienced and accepted his position in the middle of the boat because he saw it as an opportunity to do well, but l'avant considered his performance lacklustre, an opinion that grew more severe after the first portage, during which Alex was unable to carry more than sixty pounds of supplies down a rocky chute.

The Captain's men swatted at flies and exchanged looks and smirks, all except Rémi, who shook his head curtly and spat on the embers of the fire and picked up a twig and tossed it into the pine, yawning as the sunlight swept across his face but failed to lend him an appearance of youth.

Alex said his poor performance only lasted the first month of the journey. He knew he'd harmed the brigade's productivity and laboured to make up for the loss, and by the fifth week he was the strongest of les milieux and could carry ninety pounds of supplies over the portage routes, but still the men didn't like him.

'Pity that,' said the Captain, and he puffed his pipe and offered it to Alex. 'The mind of a man is too often the stuff of a flint, hard and unchanging and liable to spark when rubbed both the wrong way and the right.'

Alex took the pipe and drew in smoke and exhaled into the fire. He told them how in the sixth week the brigade had decided to shoot a frothy rapid despite the inherent danger; they had no choice, they had to make up lost time. Alex was aware as he was talking that it was indeed his own voice holding these men rapt, and he felt pride in his heart, and confidence as well, and he described the passage of larger boats down the rapids and the thump and grind of their hulls as they bumped and dragged across the rocks, and then he said his own canoe had been too small to carry itself over the most precipitous chute and all aboard were tossed into the river only to surface in time to see the boat catch a rock and split in its centre, the supplies it held briefly dotting the surface before the current sucked them away.

He gathered his wind and saw the impact of his words on the men around the fire, all of whom had surely known a man drowned over the course of their careers. Only Rémi remained stoic as he packed his pipe with another pinch of tobacco.

Alex said that he and the other men managed to swim down the chute without dashing themselves upon the rocks and once clear of the back drag they heaved themselves up and into the other boats, but Alex wasn't permitted aboard and l'avant shouted over the roar of the river that this was because his weakness had cost them not just time but now supplies as well. It was within l'avant's authority to leave Alex for dead and the men paddled off and only one of them looked back, but briefly.

'Des vrais connards,' sneered one of the voyageurs, and all the other men nodded and mumbled except for Rémi, who made no sound at all, but nevertheless Alex felt his story had been accepted, however improbably, and for this he thanked both le seigneur and Serge and the ghost of his 'tit frère too.

'Thank Christ ye survived,' said the Captain. 'I've known men to be selfish and vindictive and cruel, sure as I have, but the men in that there story rank among the worst.'

'Yes, they are bad man,' said Alex, and he noticed Rémi glaring at the Captain from the opposite side of the fire. 'But I am stronger than they think, you see, and that is how I come to be washed in on your beach.'

5

THE CAPTAIN TOLD ALEX THAT THE MEN WERE IN UPPER Canada poaching fur to bring for trade on an island called Mackinac in Lake Huron, which is where they based themselves throughout the summer. He said it wasn't the general practice of the American Fur Company to creep across the border and engage in this sort of activity, and indeed the Captain and his brigade weren't there under the company's official sanction: they'd been headed to the Saginaw River to trap fur when they were robbed by Indians at the mouth of the waterway, so now they were short of supplies for a coming expedition and needed to do what they could to return themselves to a competitive posture. They'd been advised of a rise in the beaver population living in these Upper Canadian woods crowding the river that drained into the bay called Georgian, and so now they found themselves scouring the landscape but so far to stubbornly scant avail.

'And we've officially enlisted your help.' The Captain gestured with his hand, the back of which was covered in tufts of curly black hair. 'We've given you food and shown you hospitality, and in return we think it only fair that you help us achieve our goal. Any objections?'

Alex shook his head.

Rémi stood up and cleared his throat. He looked at the Captain and said, 'I will take him with me to check my lines.' Then he looked at Alex and said, 'Viens 'vec moi. Et dépêche-toi.'

'I'm not partial to the sound of that, Rémi,' said the Captain. 'Not a bit. You stay behind and finish curing that deer. Alex here will work with Séb. As for your traps in the river, Rénard will check on those.'

Rémi's face became dark and severe, and Alex looked to the other end of the smouldering fire, where a young man of maybe twenty-five stepped forward and tightened his sash, and although his face was troubled and shy, he made an effort to smile and wink and he said, 'On y va, on y va, on y va, alors.'

Behind him rose an older man with a burst of curly hair and great bushy side whiskers that had turned mostly grey. This man didn't smile or even acknowledge the others but wordlessly left the camp and slid between the trees, a musket in one hand and the other dangling in a slackly gathered fist.

They quit the camp moments later and Séb moved quickly through the woods. He threaded trees and slid down rocks and scrambled up bluffs, and Alex struggled to keep him in sight. They climbed a small and craggy cliff and Séb kicked loose a stone and it sailed past Alex's upturned face but he didn't lose his balance. Séb had set his traps far from the camp and he looked continually over his shoulder until the two of them had gone at least a kilometre from the beach, after which he became very chatty and in French he told Alex he had a wife and two daughters back in Québec and he'd built his family home outside Trois-Rivières; it was a log house with four bedrooms et un foyer magnifique, but he came to work for the American Fur Company once a year because he had connections in the country through his bloodline, which like a river had forked when his relations moved first to France and then to Louisiana after the British banished them from Acadie in Le Grand Dérangement. Most of his family remained in the south except for his father, who as a young man in his thirties went back to Lower Canada and became a peaceful worker in the foundry at Trois-Rivières, where Séb was born, and what about Alex, ah oui, bien sûr, a man from Montréal, what more did he need to know – un gars de ville and now a powerful woodsman besides.

Alex nodded and tried to smile but knew his eyes appeared sorrowful no matter the lie of his lips, and he worried as well that he hadn't travelled so very far from Serge's body, because surely the river he'd been wading poured into the bay these men were poaching, and so it was possible that they'd discovered Serge's body and connected him to it and further presumed the connection nefarious. Or would animals have already had their callous way with Serge's meat and the site of his death be a great distance away? Perhaps, but it was further possible that, despite his confidence during the telling of his tale, the Captain's men knew it was a lie. Or were they simply unsure and Alex had only to prove himself a capable woodsman and then this new group would usher him into their ranks and take him to their island? Once there, he could find passage to Fort William and maybe farther north as well, because he wouldn't be welcome back in Montréal, at least not by M. Anderson, and he knew no other way of getting a job. Serge had been right. The only way to get money to cross the Atlantic was to work as a voyageur, though even if there was another way, Alex wanted to honour Serge's wishes by fulfilling them himself, and hadn't he grown stronger in these past weeks? Yes, and hadn't he also grown accustomed to sleeping in the wilderness and enduring the elements and posting a vigilant eye to dangers of every shape and size? Yes, and therefore he could be hivernant, or at the very least try.

He picked at these thoughts as he climbed a hill, and when he crested he found Séb leaning against a tree and packing his pipe, and in a serious voice the latter said, 'There's something you must know if you want to work for us.' He went quiet and there was only the smell of his tobacco and the creak of the trees. 'It's about Captain Jones, who maybe you've noticed isn't a captain at all but a disgraced private and further un loup-garou, c'est vrai. This is a dangerous time, I tell you, not like previous years working for the company.'

This seemed like a joke at first, and although Alex didn't think it was funny he laughed anyway, but he stopped when Séb remained earnest. Alex's maman had told him about the loup-garou when he was a boy, and he used to believe the monster might chase him out of the woods in the form of either wolf or man, but later he imagined the creature was more likely trapped in the form of his papa or M. Anderson or the sons of his maman's patron.

Séb scowled and said there was nothing funny and he puffed his pipe in silence. Then he told Alex that Rémi and the Captain were locked in a power struggle to lead the expedition. The group had been languishing in these woods and had seen few signs of life, not even fish, which some of the men believed had fled the surrounding waters as soon as the brigade arrived and now no ordinary bait would lure them back. Although it was the Captain who had all the connections with the company agents, Rémi better understood the land and also the practice of trapping. He'd been a voyageur since he was young and his mother was an Ottawa who had died, but he was in communion with her spirit and his wife was also an Ottawa, and she awaited him back on Mackinac with his child, and indeed it was his wife's brother who told Rémi about the resurgence of the beaver in these parts, and then Rémi told the Captain, who was le patron, yes, but nevertheless a man he despised, because the Captain had killed plusieurs Indiens with blasts from cannons or muskets in what he called America's Second War of Independence, and this revelation filled Alex with anger, because les Indiens had been good to Serge and Serge had been good to him, and so he said, 'Mais les Indiens sont nos amis, quoi?'

Séb tapped the embers out of his pipe and said that in America it was different, just as it was different in the British-controlled lands too, but that was neither here nor there, because at the moment it was the Captain who commanded their group and it was the Captain who knew the people to whom they'd trade their fur and from whom they'd get their money, not Rémi, who had connections with no one important and was too proud or stupid to realize he couldn't control the group even if he became its leader.

6

SÉB AND ALEX RETURNED TO THE CAMP IN LATE AFTERNOON after hiking endless kilometres throughout the rocky bush, and the weather was hot and the bugs were legion and the spiky pong of their sweat followed them like a failure. They'd checked all Séb's traps but found no beaver, only one small fox of maybe fifteen pounds, and Alex had volunteered to carry the animal back to camp, where they'd skin it and cure it and dry its fur and eat its meat as part of their dinner.

As they entered the camp they saw others both returning and recently returned, but these men had little to show for their efforts, and none of them a beaver, including the older man with curly hair who'd walked off with a musket. This man approached empty-handed and Séb introduced him as Rénard, and when Rénard shook Alex's hand, the boy winced at the man's strength and was embarrassed and averted his eyes. The Captain was seated on the beach and the sunlight had gone soft with the early evening. He held a shard of mirror and a straight razor and with water and soap he methodically shaved his cheeks and neck and above and below his lips as well.

Rémi had sliced the deer meat into long, thin strips and he'd rubbed salt into these and covered them to keep the flies away. Now he drank from a bottle of rum and spoke to the men returning from the bush, and even from a distance Alex could see him growing tenser and tenser, no doubt because their smuggling effort was going awry. They'd have almost nothing to trade for supplies, and it was too late in the season for a brigade to be so poorly equipped.

An atmosphere of despondence overtook the camp. Dusk fell and the men made cooking fires and sat around them without looking one another in the eye. The Captain stood tall and placed a hand on the golden hilt of his sabre and in the manner of one accustomed to making speeches, he addressed the group: 'There are furs in these woods, men, of that there can be no doubt. And yet doubt is a most human experience in times such as these, common as clap among whores. So let me say this: Any man who doubts our ultimate success in this forest off this beach off this bay has only to look to the bounty of deer meat and the few martens and foxes acquired today. Our luck is changing. Beaver is coming. Yes, we're going through a time of scarcity, oh yes, the result of too much hunting and God knows what else, but understand that much of the industry is undergoing a similar experience, even those celebrated men way up in the British north. It's true what they say. The trade is old and products sold to Europe and China will soon be rare, if indeed they're sold at all. I agree, lads. Rarity is a-comin' just as sure as the goddamned Devil himself. But neither has yet to arrive, and the perseverance of men like ourselves will produce much from these trees and creeks and spaces between. Therefore, we stay here until we gather a few more pelts at the very least, and then we head back to Mackinac to make our trade, and after that we put paddle to current once more, likely in the Missouri, because for us it ain't just a question of profits, no, rather it's a question of adventure. Now let the delights of the evening begin so we may forget the disappointments of the day.'

Alex was disheartened to hear the Captain's assessment of trapping in the north, but the others were lifted by his words. Several bottles of rum were opened and passed around and a few men set off to rummage through the group's supplies, and they returned with two battered fiddles, a jaw harp, and a few sets of wooden spoons. These men and others gathered in a circle around the biggest fire. The players took up a tune and a few men began to dance with their hands on their hips and they lifted their knees and kicked their legs and crossed their ankles and some of them were drunk enough to fall and others roared with laughter. Rémi stood and called on the musicians to play

'V'là l'Bon Vent' and he drank deeply from his bottle as the Captain watched warily.

Séb took gentle hold of Alex's wrist and frowned and shook his head. With his chin he gestured toward Rémi, who as the song reached the start of its first verse threw his head back and howled les paroles as the braids of his beard swung this way and that and the sun sank behind the forest of pine and mad shadows crept out of the trees.

Alex knew the song as well as any other Canadien because his mother had sung it to him when he was a boy, and it wasn't hard to see why Rémi had chosen it, what with les paroles about a prince who shoots the duck of three peasant women and extracts from its body the bounty of silver and gold and even diamonds while leaving only the bird's feathers for the peasants to stuff their pillows.

The fiddlers played the song slowly and sadly and with their upper bodies swaying to the lilt of the strings and the flat muddy tap of the spoons and the steel pops of the jaw harp, and all the while Rémi bellowed the words to the thickening dusk:

> Le fils du roi s'en va chassant
> Avec son beau fusil d'argent.
>
> Visa le noir, tua le blanc.
> Ô fils du roi, tu es méchant.
>
> D'avoir tué mon canard blanc!
> Par-dessus l'aile, il perd son sang.
>
> Par les yeux lui sortent des diamants.
> Et par le bec l'or et l'argent.
>
> Toutes ses plumes s'en vont au vent,
> Trois dammes s'en vont les ramassant.

Alex and Séb were joined by Rénard, who was already drunk and tired and whose drawn face was creased with anger but mostly concern.

The three of them passed the bottle between them and watched Rémi rile up the musicians and dancers, while on the other side of the fire the Captain cursed and leapt to his feet and grabbed a voyageur by the shoulder. The two men conferred and then the Captain shoved the voyageur aside and strode toward the musicians and dancers. He threw his arm around the fiddler's neck and caused him to drop his instrument even as the Captain unsheathed his sabre and held it to the man's throat. The latter's eyes grew wide but didn't blink, rather stared scowlingly at his friends. The dancing died off and so did the rest of the music and all that could be heard was the crackle of the fire and the buzz of insects and the heavy breathing of the men.

A sickly warm breeze blew out of the forest and rustled the branches, and the Captain's voice seemed to originate more from the breeze than his mouth as he bared his teeth and said, 'So this is what a good meal does to bad men, is it? But why am I not surprised?'

Rémi showed his teeth as well and the light of the fire reflected off the saliva that coated them and above his head shone dimly the first of the evening's stars, and though his fists were clenched he didn't advance but held his ground in a huff.

'I see,' said the Captain, the blade of his sabre pressing into the flesh of the fiddler's neck, 'that the time has once again come to remind you all that you've been indentured into my service. You all signed your agreements in the perfect absence of any kind of duress at all, and then you hurried off to your water-holes and gambling dens and frittered away your cash advances, and most of you were penniless again but a few hours later.'

Rémi jabbed one of his gnarled fingers. 'That does not give you the right to march us to our deaths in these barren woods.'

'Not entirely barren,' said the Captain, jerking his chin at the curing meats and furs. The fiddler grunted and the Captain said, 'And allow me to remind you on whose information we planned this here voyage, Rémi. But nevertheless, I see you've lost your faith yet again, of that you've made yourself clear. You wish to leave?'

'Bien sûr que oui. We must go back to Michigan and prepare a journey west. Miigwan was wrong. It happens.'

The Captain sniffed and swallowed and let his eyes flit about the fire, until finally they landed on Alex, whose head had grown fuzzy with rum and worry. 'I reckon that's possible,' said the Captain. He lowered his sabre, returning it to its sheath as the fiddler stumbled away with one hand pressed against his throat. 'But you'll have to win a little contest first. Otherwise, I won't release you from your indenture and instead see to it that no matter how far you go, the company's men hunt you down and clap your legs in iron.'

Rémi put his hand in his beard and pinched one of his braids and dragged his fingers slowly down the length of it. 'What type of contest?'

The Captain grinned. 'Why, fisticuffs on the ole beach, of course.'

7

THE FULL MOON LOOKED LIKE IT COULD FALL OUT OF THE
sky, and beneath it the Captain approached Alex and led him away
from Séb and Rénard. The waves of the bay washed lazily up the beach
and the fire popped and the pines creaked. The flames threw haggard
shadows at the woods and it seemed as if the Captain's face was coated
in stubble despite the fact that Alex had seen him shaving just a few
hours before. The musicians had taken up another tune but no one
danced and the night was thick with the coming fight.

The Captain put his hand on Alex's shoulder and his breath was
rotten as he spoke. 'Your story doesn't quite make sense, lad, but don't
worry, because there's very little out in the woods or anywhere else that
does, and nevertheless I see something in you and want time to figure
out just what it is. But first, I've a little test you must pass before your
spot in the brigade is assured, do you follow me, lad?'

Alex looked at the coarse hairs sprouting from the Captain's neck
and said nothing.

'He's a big boy, Rémi, that he is, and a constant fire under my
culet. There was a time when I could've made use of a man like
that, but old Rémi has lost sight of his place in the world, and as
often happens when a man loses sight of so precious a perspective,
he's created a fiction to fill the void, and from this he entertains a
notion of power.'

Alex began to shake. 'I don't win a fight against him. I don't have
any chance.'

'Oh? And why's that now?'

Alex shook his head in disbelief. 'Look at me! I am small and weak and he is not.'

'True, you're weak, and true, you're small, but you're also strong, because the world is just a-burstin' with contradiction and life is both enriched and impoverished by the Heaven and Hell of its preponderance.' He chuckled and opened his coat and pulled from its darkness a small dagger with a black blade. From his pocket he took a leather sheath and twine with which to tie it. Alex looked nervously over the Captain's shoulder, but they were ensconced in shadows and the other men couldn't see them. 'I'm guessing you've taken your fair share of beatings in this life, correct? You'll take another one tonight, sure enough, but not to the point of death, nor even defeat. You let that brute knock you flat, and when he stoops to finish you off, pull this knife and stab him in the ribs, not once, mind, but dozens of times, and do it quickly, and then these other men'll regard you in high esteem and never again will you be bested as you have been so many times before.'

The brigade had moved out of the woods and onto the beach and they'd found long branches and wrapped these in moss and then lit them aflame. Now the torches stuck out of the sand but still the dark pressed inward. The moon hung over the down-shore cliffs, but its light couldn't quite reach them, as if it were devoured before it could touch the sands. Alex had never known so far ahead he was about to be the victim of violence, and absent the element of surprise his fear had ample opportunity to occupy his entire body so that he felt a sinking feeling in his bowels as though he might shit himself. He watched as Rémi guzzled rum and threw his head back and howled at the sky, which swallowed his rage and gave back nothing. Alex brushed the hair out of his face and worried the knife was visible beneath his tattered cotton shirt and he couldn't imagine himself brandishing it quickly enough or even figuring out how to use it if he could. He wondered what Serge would do and knew his friend would refuse the weapon, but the convictions of a man like Serge were not the province of a boy like Alex, who had to grasp at whatever he could.

Now the Captain stood behind Alex with a handful of other men, among them Séb and Rénard, the former with eyes wide and mouth ever so slightly open, the latter still and stoic. On the other end of the beach Rémi's supporters clapped their champion on the back and puffed their pipes and passed between them bottles of rum. Rémi emerged from their numbers with his fists clenched and his hairy face held high in the light of the fire. The musicians lurched into a frenzied tempo, and Rémi roared and came dashing down the beach, his beard blowing over one shoulder and his bare feet gouging the sand.

His first fist caught Alex in the jaw, and Alex heard a loud pop from somewhere in his neck and then his body was briefly weightless and then his back thumped the beach. Seen from the ground, the many torches appeared as burning trees and their angry light obscured the sky. Rémi stood between the flames and grinned as the braids of his beard hung like ropes from his chin. Alex struggled to stand and understood Rémi had given him the space to do so, and with a shaky hand he drew the dagger and held it limply before him, but already he knew he'd done this prematurely, and indeed Rémi snorted and made a gesture with his hand and shook his head. He looked to his men, who were variously laughing or sneering or drinking or smoking, and the Captain called for Alex to attack, goddamn it, attack, and still Rémi shook his head, but now with a trace of pity.

The distance between them was slight and Alex stood there holding his weapon slackly before him and in his mind was nothing but the sound of rushing blood and the hammering of his heart, and then Rémi closed the distance. He slapped the knife from Alex's sweaty grip, and from beyond the torches the Captain swore and shouted for Alex to retrieve the weapon and attack goddamn it attack. But the blade was too black to be seen and anyway Rémi grabbed him by the throat of his shirt and caused its stitches to burst, then spun him round and held him still with a granite forearm barred across his throat. 'You think I am so cruel as to beat to death a child in the woods?'

Hand at the hilt of his sabre in its sheath, the Captain stepped into the torchlight.

'I will only hurt him,' said Rémi, 'and this as a teacher, not a pawn, and then we will go back to Mackinac and you will release the group of us from your terms.' He threw Alex to the ground and kicked him in the ribs and seemed ready to do so again, but a warm spray spattered them both and at the same time they heard an explosion and the Captain screaming until his voice cracked and peeled and scattered into the trees. Then the American fell to his knees and slapped at a gaping wound in his chest before falling quietly on his face.

Alex looked up at Rémi and the two made eye contact before Rémi's shoulder exploded and he fell to the ground as another shot echoed round the bay. Men ran in every direction and Alex crawled away from the firelight toward the woods. He saw a group of armed men slide out of the pine and they wore Hudson's Bay Company stripes and fired calm shots at the Captain's brigade, each taking a knee to pour powder down the barrels of their flintlock rifles and ramrod another ball before standing and discharging again, and though some men in the Captain's brigade had weapons, none fired back, perhaps because the Captain had died and Rémi had fallen and with them went a good deal of collective courage.

Soon there were bodies on the beach and a few men floating face down in the shallows and the faintest light of the stars reflected in the water around them. Alex had hidden in the woods and watched as one of the attackers kneeled before Rémi and looked up and called out to his partners, 'Lui, il est encore en vie.'

Another of these men snorted. 'Et alors?'

Alex heard Rémi curse and even saw him lift one of his hands, but the attacker effortlessly knocked it aside, and in disdainful French he said, 'Your company has no charter in the bay or on its shores. You know that very well, and your disrespect has sown your fate.'

The man left Rémi to suffer and joined his partners by the firepit and together they assessed the goods they found scattered about, and Alex overheard a few complain about the paucity of these offerings but heard others say they'd been watching the group for two days and knew what little they had and that was beside the point. It was about territory and anyway these few goods could be traded at Fort William, alors mieux que rien.

8

THE NIGHT WAS LONG AND EVEN AFTER THE HUDSON'S BAY
men had left, Alex was too scared to quit his hiding place. He felt
pine needles beneath his palms and a stone digging into his knee and
he listened to Rémi gain and lose consciousness and briefly the man
was brought to tears. When finally the sky began to lighten and the
moon could no longer be seen, Alex crawled out of the bushes and
winced at the pain in his neck and jaw and ribs. He made his way to
Rémi, whose eyes bulged at the sight of him but then softened and
glistened as well.

Rémi's shoulder was destroyed. There was blood and bone and the
burnt shreds of his cotton shirt and it was clear that he'd die, if not
now then within a few hours.

'Il est foutu,' said a voice, and Alex turned to see Séb standing there
with pine needles in his hair and dirt on his cheeks.

Rénard was beside him and held a musket, which he'd not fired
during the ambush. He had a ghastly cut on his forearm and sighed
and shook his head and rested the gun on his shoulder. 'We must leave.'

'Non,' said Rémi, but this was a whimper that could scarcely be
heard. 'J'vous en supplie.'

Alex stood and flinched from the pain in his neck and made his
way to the firepit, and although the attackers had thoroughly pilfered
their goods, he was able to find a tin cup half-buried in sand, and with
this he hurried to the lakeshore and dunked the cup underwater before
hurrying back. He held it over Rémi's mouth and tipped it and a small
stream soaked the man's beard and ran over his lips.

'I must die on the island,' said Rémi, 'with my wife and baby.'

'He won't make it,' said Rénard. 'We must go before we're found by another Hudson's brigade.'

Alex poured more water into Rémi's mouth and the wounded man coughed without turning his head. 'Where will we go?'

'Y'a un 'tit canot. It'll take a long time to paddle with just us three, but we can get to Mackinac and then we'll report what happened, but we'll say it happened in Michigan, not here.'

Rémi coughed again and spat on his own chest and said, 'They'll blame les Indiens.'

'Allez,' said Séb and he began walking away. 'We must prepare le canot.'

Alex looked from Séb and Rénard to Rémi. He knew the former two were right, but Rémi had shown sympathy during their fight and if they hadn't been ambushed by the Hudson's Bay men it was possible Rémi wouldn't have beaten him so badly but instead taken the fight to the Captain. 'T'inquiète pas, Rémi,' he said, and he stroked the older man's brow and felt certain he was doing the correct thing in taking his side. 'I'll talk to them. We'll make sure you see your wife. Rest now.'

Rémi's blue lips managed a weak smile and his eyes fluttered closed and he was instantly asleep.

Alex joined Séb and they found le 'tit canot in the trees and beneath it they uncovered two fishing poles as well as hooks. The boat had been made for five, maybe six men, and they heaved it out of the woods and toward the shore.

'You refuse to take him with us?'

'Rénard is right, Alex. Rémi will weigh down the boat and be dead before we reach the first islands.'

'But it's a simple request.'

'Non. I have known Rémi for three weeks and nothing with him is simple. If he regains his strength, he might harm us. Even if he dies, he might harm us. You can't even trust le cadavre of a man like that. We listen to Rénard. We leave just the three of us and we go as soon as possible.'

'Maybe he'll help us paddle.'

'He won't. Look at his shoulder. And anyway, it isn't in his nature to help. You must be firm when you're strong, and so we leave him. If you won't agree, then Rénard and I will paddle the boat alone, because you won't be on it.'

They reached the water and lowered the boat and each of them jolted when the hull knocked against the skull of a dead man submerged in the weedy shallows. Séb's words were une menace, but although offended Alex understood his life would be the sort that darkened daily with umbrage, and unlike stronger men who expressed their rage with abandon, he'd have to find a less direct means of gaining say because the world was largely deaf to his voice and doubtful of what little it heard.

In the end it didn't matter. As Séb and Alex sloshed out of the shallows, they heard a shot, and when they looked up the beach they saw Rénard standing over Rémi and still pointing the musket at his chest and the barrel still smoking and in Rémi's body was the gaping hole of the bullet fired at close range. Rénard kneeled and reloaded the weapon and then stood and walked toward them. He said Rémi had been asleep when he fired the shot and so none the wiser, and Alex wasn't sure but ultimately chose to believe this because it was good and proper to imagine Rémi had died thinking he'd soon see his wife rather than alone and abandoned on a beach with only the blasted bodies of dead men to keep him company.

But Séb grew anxious at the sight of Rémi's corpse and rushed Rénard and Alex to the boat. Rénard saw the fishing poles and chuckled and walked back to Rémi's body. He kneeled and drew a knife from his waist and cut a piece of flesh from Rémi's chest, then another and another. He walked back to the boat and tossed the flesh inside, where it landed with a splat, and when Séb gave him a look of horror, Rénard shrugged and said they'd need good bait if they were to catch any fish, for look at the failure of their efforts over the preceding days, and besides what use did Rémi now have for a few strips of his chest, none at all.

The three of them pushed off and began the arduous task of paddling le canot. Alex was in the middle and Séb was in the bow, while

Rénard took up the most difficult position at the stern. The water was green and clear in the sunlight and there were fish picking at the dead floating near the shore, but they were too small to eat and otherwise there seemed to be no life beneath the hull of the boat and none in the air either, not an eagle or even a gull. But then, as they glided away from the shore, they saw a beaver breach where the river drained into the lake and it looked at them and slapped its tail on the surface, and although Rénard raised his musket the animal dove back under before he could fire a shot.

Le canot was heavy even though it bore no supplies, and the action of paddling filled Alex's ribs and neck with sparkling pain, but this he ignored, choosing instead to set his jaw and stare down the horizon and repeat the motion over and over again. This, he realized, was a determination he'd always had, not one just arrived.

'Gardez,' said Séb after five minutes or so, and Alex looked up to see him pointing back down the beach. 'Des Indiens? J'en doute.'

They were maybe half a kilometre away and it was hard to see clearly but did appear as though two men were standing in the shallows with something limp between them and sagging and shaped like one of the bodies that had been floating near the shore. Then they tossed the body on the beach and crouched and lowered their heads and began to thrash.

9

RÉNARD AND SÉB DISCUSSED VARIOUS ROUTES, DECIDING IT safest to travel northwest at a distance from the shore so they'd appear as a blur to anyone moving through the woods. A chain of islands would rise up on their port side, and toward the end of their first day they'd come upon a tight strait between one of these islands and the mainland, which they'd creep through quickly and quietly, as there'd be Ottawa villages around and they didn't want to risk an encounter. They took frequent breaks because the sun was hot and the water of the bay seemed not to quench their thirst or cool their skin. It was hard not to think of the dead floating in the shallows of Upper Canada and hard not to interpret their bodies as harbingers of a similar fate, but Alex didn't voice these concerns because he felt a growing tension among the group.

He was hungry and exhausted, and a number of times he felt himself nodding off even as he paddled, until finally he didn't jerk himself awake but rather lost a few seconds of consciousness. When he came to, it was because Séb had cursed him and twisted around in the bow of le canot with a scornful look on his face.

'You lied about your story, it's obvious,' he said, 'because you're no woodsman, that's clear. My daughter can paddle better than you, come on.'

Rénard reached forward and grabbed Alex by the shoulder and sank one of his powerful thumbs into the flesh of his collarbone and briefly held him like this before letting go, and with his blue eyes narrowed to slits he said, 'We want the truth or we'll throw you in the lake and watch you drown.'

Not far off, Alex saw the first of the islands, lonesome mounds of pale rock with gnarled pines clinging to their surfaces because that was where God had hurled His trees to root. Alex set his paddle across his knees and hung his head and his hair fell loose and obscured his face. He imagined himself sitting there, feeble, scrawny, and once again he didn't know where he was and once again he didn't know who he was with, and while he understood these factors as common for men of his times, he also feared that unlike those men he wouldn't be able to find his place in such a confusing world. He'd been certain the Captain's brigade had believed his story and now two more of them were casting doubt. He realized the only person he'd fooled was himself, and while he'd drawn strength from that delusion the strength like its source was unreal. Perhaps then it wasn't the individual words or the whole story that had bought the Captain's favour but rather the way Alex had spoken and the way he'd told his story. Perhaps now the words had lingered in the minds of the men, and absent the way he'd spoken them, they'd begun to feel cheap and false. Or perhaps the Captain and the others obeyed dictates issued from authorities Alex couldn't fathom, or perhaps they were all mad and there was no grappling with any of it.

'Écoutez,' said Alex, and he lifted his head and shook the hair out of his eyes. He looked first at Rénard, whose face was creased and puckered, then at Séb, who wore a similar mask of anger, but less intense, less committed. 'You're right to doubt the story. I made it up. But I couldn't risk your brigade sending me into the wilderness alone or worse. I was desperate.'

Séb frowned and turned to face the islands that loomed larger and larger, and Rénard said, 'Did you lead those men to our camp?'

'Non!' cried Alex, and he felt foolish that he hadn't seen the situation as something so suspicious, though clearly it could appear as nothing else. 'I've never seen those men before. J'vous l'jure!'

Séb and Rénard said nothing and the three of them merely paddled the boat for a time during which Alex said nothing as well, until it occurred to him that he was being invited to tell the true story of his arrival in the Captain's camp, and so he began with Serge in Montréal and ended with the ghost of his dead brother rescuing him from the mysterious flood. He told them what a great man Serge had been and how he was renowned all throughout the trade, but neither Séb nor Rénard recognized the name and this ignorance Alex accepted quietly and with all the neutrality he could muster lest he make plain the depths of his love, which surely wouldn't be understood by men such as these but rather could've renewed the forces of anger and violence that had dogged him relentlessly for months. Alex would need these two to help when they got to Mackinac, and so just the right amount of truth would have to do, which happily was the bulk of the story anyway.

There was a long period of silence after he'd finished, only the sound of water sloshing against the hull of le canot and their paddles knocking off the gunwales as they laboured through their strokes.

After a time, Séb stopped paddling and shifted around so that he was facing Alex, and he said, 'Me too, I've seen the ghosts of my lost family. En effet, it was one of them who first led me from Québec to the American Fur Company when I needed work, and only this summer did I make the journey without the help of a ghost, and look at the misfortune.'

Alex was surprised to have his story so readily accepted and nodded but didn't speak because from behind Rénard filled his lungs with air and said, 'Me too, I experienced the unreal once as a young man collecting syrup in the woods of Vermont, where my older sister followed me for two days through the trees but left no footprints in the soft snow because she'd died in a storm some months previous.' His voice was shaky and he cleared his throat and tried again. 'The other time was on this very lake. It was my first year working for the American Fur Company and I was travelling with several men to Mackinac to begin the season. We were passing through the islands we're right now approaching when the water around le canot began to bubble and boil, as if we were travelling across the surface of a cooking pot, and drops of this boil flew into the boat and burned terribly the face of l'avant.' He shook his head and ran a hand through his greying curls. 'It went on for ten minutes, maybe more, and when it finally stopped, one of our crew said it had been the beast of the lake foretold by les Hurons, but I knew otherwise when I saw a fistful of my sister's blonde hair twisting in the wake of the boat. As for l'avant, he was struck blind and unable to eat or drink because of the burns to his lips and mouth, and he died a week later and after was identified as a vengeful fugitive who'd murdered several of his brigade the season before and vowed revenge on the survivors and anyone working alongside them. My sister knew. She protected me.'

'It's good you told us this,' said Séb, 'because Rénard and me, we've had special experiences in our lives. But it's also good you didn't share it with the others, because they wouldn't have believed you, not even the Captain or Rémi, who right now are les esprits des loups tearing at the bodies of those fallen men, and when they're done their meal they'll fight each other and the waves of the bay will grow high in the storm of their violence. We must get as far as we can before that happens.'

10

THEY CAME TO TRUST HIM, OR SO IT SEEMED, AND THEY told him how the American Fur Company had recently tightened its terms of indenture while simultaneously raising the rates of trade, and not for the first time, except now it had become too hard to make money in the employ of men like the Captain, who themselves went madder and madder with the passing of every season. They said the best thing was to return to Québec, and Séb said he'd work in the iron foundry at Trois-Rivières because who among them couldn't see this sort of industry as the way of the future, and as for Rénard he said he was too old to learn new skills but would leave Vermont to the Americans and return to Québec as well, and there he'd fish the rivers and in the winters tap the maples for syrup, because he knew his sister would protect him and despite his advanced years he'd take a wife, maybe even an Indian, why not, he wouldn't be the first, and in this way they'd prosper, however slowly, because the integrity of such a life would merit the whole of his sister's aegis, even if occasionally he'd been less than moral in his practice as a voyageur.

Larger islands now loomed at their port, and Séb wiped the sweat from his brow and spat in the bay and then turned around and put his paddle into the water once more. Over his shoulder he said, 'When we get back to Mackinac, I'll introduce you to some of my friends and they'll help you find a place on one of the boats headed back to Québec. It's best you return to Montréal.'

Alex stopped paddling. 'But that's not what I want. I want to go north. I want to be hivernant.'

Séb said this wasn't possible for a man so inexperienced as Alex, and anyway the trade had been languishing for decades in those environs, this because of overtrapping and disease and conflict between its various agents. 'Many hivernants are either starving or coming south now. The north has been spoiled, like the Captain said.'

Alex felt a jolt of pain in his jaw from where Rémi had punched him. He swallowed and closed his eyes, and when the pain subsided he said, 'But you told me the Captain was a liar.'

Séb shrugged. 'He was. He is. But the north is spoiled, it's true.'

'Laisse-le faire ce qu'il veut,' said Rénard. 'If he wants to live among cannibals, he wants to live among cannibals. He has his brother to watch over him, as we have our own esprits as long as we remain good Catholics. Besides, there's a bigger problem. No matter where we go or with who, we'll need money to pay our way. And we have no money, nor anything to trade, and soon enough we'll return to Mackinac just two people and one stranger from a group of fourteen. The company will want answers. They might even punish us.'

'Alors,' said Séb, 'we'll tell them what Rémi feared. We'll say les Indiens killed the brigade and we'll say it happened in Michigan Territory, and if they choose to send a search party for the bodies, they'll find nothing and their miserable relationship with les Indiens will be no worse off or better.'

'That might work,' said Rénard, 'but it might not. And anyway, they won't pay us if we have nothing to show. More than the massacre our problem is money.'

Very close to their port, an island rose out of the water like the skull of a bear and there was one ravaged cedar clinging to its rugged snout but no sign of human settlement. Rénard said les Indiens had a great spirit that lived on these islands and it was called Manitou and although he'd never admit this to his priest back home, he was nevertheless afraid the demon might be real. Séb motioned for Alex to be quiet as they paddled past the island and into a maze of similar formations, and although the day was sunny and a breeze had been blowing across the bay, here it was shady and cold and utterly still. They paddled for an hour, looking warily at the rocky lumps and shards, and after they made it through the foretold strait without incident, they were all exhausted and the sun was low in the sky, but even though the northern peninsula of Upper Michigan was now at their starboard it wasn't safe to make camp ashore, and anyway Rénard said they had to press on.

He and Séb rigged up the fishing poles but didn't offer one to Alex. Rénard plucked a rotting piece of Rémi's chest from the bottom of the boat and skewered it on his hook and cast out. He looked to Séb and flicked his chin at the flesh, but Séb didn't move to grab a piece, rather said there was no point, their fishing efforts in Upper Canada had proved hopeless, why would this be any different?

Rénard blew an irritated sigh and baited a hook for Séb. 'We were using the wrong bait. Trust me. Nature welcomes the opportunity to take a bite out of a man.'

After a long time Rénard caught a trout and drew his knife and gutted it and ate some of the viscera and then all three of them shared the fish raw. They used a third piece of Rémi's chest to catch another. Séb hooked a few pikes but said these couldn't be eaten raw, so he let them all go except two, which he tied to the side of the boat with twine from his moccasins. 'We don't want to go back with nothing,' he said to Alex. 'It's hard to trust even a friend with nothing, never mind a stranger like you.'

Their journey lasted through the night. At one point they all had to shit and Séb worried le canot would capsize if one of them simply squatted over the side, so they took turns, one man shitting as the other two leaned against the opposite gunwale. They also took turns sleeping so one if not two could keep le canot pointed in the right direction. The air turned cold and the wind blew softly and caused them to shiver, but all the same they were grateful the sky didn't portend a storm and indeed the stars shone in endless arrangements.

When he slept, Séb slid off the paddle bench and leaned his back against it and lowered his chin to his sternum. He snored raucously and spoke in his sleep, but not clearly enough for Alex to make out the words, except once, when he cried out for his belle puce. Rénard slept in total silence and almost without moving, as if he were dead.

Alex's arms were weak and rubbery but somehow he pressed on, finding in himself an inner reserve of stubborn strength, and in this he felt he was closer to becoming the sort of voyageur Serge knew he could be and he knew as well that the men were misinformed about the state of the industry in the north, just as they'd been ignorant of Serge's notoriety in the trade. Alex felt confident that Serge was watching him and like his brother would reveal himself when the time was right, and happily he realized that his maman must be watching as well, and this made him smile and blow her a kiss.

When it was his turn to sleep he tried to assume the same position as Séb and Rénard but found the edge of the seat cut into his back and kept him awake, and so instead he chose to rest with his eyes closed. During one of these reprieves, he heard Rénard tell Séb about a plan to rob the supply store of the American Fur Company on Mackinac Island. 'Many a voyageur has dreamed of such a pillage,' he said, 'because the company fairly invites it. We should be the ones to make the dream come true, n'est-ce pas?'

I I

THEY REACHED MACKINAC ISLAND LATE THE NEXT AFTER-
noon, and it was big and shaped like the back of a moose swimming
between the two peninsulas of Michigan Territory. Much of the shoreline seemed low to the green water and harassed by gulls, though here
and there they saw slate-grey cliffs and everywhere the bone-white
trunks of birch trees and the familiar spread of maple leaves, but no
sign of human settlement. Rénard said they'd have to make their way
to the edge of the straits at the southern point, and wearily Alex dug
his paddle into the current and heaved on. Over Séb's shoulder, he saw
both a smaller island and a fishing boat travelling between the two,
and as they got closer a fort came into view high on a hill, sunlight
glinting off the barrel of a bronze cannon, and even from a distance
the palisades looked shoddy and worn. Alex had been labouring all
afternoon, and with total exhaustion he heard the grumpy sound of
the hull first nudging and then gouging the pebbly beach, then the
sounds of two waves foaming and sighing and sliding back into the
lake. Later on, a drunken Séb would claim to have howled a hoot of
triumph as they arrived, but en réalité Alex knew without a doubt
that Séb had been slumped over the side of the boat, his paddle lost
to the straits and a thread of saliva hanging from the corner of his
sunburnt lips.

The long beach spilled out from the edge of a village that rambled
downhill from the gates of the fort. All along the line of trees were
tents and the beach was swarming with people, a hundred or more,
and the noises they made were thick and pitched: here a fat man in

buckskins playing a detuned fiddle; there an Ottawa woman singing as she stretched a pelt to cure; up and down the expanse there were fires burning and the smell of meat and shit as well as men shouting through transactions, and it was clear many of them were drunk.

Rénard was wide awake and expressionless and he jumped out of le canot and glared at Alex and roughly shook Séb out of his sleep. He strode up the beach all strewn with people and tents, and he motioned for them to follow.

Later, they traded their fish and canoe for a few nights in a wedge tent owned by a Canadien named Simon, who was friends with Rénard. He slept in there with an Ottawa girl of maybe fifteen and said he was holding her as collateral for a gambling debt owed by her father. The tent was small and the place stank of sweat and alcohol, but this was the condition of many such tents on the beach and the smell was leavened somewhat by cooking fires but worsened again by curing meat. Most men were Canadien and they hailed from Lower Canada and Louisiana and the farms around Detroit, and scattered among the many white and mixed-blood faces were the Ottawa, some bare-chested with colourful feathers in their sky-black hair and others with the cotton shirts and red sashes and cloth trousers of the voyageurs and still others dressed in exotic clothes, red silk shirts and gauzy scarves, which they must've procured from travellers, who in turn had procured them from travellers, and on and on it went until the world seemed somehow small and negotiable, even though clearly it was not. Alex sometimes watched this activity through the flap of the tent and other times lay back and rested his head and slept without remembering his dreams.

He awoke early the next morning, hungry but rested. He was alone in the tent with Séb, who drooled in his sleep, and Rénard, who wore no clothes and slept face down with an empty bottle of rum held slackly in one of his hands and his body stinking of sweat and his breathing laboured and sporadic, and when he did exhale his wind smelled rotten even from a few feet away.

Alex left the tent and stretched in the morning sun. He walked down the beach toward the water, where three dogs fought over scraps around the charred remains of a fire. He waded into the shore and enjoyed the water's light bite against the flesh of his ankles, and he kept wading until his trousers were soaked to the knees and then he dove in and opened his eyes and watched minnows dart from his approach. It was amazing to swim, and he offered a prayer of thanks to his brother for teaching him how. When he broke the surface and sloshed around to face the shore he saw Séb waving at him from the beach. He lifted his arm out of the water and smiled and returned the salutation, then dipped back under and felt the current stream through his hair as he swam ashore.

For breakfast Séb and Alex sat on driftwood scattered round a firepit and they ate fried eggs and ham that tasted like sulphur, passing between them a jug of warm beer. Séb said he'd gone to report the slaughter to the authorities, who'd send a small company of armed men to retrieve the bodies from the forested lands of the territory's northern peninsula, which was vast and stretched from the bottom of Lake Superior to the top of Lake Huron. He said this was less an earnest search of the woods than a gesture of good will to the families and a show of strength to les Indiens, whom Séb had blamed for the massacre.

They passed the morning drinking beer and smoking a pipe and they watched fishing boats tip through the straits and on land they saw people wander from various tents to the shore and also up the beach and into the village, where the American Fur Company ran its supply store. The store was the subject of a thick-tongued rant issued by Rénard when finally in the early afternoon he roused himself and clothed himself and lowered his thin frame to the driftwood between Alex and Séb, and immediately he extended his hand to receive the jug of beer, but when he discovered it was empty he scoffed and shook his head and spat in the sand and continued his rant against the company.

Rénard said they'd been gone two weeks and yet again the company had tightened its terms of trade and the conditions of indenture. He knew because Simon had explained it all the night previous, and any Canadien who complained had his contract suspended, and if enough men complained the company would simply recruit other

Frenchmen, for since the Second War of Independence the French had crawled across the land like lice across the hide of a cow, why shouldn't they, and if the company couldn't beguile them, then it would turn to the Ottawa, who were filthy and desperate and would accept even slavery if it meant a heel of bread in the morning and a piece of pemmican for lunch. He cursed John Jacob Astor, the real estate mogul who owned the company, a scoundrel, and his treatment of les Canadiens amounted to revenge for when they outmaneuvered his agents in the west and along the Missouri, and a man like Astor needed the armed imps of government to rescue him from his incompetence, whereas les Canadiens relied on themselves and each other and no one else.

'And yet we're not resisting the company these days,' said Rénard, 'not sufficiently. Me and Simon are disgusted. We're just sitting here and many of us are lazily forgoing our expeditions and all that results is the company recruits other men and those of us who don't go trapping owe it more money, and so everyone takes home less come winter, and the company leaves us only with the hope that next year will be better, which of course it will not.'

They spent the afternoon roving the village, which was a sad nest of muddy streets flanked by weather-beaten buildings: a schoolhouse and a tavern and a blacksmith and row of sloping homes, but not a stone building to speak of, rather everything had been built from the forest of pine and birch and maple that reared up over the settlement like a wave, and in comparison the village gardens looked tiny and haggard and lost. They brought along two axes and three hammers and first they took their tools to the church, where they proposed to cut wood for the lanky, grey-eyed reverend, but this man was a Protestant and so was his church, and he couldn't keep scorn from twisting his thin, white lips as he pronounced there to be no work for French Catholics, at least not around those most holy of environs. Rénard spat at the man's polished shoes and shouted 'Va t'enculer, 'tit fils d'pute', and the reverend turned pale and retreated up the steps of his church and the three of them walked off and grouped again farther down the swampy road.

Rénard began again to lament the lot of les Canadiens on Mackinac, because wasn't it the French who first settled this area, oui, c'est vrai, they'd built a grand fort on the mainland and it had mighty palisades and deep ditches and ramparts too, but they lost their position to the British and watched as the British lost it to les sauvages but then regained it and moved the fort to the island, only to lose it to the Americans. The fighting between these two had briefly divided les Canadiens, those to the south of the Great Lakes and those to the north, but they'd since forgiven each other the violence of war, and today the whole place was overrun with bluecoats who were neither subtle nor kind about the advantages they held. The three were now passed by an Ottawa man with a pole across his shoulders and a bucket of shit hanging from each end, and Rénard redoubled his outrage, because this was work that not even un Canadien could get but rather un maudit sauvage who'd gone to the Indian agent and disavowed his chief and was too struck blind with gratitude to realize he was merely a slave, except recently his shackles had become invisible, and so what, because how quickly the Americans had forgotten their debt to the French, oui, la mère-patrie, and how quickly they'd come to see their independence as God-given rather than supported by the French. Here Alex mentioned the Captain and the thanks he'd expressed regarding the French, and at this Rénard sneered, 'But it was the Americans who ousted us from our trading posts all along the eastern side of the continent and who overlook us daily in the west. The Captain was a liar. As for his American brothers, they're the British in blue, nothing more.'

After a time, they passed the American Fur Company's supply store and sat on the other side of the street and watched two armed bluecoats smoking cigars on the porch. Rénard said the store was full of supplies that rightfully belonged to the voyageurs but had been taken from them by the greed of the company as manifested in the increasingly outrageous rules of trade and indenture and what they should do was rally together a few politically minded men, like Simon, to whom he'd already spoken at length regarding this very subject, and both agreed that they should take their bounty off the island and back to Québec, where at least the British allowed them a region to call their own, and while there was of course interference within this region, the British didn't want another war, so it was the duty of every Canadien to return to Québec and be counted.

Séb cleared his throat and put his hand on Rénard's shoulder, giving it a friendly shake. He said that some plans were possible and some plans were dangerous and some plans were both, but he himself feared a dangerous plan, regardless of how possible, especially one that involved theft, because surely such a plan would not warrant the oversight of their spiritual guardians.

Rénard shook him off and cleared snot from his nose and said he knew of a man building a house not far away and this man was un connard like everyone else who spoke English, but he was un connard who sometimes drank with Rénard and so likely they could get a few hours' work hammering nails or squaring fresh timbers and with the proceeds they could buy food and rum for the night.

The work turned out to be hard and tedious because unlike Séb and Rénard, who chopped timbers into perfect squares, Alex was clumsy with an axe and le patron made him scrub fish barrels instead. The man never spoke directly to Alex but relayed orders through Séb and Rénard, and while the former directed him with a least a faint trace of civility, the latter was gruff and rude, and after a few hours Alex began to resent them both.

Later that evening, the heat broke and a cool breeze blew off the lake and ruffled the tents and stoked the cooking fires scattered along the beach. The sun was setting behind the forest, and the straits beyond the island's settled shore had begun to darken. They sat around a fire outside Simon's tent and Alex was sore and tired and hungry, but they'd spent most of their pittance on rum and for food they'd only managed half a loaf of bread, which they dipped in cooking oil because it was too hard and stale to otherwise chew. The rum took hold fast and fierce because his stomach was nearly empty and Alex lay on the beach and looked at the emerging stars and was about to drift off when above him loomed the figure of Simon, whose face was lit by a nearby fire that revealed his advanced state of inebriation, this man with chunks of vomit in his beard and one of his eyes pinched shut and the other peeled wide and wheeling, and in one hand he held a three-barrelled pepperbox pistol and in the other he gripped the wrist of the Ottawa girl he'd been keeping as collateral. He opened his mouth and the fire illuminated a thick cord of saliva dangling from his upper teeth, and he said, 'This girl's hure of a papa can't produce the money in a timely fashion and so tonight we'll make a bit of money in the tent, and tell me, my friend, would you like to fuck this filthy salope?'

Alex couldn't believe what he was hearing and couldn't therefore summon a response, but he did glance at the girl, who wore a cotton dress and a fur smock, and from her neck hung several strings of beads, their colours strangely muted. Her bruised face was set in a look of fierce determination, and although Simon yanked hard on her arm as he talked she refused to acknowledge him. Alex looked to Séb, who stared at his own bare feet, then Rénard, who stood and tossed Simon a copper coin he must've withheld from the day's earnings. He took the girl by the wrist and pulled her toward the tent. Séb hauled himself to his feet and staggered off, and though Alex remained still for a moment, he soon stood and followed Séb into the thickening darkness of the beach.

They gathered at the shoreline, where the waves somewhat smothered the debauched sounds of the camp, and in a panicked voice Alex asked, 'What's wrong with that man?'

Séb shrugged and looked up at the stars and then back to Alex. 'Which man?'

Alex sat in the wet sand and crossed his arms and held himself. 'Sais pas. All of them.'

'Rénard. Simon. These are men who've been pushed too far. They know not what they do.'

'But look at their behaviour. C'est fou. There's no excuse.'

'Oui, c'est vrai. But you and I and others besides will have to endure this insanity until it runs its course.'

'Why?'

'Because without Rénard, we won't get home. He's our leader now. It's just a thing that's happened, like all things that happen.'

Alex swallowed and looked up at Séb and opened his mouth and closed it, then opened it again and said, 'And what if that girl was your daughter? Would you be so accepting then?'

Séb sat down beside Alex and shook his head and heaved a sigh. 'Maybe you're too young to understand, but that girl isn't my daughter, and for that, at least, I'm grateful.'

12

THEY SLEPT UNDER THE STARS BECAUSE ALL THROUGHOUT
the night men from around the camp came to visit the girl, and the
next morning there were rumours that even bluecoats from the fort
had given money to Simon. Alex and Séb awoke with dry mouths and
sundered heads and they were tormented by flies and the wet heat of
the sun and the constant shriek of the gulls. They crawled into the
waters and floated on their backs until the feeling somewhat subsided,
after which they climbed the beach in search of Rénard.

First, they checked Simon's tent, where all around slept dishevelled
men and scattered about their bodies were empty bottles and stray
tobacco pipes and hunks of charred wood. Alex hung back while Séb
peered through the flaps, but he saw only the naked forms of Simon
and the Ottawa girl, no sign of Rénard, and this he related to Alex in
a tense whisper.

Then they wandered the beach, and when they came close to the
other end they saw a thin Ottawa woman standing outside a tent
and staring at the lake, and according to Séb this was Rémi's wife, a
seamstress, and after a time a young, sinewy man wearing breeches
and a buckskin vest emerged from the tent and put his arm around
her, and that, said Séb, was Rémi's brother-in-law, the one who'd told
of a rise in the beaver population of Georgian Bay. The brother-in-
law saw them pass and watched them with his dark eyes but didn't
otherwise acknowledge them, even after Alex nodded a shy greeting.
Once they were clear of him Séb warned Alex never to greet the man
again, for there were stories surrounding him like a deadly fog: people

said he had supernatural control over the island's Indian agent and was involved in illegal trading and gambling and once he'd killed a Dutchman in the caves on the north side of the island, this because the Dutchman had been conducting his own gambling concern, and when the man's friends went to the cave to retrieve his body, a flock of bats emerged and darkened the sky; one of the bats had the face of the Dutchman, screaming and sobbing and begging to go home.

They spent the next hour wandering the village with their pockets empty and their stomachs as well, until finally they found Rénard sitting in the shade and eating an apple across the street from the American Fur Company's supply store. Alex grimaced at the stench of him and also his appearance: clumps of mud in his grey whiskers, eyes glazed and yellow, one of his powerful hands clasping his knee with knuckles bruised and scraped, the flesh around the wounds as yellow as his sickly eyes. They stood beside him and listened to him chew until he offered them an apple as well, but only one to split.

When he spoke, he didn't look at either of them and instead jerked his chin in the direction of the store. 'You see those bluecoats on the porch there?'

On either end of a table sat two neatly shaved young men with rifles leaning against the wall close at hand. Séb said oui, he could see them, and Rénard said these two men were the only soldiers posted to the store, quelle bonne chance.

Séb took a huge bite of the apple and then another, and with his mouth full he said, 'Et v'là un problème. Those men are trained soldiers. They'll kill us if we try to rob that store.'

Rénard took a final bite of his apple and threw the core into the road, where it rolled a surprisingly long distance but then became laden with dirt and was suddenly still. He dredged his throat and spat in the street then looked at Alex and winked and said, 'What do you think, mon gars? Will they kill us? Or will we enter freely and get the clerk to unlock the safe?'

Once again Alex didn't know what to say, but it didn't matter, not to Rénard, whose influence had somehow possessed him, just as it had Séb, and while Alex longed to be free of these men and free of

70

Mackinac as well, he recalled Séb's words from the night before and understood that he'd have to be controlled for a while longer before he could be free.

Séb passed him what was left of the thoroughly gnawed apple and there was so little that Alex swallowed the whole core, as he'd done from time to time while working for M. Anderson.

Rénard yawned and stretched and said, 'They won't kill us because they won't be there. You'll be there, Alex. You'll stand there and watch the street for soldiers or any other man with a gun who might do us harm. You won't be armed, because your 'tit frère wouldn't approve and we'll need his protection. Simon and I discussed all these details last night, and he's prepared to play a role as well, and his share of our profits isn't so greedy.'

Séb attempted to speak but his voice cracked, so he cleared his throat and tried again. 'And where will the soldiers be? And what have you discussed with Simon?'

'The soldiers will be on the beach. Or haven't you heard? Simon has dared the father of the Ottawa salope to reclaim the girl before he sells her yet again, and so the whole beach is tense with the coming fight, which will likely arrive this afternoon or tomorrow morning. The Americans hate les Indiens, but for sure they'll send soldiers to the beach to stop the violence, and for sure these two soldiers will be among them, especially given that several bluecoats are wandering the territory to look for the bodies of our lost brigade. Simon will be sure to make sufficient violence to draw the soldiers, and in return we'll give him some of the money or goods we win from the store. Our timing is excellent, les gars, as it is for all men with an opportunity to win.'

13

A GROUP OF TEN OR SO MEN HAD GATHERED AROUND SIMON and his tent, inside which the girl still slept. He told them that her father was a man named Bineshi who carved birchwood canoes for the company, and because the season's new terms of indenture had affected the number of expeditions, Bineshi had begun selling fish but couldn't catch enough to support both his family and his drinking, so he turned to games of chance but was a rash and unskilled gambler and that's how he came to owe money to Simon. He was a tall man who wore a necklace of bear teeth and sometimes painted his face red and inked black lines beneath his eyes, though few of the whites found him fierce or even vaguely threatening and this because he'd become ghastly thin and was frequently drunk and when men harassed his wife or daughters he threw tantrums and issued threats but never proceeded to violence, and no one could respect that, least of all Simon. Like many Ottawa, Bineshi and his family camped on the beach during the summers so they could be near the voyageurs and the business and trade opportunities those men brought with them, even if it meant living close to the Americans, who detested the Ottawa after they'd sided with the British in the Second War of Independence. It would be best for everyone from humble Canadien to vainglorious bluecoat if the Ottawa quit the beach and returned to their villages or if they simply walked into the straits and allowed themselves to be swept away.

Simon held a musket and waved it over his head as he told his story and the men were variously armed with rusty knives and hatchets and muskets and swords, and they hooted and hollered and cheered as Simon recounted the details. He'd washed his face in the lake but even still his skin was scuffed and scabby. Alex couldn't understand why so many men were compelled by his words and supposed that the most unlikely of men held sway over their comrades, they and the likely too.

Then Simon told his audience he'd been patient with Bineshi, forgiving repeatedly the man's failure to repay his debt, but gradually he became aware that Bineshi had been taking advantage of his generosity and went about the camp in a drunken stupor accruing debt from other men even as he fished less and carved fewer canoes and sloped into the sort of destitution that ever circled his people, and so Simon had no choice but to capture the man's daughter even though he recognized this as a tactic developed by the British, who were scum to the very last red wretch, but sometimes a man borrowed from one enemy in order to put down another. Bineshi couldn't accept the terms of debt he'd created for himself and now recruited from his people to help reclaim his daughter, if such a word were even appropriate, which of course it wasn't, because Bineshi's debt neutralized any such claim he might have had, and therefore he'd be resisted, even if resistance meant blood and blood meant death.

The men agreed with this and several drank from jugs of beer and flasks of rum, and they bickered and shouted about how they'd prepare themselves for the coming violence, deciding that four musketeers would take the front of the line and discharge at will, and while they reloaded, men with hand-held weapons would dive in to chop and slice and skewer.

Alex watched all of this from a slight remove and next to him was Séb, who grew increasingly pale and consciously or not issued the occasional discontented moan, but it wasn't clear whether he was disturbed by the fight that loomed on the beach or the fact he'd soon be robbing a store or both.

Rénard was with them too, and he watched Simon with half a grin and his hands in the pockets of a black coat that hung past his knees, under which he said he'd hidden Simon's pepperbox pistol with its three gaping barrels, and from one of his pockets he produced a second pistol with simply one large barrel, and this he gave to Séb, who took it with a trembling hand. 'On loan from Simon,' said Rénard, and Alex thought that his grin was a contrivance and that actually he was afraid of what was coming, but non, there was too much light in his smile, too much joy.

With shouts and bellows Bineshi and his braves began their long trek across the beach to engage Simon and his gang. The waves beat against the shore and the sky was clear but for a bank of clouds rising on the eastern horizon. Séb and Alex followed Rénard as he turned his back to the lake and made his way to the supply store.

14

THE SAME TWO BLUECOATS HUNG ABOUT THE ENTRANCE
drinking coffee and smoking their pipes, and while they glanced
briefly at the three would-be bandits their gaze didn't linger, for they
were telling each other jokes and snorting laughter and one of them
chuckled so continuously he slopped coffee on the scuffed boards
of the porch. Rénard signalled for Alex and Séb to hang back, and
although it was only a short instant before the first gunshots rang out
on the beach it was nevertheless time enough for trepidation to creep
over each of them so that they both froze at the sound of the first shot,
even as the bluecoats snapped to attention and dropped their cups
and gripped their rifles and Rénard began a hunkered march in their
direction, his hand sliding inside the flaps of his coat.

Almost immediately their plan went awry as more shots sounded
from the beach but only one of the soldiers took off in that direction,
while the other kept his post and clutched his rifle, his face bare and
boyish and flushed with colour. Rénard moved at a remarkable pace
for a man so torn apart and was up the steps of the porch with his
pistol drawn before the American had even gauged his approach, but
rather than shoot this man he instead deployed the butt of his pistol,
whipping it back and forth across the bluecoat's face, once, twice,
thrice, and the man gave up his rifle and fell against the outer wall of
the store. By this time Séb had begun to follow, bare feet thumping
against the porch steps as he ascended to the landing, yet Alex still
couldn't bring himself to move and this was many parts fear and a
good many moral reluctance as well.

Both watched as Rénard continued to pound the soldier's face, and the sounds of the man's teeth bouncing across the porch were audible in the tight spaces of silence between this violence and that which exploded on the beach. When finally he'd finished his work, he turned, spattered with blood, and barked at the other two to follow, an order to which Séb shakingly acquiesced, his pistol now drawn, but Alex still couldn't bring himself to move. 'This isn't for me!' he shouted, his voice thick with coming tears. 'I don't want to hurt anyone!'

'Viens!' Rénard shouted. 'Tout'suite!'

Taking a step backward, Alex shook his head, staring in disbelief as Rénard aimed the pistol at his chest and did not vocalize a threat but simply cocked the hammer. When Alex still didn't move, Rénard slowly raised the gun so it was pointing at his face.

The two made eye contact across the great expanse of the barrel. They stared at each other for a long second and Alex could see Rénard's finger tighten on the trigger. He could hear screams coming from the beach, and he took one step forward. Then another. Soon his feet were on the patio steps and he climbed to the landing, which was soaked in blood and coffee, and although he didn't want to look at the soldier he found he couldn't ignore the man, who lay motionless on his back with his neck crooked against the wall and his head therefore propped up, the features of his face lost to the blood pouring from a gash in his forehead and the muck of his nose as well as the darkness of his mouth. Despite these disfigurements, Alex recognized him as the one who'd been laughing so hard just a few minutes previous.

Rénard opened the door to the store and the three of them entered and there were two men inside, one of them behind the counter and reaching down and the other in the middle of the store, as if he'd been approaching the door, and this one dressed in an officer's uniform but unarmed.

'Stop now!' screamed Rénard in English, but the man behind the counter continued to rummage and it was clear he was reaching for a weapon, so Rénard fired a shot over his head and it was deafening and a storm of splinters rained down from the ceiling and the man froze. 'Come from behind the counter. Both of you lie your faces on the floor. Do it!'

Alex felt dizzy and he was hyperventilating and he reached out to steady himself against a wooden pillar but pulled his hand away when he saw hanging there a great metal trap big enough to capture a bear. Missing the pillar, he stumbled and bumped into a cabinet of knives and this noise was enough to distract Rénard, who again turned his pistol on Alex but didn't fire, instead instructing Séb to do the same and shoot Alex in the head if he made to escape. Only the day before Alex wouldn't have thought Séb capable of following through on such a threat but this afternoon he saw a man cornered by circumstances who despite his pale and clammy face and the vein visibly throbbing in his neck would shoot as he was told, and so Alex slid to the floor and hugged his knees and couldn't stop himself from crying.

Rénard turned his attention to the other two men, who'd lowered themselves to the floor. The one from behind the counter was fat and solid and had long, yellow moustaches but was otherwise totally bald. There was a scar on his head that was thick and eerily white and ran from the top of his skull to the base of his neck, where it vanished in a patch of coarse blond hair. This man was facing the floor, but Alex could see the side of his mouth with lips drawn back and teeth clenched in anger and a thick cord of foamy saliva dangling to the boot-worn boards. The other man was thin and regal on account of his officer's attire and he had wavy hair and short, tidy side whiskers, and like the first man he wasn't so much afraid as angry, and with flinty black eyes he stared at Rénard and awaited whatever was to happen next.

'Bon,' said Rénard, who despite the ferocity of his intention seemed nevertheless briefly rattled by the situation, with ragged breathing and a look on his face like a boy who'd somehow won a fight against his older brother. He stood there with his pistol trained on the two men and looked around the store, which was now quiet enough for all to hear the muffled sounds of battle on the beach. There were muskets hanging on the walls and animal traps as well, and on the far side of the room by a flight of stairs there were several racks of fur robes.

'Son,' said the bald man, 'you've just now secured yourself a tiny piece of Hell on Earth. I've no doubt that you'll burn right before my very eyes, yes indeed, because I'll see to it that you do.'

Rénard said nothing at first but then gathered himself and spat on the man's back. 'We have protection for us that men like you cannot comprend. Where is the fucking safe, connard?'

Neither of the captives uttered a word and so Rénard kicked the bald man in the ribs and the man coughed and grunted and sucked wetly at his lips. 'There is no one coming to help you, les gars. If you want to live this situation, you will tell me where is the safe. If you want to be a stubborn man, then I will kill you and find it myself and we will get it open and take the money, or if we can't, then we will settle for those lovely robes of castor, but either way you will be dead and your friend will also be dead.'

The bald man appeared to ponder this and confessed that the safe was upstairs.

'Get up,' said Rénard.

Alex watched as the bald man struggled to his feet and grimaced beneath his moustaches. He kept a hand on his ribs where Rénard had kicked him and looked from the stairs to the man in the officer's coat and then back to Rénard. The officer lay flat but his hands trembled as though he wanted to lash out, and Rénard told him to crawl across the floor and position himself next to Alex, which laboriously he did. He then offered Alex a pitying look and whispered, 'Don't worry, son. We've only to do what they say and we'll get out of this in one piece.'

'Ta gueule, connard,' said Séb, who over the past few minutes had managed to halt his trembling and regain some of the colour in his face. 'No one talks.'

Rénard told the bald man to walk toward the stairs and he followed and the floor creaked under the passage of their feet.

'Wait,' said Rénard, who with his free hand caressed one of the fur robes there displayed. He looked at Séb and chuckled and then looked at the bald man and told him to kneel and interlace his fingers at the base of his neck.

The bald man turned to face Rénard and exhaled loudly but otherwise didn't move, so Rénard jabbed the barrel of his pistol hard into the centre of the man's forehead and this was inspiration enough for the man to kneel as he'd been told, his knees landing on the floor like rocks dropped from a great height.

Switching the pistol from one hand to the other, Rénard took off his coat and selected a robe from the rack. He slid one arm through a sleeve and passed the weapon to that hand and put his other arm through the other sleeve, and again he chuckled. 'Oh, castor,' he said to Séb before turning his attention to the bald man. 'It's the first time I wear one, you know.'

The bald man said nothing, but his eyes flamed and from across the store came Séb's voice high and strained: 'Mais dépêche-toi, Rénard!'

Rénard gestured for the bald man to stand and told him to climb the stairs and the man struggled to his feet as Rénard drew nearer. When the man was fully upright, he dropped his hands and with a roar lunged at Rénard, who fired a shot and tagged the man's arm but did nothing to slow his stampeding advance.

The man slapped the pistol out of Rénard's hand and the gun clattered across the floor and crashed into a few cast-iron pots arranged against the wall. He threw a fist straight into Rénard's chest and knocked him to the floor and then was on top of him, choking him with the hands of a colossus. Rénard writhed and wheezed and closed his fingers around the bald man's wrists, but this was a futile effort and so he began kicking his heels against the floor and after a few seconds of this Séb took his pistol off Alex and the man in the officer's jacket and shouted for the bald man to stop, but the bald man ignored him and continued to strangle Rénard and the look on his face was calm and resolved, the only sign of tension a slight creasing of his brow.

'I say *stop!*' yelled Séb, and then the man in the officer's jacket leapt to his feet and rushed him, but Séb saw the movement and wheeled around and fired off a shot even as the man buried a fist in the middle of Séb's stomach. Staggering backward, Séb tried to fire the gun again, but after hearing the hammer strike an empty chamber he dropped the weapon and called out to Alex: 'Aide-moi! Ton frère! Aide-moi!'

Alex felt as if he'd been punched or kicked in the stomach and he grunted with pain and looked down at himself and saw a hole in his shirt and also a hole in his body and from this winking burning hole came a stream of blood, and the stream came in surges as the hole continued to wink, and soon his lap was full of blood.

Dizziness overtook him and he was aware of the bald man standing over Rénard's body and Rénard's mouth was open ghastly wide, eyes bulging at the rafters and a pool of urine spreading from his pelvis. Now the man crossed the store and picked up Rénard's pistol and called out to the officer, who was wrestling Séb but released him at the sound of the bald man's call. Séb understood what was happening and moved for the door but the bald man fired the pistol and hit him in the back and then fired again and hit him in the neck and the force of the shot threw him off balance and he crashed through the door and onto the porch near the soldier, whom Alex couldn't see but nevertheless knew was dead of his injuries, just as he knew Séb was dying too, lying on his chest, convulsing and blinking at the sticky planks under the bright blue sky.

The man in the officer's coat turned to Alex and saw the blood and kneeled and called out to the bald man: 'Quick! Get a knife!' He coaxed Alex onto his back and with powerful hands groped at his waist and stomach and ribs, and after the bald man brought the knife he cut away Alex's shirt, revealing the wound and applying pressure with his palm and then withdrawing his hand as the apple core Alex had eaten emerged semi-digested from the hole and rolled into the bloody soup of his lap.

These things happened at a great distance, because although Alex hadn't left his body, he couldn't feel it either, and all he could think of, happily, was the mattress he'd slept on in the coach house he shared with his mother, and he imagined himself lying there early in the morning and waiting for the sun to come up so he could start another day of work, and this was a comforting thought because in the corner of the room he could sense his brother, who was smiling, and once this awareness arrived completely so too did Alex's attention return to the supply store, where he saw an apparition of his brother coated in a film of shimmering light as he levitated above the man in the officer's coat, and the man seemed also aware of the presence, for he looked up from his work, and as he did Alex's brother drained like water into the man's mouth. Then the man returned to the bloody task of saving Alex's life.

PART II

Foutu

SUMMER, 1831
—
WINTER, 1832

15

THE WOUND WAS ON HIS LEFT SIDE AND BELOW HIS NIPPLE, about the size of a tiny fist and flaked with burnt skin. Visible within was a bulge of lung caught on one of a few fractured ribs like a dirty sack in a thorny bush. Later Alex remembered seeing this through locks of sweaty hair and he also remembered the bald man grimace and swear and turn away. These and other recollections were nebulous and vague: his 'tit frère had entered the man in the officer's coat and then the man kneeled beside him and worked on the wound with a paring knife; amassing at the man's knees were clots of blackened flesh and the blood-soaked shreds of Alex's shirt; there was the soft and almost comical sound of air bubbling out of the wound and the harder sound of the bullet dug loose and dropped to the floor. There was also the misshapen apple core that had fallen out of the hole, and the officer held it for a moment between thumb and forefinger and looked it over and shook his head, then set it next to the bloody scraps of Alex's shirt.

He was carried up the hill to the fort and moved to an army hospital behind the gates, and there he was laid out on a wooden bed covered by a thin mattress, though this journey he would not recall. No one thought he'd survive the night and he grew feverish and sometimes convulsed, but he didn't die and the next morning awoke to a nurse who stood over him with a hose in her hand. 'You leak from the side,' she confided in a tired whisper. Her blonde hair was pulled tightly back and her green eyes were kind, but he couldn't distinguish much of the room around them, just that it was vast and grey and he was sweating and there was a fly nearby – no, there were flies all over. The nurse directed him to roll onto his side, and once he could no longer see her face he imagined her kindness hardening, but that didn't bother him, it was normal, he'd die soon anyway. There was a distant pressure behind him like when he'd slept with Serge, and he understood the nurse was inserting the hose in his rectum, though he wasn't bothered, he barely felt it – it was just a thing that was happening, like all things that happened. The nurse said he'd have to eat that way for the foreseeable future and he just nodded and lay on his side until she returned to remove the hose, after which she gave him a dose of laudanum and later he fell asleep.

It was possibly the same day or perhaps another when he awoke and his mouth was dry and his head was fuzzy and the room smelled of things foul and septic, with a faint trace of vinegar. Alex blinked and tried to focus on his surroundings and again he was struck by the size of the room and the rotted rafters way overhead, like a barn, and there was a loft up there with a desk and down below a collection of beds and he heard other patients rasping and coughing and he assumed these to be casualties from the beach. He knew he'd been severely injured and possibly implicated in the robbery of the supply store, but with death so close at hand he hardly cared and thought, almost with relief, why worry, ça vaut pas la peine, there was little he controlled, there was nothing he controlled.

'Can he speak English?'

Alex couldn't be sure if another day had passed and he opened his eyes and standing there was a tall man with his head shorn, and he wore a blue army coat with scuffed brass buttons and frayed epaulettes and a dirty gold trim. The man's leathery face was clenched into a neutral expression and next to him was a younger man with a delicate mouth and wavy hair, and he was wearing an officer's uniform as well. Alex recognized him as the man from the store who'd swallowed his 'tit frère and saved his life, and the recognition was joyful because likely his brother still hid in the darkness of this man's insides, and so would they not meet again soon, at least in death if not life?

This man looked at the bald officer and shrugged and said, 'He didn't speak during the robbery, Colonel, but I suppose he can. Don't they all, at least a little?' He turned to Alex. 'Son, do you speak English? I'm Doctor Samuel Beaumont, and this is Colonel Roland Smyth.'

Alex had the covers up to his waist and his torso was wrapped in stained bandages and he was aware of a bad smell, but it was distant, inoffensive, and he nodded but couldn't make any sounds when he opened his mouth to speak, and this strange loss of will caused him to giggle, though only briefly because a blade of pain pierced his euphoria and brought him low.

'Christ,' sneered the Colonel. He had a small but sharp nose and his nostrils flared with contempt. 'He's a fool. Of all the ones you could've saved. Our men bled out like pigs.'

Beaumont faced the Colonel and lifted his chin, and Alex wondered if this was a bravery he could summon at will or maybe a gift from Alex's 'tit frère. 'I wasn't on the beach, Colonel Smyth. As you well know. Further, in such circumstances, it's my duty to assist to the best and fullest of my abilities injured peoples as I find them. I took an oath, man.'

'Meaning?' The Colonel nodded at a passing nurse. Beaumont kept his chin aloft.

'Meaning had I been on the beach, I may have found myself preoccupied with the care of another of these voyageurs, or even an Indian, so long as they were as wounded as your lost men, and by the looks of it many such people were. All lives are human, Colonel, even those admittedly less accomplished.'

The Colonel chuckled, then frowned. 'And yet look at his face. He looks a fool.'

'He's not a fool, Colonel. It's the laudanum making him slow, and also the trauma. The wound goes right through to his stomach. Believe it or not, I witnessed a partially digested apple core in the boy's lap. It came out of the wound. I've not seen anything like that since the war. He needs a few days yet, and that's just to get over the worst of it. Fact is, he may die. I have at least one more surgery to perform, and this in the middle of a blazing summer.'

'Look, Beaumont.' The Colonel pressed the heel of his palm into his eye, then slid it down his cheek and made a fist of it next to his hip. He didn't raise his voice, not quite. 'Last week was an inferno. I've got two dead soldiers, three dead frogs, and an old Indian the savages are mourning in the northside woods. Not to mention the extent of the injuries. There were men delimbed, for Christ's sake. Right in the middle of events, I've got an armed robbery perpetrated against the American Fur Company, as if we're stationed way out on the god-damned frontier, and all this when I'm down a few men because of a search party that didn't find a thing.'

Beaumont lifted his chin again and opened his mouth, but the Colonel shushed him, clenching his jaw and raising his finger and spraying saliva through the cage of his yellow teeth, and all about Beaumont's neck was a tightening of muscles and tendons.

'I'll want to talk to your fool when he regains his tongue, Beaumont. These conscripted vagrants cling together like fish eggs.' Now the Colonel's eyes landed on Alex's face and calmly they blinked. 'The gambling is getting out of control again. The drinking and the fighting. It's what these fools do when they don't have enough work to distract them. I'll want to chat about that, and in the meantime, this hospital is for men and women enlisted in the military or in the employ of the company, as you very well know, so find another place for your fool to recover. You have a week, no longer.'

16

ALEX OPENED HIS EYES AND SQUINTED AGAINST THE LIGHT of a lantern. Still he was shirtless and still his chest was wrapped in dirty bandages and he looked down on himself in bed as though his neck were the trunk of a tree and his head lost in the rustle of the leaves. Beaumont was sitting in a chair next to his bedside in shirtsleeves, and his legs were crossed and he hunched over a small wooden table and fiddled with surgical instruments set out across its surface. Alex felt the presence of two men at the head of the bed, but he couldn't see them and wondered if they were real or perhaps spirits or fugitives from a forgotten dream.

Beaumont lifted his face and his brow was creased as he ran the tip of his finger along the edge of a knife. He hadn't noticed Alex was awake. Had the doctor's hair always been so curly? Always so dark? Alex couldn't recall. Possibly it hadn't and these characteristics were influenced by his 'tit frère, who surely was somewhere behind Beaumont's skin. This thought was for a moment sad because Alex imagined his brother struggling for control of Beaumont's body, struggling and losing, much as in life. But perhaps not. Perhaps his brother was no longer beholden to mortal weakness, rather he'd broken loose of those shackles. So why couldn't the doctor's movements be willed by Alex's brother? And maybe even his thoughts. And maybe even the things he said.

Alex shifted and winced. 'Es-tu tout seul?' he muttered. 'J'ai des questions.'

Beaumont looked up and cleared his throat and squeezed Alex's hand and returned to adjusting his instruments as if he hadn't understood, and maybe he hadn't, which meant Alex's brother was not in full control, or perhaps not there at all.

'Alex? Es-tu là-dedans?'

Beaumont looked up again and smiled without humour. 'There, there, lad. The tincture can cause confusion, that's all.' He took a last look at his instruments and filled his lungs with air and exhaled slowly. 'I'd like to apologize for the inhospitable nature of the local authorities. They're cruel. Selfish. They've had a meeting and passed a motion. Sadly, they won't expend the island's official resources on the amelioration of your plight, this because you're neither an employee of the company nor a soldier in the army nor even a resident of that squalid little village.'

Alex became increasingly awake and the hole in his side did the same, as if it had a pulse that could be felt up and down the steep red walls that made its shape. The hospital was shadowy, it was night, and Alex could hear the patter of rain on the roof and there was a man snoring and another weeping.

'We'll have to move you in a few days' time. They wish to send you home, but I've told them you wouldn't survive the trip, and that's most certainly true. You're in a very bad way. You've bits of shattered rib lodged in a number of abscesses around your wound. Bits of unstable cartilage as well. Of course these must be removed as soon as possible.' He shook his head in disgust. 'Imagine, for a moment, the risk of wilderness travel. People are too self-interested. It's always bothered me, that fact of a man. I see it everywhere.'

Alex understood very little of this. His throat was dry and his head hurt and there was a faraway burning somewhere within his wound.

Beaumont frowned and muttered. He loosely gripped Alex's shoulder and applied pressure to bend him forward, and Alex cried out but the doctor only hummed a consoling note and applied more pressure. 'To get the bandages off,' he explained. 'And I'll need to insert a plug, of course. In your side. It's so you can imbibe something for the pain without the problem of leakage.'

Beaumont unwrapped the bandages with powerful arms that reminded Alex of his papa's folded around him as a boy while tending to some small crisis of his body. Wouldn't it be nice to find himself anew in that simple place of succour and strength? But of course he couldn't, and besides it had never been so safe a place.

'As for the predicament of your lodgings,' said Beaumont, his head angled as he worked, 'I'd like to propose a solution. You'll stay at my residence. My wife is there in summers. Deborah. We have a back room. It can be chilly in winter, but she'll make you comfortable and get you settled in the house. In a few months, she'll head to Detroit for the cold season, and you'll be in my care alone. It's our duty, I'm afraid, to see you through to recovery, and that may take until spring or even beyond.'

Alex heard a touch of kinship in his doctor's tone and wondered if his brother had regained control, which seemed likely. As for the strength in Beaumont's arms, that was surely his brother's as well, not their papa's as he'd originally thought, or not precisely. Rather, it was a promised strength, passed down from their papa. In life, it would've been his brother's only if the child had grown. In death, it was his always.

The bandages were off now and the flesh beneath was damp and it stank. Beaumont took a bundle of tightly packed gauze from the round table and leaned in close and there was a pause as each of them was startled by the sight of the hole. 'This will hurt,' said the doctor. 'I'm sorry.'

Alex watched his body thrash and heard it yelp and he broke into a sweat as Beaumont, with his thumbs, pressed the plug into the hole. He could feel this but was also somehow sheltered from it, as if his body were lumpy, vague, and so too its various obligations to pain and injury, such that what he acutely experienced was vertiginous anxiety – swooping and twirling and spinning and falling.

'Now,' said Beaumont, leaning back in his chair. He reached to the floor and lifted a bottle of rum into his lap. He uncorked it and handed it to Alex. 'This will have to do for the discomfort, I'm afraid. You've been a bit too keen with the laudanum, son. Much too keen, in fact. It's a helpful substance, that's true, but dangerous. After a time, it commands a person's body. People find those commands hard to disobey, sometimes impossible.' He sighed and shook the hair off his forehead. 'Meanwhile, alcohol makes men boorish, most shamefully so. But in a surgery scenario, if the patient drinks a lot, and quickly, well, it can be a more effective inebriation than that caused by the laudanum, and far less commanding in the medium term.'

Alex struggled to raise the bottle, struggled to tilt his head, then succeeded and drank and drank some more. He lowered the bottle and gasped and then raised it and drank still more, until finally he heard a sneer from Beaumont and the doctor snatched away the rum. Beaumont set the bottle on the ground and stood up. He crossed his arms over his chest and his face seemed to ripple and settle.

'I see,' he said. 'Well. My father was partial to drink, to phrase it mildly. He was a farmer in New England and though he began his life with courage and strength, he left it as a weak and ignorant man whose accomplishments were few and insights fewer. I was lucky to escape the same fate. Hopefully my luck rubs off on you, son. You're in evident need. In the meantime, we'll have to stick to the laudanum. I'll have no part in slaking the thirst of a man's most cackling devil.' He removed a timepiece from the pocket of his trousers and consulted the face. 'We'll begin in fifteen minutes.'

Alex sat back and tried to trace the passage of the rum through his body. He imagined he could feel a tide of it rushing into the chamber of his wound, sloshing against Beaumont's plug then receding again, back into his pit where it belonged. He was again aware of the hospital around him, of its darkness and size and of the weakness of various lanterns hung from support columns and the fetid smell of the sick, and he was again aware of two people breathing at the head of his bed. He craned his neck to see them but couldn't get a full view, only a hint of one man's beard, and perhaps this was Serge, or some vestige of Serge, watching over him while he suffered. 'Grâce à dieu,' he said. 'J'vais venir 'vec vous autres.'

Beaumont paced the area in front of Alex's bed, his body wandering in and out of the lantern light. 'Your wound is most astounding. An aperture from the outer world to the inner. Amazing you survived, frankly, especially on a day so blighted by death, though of course, you've quite the battle ahead of you yet. Nevertheless, I've already begun a paper on the subject. Probably you don't remember, but there was food in your lap after you were shot. An apple core, of all things. Partially digested, by the looks of it. Clearly, young man, you present an opportunity for study, yes, an exceedingly rare opportunity to understand the process of digestion. Imagine yourself, son, as a man of the sciences. Quite a turn, isn't it?'

He checked his timepiece and paced a few more minutes in silence, though his lips continued to move and he gestured occasionally with one of his hands, and then he returned to his chair and crossed his legs and adjusted the light of the lantern so the flame burned brighter.

'Of course, if you're to fulfil this debt to science, you must continue to survive.' He took up one of his surgical instruments. 'Your road is by no means travelled. I'm concerned about the fragments of rib, about the unstable cartilage. These things pose a threat to your overall health, resilient though somehow it seems. My hope is to remove the majority presently. I'm afraid I see no other way.'

The doctor checked his timepiece again and then looked to the head of the bed and nodded. Alex felt powerful hands settle on his shoulders and hold him still. Whereas moments ago he'd been displaced from the affairs of his body, now he was captive in his flesh and he couldn't struggle without intense pain, so he lay there limply in the grip of the men. One of the hands clutching his bicep was hairy and crisscrossed by fat blue veins, and so perhaps it was Rémi come to take his vengeance for leaving him to die on the beach. 'Désolé,' Alex whimpered. 'Pas ma faute.'

'We may need to restrain his feet,' said Beaumont, and he leaned over Alex and lowered his silver instrument, and quickly a flame of agony shot to life and did not flicker but burned and grew larger and burned some more.

Alex screamed and one of the men holding him leaned forward and strained and Alex smelled his sweat and screamed again. He heard the cries of other patients rise up from the gloom as though a wretched choir, and their fear caused the lanterns to flicker as the rain pelted the roof and he detected movement in the lofty darkness above – were there bats swooping down from the rafters, or had he simply lost his mind? Where was his brother in all of this? He imagined the poor child naked and curled up on the floor of Beaumont's soul, resting because he needed it, unable to influence the events of the moment. But was his brother not beyond such fatigue? Surely he was. Perhaps his brother wasn't resting but issuing a test. Or if not a test then a lesson. Alex would endure this pain alone. If he survived, he'd grow stronger. If he didn't, he'd join his brother elsewhere, and together they'd live with Serge and their maman, and they'd all look down on his papa and wish him well.

17

BEAUMONT PERFORMED TWO MORE OF THESE SURGERIES over the next few weeks, and even though they were shorter and less invasive Alex was certain he'd die despite having somehow survived to that point, and when he was lucid enough to remember his prayers he beseeched le seigneur to take him as soon as possible, because he was too exhausted to continue.

After the first surgery, Beaumont sutured the incisions and had Alex placed on a plank so two square-jawed men could carry him out of the army hospital and down the street to Beaumont's house, and although he was only semi-conscious during this migration he was nevertheless aware of passersby stopping to watch, stopping and whispering and some of them pointing as well, and again he prayed for God to quickly guide his ordeal to its most logical conclusion.

Beaumont lived in one of the two-storey log cabins built for officers inside the gates of the fort. There was a large chimney rising from the centre of the house and the main rooms on both floors were built around it, though Alex was given the tiny servant's quarters at the back of the first floor, behind the kitchen and next to the scullery and rear entrance. Only a short time before, his world had been an endless expanse of rivers and trees and, before Serge died, the promise of so much more. But now life had shrunk to those areas immediately surrounding his skin, and even then just barely, for he was too weak to move and too tired to look around the room or else too flush with laudanum to understand what he was seeing or even to care.

The doctor appeared at his side several times daily, hale and handsome as he surfaced from the darkness of Alex's condition, and though he spoke a great deal as he changed Alex's dressing or prepared surgical instruments for each of the procedures, much of what he said was nearly incomprehensible: technical descriptions of Alex's wound, lamentations that Colonel Smyth would soon insist on an interrogation, idle chit-chat about his wife's end-of-season departure to Detroit.

Alex wondered if his brother hadn't deserted Beaumont, but nevertheless he kept as watchful an eye as his situation would allow, for perhaps it was his brother who'd invite him to the Great Beyond and it was critical he not be asleep or confused such that he missed the invitation when finally it came. The doctor's moods tended from kindly and gentle to callous and severe, but Alex began to understand these changes less as signs of struggle between the doctor's soul and his brother's and more as the sort of volatility he'd seen many times in people with power.

After three weeks, his abdomen a maze of sutures wrapped in bandages, Alex was able to take food through his mouth and started to wonder if he might not survive after all, and a feeling of immense gratitude began to stir in his chest, though perhaps he was grateful simply because gratitude was the province of the feeble. It made dependence bearable, but it wasn't the true appreciation that passed between equals.

As his stupors began to leaven, he became more aware of Deborah Beaumont's occasional visits to his room, usually to bring his meals or change his chamber pot. Every Friday, she brought along a tooth powder made of ground charcoal and apologized for its crudeness, but such was life on Mackinac, at least she'd added salt to improve the taste, and a dash of sugar too. She was tall for a woman and thin and she wore her black hair in a braid held together by a silver brooch. She greeted him when she entered, and she spoke about the food or the water or the tooth powder, but she didn't say much else and he assumed she found him revolting, so he avoided looking at her until she took her leave and her back was turned and her fingers lingered on the door before pulling it closed.

Saturdays she dragged a metal tub into the room and filled it with water fetched from the pump in the fort, as the Beaumonts wouldn't concede to bathing in the lake, and some of this water was even boiled in the scullery. She left him to hobble from his bed to the tub, his vision blurred by tears and pain, and it was Beaumont who helped him wash his scabby, sutured wounds. Alex hadn't been consciously naked in the presence of another person since sleeping in the deerskin tent with Serge, and he wondered what the doctor might think, but Beaumont was completely focused on the hole in Alex's side, nothing else, and this was as much a relief as a disappointment.

Not since the first surgery had the doctor offered Alex rum or any other sort of alcohol but instead administered laudanum, and Alex became accustomed to the drug and sometimes asked for larger doses, though these requests were usually denied. His habituation allowed the pain to grow constant, but it was manageable, and subsequently the room came into sharper focus, with flowering plants potted on the desk, which though basic had a chest of drawers on one side. There was a window above it and a crucifix above the door, and the curtains in the window were white and clean and embroidered with tiny flowers, and within these details he saw a touch not unlike that of his maman, which was a comfort at least, however small.

Once, when Alex was a boy, the three sons of his maman's patron had led him into the woods and taught him to climb a tree, a feat they performed with ease, leaping into the crotch of a maple, shimmying up a split in the trunk, then dangling from a branch before dropping back to the ground. These boys sometimes liked Alex and sometimes not, he could never be sure when their moods would change, rather he was like a fleck of cork in a barrel of water, floating calmly on the surface until everything was inevitably overturned and he was swept away.

It was a warm summer morning and the woods were thick with blackflies and Alex trailed behind them and saw a tiny wood-boring beetle crawl across the breadth of a fallen leaf, and he was privately amazed. The forest buzzed with insects and the boys slapped at their bare arms and legs and Alex hung back as the three of them hurried up and down the trunks, dirtying their breeches and giggling and spitting at one another from greater and greater heights. He crouched next to a branchy copse and watched them play, and he smiled when it seemed appropriate and laughed whenever the boys laughed, and in this way he hoped to go unnoticed in the blurry rush of their fun, a strategy he'd used many times before, sometimes successfully but sometimes not.

Possibly he laughed too hard or possibly not hard enough, but whatever the case, one of the sons halted progress up the lower trunk of an ash and leapt easily to the ground. He approached Alex and took him by the hand and pulled him to his feet and led him to the base of the tree. 'I'll give you a boost,' said this boy, whose name was Patrick, and he placed Alex between himself and the tree, very close, so that Alex could smell his musty skin. Patrick interlaced his fingers and made of them a step, and he beckoned Alex to put one foot there and reach upward and begin his ascension.

The tree was old and its bark was ridged and rough. Alex lifted himself free of Patrick's hands and scrabbled up a few feet of the trunk, laughing, but quickly his grip began to falter and then his footing too. The bark crumbled, he couldn't find new purchase, and he slid down the trunk and crashed into Patrick, both boys falling to the ground.

Punishment came swift. Patrick jumped to his feet and shouted obscenities, and Alex barely had time to curl fetal and cover his face before all three brothers formed a circle around him and began to kick him and spit on him and they rubbed dead leaves in his hair, but after a minute they grew bored and broke into a run back to the patron's estate.

Alex wandered home slowly. He looked for the beetle but couldn't find it, and he arrived at the coach house around noon, when his maman was having her déjeuner. This was not the first time he'd appeared before her with cuts and bruises, and she kissed him on his dirty forehead and he smelled her salty skin. She washed his cuts and brought him to the small table where she'd been eating her lunch. She lifted him into her lap and put her arms around him and then from beside her plate she took up a peach, from which she'd already taken a bite.

The peach came from a tree the patron had grown in front of the house, and though the cold winters were too much for most of its ilk in Québec, this was a hardy one that not only endured but thrived, and in summers Alex's maman would collect its peaches in baskets made of wooden slats. The patron spoke often of how the tree had come to be there, a story he'd recount when giving Alex lessons in English, and Alex understood that the seeds of the tree had somehow come from China and been traded to les Indiens. Colonial men then acquired them and they changed hands throughout the Spanish-held lands far to the south, eventually making their way to the Thirteen Colonies, then to the suburbs of Montréal, and so it was that things from one part of the world could be grafted onto things from another.

'Mange 'vec moi,' his maman said, and they took turns savouring the taste both sweet and sour, until finally they came upon the hard, brown stone, with bits of flesh still stuck to the grain, and his mother held this between two of her wrinkly fingers. 'C'est comme toi, ce noyau, comme toi et ton 'tit frère.'

'Mais comment?'

She smiled and put it in his hand and told him that like a peach he was very sweet and like any human being he could sometimes be sour, but most importantly, he was soft on the outside. People would be drawn to this, they would be nourished by it, and he'd have to remember that somewhere inside he was strong and hard and vital, nothing would change that.

He nodded and she hugged him and held him for a long time, until her embrace abruptly vanished and in its place were powerful fingers prodding his side and causing him pain and then the coach house was gone and he was lying on the mattress in the room at the back of Beaumont's house, and it wasn't his maman prodding his side but his doctor with features stern but studious as he inserted one of his fingers into Alex's suture-surrounded hole.

'Sorry, lad,' said Beaumont, lifting his eyebrow. 'I'd thought the laudanum would mute my examination, but of course you've become accustomed to your doses. Perhaps I should raise them, risky though it is.'

Alex wriggled and writhed but couldn't break free from Beaumont's finger so deep within.

'It's fascinating,' said the doctor, 'the way your wound is healing. It seems that the tissues of your stomach have begun to adhere to the flesh of your belly, and the wound shows not the least disposition to close its orifice but rather resembles, in all but a sphincter, that natural anus with a slight prolapsus.' He laughed and shook the curls off his forehead. 'Of course, you'll not understand so technical a description, will you? Even if you were able to speak perfect English, I suspect such an assessment would range beyond your ken. What I'm saying is that the hole in your body seems keen to remain open in the form of a gastric fistula, which is frankly astonishing, but to be honest, it's what I suspected when first I saw the apple core in your lap.'

Alex began to weep from the pain and Beaumont tenderly patted his shoulder and offered him yet another dropper full of laudanum, which despite its burning taste Alex imbibed as though water.

'Now,' said Beaumont, turning to take up a pair of scissors and forceps, 'it's time we removed these sutures.'

18

ALEX WAS RUNNING HIS FINGERS OVER THE RIDGES OF twisted flesh that surrounded his fistula when there was a loud knock on the door and in walked Beaumont and Colonel Smyth, a tension between them as if they'd been arguing.

'Well,' declared Smyth, and he took the wooden chair from Alex's desk and dragged it loudly across the floor and placed it next to the bed. He sat and crossed his legs, coughing openly, and his breath stank of coffee and tobacco. 'So you're Beaumont's miracle patient, then, are you? Got a fair portion of the village in heated confabulation about the drama of your situation, you do, and for that notoriety you can thank the doctor himself, correct, Samuel? Because it's the doctor who tells his colleagues that you constitute a research boon for an ambitious young professional, and further—'

'Colonel,' interrupted Beaumont, who'd taken a seat on the edge of the table by the window but now stood up and put his hand on his superior's shoulder. 'Please. Although Alex has overcome the most dangerous chapter of his predicament, he's still easily fatigued, and I'm afraid I'll have to ask you to keep this session succinct.'

The light of the morning streamed through the window and Alex could tell the day would be hot. Already the Colonel's brow beaded with sweat and the bare skin of his head appeared wet and flushed. Smyth produced a violent shrug and Beaumont's hand fell away. The Colonel then scrutinized Alex's face, his stare so unsettling that Alex closed his eyes to escape it, and when he opened them again he saw Beaumont returning to his seat on the table. Smyth leaned forward, and with an irritated sigh he said, 'I trust the doctor has informed you of the aftermath of the robbery, yes? And that of the violence on the beach?'

Alex could think of nothing to say, and quickly Beaumont broke the silence: 'Such information was deemed unhelpful to his recovery. He's not been informed.'

Smyth's faint eyebrows rose in disbelief. 'And wasn't he curious? Didn't he ask about the robbery himself?'

'Colonel. Please.'

Smyth shook his head and heaved another of his tremendous and foul-smelling sighs. He said both Séb and Rénard had been killed in the robbery and one of the island's two churches had shown mercy and allowed their bodies to be interred in its cemetery, and did Alex know these men, or was it truly a coincidence, however unlikely, that they'd all gone into the store at the same time?

Alex felt nothing for Rénard but pitied Séb's family and even Séb himself. And yet God's verdicts of death were beyond his appeal, he'd learned that, what was important was that despite Smyth's suspicion the Colonel seemed partially open to the idea that Alex had played no culpable role in events, and this was in fact the truth, was it not, or at least true enough.

'I wonder,' said Smyth, 'if there isn't some connection between all the events of the day. The robbery. The search party. The battle on the beach.' He removed a plain white handkerchief from his pocket and dabbed his forehead. 'Do things like that happen independently of one another? Is that how life works? Or are they nudged along by the conniving hands of men?'

Alex attempted to sit up but couldn't without wincing and he didn't want to give the Colonel the pleasure of seeing him struggle, so he lay flat and said nothing.

The Colonel folded his handkerchief so that a splotch of sweat was visible, then put it back in his pocket and said, 'When did you come to Mackinac?'

'I only recently come to look for work.'

'So you know folks who make their home on the beach?'

'I don't stay there long.'

'What? What's that supposed to mean? Make sense.'

Alex heard Beaumont stir on the table, but before the doctor could interject he said, 'I mean I arrive on the island only a few days before I am shot.'

'So you don't know what caused the fight?'

'I don't know what cause.'

'But you do know there was a deadly fight?'

Alex shrugged his bare shoulders. 'I hear some people that morning who say there is coming trouble, but I don't pay attention because I want to find work.'

Smyth twisted around in his chair and shot Beaumont an incredulous look. He turned back and leaned forward. 'How about gambling? Have you been gambling since your arrival on Mackinac? You understand the fur company mostly forbids that kind of activity here? Oh, sure, we know it goes on. But we don't condone it. Are you aware of men gambling?'

Alex coughed and clutched his side. His hair fell in his face but he didn't shake it away.

'Colonel, please,' said Beaumont. 'We're distressing my patient.'

Smyth stood and looked down on Alex then turned from the bed and made to leave, but Alex reached out and grabbed his wrist and shook the hair out of his face and said, 'There is a voyageur named Simon.'

The Colonel yanked his hand free. 'No. There isn't. Which is to say, there was, it's true, but that scoundrel was hanged for his crimes, so now there isn't.'

'He was one of them who starts the fight. He speaks angry about les Indiens.'

Smyth snorted and walked to the door and slammed it shut behind him and there came the sound of Deborah talking to him and leading him out of the house. Beaumont sighed and offered Alex an apologetic shake of his head. 'There's a man I've only recently come to understand. Allow me to impress upon you my learning in case you someday find it useful, which very well you might.'

Alex was exhausted and sore and wanted to recede into the languor of morning, but nevertheless he nodded and tried to look grateful to receive yet another of Beaumont's important lessons, for this was, after all, the man who'd saved his life.

'Authority,' began Beaumont, lifting his chin. 'Colonel Smyth believes in authority, of course, but he understands it in a more complicated way than other enlisted men, even his superiors. I know because I'm sometimes subjected to his lectures on the topic. A man like Smyth will point to the great financial costs of such conflicts as our Revolution and our Second War of Independence and even the money spent pacifying Indians all about the continent. He'll point to the costs incurred not just by we Americans but also our allies and enemies. He'll point to the enthusiasm with which these dollars are spent. He'll tell you that the fact of this spending, the fact of the enthusiasm that informs it, suggests that no one truly believes diplomacy is useful in the maintenance and propagation of power and authority. In fact, it's force that carries the day, raw and brutish.' Beaumont had worked himself into a state of agitation and now paced the room, jabbing his finger and sweeping his hand. 'A man like Smyth will see this concept applied not just to political struggles between nations but to other sorts of social engagement as well, perhaps a proprietor's wont of controlling an employee or a young man's insistence to his friends regarding the purity of his bride. It's a compelling line of reasoning, isn't it? The idea that a person who seeks to influence with his mind cannot overcome an adversary who seeks to influence with artillery. And yet, it's a primitive notion as well, and Alex, we must do our best to avoid it.'

His thoughts now fully expressed, Beaumont frowned and looked to Alex and shook his head in the manner of one friend relating to another. He bent over the bed and pressed the back of his hand against Alex's forehead and after this he moved to the door and told Alex not to worry, he was in fine hands, he'd recover, his life would present exciting new opportunities before long.

19

THE WARMEST MONTHS OF THE YEAR HAD PASSED AND THE world outside the window wasn't as bright as once it had been, and soon the darkness would grow thicker still. Alex hobbled from his bed to his desk and sat and lowered his nose to the flowers Deborah had brought to decorate his quarters. He inhaled their fragrance and turned to the window and ran the curtains between his thumb and forefinger, the embroidered flowers exquisite with faraway textures. He'd become accustomed to the idea of wintering on Mackinac, but still he longed for a modicum of freedom, such as permission to come and go from the house so he could roam the beach and perhaps visit the tavern. He remembered the burn of the rum he'd drunk with Serge in the back of M. Anderson's store, and looking around he felt that at the very least his accommodations had improved since departing Montréal. Then the door flew open and the doctor trotted in, cheeks flushed and hair in disarray, officer's coat unbuttoned and flapping about his waist.

'Fantastic news,' he blurted, waving a letter in one hand and in the other a neatly opened envelope. 'I have fantastic news. I've heard back from the University of Michigan, to whom I wrote regarding the implications of your fistula.'

Alex shuffled from the window to the bed, where he lowered himself with a grunt to its edge. He didn't care for the sound of that word – *fistula* – which to him had a frightening ring, and as Beaumont marched about the room grinning maniacally, Alex lifted a hand and pressed it gingerly against his dressing.

'The university does not itself award funding for research, but the able-minded men of its faculty of sciences have gone to their donors and expressed just how astounding your condition is. I sent them drawings and descriptions to assist in their appeal, and I've detailed for them the progress of your recovery to date. See here.'

He unfurled the letter and handed it to Alex and tapped one of his neatly kempt fingers on a middle paragraph. Alex held the letter and stared at the words but couldn't make sense of them, and briefly observing this, Beaumont registered his confusion. He offered a delicate smile, swiping at his curls with a chuckle.

'Pardon me, Alex,' he said, reaching out to reclaim the letter. 'I sometimes forget that men are not born literate.' He cleared his throat. 'The author of this letter is a giant of the United States' medical community, one I happen to know personally, thanks to Deborah's father, and he says you have a fortitude that only God can give. I'm inclined to agree. I didn't want to broach this subject with you until the funding was a certainty, but I am further inclined to wonder if such heavenly gifts don't place a burden on the receiver.' He paused, opening one of his palms in a gesture of proposal. 'Son, do you see what I'm saying?'

Alex blinked his leaden eyelids and looked into Beaumont's face, where in the arch of the man's brow he saw an entreaty he couldn't decipher, so he shook his head and wondered if Beaumont wouldn't soon administer more laudanum. But the doctor had worked himself into a frenzy and spoke at length about the extraordinary nature of Alex's condition and the opportunity it represented for the advancement of mankind.

'Perhaps I sound flighty,' he said, 'perhaps overly grand. But hear me out, lad, because I'm not given to overstatement, not a bit.'

He announced that some men believed the stomach was an organ of mechanical function, something of a crusher, while others supposed its doings were chemical, and Alex's condition – his *fistula* – provided a chance to test these theories and arrive at a definitive conclusion, and therefore he proposed that Alex stay on not just for the winter but the foreseeable future and play a central role in the history of medical discovery.

Alex looked from Beaumont's face to his own lap and he saw his hands down there and his fingers twisting and untwisting. 'Thank you, Doctor, thank you much. But I go home in the spring.'

Beaumont snorted. 'Why?'

'I should not leave in the first place.'

'And what would you do back home? Isn't it hell?'

'Maybe I work at the ports, because now I know the fur trade very well. Then maybe I go to France. My papa, he is there. Or maybe by then he comes back to Québec and we are becoming fermiers.'

Beaumont stopped his pacing and sighed. He buttoned his coat and sat on the bed, taking Alex's hand in his own. 'Listen, lad. Among the casualties of that fight on the beach were men in silk shirts and even a turban, which must have come from India, as rightly as not. And so one sees this entire industry in a nutshell, doesn't one? One sees men and women obsessed with material pleasures, yes very, and so much so that they become ensnared in the pursuit and once trapped are in conflict with the people around them. I'm offering you a higher calling, and seldom does such a calling visit the life of a man whose fate has been as yours, so you must pay heed to what I'm telling you, don't you see?'

Alex looked at the doctor's fingers gripping his hand. 'But I need money, Doctor. Maybe I go to the foundry in Trois-Rivières, because who does not see that it is work of the future? And this way I have money for land, and my papa, he can come home.'

'Alex, the fact is that such work will not be the way of your future. I'm sorry to say it. Your wound is a marvel in certain contexts, a gift, but in others, it's a handicap, a danger. You're too weak to endure that nature of work. Likely you will always be too weak. Again, I'm sorry to say it, but for your own good it must be said.'

Alex looked over the doctor's shoulder and out the window by the desk, and through the trees he saw the fort's desiccated palisades. Most likely Beaumont was right, if only for the time being, because Alex had no money and no idea how he might find his way back to Québec, nor did he have a plan for what he might do once he got there, only vague ideas, for the hope of living up to Serge's vision was lost – he'd accepted that, however reluctantly. He also struggled with the awkwardness of asking Beaumont for money, but he recognized as well that he had little choice, and he felt that if Serge were there to counsel him the advice would've been to seek from the situation at least some modest gain. 'But money,' he said after a long pause. 'How will I have money?'

A smile twinkled in the corners of Beaumont's mouth. 'We'll devise a suitable arrangement so that you can have some spending money. There's work you can do around the house and the property, and you'll be provided room and board in exchange for your participation in the research, of course. When it comes to fruition, there will easily be enough money for you to bring your father home. I promise it.'

Alex could hardly believe what he was hearing and felt a grin spread across his face for the first time since he'd wintered with Serge. Clearly his 'tit frère still had some influence over Beaumont's actions, though whether from within or without, Alex couldn't be sure. 'Vraiment?'

Beaumont frowned. 'I'm sorry?'

'I mean, you – you are talking serious?'

'Yes, son. I'm speaking seriously.'

A sense of renewed purpose bloomed in Alex's chest, and he imagined himself standing at the wharf in Montréal, his father strolling down the gangplank of a barnacled sail-ship, pride radiating from his squinting, leathery face. 'And I can go outside?' he asked, nearly laughing. 'I am inside for over a month now. I don't know how long.'

Beaumont's smile now shone, a full moon breaking through clouds. 'My friend,' he said, 'I believe we have ourselves a deal.'

The following morning, Beaumont presented Alex with a contract. They'd been changing his bandages and he was shirtless and lumps of gauze were scattered across his bed. The fresh dressing felt stiff around his ribs; it was clean and white and he was careful not to touch it, lest it be dirtied. After the procedure, Beaumont rolled his shirtsleeves down to his wrists and said he had to get something special from his study, and he returned with the document, which he placed on Alex's desk, and invited him to take a seat before a pot of ink and go over the terms. Alex swung his legs over the edge of the bed and situated himself at the desk; the contract seemed to glare up at him, an incomprehensible blur, but he understood it held the details of a better life, so he narrowed his eyes and bit his lip and brought his fingers to his mouth, but the words didn't come any clearer.

With a snap of his fingers, Beaumont excused himself and began to recite the terms aloud, though most of what he said was beyond Alex's understanding, except for the salient parts, those clauses related to payment, which would be doled out monthly, a relatively small amount at first but one destined to become significantly larger once the research was published, and in exchange Alex would help Deborah look after the house. His duties would be simple: emptying chamber pots and sweeping floors, and when his strength returned, he'd be responsible for chopping wood and fetching water from the fort's pump and supplies from its storehouse. When she left for the winter, which would be very soon, he'd assume these duties with the help of a few delivery boys Beaumont would commission from time to time, but again, only until Alex was strong enough to manage alone. As for the medical experiments, Beaumont would conduct them weekly, and these would entail the suspension of various food items into Alex's fistula. 'You'll be a man of the sciences, son. No doubt the first in your lineage to achieve a station so noble.'

Throughout Beaumont's presentation of the terms, Alex nodded and smiled even at the parts he didn't understand, and with this last remark he issued a giggle so childish he'd have been embarrassed were he not so amazed at his good fortune. At Beaumont's direction, he signed the document with a slash of ink that the law considered a signature, and once this was done he was invited to go outside and take a walk, enjoy the fort, explore the village, but not to be out for too long, as late that afternoon he'd be sitting down with Deborah. She'd apprise him of his daily duties about the house and also they'd begin some basic studies so he could be more lettered when finally he met Beaumont's esteemed colleagues in Detroit.

'Yes,' said Alex, still grinning, 'I understand, and please, my money?'

Beaumont's brow tightened. 'At the end of the month, as per the terms of the contract.'

Alex looked out the window. The sun shone but its light seemed somehow cool, and he returned his attention to the document, which lay open to the last page, his slash of a signature still shiny and wet. 'I can have some now? Just to go for my walk?'

'Those aren't the conditions of the arrangement, Alex. You understand, don't you? Shall I reread the relevant section?'

'Yes, I understand, but… please?' Again he felt a tinge of discomfort asserting himself so forcefully in the negotiation, but as Beaumont had just made clear Alex was a man of the sciences now, a man who'd survived adventure and misadventure both. He'd come a long way since living in the back of M. Anderson's store, and surely that merited at least a little bit more presence in discussions such as this.

Beaumont stepped toward the door but hesitated at the threshold, turning around and filling his lungs with air. He blew a monumental sigh, shook the curls off his forehead, and shoved his hands in his pockets. 'A small advance is fair enough, son. You're right. I'll get you a few coins.'

20

BEFORE EMBARKING ON HIS WALK, ALEX POLITELY requested a dose of laudanum, lest his wound agitate him while he was out, and Beaumont nodded and produced the vial and spoon to mete out a substantial serving, more than usual, and Alex savoured it on his tongue, the blazing bitterness and the almost imperceptible sweetness too.

He still dressed in Beaumont's clothes, though Deborah had brought them in at the sleeves, hems, and cuffs to better fit his smaller frame. Outside, the mid-autumn air braced his skin, and though moving quickly caused him pain, he hurried across the grounds of the fort, past the storehouse Beaumont had mentioned, where bluecoats wandered the vegetable stands and women filled their sacks with beets and carrots. He heard the clang of a blacksmith's hammer and saw a draft horse dragging a mill cart in the direction of the log cabins whence he'd come. Alex passed through the gates of the fort, where two soldiers stood sentry. One of them pointed and the other snickered but they didn't interfere with his passage, so he hurried down the hill past the gardens growing on either side of the road and toward the beach.

It took ten or fifteen minutes to reach the shore, not enough time for the laudanum to take hold, but Alex knew that soon it would, and the knowledge carried him along. There were fewer people camping on the beach, and the wind came hard off the strait and battered its surface into curling waves. Surely the fight between Simon and Bineshi had left tension between les Canadiens and les Indiens, but that wasn't readily apparent as men and women of the white, red, and mixed races met in various groups and pairings to haggle over the terms of clothing and boat repair and the procurement of beans and bear fat, and Alex imagined that enmity couldn't divide people who wanted things from one another – but then again, perhaps it could. He thought about this and couldn't be sure and thought some more before shrugging it off.

The beach was thick with spoken French and he noticed how sorely the language was lacking at the Beaumonts' house. It was the difference between home and forest, warmth and cold, and bientôt his smile grew slack and wide, but it wasn't just the French that pleased him, rather the laudanum had finally begun to wriggle through his system. He bought a bottle of rum from a Frenchman who wore an eyepatch and stank of his own rotting liver, but this was a friendly fellow who clapped Alex on the shoulder after taking most of his money, and together they had a glug from the bottle and the man swallowed and winced and said, 'Tu veux-tu une femme, mon gars?'

Alex shook his head, non merci, and he walked farther along the beach until he found a piece of driftwood shaped like the severed horn of a sea monster, and he sat on this and looked at the high waves of the lake and drank from his bottle. Much of the rum leaked out his side, so he bundled his shirt and pushed it into the aperture with his thumb, and though this was painful he held it in place as he gulped and swallowed and gulped again.

He didn't much feel the booze as it sank into his body, and while it was dawning on him that he'd be a little intoxicated for his meeting with Deborah, at the moment he didn't care. If later Beaumont should punish him, then it was unlikely the punishment would be severe, because the doctor was clearly excited about their deal, clearly swept up in the notion of medical discovery, and surely his gratitude toward Alex would lessen the bite of his less generous impulses, and if that wasn't his natural inclination, then likely Alex's brother would sway him in that direction.

'Partageons?' The accent was rough and strange and belonged to an Ottawa man Alex vaguely recognized, a man who held out his hand, a pouch of tobacco in his palm. 'Not that shit from Virginia,' he continued in his grainy French. 'This is from the lands far to the south, where the Spanish once controlled toutes les affaires.'

The man sat next to Alex and packed an eerily carved pipe, the bowl of which was shaped much like the face of the man himself. He lit the tobacco and smoked and then passed it to Alex, who offered the bottle in return, and the Ottawa man crossed his legs and drank and looked at the lake with squinty eyes. He wore black trousers and a string of animal teeth around his neck and a cotton shirt and leather bands around his biceps all tattooed with geometrical shapes and patterns. His feet were bare despite the chill and his toenails were chipped and dirty and he crossed his legs and sighed contentedly. He said, 'You're recovering from your bad luck, it seems.'

It wasn't a question and sounded as though spoken from a great distance, so Alex nodded but didn't respond, and for a while the man said nothing more. The two of them passed the pipe and the bottle, the pipe and the bottle, the pipe and the bottle, until after a time the Ottawa man spoke again. 'You have about you a tristesse. Like a dark cloud. It's very big and very tense and eventually it'll bring a storm.'

Alex smirked – mais comment ça, une tristesse? – but when he tried to speak, tried to tell this man just how happy he was now that he'd been recruited into the sciences, he found that saliva had built up around his lips, and as he opened his mouth it spilled over his chin, so he wiped himself and forgot what they were talking about and decided to change the subject. 'Were you angry? After the fight on the beach? Your people. Were they angry?'

The Ottawa man puffed his pipe. 'Many were angry, yes, of course. But what can they do? Me, it's not my way. Me, I waited. I watched. And when the fight was over, I went among the impartial French and made wagers that the one who started it would be hanged, and in this way something positive came out of the whole affair.'

Alex felt a bewildering exhaustion unfurl from somewhere deep in the pit of his stomach, and he looked at the Indian and tried to find his tongue. 'I'm very tired,' he said, 'and I don't know when I will be able to rest.'

The Ottawa man thought about this. 'I have a place where you can rest.'

Alex wouldn't remember standing up or following the man, but later he awoke in a tent nauseous and sore and with his head thumping and his mouth completely dry. He looked outside and saw the Ottawa man tending a cooking fire and beside him kneeled the woman who Séb had identified as Rémi's wife, her hair spilling down the shoulders of her animal-skin smock, red and black beadwork travelling up and down the seams. 'Shkuze,' the man said to her, and she glanced at Alex and frowned and looked away.

He crawled out of the tent and looked at the sky but couldn't be certain if a day hadn't passed. They were far down the beach along the forest, and from this distance the voyageur camp looked like a piece of rotten wood crawling with insects. The Ottawa man stood with his hands on his hips in front of the fire, above which a steaming iron pot hung from a tripod fashioned of branches and leather twine. The Ottawa man grinned and turned to Alex, and in French he said, 'My friend, you have about you a most powerful stench.'

Alex coughed and cried out from the pain, then coughed again. His furry tongue was glued to the roof of his mouth and his voice sounded as a raspy whisper, and he wasn't sure how to lift himself all the long way to his feet. 'What's the hour?' he asked, remembering his appointment with Deborah.

The man looked from Alex to the sky and shrugged and renewed his smile. He pointed at the dull sun and said, 'Sometime today, by the looks of it.'

Alex's stomach heaved but nothing came up and he clutched himself and stared at the ground until his nausea subsided. 'Do you have water? Please?'

The man nodded. 'There's water.'

He made no further movement and Alex was about to ask again, but then Rémi's widow appeared. She looked about ten years older than Alex, with two parallel lines faintly tattooed on each of her cheeks and two more on her chin. 'Gidahn,' she told him, a hardness in her eyes, a suspicion, and she tipped her bony hand back toward her mouth, encouraging him to drink. She had her baby bundled on a cradleboard strapped to her back, and she stepped quickly away from him and looked down with a guarded expression.

Alex balled up his shirt and plugged his hole. He took the water and tilted his head, and despite the pain in his ribs and skull he sucked and gulped and swallowed.

The man watched this with an appraising look and said, 'That's Namid. I believe you knew her husband, n'est-ce pas? My name's Miigwan.'

Water spilled down the side of Alex's mouth and he wiped his lips with his sleeve. 'I have to go home.' He handed the waterskin to Namid and stumbled to his feet and struck out onto the beach. He was late to meet Deborah and gone was his earlier insouciance, for he'd made a commitment to Beaumont, he'd signed paperwork with legal heft, and in this state of pain and sobriety, he found himself intensely fearful of the consequences should he violate the terms. He couldn't let his father down and couldn't rely on his brother to right his every wrong, he had to rise to the occasion and make the most of the opportunity, as surely Serge would've done.

'It looks like maybe someone is having his way with you,' Miigwan called out, but Alex didn't know what he was talking about and didn't care anyway. There was maybe an hour or two of daylight remaining, and his stomach lurched as he moved down the beach and into the village, and several times he had to stop and double over to clutch his knees, heaving yellow froth in the dirt of the street. He did this in front of the American Fur Company's supply store, and when the fit finally subsided he looked up and saw the big man with the moustaches standing beside Colonel Smyth on the porch and behind them two bluecoats smoking their pipes. Alex nodded, but although they were making eye contact, the Colonel didn't return the greeting and the two stared at each other a moment before Alex continued up the street.

When at last he climbed the hill to the fort and passed through its gates and lurched his way down the little wooded trail to Beaumont's home, he found the doctor standing out front with his shirttails untucked and his arms crossed tightly over his chest. He scowled as Alex climbed the steps but didn't speak until they went inside, after which he closed the door and locked it.

Alex had broken into cold sweats and his stomach was convulsing and the effort to stand was suddenly too great, so he pressed his back against the wall of the hallway and slid to the floor. He looked up at Beaumont imploringly. 'Please, Doctor,' he said in a tiny, almost inaudible voice. 'I have pain everywhere.'

Beaumont's cheeks were blotchy, his brow creased and nostrils wide. He looked more like an angry father than the handsome young doctor who'd rescued Alex from the snapping jaws of death. 'You,' he hissed, 'stink of a man besotted. It is absolutely vile.'

'I have pain everywhere,' Alex said again, looking up at Beaumont as if from the bottom of a hole. 'I feel very sick.'

'You were meant to meet with my wife two hours ago. We were about to send a soldier to find you.'

'J'étais perdu!'

'You will speak to me in *English*.'

Alex shrank away and stammered his regret, but his stomach convulsed and he doubled over as the retching took him in waves. The attacks were swift and vicious, and he couldn't always manage a breath in the tiny spaces between. He could think of nothing but his physical agony and the prickling fear that Beaumont would no longer let him be a man of science.

The doctor loomed. 'You idiot. The alcohol has ravaged you, and you're in need of the laudanum. What did I tell you? You've gone too long without it, and now you're in a very poor way.'

As the doctor walked down the hall, the floor creaked and Alex could do nothing but retch and struggle for breath. After an eternity, Beaumont returned and crouched at Alex's side, roughly gripping his arm and pushing the tiny bottle into his hand. Alex clamped his palm to his side and drank. Everything was briefly still, then Beaumont stood and ordered Alex to pick himself up, but the boy couldn't move. He lay crumpled on the floor, gasping, saliva caught in the sparse hair of his chin. Beaumont shouted the directive anew, and this time, trembling, Alex rose to his feet and followed his doctor down the short hallway to the scullery and into his bedroom.

'Go to sleep,' said Beaumont. 'I'll have to lock you in, I'm afraid.'

Alex sat on the edge of the bed, hair hanging to his chin, and though he desperately wanted to, he couldn't bring himself to ask if the experiments would still proceed. 'Please,' he whimpered instead, 'I can have water?'

Beaumont studied him for a long minute, face stoic except for his eyes, which moved about the room, deliberating.

'Please?'

Beaumont cleared his throat and stepped wordlessly into the hall. He closed the door and Alex heard him lock it from the outside, then he heard muffled voices arguing and imagined the doctor was giving his wife a lesson on the demerits of leniency. He curled up on the mattress and tried to sleep, hating himself for having been foolish enough to take his new station for granted and now preparing to do whatever it took to put things right. But although Beaumont had given him enough painkiller to rescue him from total distress, he could feel the drug threatening its own absence before the effects even took hold, and he understood then that he had a new affliction to endure, this need for a thing that assuaged the very harm it inspired.

21

HE DIDN'T KNOW HOW LONG HE SLEPT, BUT NIGHT HAD fallen and the room was dark when he awoke to the sound of a key in the lock. His body was full of pain, the constant shriek of his wound and a cruel twisting in his guts and underneath it all the irritated mumble of his legs from walking so much the day before. The hinges creaked as the door opened and Deborah entered with a serving tray upon which was a lantern and a bowl, and next to the bowl a heel of bread.

She wore a white gown under a navy blue housecoat, and her hair hung in two black sheets on either side of her neck, her throat pouring from the shadows of her face. She set the tray on the table and moved the chair next to his bed. 'Are you awake?'

He grunted.

'I've brought you some food, Alex. You must be hungry.'

He struggled to sit but couldn't make progress. Seeing this, Deborah bent over the bed to fuss with his pillows. She brought with her a cascade of hair and a cloud of salty scent and a glimpse of the flesh below her neckline, and although her skin was bright there were still shadows shifting about the details of her body, and they hid from Alex the scandal of her breasts.

Once she'd arranged his pillows he pressed his palms into the mattress and attempted to lift his back, and this was painful but possible. She saw him grimace and touched his shoulder and smiled encouragingly, and she reminded him faintly of his maman, but also something else, some vague concern that recalled Serge, but very vague, as though she wasn't aware of it herself.

'I brought you some stew,' she said, sitting next to him and taking the tray onto her lap. 'While presently it may not seem it, my husband is, in fact, a very fine man. He's charitable and kind, hard-working and fiercely intelligent.'

Alex said nothing but stared at the bowl, which was full of a thin broth he hoped his body would accept. Seeing his gaze in the light of the lantern, Deborah took up the spoon, lowered it into the bowl and, with her palm beneath, craned it into Alex's mouth. His teeth knocked against the metal and the sound was deafening in the quiet of the night. His throat barely accommodated the warmth of the broth and his stomach groaned in frustration, and a second later he felt his bandages dampen where much of the fluid leaked free from his body. But it was good, and he wanted more.

Deborah continued to justify her husband. 'He grew up poor, you understand. A Virginia farmer's son. Tobacco, of course. His father was born of a blacksmith and his mother a girl from Ireland, and both of them died only a few years ago when their farm was attacked by bandits likely sent by creditors.' She set the spoon in the bowl, and with delicate fingers she tore the bread into small pieces, one of which she passed between his lips. 'Dr. Beaumont went pale when he learned of the news. He was devastated. But there was an outbreak of fever at the time, and he was required at the barracks. Of course he put the needs of his patients far before the demands of his grief. That's always been his way.'

Alex managed to hold the bread inside as he pondered this story and didn't doubt its veracity. 'He will become angry if he finds you are here, non?'

She fed him another spoonful. 'He's very tired tonight. I am sure he'll sleep through till morning.'

The thought of going that long without laudanum made him tremble, and Alex instinctively pulled up his shirt and showed Deborah the broth-stained dressing around his wound. 'Ça me fait mal,' he said.

She held his gaze. 'I'm sorry?'

'It is hurt me. Right now. It is hurt me very much.'

She dropped her eyes to the contents of the tray and kept her silence.

'It is hurt me very much,' he said again. 'Hurting.'

'I cannot administer any medication. I'm sorry.'

Alex felt he might cry. 'But I feel bad without it.'

'No. Samuel won't allow that to happen again. You shouldn't have left his care for so long earlier, don't you see? That's why you were sickly.'

'I was not knowing what would happen.'

'Just as Dr. Beaumont didn't know you'd be gone for so long. There's much to learn about your condition, Alex. He's trying to teach you things only as they arise. It's less overwhelming that way.'

'But now? Now I have pain. I need my medicine. Or maybe something to drink. I have something to drink instead. Yes?'

Deborah straightened in her seat and placed her small hands on either side of the tray. 'I can't be of help, Alex. Not like that. What I can tell you is both God and man are watching over you now. Perhaps life to this point hasn't afforded you that degree of care. But you have it in this house. You must learn to see that. You must learn to accept it.' She stood and took up the tray and moved toward the door, pausing at the threshold to look back at him. 'Goodnight.' She held the tray with one hand and with the other she closed the door and returned the room to darkness.

Alex heard the key rattle in the lock, and then the night was quiet once more. He was alone with his pain and sat against the pillows with his bandages clinging wetly to his ribs, and while he waited many hours for the sun to rise and for Beaumont to return with the laudanum, he thought he saw a dim light floating at his side, bouncing gently off his sodden bandages, flickering and then fading away.

22

AS THE WEEKS PROGRESSED, BEAUMONT CAME TO HIS ROOM to silently change his dressing, and as the first snow neared, even this became unnecessary, because the aperture, in its own way, had mostly healed. No further surgeries were required to remove shards of rib or clumps of cartilage and even the plug became redundant, for Alex's body had grown a fleshy sort of flap that wetly covered the hole and could be pulled back with delicate fingers, a development Beaumont termed 'most astounding', but this without sparing a smile for Alex or even much of a glance.

During this time, Alex also took up his contractual duties around the house. Deborah did the bulk of the work, tidying the cabin and visiting the fort's storehouse to buy grains or the butcher to buy meat. She wandered the village to have clothing repaired and cooked their meals and cleaned their tableware, whereas Alex had only to get the things she needed to complete these tasks and was also required to carry two buckets of water to the house per day, and even though this was greatly exhausting he vowed not to complain lest he inspire another episode of his doctor's displeasure. She said this type of work had taken her time to accept because she came from a family with the means to hire servants, but she understood that it must be done in the near term so that she and her husband could prosper in the long.

There was also time for her to give him a few short lessons before she left for Detroit, and during these he learned to spell his name with letters most gracefully drawn. The sessions took place in the late afternoon after they'd done their chores, and Deborah first retired to the room she shared with Beaumont, where she changed out of her bonnet and petticoat, and in their place she wore a white blouse tucked into a plain brown skirt. Alex had two shirts and two pairs of pants and he changed into the cleaner outfit, though immediately the shirt was sullied by the grip of his suspenders against his wound, and he felt himself boyish in clothes tailored to fit his marginal frame.

They took their lessons at the dining-room table, which sat before the hearth in a pool of waning afternoon sun cast through the window, and the walls of stacked logs were lightly decorated: a large crucifix carved and stained, a simple painting of a farmhouse, a portrait of George Washington, and, over the fireplace, a long and shiny musket. Deborah neatly folded her arms at the edge of the table, and when she leaned forward to remark on Alex's work, he could smell her sweat from the day's labour, and again she reminded him of his maman. The way he rendered the letter *X*, she said, was especially stylish, with two elegantly swooping lines travelling from their remote beginnings to meet in a near-perfect centre, and where they crossed they made a lump of ink that Alex thought of as the stone of a peach. He blushed and turned away. Surely she was telling him only what she imagined he wanted to hear, because his letters appeared crude when sharing the light with hers; indeed the *D* that began her own name was a thing of majesty, at the top a flowing loop like a lock of hair and at the bottom a tighter circle extending from the base as though a dainty slipper emerging from the shadows beneath her bed.

'Truly, you're a natural when it comes to penmanship,' she told him again during their final lesson, and with reticence he described his hobby of drawing at night in the back of M. Anderson's store, and during another lesson a few days later she gave him a sheaf of paper, a pot of ink, and a wooden dip-pen with a metal nib. 'I spoke with Dr. Beaumont and he agreed that you should take up your hobby anew while you're under his care. It'll certainly help pass these coming winter months.'

Alex leaned back in his chair and sighed. 'I don't believe he is really buying me anything. He is not even looking at my face when he is taking care of me anymore.'

'Don't fret,' said Deborah. 'He'll come back around to the way he was before. Beneath his formal disposition, Dr. Beaumont is a most sensitive man, and while I know you didn't intend it – I know you intend to hurt no one – he's nevertheless still smarting from that afternoon of your indiscretion. But I also know that he's working hard on a course of research whenever he's not preoccupied with his formal duties, and I know equally that the two of you will find an easy rapport while I'm gone. When I return, we'll take up these lessons anew.'

Alex was dubious. Now certain his little brother no longer occupied any part of Beaumont's soul, he instead suspected the spirit roamed the house in the form of the light he'd seen while locked in his room after his indiscretion, and so he couldn't rely on familial oversight to imbue the doctor with mercy. And yet there were small signs of Beaumont's lessening anger, and if Alex was honest, he could see these signs trailing nearly all the way back to the event itself: his door had never been locked after that first night, Beaumont still administered laudanum even though most of Alex's pain was gone, and Alex was allowed out for walks once a day, though Beaumont strolled a few paces behind, hands joined formally at the small of his back.

Alex thought about this as Deborah examined his penmanship and he realized that she was probably right about it all, that if he maintained something of the disposition he'd had with M. Anderson he'd be able to see this opportunity through and return home to Québec a wealthy and lettered man.

23

THE NIGHT BEFORE DEBORAH LEFT FOR DETROIT, THE
Beaumonts invited three officers and their wives for dinner. The men
turned out in dark black jackets and cravats and the women wore jew-
elled headbands and dresses of seemingly endless drapery. Alex ranked
Deborah la plus belle, with her black lace gloves and rouge on her cheeks.
It was as though the company so finely attired lifted itself above the
remoteness of the island and the dreadful creep of the changing seasons.

Alex and Deborah had spent the past two days preparing a hog for
the main course as well as soups and fruit, and they tracked down several jugs of wine and the table was elegantly set. Alex was not invited
to join them – Beaumont thought it uncouth – but he was called upon
to serve the various courses and was surprised to see Beaumont sitting
quietly while the others laughed and carried on. Alex had expected to
see his doctor holding court on any number of topics, whether politics or history or medicine, but it was the other men who steered the
conversation and owned it too.

When much of the wine had been drunk and the food eaten and
the plates and cutlery strewn across the table, Alex came to tidy the
mess so the company could begin a game of cards. One of the officers
tapped him on the shoulder and everyone fell silent to observe their
exchange. This was a tall man, thin as a branch and with dull blue eyes.
He wasn't quite forty but had a cane with a silver handle, and he said
to Alex, 'This hole in your body, son, give us a peep, will ye?'

Alex looked from this man's inquiring eyes across the table to
Beaumont, who was studying his untouched wine, then to Deborah,

who gave him a smile that was both reassuring and apologetic, and so he returned a few dirtied dishes to the table. After a small hesitation, he lifted his shirt and displayed his fistula, with its fleshy covering, for all to see. Everyone turned their heads to stare, all but Beaumont, who remained focused on the wine he had yet to drink.

'May I touch it?' asked the man.

'Yes, sir, as you wish,' said Alex, knowing the man would touch his body whether he liked it or not.

The man extended his index finger and it hovered between Alex and the table. Everyone remained quiet as it inched closer and closer, and when finally it made contact, Alex was surprised at how cold it was, as if this man had no pulse, as if he'd been struck dead on a battlefield somewhere and now hobbled from dinner to dinner imposing himself on the help. 'I'm not sure what all I was expecting,' said the man, 'but he feels about as human as the rest of us, don't he now?'

There was silence and then one of the women, presumably this man's wife, with a drop of gravy on her dress she hadn't noticed, threw back her head and laughed and squeezed the man's knee, saying that he was really too funny, oh yes, much too funny indeed.

Later, while Alex was kneeling on the floor of the scullery scrubbing dishes in the wash basin, Beaumont entered, his dinner jacket removed and his hands in his pockets. He cleared his throat and crouched to Alex's level. 'Sorry for the intrusion tonight, son. On your person, I mean. I'm not one for large gatherings, I'm afraid, not generally, but I should've overcome my reticence so that you could've maintained your dignity.'

Alex looked up from his work and the two made quiet eye contact, then Beaumont stood to his full height and left the room.

24

THERE WAS SNOW ON THE GROUND BY THE TIME BEAUMONT
was ready to conduct the first of his experiments. It was early morning,
cold in Alex's room, which now felt very far from the house's centre
chimney. The sun had yet to fully rise and a gusty wind rattled the
windowpanes. Alex lay supine on his bed with his shirt off and fur
blankets folded down to his waist, and next to him Beaumont sat in
a wooden chair with his sleeves rolled up and about him a stink both
acrid and unwashed, a hallmark of his presence since Deborah had
left for Detroit a few weeks previous. As she'd indicated, Beaumont's
manner gradually returned to what it had been before Alex's indiscretion, and while Alex was relieved at this turn of events, a new tension
had taken its place, that of his fear regarding the experiments, which
Beaumont had begun talking about more and more.

Two round tables had been set up by the bed and the lantern had
been taken down from Alex's wall and placed in the centre of the
nearest table, while on the other was a plate of assorted victuals: a
piece of salt pork, a chunk of cheese, a slice of apple, all of which Alex
had prepared himself. His drawing materials had been put away for
the occasion and on the desk in their place were Beaumont's scattered
papers, an inkpot, and a few of the doctor's pens.

'Here we begin a historic journey,' said Beaumont. He leaned back
in his chair and his loose suspenders dragged across the floor. He
shoved a hand in his pocket and removed a ball of silk string and an
hourglass. He wore a slight smile, as if remembering a private joke,
and he asked repeatedly if Alex was comfortable. 'We're partners in a

scientific expedition, Alex. I only want to ensure you're as content as the procedures will allow.'

Alex glanced at the fleshy covering of his aperture. 'J'ai peur.'

'What's that? I'm sorry?'

'I have fear.' Looking out the window, he watched as the cold blue dawn gave over to day.

'I see,' said Beaumont, pensively touching his lower lip. 'But that's understandable, lad. When a man sets out to walk a snowy wood which no man has walked before, it's natural he should be apprehensive of everything therein. It's natural to be wary of danger. And while I don't mean to delve too deeply into the abstract, it's equally natural for a man to wonder how those woods might change him, you understand, really change him, for better or worse, or perhaps most dreadfully, not at all.' Beaumont reached out and gave Alex's hand a squeeze. 'Try to remember, in this instance, that we are two men entering that snowy wood together. You have only to follow closely in my footsteps as I guide the way. And in your particular case, if the walk should cause discomfort, there's a dose of laudanum waiting at the next clearing. Of that I can assure you.'

Alex coughed and nodded and focused on the ceiling. Beaumont had explained to him the basics of the experiments a few nights previous, and they were ghastly. He didn't want to call them to mind just now, but still the details eddied mere inches below his full attention, and so he stared at the ceiling as Beaumont prepared the first insertion. After a minute or so he felt the doctor's strong fingers palpitate his chest, then peel back the flap covering his hole, and there was a gasping sound as the seal was broken. Beaumont spent some time with his face pressed against Alex's abdomen, eyelashes tickling the tender flesh around the aperture, as if he were peering into a spyglass.

'Fascinating,' he mumbled, sitting up straight and shifting in his chair to tie a length of string around an item of food. 'First, we lower a piece of meat.'

Alex glanced at Beaumont's hands and saw the fingers of one pinning back his flap as the thumb of the other pushed a piece of ham into the hole, and around this piece was a length of string tied neatly.

The pain wasn't unlike that which he'd known at various intervals throughout his life, but it was stranger and mixed with an odd pleasure as well, and this he recognized from his relations with Serge and also with rum. His brow broke into a sweat but Beaumont didn't notice, or rather didn't remark, and once the doctor had sunk his thumb all the way in, he wriggled it this way and that and then withdrew it, and though the pain broke off immediately, a sort of intimacy was lost as well, and the only sign of this penetration was the string that hung out of Alex's body and dangled down his ribs.

'Now,' said Beaumont, 'we wait.'

He dragged his chair away from the bed and over to Alex's desk, where he dipped his pen and began to scribble notes, repeatedly glancing from his writing to Alex's face. They didn't speak, as Alex had hoped they would, but rather spent an hour in near-total silence, only the sound of Beaumont's scratching pen between them, until the glass emptied and Beaumont returned to Alex's side, where he pinned back the flap and with one fluid motion pulled the ham out of the aperture.

'You see?' he said, dangling the food between them, its edges softened and eroded. 'How can anyone insist this material has undergone only a mechanical process? I mean, really, Alex, if you only knew how learned men can be stubborn.'

25

BY MID-DECEMBER BEAUMONT AND ALEX HAD SETTLED INTO a routine, with the former out of the house most of the day while tending to the sundry ailments of soldiers and villagers and their wives and children. Almost every morning, as the sun was rising, Beaumont opened the door to Alex's room without knocking and set the table for his experiments. Into Alex's fistula he inserted all manner of food, from toast to salt pork, raw beans to chopped potatoes, and he came home at lunch to check on the progress of their dissolution, and this he did again in the evening. There'd be many insertions to come, and if along the way he should discover not just the manner of the process but its materials as well, then that would be most fortunate indeed, and so one morning he inserted a hose into the aperture, mumbling a distant apology as Alex flinched and clenched and drew air through his teeth. Beaumont sucked on the end of the hose, then made a twisted face and spat a mouthful of acrid-smelling fluids into Alex's chamber pot. He then angled the hose over the chamber pot and proceeded to gather a few samples in a small collection of scuffed vials.

'This,' he said, 'has never before been done, son. We truly are on the very frontier of discovery. We need to send these fluids to a laboratory. I strongly suspect the presence of a powerful acid.'

After removing the hose and again mumbling his apology, he cautiously lifted a vial to his nose and gave it a sniff, his brow furrowing, and then he brought it to his mouth and with the tip of his tongue tasted the contents. Smacking his lips, he said he'd hired a dogsled team to transport the samples to an alchemist in Detroit. He was working on a paper he planned to submit to the *American Medical Recorder* before spring, and he hoped to include the test results if they came back in time. If not, a follow-up paper would be warranted, as the information would put an end to the long-standing debate on the agents of digestion.

Alex spent the weeks performing his duties, taking personal time in the evenings to work on his drawings, one of his maman sitting down to her lunch in the coach house, but the face of this one unfinished because the memory made him sad, so another of Serge with scarred hands buried in his thick beard, but the eyes and the brow he couldn't bring himself to complete, a dishevelled secret in their composition he wasn't yet ready to reveal. While he tried to be grateful for the pens, what he truly longed for were the lumps of coal he'd had in M. Anderson's store and even in the hotel with Serge, because he wanted to look up at the cabin rafters and let his hands once again shuffle rapidly about his canvas, and that way he could see anew all the swirls and smears and smudges and whorls that had once told him so much of how he'd felt, but instead he used the pen to practise drawing the letter *D* as Deborah had done it; while the image remained firm in his memory, there'd also been a recent reminder in the form of a letter from Detroit, and how badly Alex had wanted to press Beaumont about what she'd written and if she'd asked after him and how, but something about that felt wrong, as if it weren't the sort of query one man of science made of another's dearly beloved.

And so he devoted himself to his chores, which mostly entailed cleaning a great deal, though not Beaumont's study, into which he wasn't permitted, and he washed their clothes and visited the fort's storehouse and butcher, and he cooked as well, though his meals were basic and bland, salt pork for the most part, always with beans, and once a week they had fish dried to last the winter. They seldom ate together – Beaumont took his meals in his study – but when they did sit down at the dining-room table the atmosphere was amiable, lantern lights flickering as the doctor expounded on the progress of his paper.

During his waking hours, Alex searched for but couldn't find further signs of his 'tit frère, nor any other ghosts besides, and it was as if the house itself had put them to rest, because though it was dark and dusty and in some places festooned with cobwebs he could never reach, it was full of hard details as well: the blackened heads of nails that held down the floor and the white paint that peeled off the shutters and the musket over the fireplace. These things were the products of settlement. They had a power that seemed to force away any other type of thing that didn't share the fullness of their reality, or perhaps it was Beaumont who imbued them with an unbending truth simply by living among them every day.

In sleep, however, Alex continued to meet with the dead, often in settings of horror, and while some of these episodes he knew were caused by the laudanum – he took three doses each day: morning, noon, and night – others he was less sure about. It was terrifying to relive the Georgian Bay massacre, to find himself running through a burning wood with Serge's anguished spirit in devilish pursuit, to see a pale and bloodied Séb appear before his bed, pleading to be taken home to his belle puce so he could embrace her once more. He also dreamed of a benign ball of light circling his body and thumping against his fistula, as though seeking to gain entry; he'd peel back the flap in invitation, and though the light entered, it did so only briefly before exiting in a rush, dimmer somehow, and as these particular dreams came to their close, Alex tasted river water and felt himself to be drowning.

26

ABOUT A WEEK BEFORE CHRISTMAS, BEAUMONT FAILED TO appear one morning with his notes and his string and his hourglass. Alex had prepared a number of food items and arranged them on a plate, which he placed on his desk. Ice covered the edges of the window and he could see his breath in the evenings and throughout the night, but less so in the mornings after he'd built up the fire in the hearth and the heat had managed to reach his room. He waited in bed, the sheets pulled up to his chest. He'd grown accustomed to the experiments but still found them disturbing, and depending on the size of the morsel Beaumont inserted they could be painful as well. Once they'd even caused him a fever. Still he worked hard to maintain his resolve, to remind himself that he was a man of science now and it was his duty to make his papa proud, and if ever he felt too fearful to continue he knew he had only to turn to Beaumont, his guide in this snowy wood.

But it had been eight hours since he'd had his last dose of medicine and his stomach was tense and it promised soon to buckle. He lifted himself out of his bed and opened the door and stepped into the hall, but all he heard was the house creaking in the wind and the occasional pop of a wood knot in the fire.

He made his way to the stairs and ascended to the top, where the short hallway was gloomy but warm, and again he strained to hear any sign of Beaumont moving about, and this time he did, a very slight moaning, not of the pleasurable sort but anguished – and it was coming from Beaumont's room.

Alex hesitated. Beaumont wouldn't want to be seen in the private setting of his bedroom, likely in a state of undress and potentially ill, so Alex considered returning to bed and pretending he'd never heard any signs of discomfort, but there was something wrong about that, something callous, and besides, he needed his medicine. Maybe a knock at the door? An inquiry after his doctor's health? But that would embarrass Beaumont and cause him to reject any suggestion of assistance. Perhaps it was best to simply open the door and present himself, and before doubt could erode his determination he grasped the handle and pushed wide the door.

The drapes were drawn and the air stank of sweat. The room had been built on the centre chimney and a fire smouldered beyond a black iron screen. Beaumont lay in bed with his shirt off and fur blankets twisted about his waist. His hair was damp and stuck to his forehead and his face was blotchy and his eyes moved slowly and without focus.

'Dr. Beaumont,' Alex said, his stomach cramping. 'Excusez-moi. I hear you moaning from downstairs. I am getting worried because you don't come for our experiment this morning.'

Beaumont's chest was wide and muscled and Alex imagined him labouring on a tobacco farm in Virginia, harvesting the plant as the sun bronzed his shoulders, and then the doctor pulled his sheets up to his neck and began to shiver and tremble. He glared at Alex and made to speak but burst into a fit of coughing instead. Phlegm snapped about the back of his throat and the sound reminded Alex of Serge in the days leading up to his death.

'There's paregoric,' said Beaumont, once his coughing subsided, 'in the wardrobe over there. Top drawer. Get it and bring it to me, son. Please.'

Alex approached the wardrobe, which was next to Deborah's dressing table, abandoned for the season, and he opened the drawer and saw the bottle but also a few of Deborah's nightgowns, white and neatly folded, and one of the strings that went about her neck dangled free of the pile. He let his hand come into contact with the material and it was sublime in its softness and he imagined Deborah in his place, rising from bed in the middle of the night to fetch the medicine for her husband, because even a doctor sometimes fell sick and was rendered helpless. Her hair would cover her eyes as she dug through the drawer and she'd shake it out of her face as she returned to bed.

He brought the paregoric to Beaumont and the doctor reached for it and their hands touched and Beaumont's was noticeably hot. He fumbled to unscrew the cap and Alex reclaimed the bottle and removed its lid before returning it, their fingers touching once more. Beaumont avoided eye contact. His hands shook and he threw his head back and gulped and much of the paregoric spilled down his neck. He wiped it away with sodden sheets. 'It happens,' he mumbled, studying the bottle's painted label. 'A doctor gives so much of himself to his patients. Nearly all. At times, they give something in return, and this is often some form of the very sickness we doctors labour to cure.'

Alex's stomach tightened and twisted, but he was uncomfortable steering the conversation to the subject of his needs, assuming instead that Beaumont would notice and offer some resolution. 'Me, I like to bring you something, Doctor. Water? Food?'

Beaumont tried to sit up in bed and succeeded only partially. 'I need you to go to the hospital, Alex, and find one of my proteges. Explain to him my situation and tell him to bring along the necessary instruments to perform a bloodletting.'

'Bien sûr,' said Alex, unable to mute his discomfort any longer. 'But there is a small problem because I feel myself am getting sick.'

He expected anger but Beaumont seemed surprised, and with a shake of his sweaty head he said, 'Of course, lad. My apologies. Your medication is in my study, the key to which is on the wardrobe there.' He gestured feebly with his chin. 'This won't be a regular occurrence, you understand, this practice of you administering your own medication. But this is clearly a special situation, so please, do that first and then run to the hospital to fetch a protege.'

Alex crossed the room to the wardrobe in a few strides and felt the cool of the key against his palm. He turned immediately for the door, lest Beaumont should reconsider.

'Alex?'

He paused at the threshold, trembling.

'Thank you, son. You've shown real character this morning, and real dedication to the research.'

Downstairs, the grey light of morning shone through the windows of Beaumont's study and Alex saw that like the rest of the house, this place bore the same lingering traces of the doctor's absent wife, the dry and twisted stocks of various neglected plants left to languish on the mantel above the fireplace, and comme c'était triste to see Deborah's touch so plainly forgotten.

But his gaze didn't linger, because tacked to all four walls were drawings of Alex's fistula, and they were rendered in dark pencil strokes depicting his nipple and his bony ribs and the aperture itself, which was all swirling lines and a blackened centre. It was the first time Alex had seen himself from such a vantage. He stood there, unblinking, laudanum forgotten. He imagined esteemed men in Detroit and elsewhere studying these drawings and based on those depictions they'd form an impression of him, and that impression would be grotesque.

Then his stomach lurched and he remembered his plight and looked about the office's dusty shelves and the desk so cluttered with pens and dried inkpots, and finally he saw it, the tincture. He snatched it up and popped the cork and guzzled freely. The medicine burned and he looked at the drawings once more, then left the office and quit the house.

Winter had taken firm hold of the island, with ice built up on the palisades and the sky densely grey. Huge flakes of wet snow spun down from the heavens and Alex hunkered into his coat and rushed to the hospital.

27

HALF AN HOUR LATER HE APPROACHED THE CABIN WITH
one of Beaumont's colleagues, a branchy man with round spectacles
and bright red hair, the two of them hurrying through the snow and
not a sound but the crunching of their footsteps and the occasional
whistle of the wind. Alex led the way to Beaumont's room, which
now reeked of perspiration, and he stood in the door frame as the
man prepared his procedure, first comforting the drowsy doctor and
then removing from his case a brass scarificator shaped like a cube.
He groped around under the bed until he happened upon Beaumont's
chamber pot, and its contents sloshed and spilled as he dragged it to
the bedside. The man opened the top face of the scarificator to set its
spring, then pushed the opposite surface into the flesh of Beaumont's
arm. He pressed a button on the side and there was the loud snap of
the spring, which the man explained triggered the release of a dozen
tiny blades into Beaumont's flesh, lacerating him in several places, and
from these wounds spurted a fount of blood, much of which splashed
the doctor's bedclothes, and then the man angled Beaumont's arm
over the chamber pot and directed the flow therein.

Beaumont gasped. His face grew pale and clammy and his body
seemed to wither and shrink beneath the fur blankets. Gradually, the
flow of blood became weaker and pulsed less. Alex was overwhelmed
with pity and the sort of fear a boy might feel when confronted with
the ailing form of his father, and he wanted to take Beaumont's hand
and whisper in his ear that everything was going to be all right, he was
an important man, this was just a fever, soon it would pass.

The man from the hospital cleaned up his accoutrements and took his leave, instructing Alex to look in on Beaumont often and bring up plenty of food and fluids because he'd be weak and tired and it would take him a few days to recover. Alex nodded and saw the man out, then he took Beaumont's chamber pot, filled with blood and urine and feces, and brought it outside through the back of the house, where he threw its contents into the snow, and the stain was fiercely red and darkly brown, shocking evidence of mortal illness quietly obscured by the falling snow.

Later that afternoon, with Beaumont unconscious, it wasn't possible to ask for laudanum and Alex assumed the special circumstances still held. He re-entered the doctor's office and drank from the bottle. He couldn't bear to look at the drawings of his fistula, they were too vile, but as the drug took hold he found himself inspired and spent a few hours at his desk dipping his pen and working at self-depiction. He drew himself sitting upright in bed, his shirt off and the sheets bundled at his waist. He stayed true to his ribby chest and the way his hair hung limply and the patchy tufts of his beard, because these details didn't bother him, what mattered was that he was not merely a fistula, not merely a tunnel from inside to out, rather he was his full self, Alex au complet, a full man around a hole, a man of science who'd loved and lost and seen other men suffer the same tumult, and when finally he began to outline his aperture, he found he could consider it without the revulsion it usually evoked. He was absorbed in his work and his concentration was only broken when he heard a great thump from upstairs. How long had it been since he'd checked on Beaumont? He couldn't be sure.

The steps groaned as he climbed to the second storey, and this time he opened Beaumont's door without hesitating and found his doctor prone on the floor, stark naked and propped up on his elbows. His hair was sweaty and stuck to his neck. His deflated muscles hung like loose garments. Alex kneeled at his side and put an arm around his shoulders. Panicked, he asked Beaumont what he'd been doing, and Beaumont craned his head so Alex could see his glassy eyes; he said he was late for work and Deborah hadn't yet prepared his breakfast.

Alex helped him to his feet and sat him on the edge of the bed. The sight of Beaumont's nakedness gave him pause, the dark patch of corkscrewing hair between his legs and his fleshy penis emerging from the tangle, smaller than Serge's but imposing in its way. 'You have finished to work for now,' said Alex, and he let his hand linger on the doctor's shoulder. 'You help many people and all thank you when they pray.'

Beaumont smiled and nodded and mumbled something unintelligible. Alex watched the bobbing of his chin and then sat next to him and without thinking lowered his hand to the doctor's thigh. He felt sweat there, and heat, and he felt the same forces flush his whole body, but then Beaumont slapped his hand away, and the sound of their flesh colliding gave Alex a jolt. He shot to his feet and interlaced his fingers behind his back and said, 'Please, Doctor, I go to bring you food now.'

The doctor lay on his bed and spread his arms and legs and Alex turned away and his throat seemed to be closing as he hurried down the stairs and into the scullery. He put together a meal of bread and cheese and a piece of dry fish, and though he was afraid to face Beaumont again he forced himself to return to the second storey and present to his doctor the meal he should've brought hours ago. When Alex entered with a serving tray, Beaumont was upright in bed, palefaced and covered to his waist. 'I'm... I'm in your debt for a change, son.' He licked his lips and turned his head and coughed, then wiped his mouth and looked back again. 'I'll not forget. I promise.'

28

THE BLOODLETTING HAD BEEN SUCCESSFUL, AND BEAUMONT recovered in time for Christmas Day. He didn't mention Alex's indiscretion, and Alex felt sure the moment had been lost to the haze of the fever. He was relieved, but the memory of Beaumont sitting on the edge of the bed came over him at night, and he was grateful Deborah wasn't around to clean his sheets and that Beaumont failed to note the frequency Alex brought to the task himself.

Beaumont suggested they eat Christmas dinner together, so Alex prepared a meal of salt pork and preserves. He was surprised to see Beaumont place two jugs of wine on the table and to pour each of them a generous glass, and in short order the two of them had emptied the first of the jugs and uncorked the second.

It had been nearly two months since Alex had been drunk and the sensation was somehow more joyous than he recalled, more sensational, and with great happiness he ate his preserves and he was pleased as well to see that Beaumont drank almost as much as he, and after an hour the food was done and the two of them sat merrily at the table. They were now more than halfway through the second jug and Beaumont said he'd spent the last couple holidays alone because although he was expected to make appearances at the officers' galas, he found the company disappointing and further no one seemed to want him there and indeed no one ever remarked on his absence, and so between him and his military peers there had developed a mutual aversion, and though it remained unspoken it was no less palpable. Deborah was different of course, she was a friend to every officer's wife, but in her absence Beaumont wasn't obliged to be social.

'This,' he said, leaning back in his chair and tracing his finger along the stem of his wineglass, 'has been a most pleasant holiday, however. Far and away the most enjoyable of recent years.'

Alex grinned and all throughout his body the laudanum and wine danced as lovers in moonlight, and though he felt he could look on them and protect them from division, he was distantly aware that eventually they'd separate – the moon would vanish and in its place appear a desiccating sun – but for now, at least, the knowledge was vague.

Beaumont gave the table a playful slap. 'But enough about me, son. I do go on, don't I? Yes, I know I do, and not just because Deborah often tells me as much, no, but also because I can hear it personally. Tell me about yourself, Alex. It's high time, isn't it? Let's see.' He slapped the table again. 'Aha! What sort of man was your father?'

There were many ways to answer that question. Alex regularly asked it of himself, and depending on his mood he saw his papa rendered in shades most cruel, a rough man who'd taught his son about the roughness of others before leaving him to fend for himself. Other times he'd see his papa as a man whose truest nature was gentle and loving and led him to make enormous sacrifices to provide for the people he loved, and if sometimes his behaviour tended toward the brutal, well that was merely the outside world conducting itself through an innocent man, and it was this softer version of his papa he chose to relate to Beaumont.

'When I have only three or four years,' said Alex, and he reached into the centre of the table and took the jug in his hand and filled his glass, 'before maman gets a job with her patron in the suburbs of Montréal, my family and me, we live in a small house with just one room and all around are other houses like this, and really it was complètement sale, you understand, very dirty. We sometimes walk together to a nice part of town, and one day in summer I see a toy chariot in the window of a shop, a wooden carriage made by the carpenter there, and I ask my papa to buy it for me but he says non, it is too expensive.'

He paused to collect his thoughts and Beaumont nodded and said, 'My own father never purchased me a single toy, it's true. But I'm sorry. Please continue.'

Alex offered a look of sympathy but though he could see Beaumont wanted to carry on with his story, he was keen to finish his own, not least because Beaumont had so far gained the wrong impression. 'Yes, but then some couple days later, he comes home from travail and he give me the chariot. I am so happy then. I roll it across the floor of our house and pretend there are horses and the horses love me, and then one day I lose the toy, I don't know where, and although I expect my papa to be very angry, he is not. He tries to make a new one himself. He never finish, but it is all right, because he works so much, and even that young I understand he loves me. So my papa is a nice man and someday soon I will have enough money to bring him home from Paris.'

'Ah,' said Beaumont, smiling sadly. 'That's a lovely story, son. Your father sounds like a far better man than my own, who was a mean drunk and a chronic debtor and spared no kindness for anyone, least of all his son, though I suppose his callousness was motivation enough for me to quit his cursed farm and enlist in the service and later to take up the study of medicine under the guidance of a great war surgeon, a man who'd known combat during the Revolution and the Indian Wars too, and so now I'm here, working with you on the wild frontier of medical discovery.'

Alex had been waiting for Beaumont to bring up the subject of the research, and now he leapt out of his chair and bumped the table with his hip, spilling the wine, and although Beaumont's face darkened for a moment, quickly the expression lifted, and Alex squealed, 'Attendez!' He ran to his room and from his desk he took his self-portrait. He didn't pause to admire it as he had been the past few days but rushed back to the kitchen and presented it to Beaumont. 'I draw this of myself. It is me.' Beaumont's eyebrows lifted in surprise and an appreciative look overtook his face as Alex said, 'Please, you send it with your paper you write, because I am sorry but I see the drawings in your office and they make me feel very ugly, and this drawing, it make me feel more like me, and I want to be sure the doctors in Detroit see me au complet, a real man of science, you see.'

Once he'd finished speaking Alex struggled to regain his breath. He'd wanted desperately to ask this favour, and with great, boozy excitement he registered Beaumont's hands reaching out and taking the drawing and his eyes moving slowly about the details. 'My, my, but you're very talented, son. Of course I'll send this with my paper and the drawings of the aperture I've done myself. You're right that it's essential. We need these men to view you as an equal to me, of course, and to do that they need a full appreciation of you, which this drawing will most certainly extend.'

Alex laughed and was about to embrace his doctor, but he stopped short lest he remind Beaumont of what had transpired upstairs. They spent a few more hours drinking the wine and talking about their families, and after a while, Beaumont grew tired and suggested he administer Alex's nightly dose of laudanum and not to worry about the dishes, they'd clean them together the next morning after they had rested. They didn't, but that was all right, Alex didn't mind cleaning them himself, not just because that was his typical lot in life but also because Beaumont had done him a much bigger favour, and already the idea of undergoing further experiments had lost some of its horror.

29

THE WINTER MONTHS SLOGGED ON. THOUGH THEY DIDN'T dine together any more often than they had before, it seemed as though a lasting and positive change had come to their relationship, for as the experiments continued Beaumont was gentler with Alex, less distant during the procedures and more concerned with his patient's comfort and well-being. He dangled into Alex's fistula all manner of foods and he flipped his hourglass and removed these items and recorded how Alex's stomach had altered them, and although this was as unpleasant as ever, the doctor's renewed manner made the sessions easier to endure, and then finally in late March, the test results arrived from Detroit.

'But of course I was right!' Beaumont exclaimed, exploding through the front door one afternoon as Alex was dusting the dinner table. He strode down the hall and into the room, a feverish glint in his eyes, and triumphantly he slammed a large envelope on the table, jabbed it with his finger and fairly bellowed: 'Hydrochloric acid! Just as I suspected!' He said he'd be taking his meals in his office for the next few days and the experiments would have to be paused while he redrafted his paper. He was due to post it at the end of the week, and he could surely manage that, of course he could, but what was first required was a reframing of his prose so that the indisputable nature of his discovery was clear from the opening paragraph, and such important work couldn't be delayed, no, not even for a second.

For the rest of the week, Alex didn't see his doctor in the evening nor any other time of day, but on the kitchen table, morning, noon, and night, there was his medicine, the dose poured into a dented tin cup. Alex went about his cooking and cleaning and drawing. He left meals outside the door to Beaumont's office and empty dishes appeared in the same place a short time later. Twice or thrice the house was visited by one of Beaumont's colleagues, and Alex would lead these men to the threshold of the study and notify Beaumont through the closed door of their presence, but the doctor wouldn't answer and instead these colleagues would leave Alex with a message, something menial about the progress of a patient or the dwindling of supplies, and Alex would relay these messages, again through the closed door, but again Beaumont never deigned to respond.

Not until late Friday morning, while Alex was on his knees scrubbing the floor of the dining room, did Beaumont burst out of his office, and Alex caught a glimpse of him as he ran down the hall, his shirttails untucked, his hair dishevelled, his suspenders flapping about his waist. He had a sheaf of papers under his arm, and then the front door slammed and the whole house shook.

Alex raised himself from the floor and felt a surge of pride that Beaumont had managed to complete the paper on time. He imagined his doctor arriving at the post office and packaging his document, smiling and whistling as he strolled back to the house. Surely Beaumont would like to return to a tidied office, and so Alex took his feather duster into the study, and it was musty and dark and scraps of food lay scattered about the legs of Beaumont's chair. Embers glowed faintly in the fireplace and shreds of bark curled on the floor, and one or two twisted logs remained to be burned. Alex thought to open the window and freshen the air, and when he rounded the desk he saw, roughly folded in its centre, the self-portrait he'd made, which surely Beaumont had forgotten, and he thought to gather it up and run as fast as he could to the post office, and he even reached for it to do so, but then he noticed that all the other drawings had been taken off the wall, every last one, and he stood there for a moment, arms limp at his sides as he regarded the bare wall, and a sort of dizziness overtook him such that he had to sit in Beaumont's chair lest he fall over, and as he did he realized that Beaumont hadn't forgotten it, no, impossible, because this was a man who forgot nothing he deemed important, this was a man whose focus never wavered from the ambitions that commanded it.

It became difficult to breathe as Alex was assailed by blurry recollections of Christmas dinner, when Beaumont had studied his portrait and agreed it was essential, agreed that his colleagues had to view the two of them as equals, but now sitting there on the filthy desk was the discarded means of doing that very thing. He picked up the portrait and unfolded it and looked it over: his limp and ugly hair, his thin and bony chest, and the vulgar darkness below his left nipple. A series of reckonings visited him as he sat and contemplated Beaumont's behaviour throughout the winter from greater and greater remove, and though it pained him enormously he couldn't help but wonder if he hadn't been a fool all these months, a lowly houseboy with delusions of grandeur, delusions fed to him by the self-serving determination of a man who'd seen in Alex a rare opportunity and had taken it solely for his own benefit, for his own advancement, because why else had he been so rough during so many of the experiments, so distant, and why else had he been so punitive when Alex had been late that autumn afternoon, locking him away as if he were some kind of criminal? The answer now appeared as naked and sickly as Beaumont had been in the weeks before Christmas: he saw in Alex only a stupid, illiterate child, weak and pliable and ever so far from home.

PART III
Nouvel Espoir

SPRING, 1832

30

ALEX DIDN'T WAIT FOR BEAUMONT TO COME HOME. HE tacked his drawing to the wall, crookedly, then spat in the fireplace and quit the office for his bedroom. He rifled the drawer of his desk until he came across his savings, which had accumulated over the winter, but insufficiently, for all this time he'd been little more than a slave, but blind to the situation, stupidly blind. He gathered his coins and they clinked in the pocket of his trousers as he donned his boots and his coat – Beaumont's coat actually, a frayed old thing, long and black and dug out from the bottom of a dusty chest and presented to him by Deborah as though a gift when to its owner it was merely rubbish. He entered the scullery and threw open the back door, left it gaping, but at the edge of the property he doubled back and tracked snow through the house and into Beaumont's office, which he plundered in search of his medicine, knocking a few books off the desk and leaving them on the floor, why bother. At last he came across a bottle of laudanum in a drawer next to a few letters from Deborah, the salve of her cursive useless against the burn of his anger, and he uncorked the bottle and took a mouthful before stuffing it in his pocket. He left the house again, this time slamming the door, and the clap of wood split the morning like a gunshot.

The sun was up and the air was warm in his lungs. Snow melted off the edges of the roofs and the ground was a patchwork of loosening ice. Had he really believed Beaumont would include his drawing in the research? Had he really believed he'd been welcomed into the sciences? Yes, he had, like a fool, but how could he have been so stupid? Just because the man had told him as much? Had been stricken by fever and briefly reduced? Just because they'd drunk together at a dinner table? These things made Beaumont trustworthy? These things filled him with the lasting spirit of inclusion?

Alex walked down the hill to the village, slipping and sliding and regaining his balance only to lose it again. He didn't greet the people he passed, didn't even look up from his feet. He hadn't wandered that far from the house since autumn, and it felt good to be free of Beaumont and his shadowy den. He'd been a fool, a weakling, and not for the first time, because hadn't Serge essentially fooled him too? He hadn't thought about it previously, hadn't wanted to examine the contours of their relationship, the uncomfortable contradictions easier left ignored, but now that he couldn't turn away from them, questions had to be asked: Why hadn't Séb and Rénard ever heard of Serge if indeed he'd been so famous in the trade? And why had André l'avant so ably beaten him on the beach if Serge had been even half as fierce as he'd self-described? Alex saw clearly now that Serge had wanted him only for company, had seen him as a simple boy he could control, a boy he could hold close when he felt lonely and penetrate when he was aroused, and of what importance was Alex's safety to the plans of men like Serge or Beaumont or Séb or Rénard, and were these men so different from even the likes of M. Anderson? The answer struck him as obvious, and so did the solution: All he could do was change. He vowed that when later he saw Beaumont he'd make this change known, he'd declare it, he'd stand firm in the hallway, hands on his hips, and he'd spit forth each and every word, and when he saw a tattered American flag fluttering outside the tavern, he decided to spend the afternoon developing the terms of his declaration right there on the bar.

Inside there were paddles painted aqua blue and forest green and they hung from the walls like swords, and there was even a battered birchbark canoe lashed to the rafters and here and there the heads of deer mounted on plaques of pine. A man served drinks from behind the bar and wore a pistol on his hip and a filthy rag over his shoulder, and his cotton shirt was stained with food and beer, and he had a mole on his cheek that looked like the pelt of a beaver. Alex ordered rum and it was served in a tin cup, and he paid and the man took his money without smiling.

The tavern was busy though the day was young. At one table sat a number of soldiers gambling with dice and at another a group of men wearing dirty suits and playing cards with stoic faces. Scattered at others, variously alone or in silent groups of two or boisterous gatherings of three were disparate men of the island's working class: a soot-smeared blacksmith ate gruel with a heel of bread; a cooper lowered his shaggy head to the table and clutched a half-empty bottle of rum, next to which was a rusty handsaw and chipped mallet; a few labourers stood in a semicircle around a piano but didn't play it, instead roaring in sloppy unison, swaying from side to side with their beer sloshing all over.

Sitting at the bar was l'Indien Alex recognized as Rémi's brother-in-law, the man named Miigwan. He wore a flowing black robe and a plethora of colourful beads around his neck, green and red and blue and yellow, and his long hair was gathered up on top of his head and mud dripped from the soles of his boots and pooled on the floor. He regarded the carpenters with gentle scorn and then turned and made eye contact with Alex and raised to him a jar of beer. Alex nodded, slowly, but sat a few stools away, taking off his coat and hanging it over the backrest. Apparently undeterred, Miigwan emptied his glass, stood up, and took the stool next to Alex. The barkeeper brought him another glass and for this he paid nothing. 'Perks,' Miigwan said in French. 'Faut en profiter.'

Alex didn't feel like talking, so he nodded and emptied his cup and signalled to the barkeeper for another, and the man with the pistol shifted back down the bar and exchanged a look with Miigwan, then poured Alex his drink and waved dismissively when he attempted to pay.

'Faut en profiter,' Miigwan said again, shrugging and clapping Alex on the shoulder, then looking out on the bar. Alex finished his drink and ordered another and again his money was refused, though this time he pressed because he didn't want to fall into Miigwan's debt, and anyway he could afford to buy his own rum. But the barkeeper was resolute, and Miigwan leaned over to Alex and said, 'Enjoy, my friend. Haven't you earned it, even if not directly from me?'

'And in return? You'll want something from me, of course. Everyone does.'

'Me, I only want interesting company. C'est tout.'

'I have money.'

'Then perhaps you'll buy me a drink later.'

'And until then?'

'Until then we'll get to know each other.'

'Non. Today I have nothing to say to anyone, and maybe never again.'

Miigwan drank his beer and considered this with two fingers pressed into the pit of his chin. 'Then you don't have to say anything. How about that? And besides, I've already gotten to know you, albeit from a distance, just as most people on the island know you. En plus, for me, it's a bit different, because I've dreamed of you too.'

Alex sipped his drink and glanced at Miigwan over the rim of his cup. They stared at each other and Alex put his cup on the bar and twisted around to reach into the pocket of his coat, from which he removed the bottle of laudanum. He popped the cork, mixed a portion of the tincture into his rum, and slid the bottle back in his coat.

Miigwan raised an eyebrow but didn't comment, rather said he owed Alex a story, and this would be a pleasant debt to repay because his people had gathered countless stories over the years and they'd told them to one another as well as to foreigners. This they'd done in lands reaching from the St. Lawrence to Lake Superior, so their power to tell a tale was like a Frenchman's power to cross a sea to a faraway land. 'My favourite story,' he added, 'is about me.'

Alex caught a glimpse of the barkeeper, and though they were speaking French this man appeared to understand, for he rolled his eyes and scratched his mole and slunk away. Alex shrugged and motioned with his drink for l'Indien to begin his story, and Miigwan spent an hour or more unpacking the details of his life.

'My people are known as traders,' he began, 'but me, I come from a family of warriors. Except I didn't want to fight. Comme toi, je suis spécial.'

He called his people Nishnaabe and said they came to the Great Lakes a thousand years ago from the eastern edge of the continent, and since then they'd fought a people Europeans called Mohawks for a stake in the fur trade and later they sided with the French against the British and then with the British against the Americans, though perhaps this last alliance was poorly chosen because now the Americans held much of their lands and sought to remove them from what little they'd yet to lose. Like paupers, many of his people went to Detroit once a year to collect a few small coins in return for all this lost land, and Miigwan had done this a couple of times himself, but no longer.

He'd known battle, bien sûr. About fifteen years before, not long after the hair had first appeared beneath his arms, his people allied with the British to battle the Americans and he heard the booming of muskets and hid beneath the arcs of arrows, all this not especially far from where they now sat. He'd even been forced to fight a bluecoat at close range, and the man stabbed him in the side and the blade slipped easily through the slats of his wooden armour. Here he lifted his robe and showed Alex his tattooed skin, and up around his ribs, near the same spot where Alex himself had been wounded, was a pale white scar that rose from his flesh like the bud of a flower.

'I fell in the long grass and saw my blood run down the stalks, and when I looked up the American was standing over me, a boy really, like me, his chest heaving, and in one hand he held a bloody knife and with the other he drew a pistol from his waist, and I thought then that I'd die.'

The bluecoat took a knee and forced the barrel of his pistol into Miigwan's mouth, but before the boy could commit further harm he was felled from behind by Miigwan's brother, and this via a spear pierced through his back and his lung and his chest. Then his head was clubbed and a piece of his skull dislodged, and in the brief second of silence between this event and the next, Miigwan heard the buzzing of flies and thought himself dead as well.

His brother returned immediately to the throes of combat and Miigwan stood up and slowly cradled his injury and looked about the battlefield. He saw dead men with their mouths wrenched open and dying men with their intestines in their rigid hands and injured men lying in the grass and blinking at the sun.

He'd seen this very sight in a vision quest a few years before. He was taken to a place in the forest where he fasted until he was visited by a manitou that took a form he couldn't comprehend. This spirit told Miigwan that when life presented him with the carnage of the battlefield, he'd achieve an understanding: such fighting was foolish; it was driven by gain, and while he didn't disavow the notion of gain, non, jamais, he judged these methods not just beastly but futile, because consider Pontiac's bloody campaign, which resulted in a silly wampum belt and a Royal Proclamation no one took seriously, and even Tecumseh had fought and died and gained nothing more substantial. Miigwan remembered this lesson from his manitou and reflected on it as he limped off the battlefield and returned home, where Namid tended to his wounds. 'You remember Namid, n'est-ce pas? The widow of your voyageur friend? She's my sister.'

Intoxication had overtaken Alex as a light rain across a parched meadow. 'Rémi wasn't my friend. He hit me.'

Miigwan licked his lips. 'He hit Namid as well, from time to time. Me too even, on occasion. But most men are coarse in one way or another, don't you agree? And it must be said, for a man so rough, he was surprisingly gullible.'

Alex nodded and drank and Miigwan continued his story, raising his voice to be heard over the bellowing carpenters, one of whom had taken a seat at the piano and pounded the keys in a perfect absence of artistry or ken. Namid had been studying to be a medicine woman when Miigwan was injured but she stopped her lessons to shelter him from the outrage of their father and brothers. He told her of his battlefield revelation and she was compelled by his vision of peace. She tried to sway their family, but they'd judged Miigwan a coward and were ashamed of his failure, and they spoke to their Elders and agreed he'd betrayed the sacred value of bravery, and after a week of convalescence he'd be banished, for how could they rely on him when their lands were being subsumed by the Americans? Namid again rose to her brother's defence. She repeated that he was a prophet of peace, that he'd seen a better way forward, but their father said this was a lie and an insult to their spiritual leaders, and now Miigwan had betrayed another sacred value, that which honoured truth. He'd have to leave immediately and was permitted to take with him only a bow and some few arrows, and if he should be met on a battlefield going forward, there'd be no distinguishing him from the enemy.

For the first few nights of Miigwan's banishment he hung about the boundaries of the village, still too injured to hunt alone and too fearful of roving American troops, and when Namid went to gather plants and herbs for her lessons she also brought him food and reported that their father's resolve had weakened not at all. On the fourth evening she was followed by one of their brothers, the one who'd saved Miigwan on the battlefield, and when the news of her betrayal got back to their father she was banished too.

'But Namid, she's no fool. I left empty-handed, whereas she gathered up a few goods, some cups and beads and arrowheads, plus a ceremonial drum, and best of all, a rifle my grandfather had taken from the body of a dead Englishman. She knew the theft would never be forgiven, but like me she saw the futility of our people's conflict, and so her banishment seemed like a new beginning. She brought these goods into the wilderness, and because we didn't have much food it was easy for me to fast, and she beat the ceremonial drum while I sought advice from my manitou, which directed us first to the forests around Detroit and then to Mackinac Island, lands already devoured by the Americans and their treaties, yes, but lands also home to our Gitche Manitou, our Great Spirit, and both the Great Spirit and my own manitou spoke to me in one voice, and they said I'd prosper on Mackinac and eventually my people would see my success and understand the truth of my prophecy. And so we began to travel, trapping our food in the forest and eventually trading our arrowheads for spots on a boat paddled by Canadiens such as yourself.'

They arrived on Mackinac hungry and destitute but for their few remaining goods. Miigwan was able to trade the rifle to a besotted Canadien in return for a purse of coins, and he took those coins to this very tavern, where he won several games of chance against bluecoats and voyageurs and each time he bought a drink he gave a little extra money to the barkeeper, whose name was Blake and even then wore a pistol on his hip, and when some of the white men became sore over their losses and sought to make violence with Miigwan, the barkeeper drew his pistol and fired a shot into the ceiling, and in this way a tense calm was restored, a calm that had persisted ever since.

'Et ton père?' asked Alex. 'Il te manque pas?'

'Yes. Sometimes. Sometimes I miss him and all the rest of my family too.' Miigwan saw his father a few years ago in Detroit, where both had gone with hundreds of other Nishnaabeg to collect their annuities. His father wore a dusty black coat and his hair was a tangled mess and when he made eye contact with Miigwan he didn't recognize him, or at least that's what he pretended.

Alex and l'Indien fell silent and drank in acknowledgment of the quiet humiliations endured by aging fathers.

Once, continued Miigwan, there'd been an important Nishnaabe village on Mackinac, though now there were only camps, and he and his sister wandered the woods of the island until they found a suitable place to make their own, and indeed they moved it from time to time as their intuition guided them. They kept cordial relations with the other Indians living in the forest and in the village, and Miigwan emerged a respected but illegal operator of several games of chance played in the tavern and elsewhere as well as an illicit trader of many goods, and while the American Fur Company sometimes sought to halt his activities, he had the protection of not just his personal manitou but also the Gitche Manitou, and he'd dreamed of Alex and the role Alex would play in these endeavours and though he couldn't yet discern the specifics of this role, he felt sure it would be both positive and profitable. 'Alors,' he said, tapping his empty beer glass on the bar. 'Nous voilà. That's my story.'

Alex threw back the rest of his rum, and although he'd been annoyed with Miigwan at the beginning of the story, he'd begun to see similarities in their lives. They were both orphans of a type. They'd both survived damning injuries. And they'd both come to Mackinac in dire condition, only Miigwan had been there longer. He'd managed to shake off the controlling grip of other men, and maybe Alex could learn something from him if he was cautious, if he kept up his guard, because when it came to Beaumont he knew he'd never be in control, not for a minute or even a second, and he'd been a fool with his stupid drawing to think otherwise. He flagged the barkeeper and ordered drams for himself and Miigwan, and when l'Indien refused the offer, Alex insisted, saying it was only decent for one friend to return the generosity of another.

'Meegwetch,' Miigwan said, smiling and gripping Alex's shoulder and giving it a squeeze. 'I've certainly worked up a thirst.'

Alex smiled back and again retrieved the laudanum from his coat and made to mix it into his drink, why not, he'd come this far, and what did it matter what Beaumont thought, he'd never let Alex be a man of science, that much had become painfully clear. But no sooner than he'd unscrewed the cap and placed it on the bar did Miigwan, with a quick but gentle hand, reach out and stay his pour.

'That,' said l'Indien, 'you got from your doctor, yes?'

'Yes, of course.'

'And you don't find it a bit strange? You've experienced the withdrawal?'

'Why,' said Alex, a realization dawning even as he uttered the question, 'is it strange for a doctor to give his patient medicine?'

Miigwan clucked and fingered his beads. 'You should give it up. You've recovered from your injury. That's not medicine anymore. It's something else.'

Alex looked down at his legs hanging off the stool. He didn't even have a pair of pants to truly call his own, instead he wore Beaumont's trousers, spattered from the scullery. He nodded, hair hanging in his face as he studied his hand in his lap, the open bottle of laudanum in his palm. Of course it was just another means through which Beaumont asserted control, much like the meagre wages he doled out each week, and Alex had been a fool yet again not to see it for what it was, but nevertheless he extended the bottle and poured some into his dram, for that was simply what his arm insisted on doing. Then he put the cap back on the bottle and the bottle back in his pocket, and he raised his eyes to Miigwan and shrugged. 'He made me think I was special.'

'You are. But not the way he thinks. You have to start resisting him.'

Alex threw back the dram, wincing as the mixture seared its way down his throat. 'But how? There's nothing I control.'

'And suppose there was? What would you do then?'

Alex set his cup on the bar and thought about this as the burn subsided. Then, from the ambition-bereft expanse of his imagination, there rose an idea of such perfection he was ashamed it had never occurred to him before. 'Me, I want to grow a peach orchard in Québec with my papa.'

L'Indien raised an eyebrow and pursed his lips and looked Alex in the face for a long minute. 'It's a beautiful vision, my friend, easily within your reach, and tell me, have you ever heard of the moccasin game?'

Alex shook his head and Miigwan said it was a classic game of chance, one he often played here in the tavern and during summers in the beach camps as well, and it consisted of hiding a small item beneath one of three moccasins and then another man would come along and wager to guess which moccasin hid the object. If he won, the bank would pay him out. If he lost, he'd pay the bank.

'Want to see it played?' asked Miigwan. 'It comes from my people, but I bring a simplified version to the tavern. It's one of a few games I run in here, but quietly, because the fur company might hear the money landing in my purse as opposed to theirs.'

Alex hesitated, suspicious. 'I only have a few coins. I don't make much money working for the doctor.'

Miigwan raised his hands, palms out. 'Today is a day for showing, not for betting. A day for betting will come, rest assured, but today is not it. In my dreams, I see you have the strength to learn this game, and I see that learning it will help you find your way to this peach orchard with your papa. Your strength, it comes from a manitou that takes a vague form, a brightness of some kind. A light. You just have to welcome it.' He stood and drained his glass and winked at the barkeeper, who turned and took a bottle of rum from one of the shelves and handed it across the bar. 'Viens,' said Miigwan. 'I want to show you two things.'

31

THEY MADE THEIR WAY THROUGH THE VILLAGE'S MUDDY, fetid streets, filthy mounds of snow melting on either side and a warm breeze playing at the hem of Alex's long coat. He had to hurry to keep up with Miigwan, who also wore a long black coat, and Alex imagined them as two of a kind, men who'd been tossed into exile and injury by forces infinitely larger than they were and seemingly beyond their control, but only seemingly – for were they not, the two of them, bursting with inner strength? Were their dreams and visions not within easy reach?

The mid-afternoon sun shone on their passage and warmed their journey, and when they left the slumping buildings of the village behind, Miigwan wheeled around and pulled the rum from inside his coat, and truly he cut an impressive figure with his lapels open and his beads swinging and strands of his hair fluttering in the wind. He took a pull from the bottle and handed it to Alex, who did the same before handing it back.

'Bon,' said Miigwan, sliding the bottle back into his coat. 'We must take something of an indirect route to my camp, tu vois, because I don't like leaving obvious tracks in the snow. Are you up for a bit of a walk, my friend?'

Alex laughed and nodded, giddy from the rum and, if he was honest, happy he'd taken some of his medicine in the tavern, for would he have felt so good without it? So happy? The two of them struck into the woods, their breath billowing over their shoulders as they kept to a well-trammelled trail, Miigwan whistling an angular tune and swatting pillows of ice-encrusted snow from the drooping conifers. Alex soon began to sweat and was grateful when Miigwan stopped where the trail ran past the base of a cliff, on one side a snowy chute and on the other a stand of pine. He told Alex to jump from the trail into the stand and to push himself against the rock face to keep out of the snow, and then he returned a dozen or so metres down the trail and kicked at the snow the whole way back, obscuring their footprints because, as he called out, they were going someplace special. Then he jumped to the exposed ground at the base of the cliff and led them deeper into the forest, instructing Alex to keep close to the rock and avoid knocking snow from the branches.

The terrain unfurled uphill, the height of the cliff gradually diminishing and the effect of its awning increasingly lost, which caused the snow to deepen again, all flecked with conifer needles and shreds of lichen and crumbs of bark, but as the snow built up anew, so did a trail through it emerge, and when the cliff was only as high as Alex's knees and they were again completely surrounded by trees, he smelled smoke. Miigwan turned to him and grinned and withdrew the rum from his coat, and they both drank deeply from the bottle.

L'Indien wiped his lips with his sleeve and spat in the snow. 'She's been through a difficult time, my sister. Many years of challenge.'

'Je vois,' said Alex, remembering what Miigwan had said in the tavern about Rémi hitting her. He hadn't thought much about it at the time, but standing there in the woods listening to the trees dripping and creaking and the beating of a bird's wings, he remembered how Rémi seemed equal parts harsh and pitiful, the sort of man who'd strike his wife with both fists and later long for her with his last breath.

Miigwan gave him a meaningful nod and started walking again. 'Difficult times,' he said over his shoulder, 'make difficult people.'

After another twenty or thirty minutes, they entered a small, sunbathed clearing with a firepit in the middle, and over it stood a tripod of branches lashed together with leather thongs, a cast-iron pot hanging from the centre and thin tendrils of smoke rising from a bed of cinders. There were logs arranged around the firepit like benches and stump-length pieces with backrests carved into them like chairs and a couple small tables fit for eating a meal or playing cards. Behind this arrangement, near the perimeter of trees, there were stacks of firewood covered in ice-encrusted skins and next to that a few sledges leaning upright against a collection of other supplies concealed with tied-off hides. A wigwam made of wooden poles and strips of birchbark stood next to these, and on the far side of the camp, almost directly across, there was another, wisps of smoke trailing from the top, and the doorway was pinned open and Alex could see furs covering the floor.

'We've been wintering in this spot for a few years now,' said Miigwan, holding out his hands as if to gather it all up.

Alex noticed a birch tree a few feet away with deep gouges in the trunk, and he tilted his head trying to imagine what could've caused such damage.

'Rémi took an axe to it after one of his failures to contain himself,' Miigwan said. 'He was often frustrated. Imposed himself on his surroundings sometimes. Tried to other times. You might start to notice them, the victims of his eruptions. They're scattered all over.' He gestured to the trees beyond and around, and indeed a good many bore similar scars and one in particular appeared especially abused, with fungus-infested wounds running from the base to shoulder height. 'A spirit in that one,' Miigwan said. 'Vengeful in its state of desecration.'

Alex looked over his shoulder, and Miigwan met his eyes and shrugged, then cupped his hands to his mouth. 'Namid?' he called. He walked to the firepit, and then there came a sound like something hissing through the air and then another like a slap and a thud and a twang all at the same time. Alex looked left to right and back again, and even Miigwan did the same once and twice before raising his eyebrows and issuing a low whistle, pointing at one of the benches by the fire: an arrow, still vibrating from impact, its fletching of blue feathers bright against the background of white and grey.

Blinking at the arrow, Alex heard footsteps in the trees behind him, and he whirled around to see someone in a hooded fur coat exiting the forest and entering the camp on snowshoes, a large parcel strapped to their back and a bow brandished in one hand. Then this person swept back their hood and it was Namid, scowling, the tattooed lines under her eyes diving toward the ground. She threw the bow aside and began yelling in Ottawa, and Alex took a few steps back before he felt Miigwan's hand fall lightly on one of his shoulders. 'You better take a seat, my friend. She's been following us. Probably from the top of the cliff. I was supposed to bring meat from the butcher.'

Alex lowered himself to the log that bore the arrow and watched as Namid stamped in his direction and shrugged the parcel off her back, leaning it against a stump next to Alex, and then she crouched to unfasten her snowshoes, all the while yelling at Miigwan, who wore a patient expression on his face but with a touch of mockery, as if he'd seen displays like this before and wasn't so impressed by them as maybe once he had been. Alex glanced at the parcel and was struck by the revelation that it wasn't a parcel at all but a small, ruddy-faced child in a cradleboard covered in beaded furs, his little hands clenching and unclenching as he watched his mother step out of her snowshoes.

Miigwan began talking and nodding and gesturing at Namid to calm down. He pointed at Alex and then at the wigwam with the open door, then lifted his hands to his face as if washing it. Namid tucked her chin and looked from Miigwan to Alex and back again. She nodded and turned and went into the wigwam, and seconds later three moccasins flew out the open door like flushed birds, arching over the camp and landing in front of the supplies.

Miigwan strode over to collect first the moccasins and then a piece of firewood. 'My friend,' he said, circling back around. 'I had to tell her that the next time you come, it will be with arms full of meat.' He shrugged and eased a log onto the coalbed, then pointed to the child. 'I see you've met Biskane.'

Alex looked at the boy, who shook his little fists and seemed to be laughing at him. 'Armfuls of meat?' He narrowed his eyes and reminded himself that he barely knew this man, that he'd allowed himself to be led to a strange camp in the middle of an unknown forest somewhere on an island he'd never heard of in the middle of a lake he couldn't have found on a map.

'Biskane is her son,' said Miigwan with a solemn tilt of his head. 'He seems much happier without his father around, even if Namid has been taking her time getting used to things.'

Namid came back out of the wigwam wearing a fluffy rabbit-skin dress. She marched up to Alex and he involuntarily shrank away, dropping his shoulders and lifting one of his hands to shield his face, and at this she raised her eyebrows before bending down to collect her son, then walking back to her wigwam and ducking inside.

Staring after her, Alex slowly let go his defensive posture. 'Go talk to her,' he said. 'I don't have money for armfuls of meat.'

'Ah,' said Miigwan. 'But you will. 'Garde.' He sat on one of the stumps and positioned a table in front of him, tossing the moccasins on the surface and reaching into his coat and producing first the rum, which he flung to Alex before reaching in anew and coming out with an arrowhead, which he held up between thumb and forefinger. He put the arrowhead on the table and made a big show of covering it with one of the moccasins. 'This is one of the games I like to play at the tavern. After a few drinks, men like to wager on which moccasin conceals the arrowhead. Harmless fun really, but never underestimate the competitive nature of a man in his cups. If his pride is on the line, he'll bet against chance and trickery both. Now look close. You see the arrowhead?'

'I see it,' said Alex, uncorking the rum.

Miigwan positioned the other two moccasins on either side of the first. He threw back his head and began simultaneously singing to a patch of blue sky far above and shuffling all three moccasins rapidly around the table, his hands a blur as they moved from one to the next. Alex froze, the bottle raised halfway to his lips as he was transported to the back of M. Anderson's store, staring up at the shadowy rafters while he dragged his lumps of coal across his scraps of wood, smearing out abstractions of sadness or anger or longing.

Then the moccasins slowed and came to a halt and Miigwan broke off his song and leaned back from the table. 'Now pick,' he said. 'Which one conceals the arrowhead?'

164

Alex took a drink and shook his head, looking from the table to Miigwan.

'Which one?' l'Indien asked again, tapping his foot against a log.

'Those motions,' said Alex, his voice a whisper.

'Did you lose track?'

Alex shook his head, still a little dazed. 'The middle one,' he said. 'Je pense.'

Miigwan grinned and lifted the middle moccasin, revealing only the grain of the table. 'Guess again.'

'À gauche.'

Miigwan lifted the left one, again revealing nothing. 'Must be the right, then, yes?' But when Miigwan lifted that moccasin, there was nothing beneath it either. He then snapped his left wrist, raising his hand in front of Alex's face, and there was the arrowhead between his thumb and forefinger again.

Alex hauled himself up from the log and drank the rum and looked down into Miigwan's face. 'Mais comment?'

'It can be anywhere you want it to be. Come on my side. Watch closer.' Miigwan hid the arrowhead under the centre moccasin and put his hand on the heel, his fingers curling so the little one was touching his palm and hovering over the table. He gave the moccasin a sudden push forward and paused, encouraging Alex to study his hand from all angles. The arrowhead had somehow come out the back of the moccasin, and Miigwan held it ever so delicately between his ring finger and his little finger. Then he brought that hand to the next moccasin, and even as he pushed it forward he slid the arrowhead under the heel. 'C'est comme une danse,' he said. 'Somewhat difficult at first, somewhat awkward, but with practice a man can easily shuffle all three moccasins, moving the arrowhead from one to another as he chooses. Would you like to try?'

'Bien sûr,' said Alex, 'and actually, I know motions something like these. I... I like to draw.'

Miigwan laughed and reached for the bottle. 'Vraiment? And you move your hands like that to draw pictures?'

'I... I do, yes. En effet, sometimes I do.'

'Ah well.' Miigwan shrugged. 'You see how life fits together every now and then.' He stood up and motioned for Alex to take his seat. 'Pretty when that happens, isn't it?'

Alex sat and took the arrowhead from Miigwan and put it under the second moccasin. He'd never drawn with three pieces of coal before but the idea didn't seem so daunting, and soon enough his hands were a blur all over the table, moving from one moccasin to the other, the arrowhead dragging audibly along the grain.

'Very good,' said Miigwan, lowering himself to one of the logs around the fire. 'Now try letting the arrowhead out.'

Alex tried half a dozen times but couldn't even get the heel to lift, so he tried again and again until it happened just once, but the arrowhead slipped free of his clumsy grasp and slid off the edge of the table. Thinking he'd failed he sat sheepishly back on the stool. 'It's much harder than it looks.'

'C'est vrai,' Miigwan agreed, poking the fire with a stick, 'but only at first. And I can tell from what you've just demonstrated that you'll learn quickly, even if it doesn't seem so right now. That's why I want you to have those moccasins and this arrowhead, mon ami. They're yours. Practise a little bit every morning and night, and you'll master the sleight in no time. Trust me. Then you can perform it in front of the villagers and make a few extra dollars, and with those you can make still more in other endeavours. You can invest in the gamut of my games, maybe even a big party I'm planning once the snow is gone, for if there's one thing I've learned since my exile it's that this island is simply teeming with opportunities. You only have to reach out and seize one.'

'But,' said Alex, casting his eyes to the firepit, 'won't people notice? If they look hard enough?'

'Oh, bien sûr,' said Miigwan, tossing aside the stick and rising to his feet. 'They'll notice. Most of them already know the game is something of a fiction, because like many fictions it's taken many forms across many cultures over many years. But everyone expects at least a little bit of deception as they go through their days and nights, and let's not forget that pride I mentioned earlier. As long as you leave the arrowhead on the table, which you must for the final reveal, there's a chance of winning nevertheless and that's why men choose to play, especially men in a tavern.'

Alex thought about this and nodded and reached into his coat to retrieve his laudanum, and he was reaching for the cork when Miigwan's strong hand landed on his shoulder and gave it an arresting squeeze.

'Wait,' said l'Indien, his eyes probing in their journey first across Alex's face and then down his shoulders and then down his arm. 'So far you've learned one thing, but remember, I brought you here for two.'

Alex had forgotten Miigwan's scolding focus on his laudanum back at the tavern, and he felt his fingers squeeze the glass protectively. He yanked his arm away, and before Miigwan could object he popped the cork and took a long, burning pull from the spout. 'Fine,' he said, grimacing as the tincture sank into his body. 'What else do you have to show me?'

32

IT WAS WARM INSIDE NAMID'S WIGWAM AND ALEX OPENED his coat but felt too shy to take it off, as though there were something presumptuous in such a gesture, something disrespectful. The walls loomed up and above, rising to a conical point overhead. A firepit had been dug into the middle of the frond- and fur-covered floor, and smoke wafted up and out of a hole in the centre of the ceiling. The walls had been covered in hides decorated with long, twisting patterns of beads all red and blue and black, and along the bases of the walls were piles of animal-skin clothing and moccasins and bundles of leather twine and bowls of loose beads. Biskane, free of his cradleboard, sat in the fronds with a doll in his lap, kicking his feet and watching the smoke as it funnelled overhead. Miigwan, stripped to his shirtsleeves, rested his chin in his palm and sat quietly next to Alex, and on the other side of the firepit Namid had crossed her legs in what appeared to be her bedding, hair covering her face as she hunched over a wooden bowl full of plant stems, and these she gathered up into a cylindrical bundle, which she bound tight with thin strips of leather.

After watching her do this for what seemed like an eternity of silence, Miigwan said something like 'Meenuhzgo?' And at this Namid issued a drawn-out sigh and flipped her head back and glared at Miigwan for a second, before leaning forward and touching the bundle to the fire and holding it there until it caught and began to smoke. Then she set the bowl in front of her legs and passed her hands through the smoke and brought them to her face as if she were washing it, as if she were rubbing the smoke into her flesh.

Miigwan leaned over and whispered in Alex's ear: 'It's sage. Purifying medicine. She's smudging her mouth so she can do the ceremony with a pure voice.'

Alex watched as Namid brought the smoke now to her long, thin neck and then down her fur-covered chest and then to her thighs and calves clad in tanned-leather leggings, and then she fixed him with her dark eyes and began speaking rapidly in Ottawa, taking the bundle from the bowl and rising to her feet, walking around the fire and standing over him, and Alex felt confusion contort his face as he looked up at her.

'She wants you to stand,' Miigwan said, nudging him in the back.

'She doesn't speak French?'

'She does. English too.'

He turned to Miigwan expecting to see a grin, but l'Indien just nodded at him and moved his mouth as if to say, vas-y, lève-toi, so Alex stood and shifted his weight from foot to foot, then took a step back and cleared his throat and looked at the ground. He smelled smoke from the bundle, and in his peripheral vision he could see Namid moving her hands in the air around his body, as if washing him in the smoke.

She bent down and Alex watched her small shoulders shift and dip as she guided the bundle around his boot-clad feet, speaking all the while, and Miigwan told him she was purifying his feet so that he might walk upon the land with more respect and that he might tread the floor of his doctor's home with more integrity. Then she rose up to her full height, a couple inches taller than he was, and with one hand she brought the bundle close to his face and with the other she guided the earthy smoke to his ears, and here Miigwan said she was cleansing them so he could better hear all the opportunities in his life, the clamour of their abundance, and then she brought the smoke to his eyes and Miigwan said she was preparing Alex to see all the good things that lay before him, and though the smoke had coaxed a veil of tears over each of his eyes, Alex saw Namid before him, the earlier harshness drained from her features and replaced by something gentle and consoling, and when her lips moved again the words came at him slowly, like a dark song turning gradually brighter.

'Now your coat,' said Miigwan. 'She wants you to take it off. And your shirt. She wants to smudge where your injury has healed.'

And whereas five minutes before Alex would have never conceded to such an instruction, he now found himself shrugging and shaking his arms and when the coat landed around his ankles he heard the bottle of laudanum clink against a piece of wood down there, and how filthy it sounded, how impure. He saw his trembling hands rise up to his throat and untie the laces of his shirt and everything went dark for an exquisite second as he pulled the garment over his head. When the light returned he looked down at the pale and bony expanse of his chest, saw a few dark hairs curling out of his left nipple and below that a warren of scars roaming to and from the puckered red lips of his fistula, this thing Beaumont had drawn from every conceivable angle, then Namid's hands were guiding the smoke first against his navel and then up his abdomen and over his ribs and across his chest, and it was like he could feel the wisps reach through his pores and wrap around his muscles and bones and squeeze out all the fear and pain and despair that had roosted in those places. His shoulders shook and he began to sob, but the sound was sweet to his ears, a gasping relief, and he tasted the salt of his eyes on his lips and then his legs gave out and he stumbled and fell backward and landed in the fronds next to Biskane, who giggled and snorted as Alex looked up at the ceiling, way up at the beautiful hole through which the smoke from the fire and the bundle both slowly wafted, twisting together, and beyond the wigwam spread the sky so clear and deep and blue. He closed his eyes and saw his maman emerge from the blotchy darkness of his eyelids, not the gaunt and pallid expression with which she'd left him but the hale and loving features he'd otherwise known all throughout his childhood, and she was holding a glowing child in her arms, dark hair swirling about his head as if he were suspended in water, and this was his brother, his beautiful brother. Alex wanted to apologize to them for his behaviour of late, for his weakness, his fear, but his 'tit frère wriggled free of his maman's embrace and began to float toward him, and his maman shook her head and said that a young man like Alex, who'd known what he'd known, who'd seen what he'd seen, who'd endured what he'd endured, a young man like him had no obligation to apology, had only to join with his brother and open his eyes and stand up and do his best to do better, only that and nothing more.

He opened his eyes and looked into Namid's face. She smiled and held out her hand and he reached for it and she pulled him upright, tears still streaming down his face.

'Alex?'

He heard Miigwan's voice off to his left somewhere and nodded and wiped the exquisite tears from his eyes and said, 'Oui? Miigwan?'

L'Indien was holding the bottle of laudanum, its painted label vile and obscene, the reddish-brown tincture inside like rotting blood. 'You should pour it out, non? If you ever want to get home, ever want to have your peach orchard, you should pour it out.'

'But...' said Alex, shaking the hair out of his eyes, looking from Namid's face to Miigwan's. 'But I get sick without it.'

Miigwan gave the bottle a shake. 'Is that why you brought this to the tavern today? To avoid getting sick?'

Alex was about to say mais oui, clairement, but he held his tongue because of course that wasn't rightly so, not at all, rather in truth he could've waited until his stomach started to declare its want of the substance and then he could've hurried back to Beaumont's to imbibe just enough to allay the withdrawal and thereby lessen its intensity the next time it reared. But he could see plainly now that he'd not made such a decision, could see that he'd wanted the peculiar thick-tongued escape the laudanum always bestowed, and he'd wanted to mix this strange quality with that which was offered by an abundance of rum. He'd wanted to do this because of how it felt and because of how it would make Beaumont feel, knowing that Alex had taken his medications himself, that he felt free enough in the wake of betrayal to do exactly as he pleased.

He reached for the bottle and took it from Miigwan, hearing the awful sound of the tincture as it sloshed against the glass walls. He pulled the cork and grimaced as a toxic smell rose into the otherwise untainted air of the wigwam, and then in a series of rapid movements he was on his feet and rushing to the door, throwing back the heavy fur that kept out the cool spring air and hurling the bottle toward the firepit, watching as it turned end over end, disgorging its sickly amber before landing in the flames and causing them to burst in excitement.

Now he turned back to his hosts and saw Miigwan standing behind him, holding his shirt and coat and nodding in approval. Alex took his shirt and pulled it over his head and felt the way it rested against his frame as if his body were somehow newer, somehow stronger, and when next he took his coat he felt how light it was without the bottle, how easy it was to slip his arms inside and let the gentle weight of it fall over the small of his back.

'You have to play a little game with your doctor now,' Miigwan said. 'Tu vois? You can't stop right away, but you can take less and less, even if you have to hide it. You can come here for more smudges and Namid will help you with other medicines, and very soon that man will have no such hold over you any longer. And in the meantime, practise the moccasin game, get that arrowhead secure in your fingers, because soon the warm season will be here, and you'll see – my party, it'll be a turning point for you. I promise.'

33

IT WAS NEARLY DARK BY THE TIME HE RETURNED TO THE village and made his way up the hill to the fort. The day had cooled as the sun went down, but nevertheless spring remained on the edges of the breeze. He imagined Beaumont waiting for him, maybe in the kitchen or Alex's room or maybe in the entrance to the house, scowling, his lungs full of a reprimanding wind. But that wasn't the case: the house was quiet and on the counter in the scullery was bread and cheese and dried fish covered with a cloth. There was also some laudanum in a tin cup, apparently Beaumont kept a reserve, and Alex lit a candle and sat down to eat and stared at the cup the whole time, finally deciding to drink only half of it; the rest he took to his room and poured out the window, and he brought the cup back to the table and set it there and beheld it, the traces of tincture clinging to its sides, pooling in its bottom, and then he extinguished the candle and went to bed.

His stomach felt cramped in the morning, as though insects were crawling around inside, getting bigger and smaller, but rather than dwell on the sensation he spent fifteen minutes shuffling the moccasins around his desk, ignoring the sound of Beaumont stamping up and down the stairs, into the study and the dining room and back up the stairs. The arrowhead sounded quietly off the desk, and though Alex still couldn't take secure hold of it, he also felt a certain dexterity in his fingers that hadn't been there the day before, or if not a dexterity then the premonition of one.

After half an hour he dressed and went about his routine, again taking only a small amount of the laudanum Beaumont had left in the dining room and tossing the rest in the snow outside his window, deciding that yes, this would be his pattern for now, this volume of the substance only, and once he became accustomed to that, he'd reduce the volume yet again, and in so doing he'd soon be free.

When finally he crossed paths with Beaumont departing for the hospital he was surprised when the doctor still didn't berate him for tearing up the house and study but instead asked if the two of them could speak a moment. He said he wanted to take a new step in their experimental course and extract weekly some of the gastric fluid he'd discovered inside Alex's stomach.

'Likely,' said Beaumont, tugging on his coat and tossing his chin, 'you'll find this process of extraction somewhat more discomforting than you did the insertion of victuals. The hose will be bigger than the string, of course. You already know from experience. However, the frequency of insertion will be less. And yet, even given your reduced involvement in the research, I've decided to increase your payment as well. After all, we wouldn't be here without you, would we?'

Alex, with an apron around his waist, nodded but didn't smile. His back ached and his legs felt stiff and sore and even the muscles in his forearms protested as he moved his fingers or angled his wrists, and he knew this was the spirit of the laudanum calling for the return of the substance – but the call, no matter how shrill its pitch, would go unanswered. He looked at Beaumont and wondered if the doctor could sense the change in him, the exact quality of the distance between them, and a wave of trepidation briefly overtook him, for though Beaumont seemed oblivious now, there'd come a time when the knowledge would be revealed in its totality, and it would be Alex who would have to reveal it, have to declare it, have to insist on it, and whereas he'd felt more than capable of doing precisely that as he stormed out of the cabin yesterday, today he felt more like himself, which is to say he felt scared and uncertain, and the thought of confronting his doctor caused the saliva to dry on his tongue.

They regarded each other across the short distance of the front hall, one man large and muscled and strong, the other small and thin and seemingly weak. Beaumont moved for the door and gripped the

174

handle, but hesitated. Without turning back, fingers still caught on the brass, he said, 'About the drawing, Alex. I know you came across it in my study yesterday morning. I know it upset you. And of course I appreciate why. But understand it wasn't carelessness on my part. It wasn't absentmindedness. Actually, I realized the drawing would only serve to distract my peers and the general public from the focus of the research – and that is our fistula, you understand. About the house and out in the community, you are yourself in your entirety. But when it comes to the research, I'm afraid such a comprehensive depiction isn't helpful.' He cleared his throat and opened the door. Outside the day was warm and the melting snow was dripping. 'It was a difficult decision, son, but I'm confident I made the right one. I'll present the terms of our new agreement upon my return.'

With cordial formality, Beaumont kept his word, and though the increase was a pittance Alex wasn't surprised and chose not to complain. He understood that he could master the moccasin game and grow his money in the tavern, and he couldn't help but imagine himself holding men rapt with his movements at this party Miigwan had mentioned, for the snow would soon be gone and the first of the voyageurs would arrive within a month, maybe sooner. He had only to endure his situation until then, after which he could amass income in earnest, and perhaps he'd return to Montréal come autumn, before another winter ensnared the island, and from there he could buy fertile land along the St. Lawrence, so that when finally his papa came back from France the two would have a thriving peach orchard to call home.

Beaumont began his new course of research that very Saturday, and though Alex had prepared himself to endure whatever the experience might entail without taking more than the reduced amount of laudanum, he'd failed to consider that Beaumont would personally administer the medication, and he found himself presented with a large tin cup full of the tincture; he couldn't summon the fortitude to decline, the bravery to declare himself finished with the tincture and to endure whatever pain was produced by its absence, so he took the entire dose and lay back miserably in his bed, waiting for the effects to take hold.

No sooner than he felt his face slacken and his attention drift did Beaumont insert a hose into his fistula, sucking on the end of it and spitting a mouthful of gastric fluid into Alex's chamber pot, then filling vials with the acrid liquid that emerged, and lying there in a quasi-stupor he wondered if he'd been a fool to imagine he could endure this kind of invasion without laudanum to dull the intensity of its imposition.

Seemingly oblivious, Beaumont told Alex that testing the efficacy of the fluid outside the organ that produced it was necessary, because despite the conclusive nature of his research there'd still be men in the sciences who'd cling to silly notions about the human body, men who believed its abilities were products of the supernatural. These men would be hard pressed to peddle their superstitions after the publication of Beaumont's second paper, which he planned to supplement with a trip to Detroit, where he'd demonstrate to all the power of the fluid.

'Further to my mind,' said Beaumont, holding a vial to the light of the window, 'this presentation will only benefit from your presence, Alex, because the audience will need to see you to believe you, will they not? They'll need to see your fistula, and of course see me extract the gastric fluid, and then finally see its effect on, say, a single fried egg. And this will serve a dual purpose, this production. On the one hand, it will cement my research in the popular imagination, while on the other, it will introduce you to the public in your entirety, just as you've been wanting.'

Despite himself, and despite the lingering pain from the insertion of the hose, Alex was briefly carried away by this notion, for these men in Detroit seemed a crowd predisposed to respect, perhaps even amity, and what a feeling it must be to bask in such a silky attention – Beaumont enjoyed it daily, and why shouldn't Alex as well? But quickly the idea lost its power. He'd never enjoy the admiration of men like that, not as did Beaumont, and he felt an urge to hit his doctor, but he didn't dare, he'd be defenceless if Beaumont struck back, and he later focused the energies of his resentments on the shuffling of his moccasins, devoting mornings to the practice after he finished vomiting in his chamber pot, his stomach twisting itself into knots before exploding upward, and within a few days he was able to capture the arrowhead, however clumsily, between his ring finger and his little finger, almost just as Miigwan had done.

34

THE TEMPERATURE CONTINUED TO RISE AND THE SNOW
continued to melt, and when Alex wasn't required at home, he slipped
out of the fort to visit Namid, finding the cliff at the edge of the trail
and ensuring he hadn't left obvious footprints before striking out into
the forest. The first time he arrived not in possession of an armful of
meat but just a few pieces he'd bought from the butcher in the fort;
he'd spent a good portion of his savings on these, and Namid received
them with a laugh and cut them into strips and hung them to smoke
over the fire in the centre of the camp.

She invited him into her wigwam and served him cedar tea, for he
was regularly congested now and often felt flushed and even a little
feverish as his body adjusted first to the lower doses of laudanum he
took during the week and then to the higher doses Beaumont gave
him on weekends and then again to their absence as he returned to
the lower doses. The tea, said Namid, would help him get back home
to Québec, and wasn't he lucky to be returning there, she wished she
could do the same someday, take her son home and introduce him to
his grandparents and his aunts and his uncles and the whole of his
community, and she could practise her medicine there and heal her
people instead of sitting around this fire sewing garments for voyageurs while her son crawled around the furs and fronds and played
with his toes and his dolls and the loose lengths of leather or bowls
full of beads, quel ennui, quelle misère, but their life was here now, not
there. It was here in this camp and along the beach, here watching
Miigwan build up his various concerns.

There was a bitterness in her voice that made Alex uncomfortable, and feeling as though he was doing something furtive he asked where Miigwan was, and Namid tossed her small shoulders and shook her head and stared furiously down at her beads. 'Where is he always? Conniving in the tavern, filling people's heads with fantasies.'

Alex didn't respond but saw in her furrowed brow a sadness and frustration he wished he could address, and he wanted to reach out and touch her but instead turned his attention to Biskane, who was sitting upright, gripping his toes, watching his mother with a look of worry. Alex finished his tea and Namid gave him more in a leather skin he could bring back through the village and to Beaumont's cabin, and she told him to drink it when he felt ill, and the next time he came she'd perform another smudge ceremony because he'd need to be purified regularly over the next few weeks.

The furtive feeling stuck with Alex over the next few days as he fed Beaumont and cleaned up the cabin and stole quiet moments in the mornings to either draw or practise catching his arrowhead as it slid out from beneath the heel of the moccasin, and was this because Namid had revealed something of Miigwan that he himself had elected not to show? Or was it something else? Was it possible Namid was simply tired of spending so much time in close confines with her brother, tired of looking after her son alone? Was it possible her opinions of Miigwan were mercurial and passing and not based on anything of much substance, for when Alex drank with Miigwan at the tavern his new friend was always sensitive to his situation and optimistic of its outcome, and truly Alex enjoyed leaning against the bar and watching Blake serve drinks as Miigwan told stories – and if Alex's own brother had not died so young but had grown into the fullness of manhood, would he not have rankled Alex from time to time as well? Was this not what siblings did to one another? Had he not seen evidence of this very thing in the sons of his maman's patron? Alex felt sure he had, and so the real source of his unease must have been the looming change he was concealing from Beaumont, who despite his bottomless self-involvement was nevertheless the man who'd saved Alex's life not even a year before.

One morning late in the week, he was wrestling with these thoughts as he washed chamber pots in the scullery, when Beaumont, voice hoarse with excitement, called for him to take a seat at the dining-room table, where he'd hung his officer's jacket over the back of his chair and rolled his sleeves up his veiny forearms and spread out a series of letters before him. On one of the envelopes Alex recognized Deborah's artful hand, and rather than take comfort he drew from the sight more anxiety still, for what would she make of him if she knew the fullness of his heart over these past weeks?

'Throw a log on the fire,' said Beaumont, rubbing his palms together, 'and know it'll be among the last of the season. With the coming of spring blooms a change in my fortunes, Alex, and I owe a great deal of my good tidings to you.' He motioned to a chair across the table, and Alex landed in it heavily, knitting his fingers in his lap. 'I have before me some very important correspondence, son. Let us go through it, shall we? First, and much as I'd expected, a warm acceptance letter from the *American Medical Recorder*. They'll of course publish my first paper on gastric fluid, for how could they not? They've even described it as "paradigm shifting". I sent a copy of the materials to our benefactors associated with the University of Michigan, and also as expected, they were thrilled at the discovery. The dean of the faculty of sciences responded personally, and he called the research historic. He said he was so impressed that he petitioned the *Democratic Free Press* in Detroit to send a reporter to Mackinac, and this man will undertake the writing of an article. Imagine! It's just as we'd hoped, Alex. We're changing the world even as we speak.'

Alex nodded but didn't lift his eyes to study his doctor, instead kept them low and focused on his apron, which was spattered from the cleaning of chamber pots.

Beaumont dredged his throat and when next he spoke his voice was searching and warm. 'No doubt you're still upset about my decision to exclude your self-portrait from the materials. Son, I completely understand. I know it meant a lot to you, and perhaps this latest turn is but fresh salt in what we must now consider an aging wound, but allow me to suggest that the arrival of a newspaperman on Mackinac is as fine an opportunity for you to achieve a similar end. I mean, think of it, Alex. You'll have every chance to introduce yourself completely to this man, and should you impress him, as I'm sure you will, then his article will detail not just the evolving science but also the character of the young man who helped make it possible. Once that's accomplished, just imagine how you'll be received when we arrive in Detroit.'

Alex looked up from his apron and shrugged. He admitted that indeed there was such an opportunity, but his voice lacked excitement. Beaumont frowned and gathered his letters. 'Tell you what, Alex. Why not take the rest of the day off? Have a shot of your medication and enjoy some time at the tavern, perhaps? I'd say you've earned yourself a few hours of fun.'

Refusing to produce the hoot of excitement and gratitude he knew Beaumont was expecting, Alex untied his apron and went to his room to change his shirt, telling the doctor he'd be home in time to serve dinner. Miffed, Beaumont offered a stiff nod and told Alex to idle freely and be sure to enjoy himself, for clearly he'd earned some time to do exactly that. Then Beaumont went to his study, fetched Alex a tin cup full of laudanum, and said he had papers to revise and would expect his dinner not long after sundown. Alex nodded and went to his room and poured almost the whole of the cup out the window, because it was late in the week and he'd recovered from the renewed grip of Beaumont's weekend administration, though he'd be in its vise again soon enough. He took his wineskin full of cedar tea and drank the last of it, then slung it around his shoulder and put on his coat and left the cabin to visit Namid. He thought about stopping by the tavern to greet Miigwan, but then he'd find himself drinking at the bar, much as Beaumont had effectively commanded, so instead he made his way out of the fort and through the village and down the trail to the cliff.

After the smudge ceremony, they sat around the fire, Namid in the furs of her bedding and Alex with his shirt still off, the purified air of the wigwam bracing his exposed flesh. He'd crossed his legs and wedged a cup of cedar tea between his ankles, and he was picking at the thinning fabric over the knees of his trousers, stealing glances at her from the corner of his eye, watching as she brought Biskane close and lowered her rabbit-skin dress to offer the child her nipple.

'Are you feeling better?' she asked. 'As the days go on and on and on, are you feeling the laudanum let you go?'

Alex couldn't bring himself to look at her with her breast exposed, so he kept picking at his trousers. 'Sometimes, oui, but every weekend he gives me those big doses again, tu sais, for the experiments, and then on Monday, when he goes back to work, it's like starting over again. I can't keep my stomach down the next few days, and I feel it in my sweat and under my skin.'

'It sounds like the time is coming.'

'What time?'

'To tell your doctor you don't want the medicine anymore.'

'Oh,' said Alex, lifting his eyes to her face. She was looking right at him, cradling her son, tilting her head, blinking. 'Do you miss him?' he asked, looking down again.

'Who?'

'Rémi.'

She didn't say anything for a long moment, long enough for Alex to regret asking, to wonder what had even come over him that he'd thoughtlessly posed the question. He looked up again and saw her staring at the bundles of fur and the hides lining the sides of the wigwam. 'It was easier to get materials when he was around,' she said. 'Now, when I want to make something to sell on that filthy beach, I have to negotiate with one of the fools who calls it home. Miigwan isn't much help.'

'He brought you furs and hides, Rémi?'

'He liked trapping. I liked it when he trapped.' She lifted Biskane away and held him over her shoulder, patting his back as she rocked from side to side. 'What did you think of him? When you met?'

Alex drank from his tea, bit his lip, drank again.

'Well?' she asked.

'Je... sais pas. He scared me at first. He was angry. At everyone. And he hit me. He hit me really hard, but it was as though he didn't want to. Maybe. As though there were other forces at work.'

'Ah,' she said, rubbing Biskane's back. 'I think I understand what you mean.'

'And he seemed sad at the end, sad and lost.'

'Ah,' she said again. 'Sounds like the man I knew.' She put Biskane on the ground and watched him crawl off to his toys. 'Come here.'

Alex looked at her, tried to read the expression on her face but couldn't, and he put down his tea and stood and walked around the fire to her bedding and continued to stand. She lifted her hand and beckoned with her fingers and lay down on her side and beckoned again. A rush of giddy confusion spread from his chest all down his arms and legs, and with a light head he lowered himself to the furs and lay down on his side, facing her, his arms folded against his chest.

'Turn around,' she said. 'Face the fire.'

He propped himself up and turned around and lowered himself and faced the fire, and then he felt her pull a fur over them and ferret her arm underneath, wrapping it around his chest and pulling him close. He reached for her hand and took it in his own and stroked her thumb and listened to air drift across the embers of the fire, and even though he wanted to turn around and press his lips against hers, he understood he was meant only to lie there beside her, to lie there and stare into the fire and appreciate the warmth of her embrace.

35

A FRIDAY AFTERNOON IN MID-APRIL, AND THE TAVERN WAS
crowded with men who'd finished the week's work and were confident
in the season's promise of more. A group of carpenters was among the
most boisterous, their cracked and oily tool belts draped over their
chairs as they shouted the words to a song Alex had never heard,
throwing their heads back and stomping their feet:

> Oh, say, bonny lass! Will ye go into battle?
> Where dem drums are all beaten and dem cannons do rattle?

One of the larger men twirled clumsily into the centre of his friends,
his hands covered in scabs and his nails crushed flat and his hairy
stomach hanging below the hem of his tattered shirt, and affecting a
piercingly girlish voice he sang:

> Oh, yes, me bonny lad, I will share all thy harms!
> And when thou be killed, I will die in thy arms!

The song broke down as the men bellowed laughter and threw their arms
around one another's shoulders and smashed their beer mugs together
and cared not at all for the great quantities of the stuff that splashed
on their chests and foamed on the floor, and then in short order they
picked up another tune and began to shout this one at the rafters as well.

Miigwan was sitting at the bar in an extravagant cotton shirt with
frills about the sleeves and neck and over this a fine buckskin vest

and hanging at his side a deerskin bag, and across from him Blake hunched over a glass of beer, arms folded on the bar, exhaustion in his puffy eyes. Alex pulled up a stool, trousers blotchy with brine from the dinner of salt pork he'd left for Beaumont before going out, and Miigwan tossed his chin at the hollering carpenters. 'New arrivals, et les gars s'amusent. They know there's money to be made repairing the fort, tu sais, the palisades and everything else the winter has ravaged. And because there's new money coming, they're compelled to spend that which has already arrived, and this they must do before the night is out.'

He winked at Blake and motioned for Alex to follow him into the back room, which was barely bigger than the Beaumonts' scullery. Cramped within was a table covered in stains and burns, and it was surrounded by chairs with various parts of them broken, here an arm and there a back support. At the far side of the room, beneath a tiny window, there stank a chamber pot full of piss, and on the surface of the table a few short candles in blackened mounds of wax, but Miigwan left these unlit such that only indirect daylight filled the room. The walls crowded the table and were speckled with what appeared to be dried blood, but Miigwan laughed and said no, that was in fact broth from a bowl of stew hurled in pique the night before.

L'Indien sat on one side of the table and from his bag removed three scuffed but colourfully beaded moccasins and a blackened arrowhead. 'You've been practising?'

'Oui,' said Alex, 'tous les matins. I'm getting better, I think, but the arrowhead… I'm still a little clumsy.'

Miigwan waved his hand. 'Not to worry. You'll get the hang of it soon. And the medicine?'

Alex turned his attention from Miigwan to the chamber pot, then to the stain on the wall. 'Namid, she helps me a lot. But tomorrow… the experiments…'

'Ah, yes. She's right.'

Alex turned back to Miigwan and watched him take a sack of coins out of his deerskin bag. 'She is?'

'Bien sûr. You have to tell him. Otherwise every Saturday is a setback.'

Alex said nothing, just lowered himself to a rickety chair as Miigwan began counting coins.

'You need a little taste of victory,' said Miigwan. 'Am I right? Why don't you invest some money in the bank here? It's time you see the moccasin game in action, n'est-ce pas? Blake is out there extending invitations as we speak.'

Alex considered for a moment, unable to fully put aside what Namid had told him about Miigwan filling people's heads with stories, but of course she hadn't meant Alex, for what sense would that have made? What sense for Miigwan to bring Alex to the sanctum of his home and expose him to the salve of his traditions just to swindle a paltry sum in a tavern full of besotted marks? No sense, Alex was sure, and he reached into his trousers and withdrew a few coins and selected from his palm thirty cents, which he placed on the table, and together he and Miigwan waited in amiable silence until two among the carpenters arrived, the fat one who'd been singing as a woman and a thinner one who was filthy and malodorous with teeth black and yellow and clothes sodden and torn, and truly they were débauché, all shouting their songs and spilling their beer and punching one another in the shoulders. They filled the tiny room with their beards and their fists and their stench, and they introduced themselves as the O'Grady brothers, freshly arrived from New York City and keen to partake in a harmless bit of gambling, why not. The fat one said he was the eldest, named Liam, and with a faintly irritated snort the other said his name was Finn, and aye, he said more to his brother than anyone else, he was the youngest, what of it?

'Ev'rythin' a it,' slurred Liam as he lowered himself into a chair that couldn't support his bulk, and he went crashing into the wall as the legs gave out. Finn roared with laughter and slapped his knees and gripped his stomach, and when Liam managed to regain an upright position, he stumbled past Alex, belching, and he took out his grey-hued penis and pissed a thick, clear stream against the wall above the chamber pot before adjusting his aim. He then returned his penis to his trousers and smiled and waved his hand dismissively and said, 'Ah, but fuck it.'

Miigwan called for order, rising out of his chair and pointing at the men individually and admonishing them and declaring that the game wouldn't begin if they couldn't rein themselves in at least while they occupied the back room. They were in fine enough spirits and found this a reasonable request, and but for the occasional burp and sigh they fell quiet.

Finn lightly kicked away the debris of the broken chair and grabbed another, lowering himself gingerly across from Miigwan, and Alex was struck by the spirit in his eyes, they looked innocent somehow, joyful, and they softened his otherwise haggard features almost to the point of beauty. Alex quietly wished good fortune to the soul behind them, and to himself too.

Miigwan raised his arms again and shook his hands so the sleeves of his regal shirt slid down his wrists. He leaned over the table and showed the arrowhead to Finn, who nodded, and then he held up his empty palms and Finn nodded again. Now he concealed the arrowhead beneath the centre moccasin and said, 'Don't lose sight of it, sir. And coins on the table, it goes without saying.'

Finn nodded yet again, very slowly, before reaching into his pocket and tossing a coin on the table, and immediately Liam began to jeer, offering his personal services if later it came time to seed Finn's wife back in Ireland, lest bravery wasn't the only flaccid aspect of his personage. A dark look crossed Finn's face, but then he chuckled and smiled and produced another coin, nodding at Miigwan. L'Indien began to shuffle the moccasins and intone a song not unlike the one he'd sung at the camp a few weeks before, and the carpenters at first looked at him appalled before snapping their attention back to the table. Miigwan's hands were a steady blur, and Alex watched as closely as he could, just barely spotting a jolt to the heel of the leftmost moccasin and then another to the one on the right, and then Miigwan broke off his singing and lifted his hands from the table, crossing his arms over his vest and leaning back in his chair.

Both Liam and Finn had a theory as to which moccasin hid the arrowhead, and they debated the likelihood of their options in voices that grew louder and more belligerent by the syllable, until finally Miigwan yelled again for them to be silent, and returning his attention to Finn he said, 'You must choose alone.'

Finn swallowed and cleared his throat, and with his index finger extended, he leaned forward and hovered his hand over the centre of the table. Liam kept a silence, but tensely, and Alex found the suspense even thicker than when he'd played himself, so keenly did he want Finn to win.

Miigwan's face remained blank as he allowed Finn much equivocation, until after a minute or two Finn chose the centre moccasin, touching the leather sole with the tip of his finger. Miigwan lifted the moccasin, no arrowhead beneath, and even as he revealed it beneath the rightmost moccasin and a look of raw disappointment washed over Finn's face, Liam erupted into a cacophony of mockery and scorn.

'T'ank God ye haven't the stones to bet like a man, young Finn, but even still ye'll be needin' us to buy ye a pour much as always now, won't ye?'

Finn's face was a portrait of misery and shame as he declined Miigwan's invitation to try his luck again, and before he had a chance to clear the way Liam was shooing him aside, noting that it was up to a real man to win enough money to buy a round of beer for his friends and family, and Finn, with a rueful shake of his head, stepped clear of the game.

Miigwan looked to Liam with a slight grin and told him to mind the chair, and Liam scowled and kicked it against the wall and said fuck it, he'd win on his feet, he had no need of chairs, he pissed on them, and further he'd already heard the stories about the Dutchman in the cave and he put no stock in them, he had no fear of Miigwan, no matter what devilish incantations he should holler, because Liam O'Grady was Catholic through and through and his vision of God didn't permit pagan nonsense the likes of which was rife on this side of the Atlantic. He took from his pocket a handful of coins and slammed them on the table, glowering down at Miigwan, who showed him first his empty palms, then lifted the leftmost moccasin to reveal only the bare table, then covered the arrowhead again with the rightmost. He inhaled casually and began shuffling and singing anew, and once again there was the blur of hands and leather, and Alex watched closely but this time saw no tell of the sleight, not even a whisper.

Liam swayed over the table and closed one of his eyes, then dredged his throat and spat in the direction of the chamber pot but missed. 'Leftmost,' he said. 'And ye best not be makin' clever.'

Miigwan's face fell almost imperceptibly, but Alex saw and knew that this round had been lost, and as soon as the arrowhead was revealed, Liam began to stomp his feet and cheer and even Finn joined him in the celebration, the table rattling about the floor and the chamber pot shuffling in a tight little circle.

L'Indien proposed a round of double or nothing and Liam gave his belly a pensive stroke and said, aye, he could see his way clear to taking more money from a godless savage, and again there was the placing of coins on the table and the rapid shuffling of moccasins and the singing of Miigwan's song, and this time Alex saw what he worried was a hand movement too obviously contrived, and he braved a quick glance first at Liam and then at Finn, but neither seemed to have noticed and as the moccasins came to a rest and Miigwan broke off his song once more, Liam snorted and swallowed and said, aye, he'd never lost sight of this one for a second, it was the rightmost, he was sure. With a sober nod Miigwan reached for the moccasin and lifted it and revealed the bare table beneath.

At the sight of his loss Liam choked out a wordless expression of fury and surprise, and there was a look in his eyes that declared his violent intentions toward Miigwan, but then Finn began to snicker as if he'd been repressing an exquisite amusement that had grown too sparkling to contain, and at the instant of its expression Liam turned on Finn and the two began a sloppy, lurching combat that saw them crash into the walls and the table as they bellowed obscenities and issued the most heinous of threats.

Alex was frightened and shrank toward the rear wall but Miigwan kept his seat and watched stoically, until after a minute Blake appeared and fired a shot into the floor. The two brothers instantly froze, and in the ringing, smoke-filled silence that followed, the barkeeper said, 'Best get home and sleep it off, lads. Yous are welcome to return, most assuredly, but only on your most gentlemanly behaviour, for I always lose sleep when I have to shoot a patron, and I'm a man who enjoys his rest, what with the late hours required of my work.'

The men left sheepish, and Miigwan sorted through the coins on the table, returning to Alex not just the thirty cents he'd invested but an additional fifteen as well. 'Tu vois?' he said, grinning. 'Pride pays, so long as it's not your own.'

36

THE SUN WAS BRIGHT THE FOLLOWING MORNING, ITS yellow rays falling on Beaumont's hoses and vials and the tin cup next to a sheaf of drawings on Alex's desk. He'd allowed himself the high dose this one last time, reasoning that he needed it not because the extraction of fluids would be painful – which of course it would, there was no escaping that – but because enduring the pain might have lessened his resolve to declare to Beaumont that he'd no longer take the medicine, that he'd recovered from his tribulations and no longer had any need of narcotic assistance, and after Beaumont retracted the hose and set the vials in their leather case and began rolling down his shirtsleeves, the words simply came out of Alex's mouth so quickly that he couldn't understand why he'd been so reluctant to speak them in the first place.

Beaumont snapped his head in Alex's direction, his brow furrowed. 'No longer... I beg your pardon, son?'

Alex sat on the edge of the bed, his shirt still off. He absently fingered the fleshy patch that covered his fistula, and it made tiny sucking sounds when he broke its seal with his body. Beaumont exhaled and leaned against the edge of the desk, hand engulfing the bottle of laudanum, and he looked from the bottle's cork to Alex's face, back and forth, his eyes sharp and angry.

'I don't think it help me anymore,' said Alex. 'I don't want it again.'

Beaumont shook his head. 'This, Alex, is a most imprudent course of action, and for a number of reasons, not least of which is the sickness you'll endure if you stop taking your medication but also the likelihood of increased pain during our sessions. Of course I advise against it.'

Alex realized he'd appear more assertive with his hands folded in his lap, and with great focus he brought them under control. He was prepared for precisely this argument, had turned it over in his head all morning, even as cramps of both withdrawal and anticipation rippled through his guts. He'd decided not to tell Beaumont about the medicine he'd been taking with Namid but to focus on the doctor's moral fibre instead, that and his sense of public worth, neither of which favoured reliance on alcohol or any other type of substance and both of which were ever on guard against the scorn of others. 'Me, I ready myself to be sick. It is better to be sick for a short time, yes?' He heard the words float from his mouth and alight in the room as though a hawk on a branch at the edge of a meadow. 'Because when we visit to Detroit to show my hole to your friends, then I will be more better and your friends will not be, what you say, disgusted by me for taking this medicine.'

Beaumont pinched his nose and sighed. He opened his mouth as if to say more but then snapped it shut again and shook his head again, issuing another long sigh. He set the bottle on Alex's desk and put his hands in his pockets, then removed his timepiece and clucked his tongue at the face. 'I appreciate your dedication to the research, son, but nevertheless, it's my duty to inform you, as your doctor, that this is not how things are done. One does not simply discontinue one's regimen, not without dangerous effect. It would be most prudent for me to lower your doses over time and thus lessen the harmful impacts of the medicine leaving your body.'

Alex summoned a smile. 'You think of my health always, Doctor, et je vous remercie. But I cannot take the medicine anymore. I don't feel good to take it.'

Beaumont stood up from the desk but didn't collect the bottle, which was more than half full. 'I can't force you,' he said. 'That wouldn't be right. And as I've said, I admire your dedication to the research, and further, I admire your desire to be free of a harmful substance. I must admit that I'm disappointed this desire doesn't extend to alcohol – you spend far too many of your evenings at that blasted village tavern – but nevertheless, I suppose I should be happy you have any such desire at all, because let's be honest, you seem the sort who'd be quite content to live out your entire life in a quasi-stupor, so long as the means were provided for you to do so. I'm going to leave you this bottle, and that way, when the withdrawal begins and you realize the mistake you've made, you can administer it to yourself. I'd also like to remind you of your contractual obligations when it comes to the matter of the research, with which your sickness cannot interfere. Are we in agreement?'

Alex maintained his smile and nodded with enthusiasm, and Beaumont gave him a commanding flick of the eyebrows before leaving the room with a pained expression. Alex heard him hesitate in the scullery, and then his footsteps continued through the dining room and down the short hall to the front entrance.

In his dreams that week, he began to see his little brother again, his manitou, an infant with stormy black hair, sometimes in bed with him, curled against his side like a pet, snoring softly and his skin aglow with a bright white light, shimmering, and the light streamed in and out of Alex's fistula, and when he awoke he felt replenished and replete with gratitude for the myriad ways Namid had tended to him in her lonely camp in its lonesome forest.

He continued to practise with his moccasins over the next few weeks, and he studied Miigwan when they combined their finances and played in the taverns at night, and gradually he noticed how fast and smooth his own movements were becoming, and when finally he was ready to show Miigwan he even managed to misdirect l'Indien once, though he wasn't sure if this was genuine confusion on Miigwan's part or rather a motivating performance, but nevertheless he felt his confidence swell as Miigwan spoke aloud of the party he was planning, of the wigwams he'd have to build and the firepits he'd have to dig, and how easy it was for Alex to imagine himself stationed at a table with his moccasins set out before him and between his thighs a heavy purse fattening with the proceeds of other men's pride.

At home he decided to let Beaumont think he continued taking the medicine, that he sneaked sips from the bottle throughout the day and in particular before their extraction sessions. He thought it risky to disabuse his doctor of the notion, though this was particularly challenging when Beaumont came with his hoses and vials, because the procedure could be excruciating: Beaumont's rigid fingers plucking the flap of his skin, peeling it back and shoving the hard hose inside his body, then ten or so minutes of living with the thing lodged in there before Beaumont finally scraped it back out. There were times when Alex found this procedure immensely disturbing, as if the doctor were trying to suck out his soul or that of his little brother, but when he visited Miigwan and Namid in the aftermath they assured him that only the fluid had been extracted. Beaumont simply wasn't able to remove anything more.

Aside from these moments, it was surprisingly easy to maintain the deception. Though his doctor wasn't above placing bottles of the tincture in his desk drawer, Alex emptied small amounts out the window each morning, afternoon, and night. Beaumont never suspected anything beyond the status quo, almost certainly ascribing Alex's declaration of freedom to self-delusion brought on by the drug itself, and Alex took private pleasure in defying that belittling presumption. He felt within himself a strength he'd never known, a thing he could visualize in the centre of his guts, hard and round and glowing ever more brightly, and he realized that perhaps for the first time in his life he was proud of himself, intensely proud. It was so easy to live this way, so marvellously easy, that he was ashamed for not pushing himself in this direction sooner, but non, shame was a useless emotion, it ferried fortune to no man, rather he had to make up for lost time, because opportunities swirled about the island and he had only to pluck one from the ether and make it his own.

37

BY MID-APRIL THE SNOW WAS LARGELY GONE AND PEOPLE
started arriving from Detroit and elsewhere in the region, and among
them came Deborah late at night, after Alex had gone to bed. He
awoke to her moaning in congress with her husband but didn't recognize her voice at first. Before long, however, he understood what
he was hearing, and it wasn't Beaumont who appeared out of the
darkness of his imagination, or rather not only Beaumont, his biceps
shaped like rolling hills and his chest hairless and white and his
pubic hair black as coal, not only him but Deborah as well, and
she straddled her husband's hips and gripped him with her thighs.
Her hair hung like ropes in her face and she clutched one of her
small breasts and with the other hand she braced herself against his
chest while he lifted his hips and let them drop, lifted them and let
them drop. Alex soaked his sheets and cried out, and afterward the
sound of them was not arousing; it hurt his feelings somehow, and
he couldn't ignore it.

The next morning, after practising with the moccasins again, he left
his room to begin his chores and Deborah greeted him in the hallway,
smiling. She wore her apron and bonnet and told him how healthy
he looked, and she said his medicine awaited in the dining room; he'd
better take it before they got started, and here he had to engage in a
bit of subterfuge he wished he could've avoided, for it was wonderful
to see her before him again after such a long winter. But of course he
couldn't take more of the tincture, and so he simply nodded and said
he'd take it in a moment, that he'd forgotten to put his drawing tools

away after his morning session. He carried the cup into his room and felt that he couldn't risk her hearing the noise of the window opening, so he dashed the contents at the foot of his mattress and watched it soak into the straw, feeling that if she could see into his heart and know him in his entirety, then surely she'd understand the need for deception, surely she'd hold nothing against him.

Throughout the day, he peppered her with questions about her time in Detroit – was it cold and what did she do and did she miss the island or was she happy to be among her family – but she gave him only short answers and told him they'd speak at greater length during his lessons that afternoon. Cleaning occupied most of the morning, and Deborah didn't complain about the state of the house, but Alex noticed right away how inadequate his attention to detail had been and he felt a flush of embarrassment that he hadn't kept the place in better shape while she'd been gone.

When it came time for their afternoon lesson, Deborah arrived at the dining-room table in the same schoolmistress's outfit she'd worn the previous autumn, except this time she'd gathered her hair tight at the nape of her neck, like a river-worn rock. A teapot steamed between them, but only she had a cup. Her eyes were sunken from fatigue, and Alex imagined Beaumont working at the hospital, tending to the afflicted, his attention wandering because of the long and bawdy night he'd spent with his wife newly returned. Alex took his seat and slid a collection of his drawings across the table so that Deborah might praise his talent.

'You've been busy,' she said, taking up his work. 'In his letters, Dr. Beaumont told me of the progress you've both made.' She poured herself a cup of tea. 'Not without the occasional setback, of course, but life is sometimes a series of setbacks one must overcome, is it not?' She held his drawings but wasn't looking at them, not yet, rather she blinked across the table and studied his face, awaiting his reaction. The mention of letters made him uneasy, and a flush of foolishness overtook him, for though he'd seen her letters arrive at the cabin and had generally been able to draw comfort from the character of her penmanship, he'd assumed the doctor's return letters would be sparse and limited only to the progress of his research or perhaps the inadequacies of the bumbling men he worked with, but now it seemed likely that Beaumont would've kept her abreast of changes in Alex as well, and how could he have overlooked something so obvious, how could he have failed to devise a plan to reingratiate himself upon her return? The laudanum had dulled his mind, just as it had damaged so much else, and impulsively he reached across the table and took his drawings and shuffled them in an arrangement perhaps more strategic; then he handed them back across the table again, trying hard to ignore the slight frown that had taken hold of her mouth.

'And do you like them, my drawings?' He'd positioned a portrait of Beaumont at the top of the pile, and it was imperative that she see her husband in his sickbed, his sweaty hair and bewildered eyes and the feeble hanging of his limbs, the saviour reduced.

She looked down and raised an eyebrow and nodded once. 'He wrote me of his illness. The first such occurrence in years, if I'm not mistaken. His fortitude is generally unassailable. You must've been frightened.'

'No,' said Alex. 'Pas vraiment. When he is sick, Dr. Beaumont treats me very nice. Better than when he is well.'

Deborah looked through a few of his drawings, face impassive. Alex had included portraits of Miigwan, Serge, and even Rénard, most elegant in a robe of beaver fur, his pistol in one hand, a paddle in the other. She offered no comment on any of these, instead arranging them in a neat pile and setting them next to her. 'I'm surprised to hear you say such a thing, Alex. Dr. Beaumont holds you in such high regard. He's told me as much a number of times. It wouldn't be a stretch to say he considers you as a son, and imagine how that warms his heart, a man who wishes to be a father. And imagine how it warms my own, a woman who wants nothing more than to be a mother. The island is simply too remote to raise children in the proper way, but of course we feel lonely as a result, and of course you've banished that loneliness.'

'Non,' said Alex, reaching across the table and reclaiming his portraits, determined that Beaumont not escape this exchange with his esteem unsullied. 'You are saying as if he loves me. But he does not love me. He uses me. That is what he does.'

'Why do you think so?'

He told her about the self-portrait Beaumont had excluded from the research materials. She brought her mug to her lips and blew on the tea and took a sip. 'You know,' she said, returning her cup to the table, 'my father is a benefactor to the University of Michigan, among other concerns. The family has made fine money over the years, much of it in shipping. He began his business empire in New York, and as the country expands, so does he. What's more, my father believes it right to invest in the surroundings that have given him so much.'

'Your husband, he does not invest in me. He only takes.'

Deborah raised a pale finger to silence him, and Alex couldn't help but scowl, though this she ignored. She said she'd met Beaumont a little more than fifteen years ago in New York, before he began his studies in medicine. They were both so young. He was a farm boy from Virginia, enlisted in the United States Army and a veteran of the Second War of Independence, which had only recently concluded. He'd not yet gained the rank of officer, but back then he was a favourite of men who held such positions. 'Not like now,' she admitted with a smile, 'although their disdain is defensive, naturally. It's merely the pathetic anger experienced by high-standing men when a lower specimen first achieves and then surpasses their rank.'

In any event, they met when her first marriage was crumbling. It was a tender union, barely two years old. Her husband was the son of a prominent politician; she'd taken his hand when she was just seventeen. But he turned to philandering after Deborah miscarried two pregnancies. She appealed to her father, pleaded with him to help her find an honourable way out of her vows, and reluctantly her father approached her husband's father and the two negotiated the terms of divorce.

The talks were ongoing when she attended a summer gala. Because the divorce was an open secret, no man would speak to her, no man, that is, but Samuel Beaumont, who came as the guest of one of his officer friends. It was at great risk to his social standing that he approached her and offered her a flute of champagne and together they chatted about the happenings of the day, in particular the Treaty of Ghent that had ended the war, but also the devastation he'd seen wrought upon the bodies of men strewn about the battlefield and how those sights had filled him with the urge to help.

'So he loves you right away,' sneered Alex. 'Please, madame. I know this man. You forget that I do.'

She shook her head. 'No. That's not what I'm saying. You see, his officer friend had told him who I was, had told him who my father was. Ambition has burned long and bright in my husband, and he saw in me an opportunity under the auspices of my father, for we had the funds his family would never have, to say nothing of the connections.'

Beaumont, then, had gained his education through the largesse of Deborah's family. Alex had to chuckle. 'Mais écoutez-vous, donc. You know the way he is. You know he uses us to make a future for himself.'

Deborah smiled patiently. She said Alex was young, and despite the journey he'd undertaken to arrive on Mackinac and the ordeal that had befallen him hence, he was a sheltered boy, was he not, so how could he understand the many angles a thing might have, the many facets? She took his portrait of Beaumont and set it between them. 'Love is one of those things. It roots itself not just in a pure soil but a rocky one as well. Indeed, there are very few pure soils in the world today, and who can say if the future will bring more. Most of us are stuck with the rocky sort, and with its coarseness we make do. What I'm saying is Dr. Beaumont does feel strongly toward you, Alex, he does care deeply, no matter the focused nature of his broader intentions. It behooves you to remember this. You would fare far worse without him.'

Alex lifted his elbows off the table and sank back in his chair, his lips pressed together as his chin fell toward his sternum. There was an awful familiarity to what she said, and to the way she said it, and he heard in her weary resolve something like the tone with which Namid had spoken about Rémi and even Miigwan, but the truth of her speech expanded from there and came to encompass his relationship with Serge as well, and it also somehow explained the absence of his papa, revealing the sweepingly contractual nature of relations that only his maman and 'tit frère had barred from their love. He raised his head and motioned for Deborah to return his drawings, and he gathered them and stood, lingering at the entrance to the room. 'Why are you sure the doctor loves you? How can you know?'

'Because I feel it.'

'That is all?'

'Yes,' she said, and she stood up now too. 'Is that not enough?'

She looked down to collect her teapot and cup, hesitated, and left them. Alex felt an urge to gather them and take them to the scullery for washing, but he resisted, leaving the room under a cloud of resentment. Half an hour later, he returned to tidy up before dinner.

38

'KYLE CUTHBERT REED,' SAID THE NEWSPAPERMAN FROM Detroit, feebly taking Alex's hand and leaving behind a cold film of sweat where their palms had touched.

Though it wasn't yet noon, Beaumont was dressed in evening wear. His cravat had been hastily knotted, for no doubt he'd impatiently brushed aside Deborah's helping hand, and now it threatened to flutter over his shoulder as he whirled away from the front door and led Alex and Mr. Reed down the short hall to his study. There, he sat behind his desk with his fingers interlaced in its centre, and whereas normally his office was in disarray, today he'd arranged it neatly, with his inkpot and notes occupying one side and on the other, two vials of gastric fluid, a bowl, an hourglass, and a cutting board with a few links of sausage, a hard-boiled egg, and a slice of white bread.

Alex took a seat on the opposite side of the desk, next to Mr. Reed, and he watched the journalist quickly take in the room, not just Beaumont and the desk but also a few diagrams of Alex's fistula, which Beaumont had fastened to the wall behind his chair, and without surprise Alex noted the absence of his self-portrait.

Mr. Reed appeared at first middle-aged but upon closer inspection extremely old, though perhaps wearing some kind of facial powder that concealed his wrinkles from a distance. He seemed lost in the folds of his suit, and although the weather hadn't yet turned especially warm, the man's brow perspired. He dabbed it with a plain white cloth, repeatedly, over and over, his eyes flitting from one object to the next, while Beaumont and Alex simply watched. It seemed as though

Mr. Reed might never cease mopping his brow, until after a minute he knocked loose his spectacles and they fell to his lap, and frantically he gathered them up and set them roughly on his nose, bending them slightly, and then he ran his fingers along his slight, black moustache and said, 'A pleasure to be here, gentlemen, even if the journey was a trifle lacking in comfort.'

'Indeed, it can be an ordeal,' said Beaumont, smiling grotesquely. 'Thank God you've arrived safely, and of course my offer to accommodate you still stands. We've a room at the back of the house. An old servant's quarters, but not nearly so crude as it sounds, particularly now that the warmer weather is upon us.'

This was the first Alex had heard of Mr. Reed potentially occupying his quarters, but he didn't lose composure, rather stared unblinkingly at Beaumont, mentally urging the doctor to turn and witness the quiet totality of his displeasure, but though he was certain Beaumont could see him peripherally, the doctor made no such acknowledgment.

Mr. Reed said, 'Very kind of you, sir, but no need. I have my room at the inn, fetid though it is. I like to be alone, you see. I like to have my own private space in which to contemplate the details of a story before I undertake its composition on the page.'

Beaumont nodded slowly. 'Yes, of course.' He reached out and took up one of the vials of gastric juice and gave it a shake. 'Shall I begin the account of the research, then, sir?'

Mr. Reed asked Beaumont for the use of his inkpot, then took from his valise a cedar box and from this he removed a black fountain pen with fine gold flourishes. 'And some paper,' he said, looking up at Beaumont with a tiny frown. 'I've forgotten my paper in Detroit.'

In a flurry of movements, Beaumont slid his inkpot to Mr. Reed, along with a few sheets of paper, after which he brought the cutting board to centre table and isolated a link of sausage from the other items. Next to this he placed, a little too firmly, the vial of gastric juice. 'Allow me to start from the beginning,' he said, and he filled his chest and seemed childishly eager, cheeks flushed and cravat ever askew. 'You see, sir, despite the long history of mankind and the many advancements in disciplines such as astronomy, seafaring, and war, the stomach has remained too complex a—'

Mr. Reed held up his hand. His moustache was so very slight, it seemed to vanish when he spoke, and in its place appeared his yellowed teeth, their gums receded. 'Pardon me, Dr. Beaumont. I'm sorry to interrupt, really I am, but the problem is the journey yesterday and the poor sleep last night have combined to make me rather tired, and so I must ask you, humbly, to proceed to the demonstration.'

Beaumont made a little gasping sound and tilted his head and gestured inchoately across the desk at Alex, hands then flying up to his cravat and pulling at the knot. He cleared his throat and said, 'I understand completely, Mr. Reed, having made the trip many times myself. Allow me, then, to hasten to the point. Alex, your shirt, please. Take it off so Mr. Reed can see the fistula – unless, of course, he's too fatigued for this introductory stage of the demonstration.'

Mr. Reed looked at Beaumont and his nostrils flared below the bridge of his spectacles. Then he turned to Alex and said, 'Please, son. If it's no intrusion, of course.'

'Pas du tout,' said Alex.

Mr. Reed clapped his hands in delight. 'A Frenchman! Your notes to the university omitted the fact, Doctor.'

Alex smiled and shrugged and said, 'Oui, monsieur. Suis Canadien.'

'Hearty folk,' declared Mr. Reed with an emphatic nod of his tiny head. 'Most honourable. I always enjoy a weekend walk along the Detroit River, where many of your people have settled into the agricultural life. I like to practise' – he filled his chest with a showman's breath – 'la langue française.'

'Bravo!' Alex applauded and glanced across the desk, where Beaumont, with stony eyes, mumbled something about pertinence. Alex pulled his shirt over his shoulders and hung it on the back of his chair, then angled his fistula at Mr. Reed, who clicked his tongue and made a spout of his lips. Beaumont stood up. He rounded the desk and crouched beside Alex, pinching the flesh that covered the aperture and drawing it back. He began to explain the original experiments, but

Mr. Reed interrupted him to say he'd reviewed the materials supplied by the university and was therefore aware of them.

'Of course,' said Beaumont, increasingly flustered. 'I'd thought a refresher of matters so complicated might be of service, but allow me, if you will, to move on to the demonstration. Suffice it to say that the gastric fluid you see before you was extracted from this hole in the boy's side, more properly called a fistula, a fusing of the organs, in this case the skin and stomach, you see, and let me add that this, as with the previous experiments, had never been done before in the history of medical science.'

'Yes,' said Mr. Reed, not taking his eyes off Alex's side. 'Most impressive, Doctor.'

Beaumont rounded his desk again and lowered himself stiffly into his chair. He said it was of primary importance to prove the efficacy of gastric fluid outside the body. He placed the piece of sausage into the bowl and uncorked one of the vials, dousing the meat in fluid. He flipped the hourglass, slamming it on the desk but startling no one. 'As you'll observe, Mr. Reed, though it takes some time, the fluid works perfectly outside the host body. In fact, the time it takes outside isn't much different than that which it requires within, and those results you'll recall from the findings of my original experiments.'

Mr. Reed nodded and said that indeed he did recall, but still he remained focused on Alex. 'Tell me, boy, how is it you've become mixed up in all of this?'

'Sir,' Beaumont interjected, 'if I may guide your attention to the demonstration in progress.'

Mr. Reed glanced at the meat in the bowl and nodded with an interest most obviously feigned. 'Yes, Doctor. Truly a fascinating spectacle. Fret not, for I shall position it prominently in the article.' Mr. Reed turned back to Alex and cleared his throat and in a fumbling accent began to speak French: 'Qu'est-ce qui s'est passé?'

The two of them embarked on a long conversation, almost entirely in French, during which Alex spoke about his maman and his papa and leur vie dure à Montréal, and he offered an edited version of his recruitment into the fur trade, quel défi, but he excluded his affair with Serge and the massacre in Upper Canada. Beaumont watched all of this with his mouth slightly open and his fists tightly clenched. In front of him, the gastric fluid worked away at the meat, gradually eroding its shape. Alex told Mr. Reed how it was that he'd come to be so grievously injured and, with a generous nod to Beaumont, he sang his doctor's praises, un vrai sauveur, kind and generous too, then he moved on to the topic of his brother, whom he'd never met, but still, Alex felt a strength within him always, which he knew was from his 'tit frère, the bravest child who'd never grown.

Mr. Reed scribbled furiously throughout Alex's account, dipping his pen dozens of times, and by the time he'd finished his note-taking Beaumont's inkpot was nearly empty. 'Doctor,' he said, finally deigning to glance at what remained of the sausage, 'you live in a most fascinating circumstance. I thank you wholeheartedly for inviting me into your home that I might record it for posterity.'

Beaumont offered a nod, tightly restrained, though to Alex it seemed as if he might lunge across the desk and throttle the delicate Mr. Reed, who yawned and in so doing gave the room a long view of his receded gums. He said he'd head back to the inn now, as the walk out of the fort and down the hill to the village would sap the last of a late afternoon's energy. 'When the article is published, I will ensure a few editions of the paper are posted to this home. Gentlemen, c'était un plaisir.'

'Alex,' said Beaumont, 'see Mr. Reed to the door, won't you?'

The journalist stood slowly, his knees cracking like sticks, and during the time it took him to shuffle to the door Beaumont fixed Alex with a burning stare, his jaw clenched, his nostrils wide, and when Alex and Mr. Reed left the study Beaumont slammed the door behind them.

'You know, son,' said Mr. Reed, lingering in the hallway, 'your presence is most palpable. One feels it from across the room. It's my hope you find your way out of this situation very soon so that you may live a life more fully your own.'

39

THE FIRST OF THE SEASON'S VOYAGEURS BROUGHT WITH them a seemingly endless celebration of song and dance. They came overland from elsewhere in Michigan as well as Ohio and Vermont and nearby locales, and still others crossed the frigid waters from Upper Canada and even the Red River Colony. They hauled their boats ashore and unloaded parcels for trade, and for a brief time at least, supply and demand would work in their favour, but soon enough brigades would arrive from Montréal and New York City and elsewhere besides, and Mackinac would be flush with goods once more. These men meted out their pemmican and all throughout the camp they lit their pipes and guzzled their rum, and those of them who drunkenly collapsed in the shallows stood up again as runnels of water poured down their beards and soaked their bare chests. The first week of their arrival brought with it a celebration so debauched that newly indentured men awoke with their legs in the lake and their pockets bereft of their advances, and a few of them bore blackened eyes and blood-encrusted lips.

Although the labour unrest from the previous season went largely unmentioned, even Alex could sense it bulging below the surface of activities, a scar on the morale of the older men, and once the season wore on and the initial excitement of its first weeks subsided, likely these men would return to brooding and the company would once again position itself against them, and the bluecoats would be there to help. In the interim, a parade of voyageurs marched from the beach to the supply store and then back to the beach, where many Ottawa had come looking for work repairing boats or clothes or to barter for goods or marriage, and it was one of these men who brought to Miigwan the news of a white man named Pierre who'd become destitute over the course of the celebration and heard from his friends about Miigwan's reputation as a seasoned trader. Pierre wished to return himself to a position more prosperous, for the celebration hadn't yet run its course and the thought of sitting out that which remained filled him with a sadness too great to endure. It was Sunday, Alex's day off, and he and Miigwan had been roaming the camp in search of illicit traders and would-be gamblers, and neither was especially moved by Pierre's plight, for such a story was all too common, but when they heard he had half a dozen peach stones at the bottom of a pigskin bag, they sent word and quickly organized a rendezvous.

Pierre was tall and thin, maybe forty years old, with his cotton shirt sullied and torn and his trousers speckled with blood and there was a slight, purplish swelling around his temple. He wore his dirty blond hair comme un Indien, with the sides of his head shorn to the skin and on top it was long and fashioned into spikes with bear grease or the like, and there were tattoos on his neck, a poorly wrought compass on one side and an exploding mountain on the other. The three of them sat on a log overlooking the lake, and the stink of alcohol on Pierre's breath hung about their heads as a dark cloud lingering in the wake of a storm.

After packing his pipe with tobacco, Pierre lit it and passed it to Miigwan, who looked kingly alongside the Frenchman, with fine new moccasins Namid had made for the season and a leather thong of animal teeth hanging down to his chest and beneath the teeth a cotton shirt, completely unblemished, and Alex was proud to be associated with his friend, and within himself he continued to feel an ever-expanding fortitude. How satisfying that Mr. Reed had noticed as well, and as for Beaumont, tant pis, let him mutter and glower and stomp about the house with his sense of self so shaken, c'était bien juste.

Alex drew upon his fortitude to contain his excitement when presented with Pierre's bundle of peach stones, for truly he wanted these more than he'd wanted anything in a long time, but equally he didn't want to encroach on Miigwan's position, which was far more expert than his own, and further it was crucial Pierre not sense Alex's desire lest the terms of trade be wrenched from their favour.

Together, Miigwan, Alex, and Pierre sat in the warm sun and smoked Pierre's tobacco and listened politely as the man unravelled his story. He was low-born in France and his father was a fisherman with connections enough to secure young Pierre work as a tar aboard a trade ship pursuing sugar and rum from the West Indies, and from there Pierre built a life in the service of such companies and had been to all the world's ports and many of its hostile environs as well, and true enough he'd survived a great many perils, such as squalls and pirates and cannibals, whereas if he'd stayed in France he would've been recruited into Napoleon's Grande Armée and likely as not a Prussian cannon would've blown his chest apart, or perhaps he would've starved instead on the long road to Moscow. But that hadn't been his fate, rather he was born to survive, and only two years previous, during a voyage to the Orient on a day so fine as this, he'd witnessed a giant fleshy creature with many tentacles and the beak of a bird rise from the ocean and attack his crew, lifting their captain from the poop and tossing the poor man into the sea, where flailing he drowned. Many of the crew hurled first their reason and then their bodies to the frothy waves, and those who survived the tentacled creature fell prey to a swarm of sharks. The water about the ship was red with blood, and the limbs and heads and torsos of the dead bobbed as debris.

Pierre and a Spaniard survived this attack by lowering a small boat to the sea, and they rowed away from the horrors, focusing on the watery horizon, and though their paddles knocked against the bodies of their brothers-in-trade, their courage held fast and soon they'd put distance between themselves and the carnage, but they'd both been weakened by the effort and they fell asleep as the sun rose high in the sky, and when Pierre awoke, there was land on the horizon and the Spaniard was dead.

He knew the little boat wouldn't survive the breakwater, so when he was as close as he could get, despite his terror that the beasts of the sea would attack him anew, he leapt into the salty water and swam ashore, and sure enough he made it, though truly he was exhausted, and he looked over his shoulder and saw the little boat battered about the breakwater, and he said a prayer for the soul of the man with whom he'd escaped. Then he collapsed on the beach and fell asleep as the surf broke over his legs.

When he awoke, it was nighttime and he was in a hammock and there was a fire burning and the smell of food, but though he was famished, fear inspired him to feign a deep sleep and observe his situation, and soon he understood that he'd been found by Indians who nursed him to health and he lived among them for a short time, playing their sports and sleeping with a prodigious number of their women and helping the men catch fish, until finally a trade ship came near shore, and les Indiens gave him gifts in a pigskin bag and one of their young took him in a fishing boat to meet the captain of the ship, who was an Englishman, but kindly so, and Pierre returned to France so happy to have survived that he vowed to find work less perilous, and here he offered an ironic chuckle, because he'd chosen to travel to British North America and participate in the fur trade, and that was how he'd come to meet them today, penniless, oui, trop vrai, but with gifts to trade, gifts from just that tropical island, transported in exactly that pigskin bag.

Miigwan was greatly impressed with this account and after its telling he puffed the pipe and looked pensively to the sky, then told the story of how he'd arrived on Mackinac with Namid, a tale Alex had heard many times over the past few days, his mind turning to Namid each time it was told, and he imagined her making her own way along the crowded beach, Biskane on her back as she hawked her clothing and longed for home, and it was sad to see her trudging through life so dejected and sore, but he reminded himself of what she got in return and of what was promised her still, and so what use were his sympathies when her future augured so fine and he had his own to improve as well? In any event Pierre enjoyed the story, nodding and shaking his head throughout, his green eyes wide and his mouth twisting this way and that depending on the events of the tale, and because they were all getting on so well Alex decided to uncork a bottle of rum and pass it around.

L'Indien eventually arrived at the conclusion of his story, and this he changed slightly each time he told it depending on the listener: he revealed his gambling concern to some, chose only to trade with others, and left still others with merely the account of his odyssey. It all depended on the countenance of his audience, and in the case of Pierre, Miigwan extended both invitations. 'First,' he said, looking from the lake to the sailor, 'let me see these peach stones, my friend.'

'Bien sûr,' said Pierre. His was a black-toothed grin as he drew from his pigskin sack a bolt of bundled cloth, and this he unwrapped to reveal six stones nestled in the folds of the fabric, and here Alex lost himself slightly and his breath hitched as he leaned over to gather a closer look. They were large, ces noyaux, larger than the ones that came from the tree of his maman's patron, and each of them was the most beautiful shade of brown, like Namid's eyes, and they were extravagantly furrowed, with grooves twisting in a manner that was busy, fluid, swooping, and at the top of each stone a little flourish, like the crest of an elegant bird.

'Lovely,' said Miigwan, and Alex was so struck by the stones that his friend's voice seemed to come from a great distance away, as if over a hill and across a breezy meadow. 'And what is it you want in exchange?'

Pierre cleared his throat and reiterated the exotic origins of his goods, noting as well that they'd been blessed by the island's chief and would remain fertile for generations, and as such their sown maturity promised a bountiful harvest, even in climes so sadly less tropical as these. Having said this, he looked out on the lake with his lips pursed, and when he returned his attention to Miigwan, he said he'd take two dollars for the bundle; he could only part with them in such a grouping, lest their value diminish in pairs or some other configuration.

Alex felt his heart stutter and stumble and threaten to stop altogether, for surely this was a price too dear. He'd seen Miigwan navigate at least a dozen of these transactions and knew well his friend's prowess in matters of bargaining and also his stubborn unwillingness to accept profits of less than one hundred percent. Was it possible to both lower Pierre's price in a manner suitable to the sailor while at the same time satisfying Miigwan's sense of gain? Unlikely, for already Alex could hear arguments against acquiring the stones, because who could be sure they'd bear seed or that said seeds would be fertile, and further who could be sure that these peaches were indeed of such exotic Oriental origin and not instead the kind that had long existed in the Americas, if only farther south?

He began to take stock of his own savings and calculate his own entry into this transaction, and he found he had enough to purchase the stones without overly harming his financial position, and he stoked himself to await Miigwan's rejection of the terms and then open negotiations himself, but this turned out to be unnecessary, for his friend peered at the stones in Pierre's cloth-covered palm and nodded and said, 'You have a deal, mon ami. I'll buy them. It's a good deal. And let me develop our friendship further by inviting you to a festival of gambling I have planned in the forest next week, a most special festival for which I'm almost done building the camp, special not just because there'll be much trading beyond the rapacious reach of the company but also because my friend and partner Alex will try his hand at a traditional game of my people, one which I've taught him myself.'

Pierre grinned and extended his filthy hand and with the other he reached for the rum and brought the bottle to his lips, the glass knocking against his rotting teeth as a breeze blew the smell of him clear.

Later, as Alex walked all through the village and up the long hill to the entrance of the fort, he kept his hands in the pockets of his trousers, fingering the three peach stones Miigwan had given him at no price at all, just because they were friends. They felt hard and ridged and powerful, and Alex could recall no purer pleasure than squeezing them as he walked, acquainting his flesh with their swirling grooves.

Inside, the house smelled of fish, and Alex paused in the hall by the door to his room and tilted his head toward the kitchen, where Deborah was working, her hair gathered loosely and hanging in the middle of her slender back, obscuring the stained-to-brown fabric of her apron ties, which he could imagine even though he couldn't see, so often had he washed her clothes, but he decided not to share with her the gift of his peach stones, rather he went to his room and hid them at the back of his desk drawer.

He sat in his chair and found a drawing he'd made of her lying in bed, her hair spread over the pillows like a storm cloud breaking into wisps. He hadn't taken a lesson with her since she told him the story of how she'd come to be with Beaumont. She hadn't asked. He hadn't pressed. Their relationship wasn't like before, when he'd been infirm and she helped him recover and reminded him of his maman and even aroused him as well. Now he saw her mostly as one of Beaumont's able appendages – lovely, complicated, sometimes even tender, but firmly under his control, no matter what she thought – and yet this didn't sadden him, pas vraiment, it was just an observation, just an understanding, there was no call to mourn. He was conducting a trade with the Beaumonts, c'était tout, and he understood that emotion would only stunt his advantages, and as well he'd learned to accept the occasional resort to deception, such as shifting the arrow from one moccasin to the next and the continued pouring of small doses of laudanum out the window of his room, which he did now, for his keepers still thought their grasp on him firm though in fact it was ever loosening, and soon it would slip off altogether. In the meantime he'd take from them those things he found useful, such as watching Deborah care for plants: the way she watered them just so, the way she pressed her fingers into the soil, moved her lips with whispered encouragement, and now that he'd seen her do this many times, he too could coax from ordinary soil an extraordinary life, and he too could watch it grow strong.

40

THE FOLLOWING SATURDAY, EARLY IN THE EVENING, HIS fistula raw from the morning's extractions, Alex followed Miigwan down a path through the woods west of the fort, far from his camp with Namid and into a rocky clearing, small and flat and surrounded by pines, where he'd built three large wigwams. They sat around a table inside the central structure and there was a small fire burning in the middle of the enclosure, a column of smoke rising up and out a hole in the ceiling. They were alone, but soon the area would swell with the boorishly drunk, and it wouldn't be safe for Namid and Biskane, who spent this night at their usual camp.

He listened as Miigwan described how men would play cribbage in one tent, dice in another, and all fours in the third, while outside, seated at a sturdy table of milled pine, Alex would entertain the men looking for lighter pursuits. Miigwan had carved torches and planted them in the ground a few feet behind the table, but not too close, as Alex would be better able to achieve his sleight in the jerky dancing of shadows cast, and he'd be given a bottle of rum as well, free for his enjoyment, and at the end of the night he had only to pay Miigwan half his share, which was standard, this not just for the training but also the ready access to a clientele.

'Celà me rend nerveux,' said Alex, watching embers pop free of the fire and land on the dirt floor and flicker out.

'But why? You handle the game very well. And do you have a song ready? To distract them?'

'Oui, I'll sing "V'la l'Bon Vent", but will it be enough? What if I make a mistake and anger the men?'

'T'inquiète pas,' said Miigwan, who leaned back and lifted his shirt to reveal a pistol holstered in beaded leather, and he said Blake would be patrolling the wigwams as well as the gathering outside; he'd have two pistols on his waist and his hands ever near the handles, lest he need to draw them in haste. Further, said Miigwan, most men understood their wagers were destined to be lost, and though bested betters might tend to outrage or bravado in the immediate wake of defeat, few escalated beyond the performance, for in their hearts they felt themselves small and powerless and deserving of failure. Further still, Miigwan had made numerous tobacco offerings both to his personal manitou and Gitche Manitou as well, so much so that the fires of his camp swirled with tobacco smoke, and the shores of the island were laden with offerings too, and besides Alex now had his own manitou to draw on, and surely it was only too eager to help.

Alex was reluctant, but he reminded himself of everything Miigwan had done for him, and he thought as well of the comfort Namid had conjured by her fire, and so later, when men began to arrive at the wigwams, he sat at his table and sipped his rum and contemplated the moccasins that Miigwan had given him, the torchlight bringing the beads and soles in and out of gentle relief. Amid the clutch of drunken voyageurs he recognized Pierre and Liam and Finn and many other patrons from the village tavern, and all around them were men hollering in French and others playing their fiddles. Miigwan circulated among them, pointing to the wigwams and collecting money and telling the men of Alex's show on the side. Above him shone dimly a hunk of moon, and behind him the torches threw staggering shadows across the table.

Two men approached and Alex took a deep pull from his rum in order to gird himself for their arrival, and then he sat up straight in what he hoped was a convincing imitation of Miigwan's posture when l'Indien conducted the game. And although Miigwan was nowhere to be seen, Alex nevertheless engaged these men, looking up at one whose legs were comically thin despite the immensity of his torso, and with an almost steady voice Alex asked him to tender a wager and guess which moccasin concealed the arrowhead, and when the man pledged a three-cent bet, his younger friend, who was brawny and hairy from his bare feet to the top of his shaggy head, matched the sum and said he had the sharpest eyes of any voyageur on the continent and he was ever alert to any and all sleights of hand or any other trickery besides, none of which he'd countenance, non, not a bit.

Maybe it was the rum or maybe a bolt of confidence borrowed from his 'tit frère, but Alex was surprised to find that this truculence fazed him not at all, rather now that the game had finally begun he was keen to bring his newly developed skills into service. 'Du calme, les gars,' he said, and he sipped his rum and nodded and showed the men the location of the arrowhead and the emptiness of both his palms and the other two moccasins. And then he was moving them smoothly across the pine, shouting his song at the tree canopy as he easily extracted the arrowhead and delivered it to a neighbouring moccasin, the shifting torch flames and dimness of the moon working with his song to abet his deception.

'Bon,' he said when he was done. 'Take your pick, messieurs.'

The man with the burdensome gut went first, pointing to the left-most moccasin, and though chance privileged the decision, for the arrowhead indeed lay there concealed, Alex kept his expression neutral while the brawny gambler chewed his lip and studied Alex's face before pointing to the centre moccasin. His brow furrowed when Alex revealed the bare pine beneath and he took an aggressive step forward, but his advance was halted by a hoot from the larger man, to whom Alex quickly revealed the arrowhead.

'Come,' said the victor, taking his disgruntled companion by the wrist. 'Let me give you a penny for all fours. You'll have better luck there.'

The man gave Alex a wounded look and reluctantly turned to follow his friend into the crowd, and even though Alex had emerged from the betting in only a neutral position, he congratulated himself on his handling of the moment's psychological dynamics, and with a hearty sip of rum he prepared for more. He came out on top the next two rounds, struck even on the third, lost on the fourth, then went on a winning run of half a dozen rounds. The night progressed in this fashion and Alex became increasingly drunk but didn't lose control of the moccasins or the arrowhead, and he felt immensely proud when Miigwan came by the table and stood with his arms folded across his chest and studied Alex's craftsmanship, the corners of his mouth turned slightly upward.

Most men preferred cards or dice, but before long people learned that Alex was the boy who'd been shot during the supply store robbery the season before, and a crowd of broad-shouldered gamblers developed around him, their teeth shining in the night, and soon enough a fiddler came to play exclusively for the event, and the whole mess of men reeked of sweat and booze and a more generalized foulness besides.

Through the throng, Alex saw Liam and Finn stagger out of the dice tent and head toward him, the former boorishly drunk with dark blotches on his shirt and pants that the jagged firelight revealed as vomit and piss, and he shoved his brother forward and roared to all that Finn was assuredly the most unlucky man on the island and likely even in the territory, but he was ever blind to the fact, so who would like to bet that he'd fail to locate the arrowhead four times in a row? In the unlikely event Finn should emerge victorious, then Liam would pay out the winnings, but as Finn stood no chance, of course it would be him who paid what was owed, even if that meant borrowing a bit of money from his kindly older brother. The men grumbled about this, and more than a few jeered at the weakness of the prospect, but apparently there were others who thought that even a man so unlucky as Finn would prevail at finding the arrowhead at least once over the course of four tries, and so bets were wagered and hands were shaken and in short order Finn stood swaying before Alex's pine table.

The arrival of the brothers disturbed Alex's poise, and he searched the men for Miigwan but saw only Pierre appear on the edge of the crowd, his face creased with concern at the sight of Liam, who'd begun arguing with someone about his ability to remember the sums of currency he'd been given. As this dispute tapered off, Alex looked into Finn's eyes and again saw the faint glow of persevering beauty that not even wretched alcoholism, relentless mockery, and unabating squalor could extinguish, and he felt sorry for himself and Finn both, two kind souls lost in a world bursting with insult and cruelty, and he wished more than anything that the two of them could find a quiet place on the beach and lie down and embrace each other till morning.

But that wasn't possible, so he proceeded with his ministrations, showing Finn the underside of each moccasin and the bareness of his palms and the position of the arrowhead, and just before he started shuffling, he glanced at Liam and saw avarice writ large on the man's flushed and filthy face, and Alex simply knew that whatever money Liam lent to Finn would come at a high cost, as Liam was nothing like Alex's brother, c'était bien trop clair, rather he cared solely for himself.

Then the game was in motion and Alex decided not to shift the arrowhead from the centre moccasin and also to ever so slightly slow down his movements, and in this way surely Finn would be able to track the winning choice, point it out, and put a stop to Liam's heartless scheme. But after completing the shuffle, Alex looked up and saw only bewilderment and frustration on Finn's face as he stumbled from side to side and slowly raised his arm and extended his finger and pointed to the incorrect moccasin.

Men broke out in cheers and Liam threw back his head and roared his pleasure at that moon, and he clapped his brother on the shoulder hard enough to knock him into the table. Alex took a long pull of his rum and called for calm, but no one took heed until Miigwan stepped forward and did the same. And then all that could be heard was the sound of the moccasins and the arrowhead sliding and scraping over the pine, and once again Alex declined to shift the arrowhead and ensured his movements weren't overly quick. When he finished, he stared meaningfully into Finn's eyes and was so bothered by their aspect of utter misery that before he could help himself he raised his right knee and gave the far side of the table a bump he knew all had seen even as his foot came back to the ground.

Finn's arm made its long way to the moccasin during a protracted moment of silence, but Liam slapped his hand away and shouted, 'But wait a goddamn minute. Why did ye bang yer fuckin' knee against yon fuckin' table?'

Alex felt his jaw tremble as his voice escaped him, and Liam snorted in disgust and addressed the crowd: 'Friends, there's a strong reek of shit about this silly amusement, aye, but do none of ye smell it?'

He grabbed the rightmost moccasin, revealed the arrowhead beneath, and tossed the beaded leather into the darkness of the night. Alex watched it tumble through the torchlight, and suddenly Liam's hands were gripping his shoulders, yanking him out of his seat and over the table and right up into the brute's snarling face, his breath a carrion wind.

A melee ensued. Alex was the target of its initial brunt, men tossing him from one to the next and raining blows on his face and the side of his head and against his ribs and all down his abdomen, and then he fell to the ground and could no longer see the treetops, rather just the bearded faces of betrayed gamblers, the darkness of their jeering mouths, the insanity yawning in their eyes, but then he heard Pierre's voice, deep and thunderous: 'Arrêtez! Arrêtez-vous! This is an honest man!' He scrambled for shelter first beneath the table and then behind a tree, and when he braved a look into the violence, he couldn't see Miigwan, couldn't see Pierre, couldn't hear either of them, until finally there was the crack of a pistol shot, and then another, and then a third, and then the brawlers began to disperse.

Alex wiped blood from his face and cautiously emerged from hiding only to see Pierre curled up on the ground not far from the firepit, both hands pressed against a wound in his abdomen and his fingers slick with a dark fluid. Standing over him was Blake, pointing one of his pistols in the air, and there were men emerging from the wigwams and others sprinting into the woods, and a gambler thus harried ran into a tree and the crack of his skull against the trunk sounded as another shot from Blake's still-smoking pistol.

Miigwan appeared and crouched beside Pierre and held the sailor's head in his hands and whispered that Pierre would be all right, yes, that was a promise, he'd survive not just the night but many days ahead, all of which had been foretold in a dream.

'But tell me,' he said, lifting his head to look at Alex, 'why did you knee the table?'

Alex swallowed and held himself about the ribs and heard in his head the roar of violence and intoxication. 'Je – je sais pas,' he whimpered. 'I'm drunk, c'est tout.'

Miigwan stared, eyes narrowing as they filled with a certainty that caused Alex to tremble with humiliation and despair; then he turned back to Pierre and stroked his sweaty forehead.

They removed Pierre's shirt to ascertain the extent of the damage, a deep and puckered slash to the abdomen that had somehow missed his intestines, and they saw all over his tattooed chest a tangled mess of scars that told of similar encounters with obstinate men, and Blake issued a low whistle of admiration. 'By Christ, that wretch was lucky to reign it over you.'

Miigwan said they had no choice but to bring him to the hospital at the fort, and what was equally important was that they agree to tell the authorities they found him this way in the streets outside the tavern, nothing more. They carried him through the woods and he didn't cry out despite the uneven terrain, and they hurried through the village and up the hill to the fort, where the guards, unmoved, bade them enter.

It was Beaumont who performed the surgery, roused from sleep and summoned to the hospital by a breathless underling. Alex stood with Miigwan and Blake outside the building and Beaumont spared them only the most withering of glances as he hurried to the operating theatre. Despite his recent victories over the doctor, Alex felt nevertheless disturbed by Beaumont's involvement in the incident, and he listened quietly as his friends explained to a soldier how they discovered Pierre brought low not far from the tavern. The soldier had about him a recently expired youth that had dried in the wrinkles around his eyes as well as in the corners of his tiny, peeling mouth. He nodded where appropriate and said he'd convey the details to Colonel Smyth when next they met, and then he lit his pipe and puffed to life a magnificent bed of embers, and with these smouldering he stepped into the night.

Blake and Miigwan left the fort without a parting word to Alex, nary even a backward glance, and in their absence the spring night became almost totally quiet but for one of the guards in the bastions coughing wetly at regular intervals. Alex was still vertiginously drunk, though flatly so and miserably bereft of the spurting, joyful founts that rum usually produced in the chambers of his heart. He'd made a terrible mistake. He could see that. Removed from Finn's sadly sweet eyes, he clearly understood that he'd confused his allegiances and revealed to Miigwan a truth he hadn't fully realized he was concealing, and the scope of the damage couldn't yet be known.

41

HE COULDN'T REMEMBER ENTERING THE HOUSE OR EVEN HIS room, nor could he remember taking off his clothes and collapsing in bed, though evidently he'd accomplished each of those things, for there he was, sprawled on his back atop the thin mattress. A cruel burst of morning sunlight filled the room, all about which his garments – Beaumont's garments – lay scattered, stinking and soiled, and the only reason he'd taken stock of the situation was because he'd been awoken by Beaumont, who stood in the doorway, his officer's coat elsewhere, muscled arms crossed over his chest and his shirt spattered with blood. The sight of him called to Alex's mind the horrors of only a few hours earlier, and just as those memories began their bombardment so too did Beaumont step fully over the threshold and permit the passage of Colonel Smyth.

Smyth's boots landed on the floor as claps of approaching thunder. He crossed the room, plucked the chair from behind Alex's desk, and in the same motion swung it into position next to the bed. But he didn't sit, instead lifted one of his oily black boots and brought it down on the seat of the chair, seemingly unbothered by the muddy water flowing from its sole. He propped one of his elbows on his elevated knee and braced his stubbled chin between thumb and forefinger, and with his other hand he adjusted the hilt of his sabre. 'Here we are again, now aren't we, lad?'

Alex grunted and moaned and felt his tongue become stuck to the roof of his mouth and then, as though a tuft of trampled cotton, unstuck. His lips were cracked and his skin felt tight all over his face, and there were swollen bulbs of flesh all inside his mouth from where men had mashed his lips against his teeth.

Smyth doffed his hat and his shorn head caught a ray of morning sun. 'You don't look well, son. A long night makes for a rough morning, doesn't it? Hell of a do, I'm told. Barrels of beer and buckets of rum. But sit up now. I don't like talking to a man on his back.'

With great effort, Alex righted himself, wincing as the veins in his temples were beset by a sudden rush of blood. He looked the Colonel straight in the eyes and the Colonel stared back, but not angrily, rather he was clearly amused.

'Your doctor tells me you've been fighting and gambling,' said Smyth, twirling his hat.

Beaumont cleared his throat and Alex glanced at him, saw him leaning against the wall and nodding with his arms still crossed. Like the Colonel, he seemed pleased with all that was going on.

'No,' said Alex. 'Me, I don't make enough money working for Dr. Beaumont. I don't make enough money for gambling.'

'He's lying,' said Beaumont, stepping forward. 'If you look in his desk there, you'll see. He's amassed more money than I've been paying him, at any rate.'

'Ah,' clucked Smyth. He pursed his lips and gave a judicious nod. 'And a bit too much of a lushington to carry a second job, am I right?'

'One might say, Colonel.'

Alex cleared his throat and made to protest, but Smyth silenced him with a flick of his hairy hand. The Colonel removed his foot from the chair and let it fall heavily to the floor. He grabbed one of Alex's garments, wiped the seat, and sat, crossing his legs and tilting his head. 'Another man injured in your company, son. Can't have that, see.'

'Non,' said Alex. 'You mean Pierre? We find him all bloody. We save his life.'

A snort from Beaumont.

'As I told you when last we met,' said Smyth, 'any gambling on Mackinac is to be sanctioned by the American Fur Company, to say nothing of trading. What you were engaged in last night was illegal, I'm afraid. In fact, I'd say you've been cheating the company on the regular, am I right, son? Now listen. As I told you before, it's not that we're unaware of illegal gambling. We know of it, and we even know the people at its centre. We'd like to turn a deaf ear, so long as no one makes too much money, but the level of violence is becoming a problem. We like to keep it at something of a murmur, but over the past year, it's been gathering itself into more of a holler, and that's forced our deaf ears to hear. The violence is like a fever, you understand. For example, one man gets stabbed and now he's got that fever. He's off to stab another man, and then that one feels his temperature rise, and off he goes, knife in hand. You follow me, lad?'

Alex looked to Beaumont, but the doctor did nothing to intervene. He'd have to fend for himself, and whereas only yesterday he would've felt poised for just such a fight, this morning his position felt tenuous, imperilled, and through his scabby lips he said, 'Suis désolé, mon Colonel. I don't know what you talk about.'

Smyth exhaled sharply. 'You know very well.'

'Alex,' said Beaumont. 'It's time to stop lying. Colonel Smyth can help you, but you'll have to cooperate.'

Smyth leaned back in the chair and put one of his boots on the edge of Alex's bed. 'Look, son. Here's what I know. Last night, you made yourself the centre of a small fraud. You know what I'm referring to. So does Dr. Beaumont here, so don't look to him for protection – he can offer none, if even he were inclined. See, more than a few cheated men furnished me with the information this morning. The allegations aren't especially serious, but they're enough that I'm going to have to confiscate all your money, you understand. All of it. And as likely as not, I'll have to make arrangements with the doctor here to seize some of your future earnings as well.'

Alex blinked at Smyth's boot, could see already the resulting dirt on his sheets. He'd been a fool to leave his money in the drawer of his desk, for hadn't he known that Beaumont rustled about in his personal space, if only to stock the room with laudanum? How could he have thought the doctor's interest would end there? His stupidity threw a shadow across his thoughts, and on the edge of the darkness, with frightening clarity, he imagined his peach stones sitting vulnerably in the very same drawer. What if these men planned to rid him of those as well? 'Please,' he said. 'We talk more later. For now, I must get dressed and begin work.'

Smyth shook his head. 'No. We talk more now. I'm going to make you an offer, son, and I suggest you give it due consideration. See now, the folk of this island neither like nor respect you, as you're sickly and weak and something of an aberrant to boot, which rightly puts off a hard-working lot such as those who populate this here locale. Accordingly, they're all too willing to incriminate you before the authority of my office.'

'But they are not speaking the truth.'

'Yes. They are. And I suggest you leave any further denials unspoken, as I find within myself an urge to strike you. Should I find this urge in command of my better judgment, well, let's just say your face will never look the same. Best you not speak. Best you consider this instead. You're of no great interest to me. You're an oddity and an amusement and something of a revulsion, but not much more. In fact, I'm interested in one of your friends. That slick little Indian feller, him and the barkeeper at the tavern. Now, that savage – there's a man people respect, or maybe they fear him, I don't know. Doubt there's much difference most of the time. Point is, the men who so freely condemn you to my bad graces grow mute when I turn the conversation to the topic of that particular devil, and not even the Indian agent has a word to say about him. Nor does anyone cast aspersions upon the barkeeper, perhaps because of the pistol he's been known so ably to wield, all of which makes it difficult for me to confirm what I know to be true.'

'I don't know them very much, Colonel. I only see them at the tavern.'

'Another lie, is it? You're close to the both of them, and the filthy little savage especially – that's obvious to anyone with eyes. Time was I'd just round up the Indian and beat from his face a confession, but as we've seen with the Seminoles, the savages are not deaf to treaty. It behooves us, initially, to peaceably pursue our destiny when it comes to the reds, so long as they don't take advantage of our kindness, of course, and that's where you come in, and it's where your money comes in too. As for the barkeeper, I can't rightly countenance an American citizen forming allegiance with a pagan, but this man is all the same one of our own, and accordingly I'm even less inclined to batter him than I am the Indian. So let me come to it. You tell me what you know about those fellers, hard details, hard as a cannonball, and I'll make you whole again. Do you or do you not understand?'

'Je peux pas.'

'English.'

'They are my friends.'

'Ah, but only a second ago you barely knew them. Well, let's suppose they're your friends then, shall we? In particular the Indian. Aren't you worried about him? About his health? About his safety? See, the company wants this business resolved sooner as opposed to later, and if I'm left with no choice but to resort to older methods of investigation, then that'll be my prerogative, won't it? Problem is, it won't end well for the pagan.'

'I don't understand.'

'It's that fever I mentioned, lad. I'm afraid I ain't protected, treaties or no.'

Alex fell silent and returned his gaze to Smyth's heavy boot on the edge of his bed, and after a few tense moments the Colonel stood up and cleared his throat and said Alex could have a handful of days to think things over, no longer. The Colonel approached his desk and yanked open the drawer and rooted through all the contents, plucking up Alex's sack of coins and every stray piece as well. Then he closed the drawer and stooped over the desk to regard a few of Alex's portraits, and at these he snorted before crossing the room once more. He and Beaumont stepped into the hallway and one of them slammed the door and Alex was alone.

There was laudanum in his desk drawer – of course there was – and he imagined the bottle resting on its side, the reddish-brown tincture within, oh so bitter, oh so sweet, and why not, if he had just a few sips, why not, if he sought to lessen his misery, to diminish his pain, because who could blame him, no one could blame him, and then his legs lifted him off the bed and his feet carried him to the desk and his hand pulled open the drawer, and now the light of day fell on the bottle and glittered against the contours of the glass, and Alex licked his cracked lips and closed his bruised eyes and stuck his trembling hand in the drawer.

But he didn't take it up. Rather, he scooped his peach stones from the drawer and regarded them with worry. Clearly Beaumont went through Alex's belongings whenever the inclination took him and clearly the Colonel was unbothered by any notion of Alex's privacy as well. Quelle menace. Alex would have to hide his stones, and he knew just the spot, though he couldn't accommodate all three. He chose the largest one, with the most elaborate grooves, and he lifted his shirt, pulled back the flap of flesh covering his fistula, and inserted it within. The rest he could risk.

42

HE DIDN'T LEAVE THE HOUSE THAT DAY, NOT EVEN TO VISIT Namid, though he longed for her touch and the care she might extend to the suppurating wounds all over his face, but how could he after seeing that look in Miigwan's eyes, that look of probing assessment, that look, he feared, of disdain, maybe even dismissal? It was that same look that kept him from going to the tavern and confessing his predicament to Blake and Miigwan, because how could Alex be sure whatever emotion lay behind that look hadn't intensified, hadn't grown more disdainful still? And yet the reckoning of the Colonel's ultimatum drew ever closer, and suppose, for a moment, that Alex told him what he wanted to hear. What would happen not just to Miigwan but also to Namid and Biskane? Now suppose the inverse, suppose he told the looming Colonel nothing – what would happen then? He'd not have his funds returned, that much was clear, and so gone all the same would be his dream of owning land, of planting peach trees, of basking in his father's pride and admiration, and likely the Colonel would harm Miigwan anyway. Alex would be trapped there in that cabin until Beaumont's ambition had run its course, after which he'd almost certainly wind up penniless, for previous promises of benefitting from the completed research now rang utterly false – there'd be nothing for him at the end of that road, probably not even the job he had now.

And though it was Sunday, his usual day off work, he was required to set about his chores, for Deborah had deemed the house in need of special attention due to Alex's recently lacklustre attentions, and his thoughts harried him as he worked alongside her in an aching, booze-bedraggled silence, just a weary breathing between them, the irregular sounds of their footsteps, the clattering of dirty dishes in the basin and the scrape of chair legs across the floor.

That evening, as Alex lay exhausted in bed, Beaumont knocked on his door to announce an unexpected extraction, saying he had to test a theory that Alex's gastric fluid changed properties as its host changed moods, and as he delivered this news he also rummaged through Alex's desk drawer, a slight, insulting grin on his clean-shaven face. 'Sorry for the intrusion, lad, but I'm afraid it's become necessary. The Colonel wants me to keep an eye on your belongings, you see, and also to remind you the time for your decision, with the passing of every second, is ever more nigh. Don't be foolish, Alex. Do what's in your best interest.' He stood up straight now and revealed an empty vial in his palm. 'And how does this make you feel, pray tell?'

Beaumont greeted Alex's silence with a smug lift of his chin, told him to remove his shirt, and left the room to fetch a tray of vials from which the insertion hose hung with languid menace. Pulling a chair up to the bed, he stated, almost absently, that Alex wouldn't be working alongside Deborah the following day, for she'd chosen to draw up two lists of chores and her wish was that Alex pursue his share in solitude. 'She's come to find your presence a bit burdensome, Alex, the cuts and bruises about your face too much of a distracting reminder of your recent choices. So tomorrow, and likely from now on, you'll be required to work alone. Scrub the chamber pots. Visit the store-house and the butcher. Cut wood for the cooking fire. That manner of thing.'

Alex absorbed this news with a sting. He'd known Deborah would ultimately position herself against him, but he was all the same taken aback by the totality of their separation now that it had arrived, and while previously he'd faced this future with an entrepreneur's absence of emotion, given the tumult of the weekend he now felt within himself a storm of grief, and this feeling must've settled on his face, for Beaumont, with arms akimbo, said, 'There, there, son. Try not to take it personally. We in this house have tolerated a great deal of your difficult behaviour. We're entitled to a little fatigue, wouldn't you say?'

Alex offered no rejoinder. Beaumont began preparing for the procedure, musing about the implications of his theory, and of course he'd have to explore it thoroughly in his book, the progress of which was most prodigious, oh yes, how the pages piled up, towers on either side of his desk, a tremendous and scholarly effort, though Beaumont wasn't surprised at his own achievement, not a bit, for so blew the gales of an inspired wind.

There was much about these events that offended Alex, the abrupt announcement that he'd be completing his housework alone as well as the presumptuous manner with which Beaumont went about the insertion, and this was further complicated by the fact of the peach stone Alex had hidden inside, and he cursed himself for having forgotten to remove it when Beaumont went to retrieve his vials – he'd been too tired, too distracted, too assailed to even think of it let alone undertake the action of forcing the stone back up through his conduit – and now it became an obstruction as Beaumont pushed and poked, with his fingers and thumbs, the red and irritated rim of Alex's hole, occasionally forcing his pointer finger inside before trying to thrust the hose down once more.

'Seems to be something blocking the canal,' he said, a frown forming beneath the veil of curls cloaking his eyes. 'Are you doing that on purpose?' Again he shoved the hose into the aperture, grunting as he tried to force it down. 'That's enough now, Alex. Please.'

The pain was immense as Beaumont pushed harder yet again, and for the second time he told Alex to stop whatever it was he was doing, for they had a contract, the two of them, and if Beaumont couldn't perform his experiments, then what use did he have of Alex? Why would he continue to open his house to such a troublesome young man?

Alex couldn't summon the focus required to speak as still Beaumont pushed harder on the hose, and it seemed as though his brother's inner shrieking would cause his body to burst. He whimpered and sobbed and then finally, deep inside his torso, he felt the peach stone scrape against the sides of his fistula and into his stomach as it yielded to the force of Beaumont's invasion. He belched and came to realize he'd been sweating profusely.

Beaumont leaned back in his chair and massaged his hands as though they'd endured a terrible strain. 'There, there,' said the doctor, making no effort to conceal his bothered tone. 'Not at your finest, are you?'

43

THE NEXT DAY, THE PRESSURE EVER BUILDING, ALEX KNEW he had to visit Miigwan and try to make amends, but first he wanted to look for the peach stone Beaumont had shoved into his stomach, so he crouched over his chamber pot and emptied himself, and then he stepped outside the scullery and with a long and curving stick poked through his soil, holding his breath and squinting his eyes. It seemed he'd yet to pass it, so he carried his waste and that of the Beaumonts to a foul-smelling creek that ran under the palisades and down the hill before draining into the lake. He dumped the contents, gagging, and took the pots back home to rinse in the scullery. He went about the rest of his chores in silence and solitude, haunted by that look in Miigwan's eyes and worrying that he'd be confronted with it yet again when he went to the tavern that evening. The feeling was one of great loneliness, though he did have company of a sort, this being the residual pain in his fistula from Beaumont's extraction as well as the occasional bump or thump from Deborah as she worked in some other part of the house, for though it was a small structure, she was nevertheless able to avoid sharing a room with him.

He finished his chores and left the house. Hands in his pockets, he walked through the gates of the fort and felt the guards smirking, but he ignored them and hurried down the hill and through the village. He hesitated outside the tavern next to the American flag, which fluttered from its pole in the soft, slow breeze, and it occurred to him that on the other side of the battered wooden door there could be men from the forest and perhaps they'd mean him vengeful harm. He swept the hair off his forehead and looked up and down the street, and though there were people milling about, they paid him no mind, so he pressed his ear against the tavern door and heard not a hint of the welter that usually rang from within, and this made sense, because most of les Canadiens would be trapping in the bush or along the rivers wild, and as for the villagers, spring and summer were often too busy to permit an afternoon of total intoxication, rather such abandon was reserved for evening. Cautiously, Alex opened the door and stepped inside.

On the far side of the tavern, dressed in buckskins, Miigwan was leaning over a newspaper opened on the bar, across from which was Blake, his arms folded next to the paper and an oily sheen to his pelt-like birthmark. Next to Miigwan, cradling himself in the manner of an injured man, was Pierre, who with a plummeting frown was first to lock eyes with Alex. He even made to stand up, but Miigwan stayed him with a single shake of his head, and Pierre's frown deepened further still. He ran a hand through his long and asymmetrically styled hair and turned from Alex to his beer, into the thin suds of which he glowered.

Alex forced a smile as he drew nearer. 'Salut, les gars.'

L'Indien whistled and grinned, and Alex searched his eyes for their probing aspect and couldn't yet decide whether it was there or not. Miigwan lifted the paper off the bar and ruffled its pages, and in English he began to read: '"A young man with a strength of spirit most palpable…"' He glanced at Blake as Pierre chuckled, then pointed at another spot on the page and lifted his chin as though impressed: '"…this young man, who longs to see his father once more, and whose inner strength is so outwardly clear…"' He looked up from the newspaper and raised an eyebrow, comically, and Alex couldn't help but smile, because Miigwan was reading what could've only been the *Free Press*, and the article was about him, about Alex, not Beaumont, and further the simple fact of Miigwan's reading and smiling and encouraging the others to make merry must've meant that Alex's transgression had been forgiven – these men were still his friends, grâce à dieu.

Alex sat on a bar stool and smiled. He asked Blake for a glass of beer and then turned to Miigwan, who smiled as well, and in French l'Indien said, 'It's been out a week or more, and all over the region. Imagine what people must think of you now!'

Alex giggled and reached for the paper. 'Fait voir?'

Miigwan put his palm flat on the page and turned to Alex. 'The problem is that we know different, don't we, les amis? We know you to be weak, despite this depiction of strength.'

Blake, who hadn't yet moved to fetch Alex's beer, grunted in the affirmative, and Alex felt the smile die on his face. Pierre grinned now, teeth all crooked and black.

'But...' said Alex. His voice cracked and he cleared his throat and tried again: 'But your dreams, remember? You dreamed of me.'

'Sometimes,' said Miigwan, with a casual tilt of his head, 'I'm confused by my manitou. Sometimes, it seeks to confuse me. And sometimes, a dream is just a dream. I'm no longer certain of the truth with you.'

Pierre stiffened and looked sharply at Miigwan, who touched his arm in a manner that must've been reassuring, because the wounded sailor relaxed and smiled to himself, then raised his glass and drained it of beer. Blake served him another.

Miigwan's eyes had taken up anew their disturbing inventory of Alex's face, and so the latter dropped his gaze to the filth-benighted floor, where gobs of tobacco-tainted phlegm had left countless stains, and only with great effort did he manage to lift his head again and look at Miigwan. 'I'm so sorry,' he said, voice catching in his throat. 'I'm truly so sorry. You're my friend. The gamblers, they'll forget the trickery. They'll come to trust you again.'

'Some will,' said Miigwan with a nod. 'As I told you, that's life for these men, and anyway they live in an almost perfect absence of memory. What concerns me more is you, and do you know why that might be?'

Alex wiped his mouth with his wrist and shook his head and shrugged.

'You met with Colonel Smyth,' said Miigwan, pursing his lips. 'And he's left you with a decision to make very soon now, isn't that right?'

Before he could think better of it, Alex found himself lying: 'Non! C'est pas vrai! J'ai jamais parlé 'vec lui! J't'l'jure!'

Pierre's stool clattered to the ground as he sprang to his feet and loomed over Alex, his chest heaving, his breath appalling. 'Allow me to hit him,' he pleaded, green eyes wide and beseeching. 'Please. Allow me to take him to the back and spread his teeth across the floor.'

Alex closed his eyes and shrank away, but then he heard Miigwan tell Pierre to return to his stool and drink his beer and maintain his calm until he was called upon to abandon it, and then Miigwan closed one of his strong hands over Alex's knee and said, 'You forget that I'm known all over this island, known and respected. My interests borrow the eyes and ears of a great many men and women, and what they don't know I discover in my dreams.'

Alex leaned forward and grabbed Miigwan by the biceps. 'C'est vrai! The Colonel wants to harm you! And Blake too! He wants me to provide information, but he already knows what you do. He wants evidence to have you arrested!'

'And what do you plan to tell him?' asked Miigwan, his voice quiet.

'Je sais pas. Nothing.'

'Which is it?'

'It's nothing. I promise.'

'You won't signal him somehow with your knee?'

'Please,' said Alex, gripping his stool between his legs. 'Please, you and me, we're friends. I'm so sorry. I'm so sorry, Miigwan. I get lonely, tu sais? That's all.'

At this, Pierre leaned forward, dredged his throat, and spat a coal-black rope upon Alex's shirt.

'Forgive him,' said Miigwan with a sad smile. 'He longs very much to please. But I think it's best you go so I can consider in quiet what to do with you now.'

44

OUTSIDE THE TAVERN ALEX BENT OVER AND GRABBED A
handful of sand and dirt and used it to wipe the spit off his shirt, his
teeth chattering, his breathing hard to control. He trudged up the
hill to the fort and a dog crossed the road and bared its teeth and he
kicked a stone but missed its head. The joy he'd felt over the article
in the *Free Press* had been brief. His friends no longer cared for him.
Pierre had taken his place, but based on what merit, simply because
he'd thrown himself into a crush of woodland violence? Was Miigwan
blind? There was ample evidence of Pierre's incompetence, the knife
wound and the scars surrounding it, and furthermore, he was obse-
quious and his breath was foul and Alex hated him. And wasn't he
required on an expedition? He'd told them he was indentured with the
American Fur Company and like all indentured boors he'd squandered
his advance, which meant the company would clamp his legs in iron
if he failed to fulfil his duties. Or did Miigwan's influence extend into
the ranks of the company's clerks? Or maybe he'd lent Pierre enough
money to repay the debt. Alex would never know, but the details
didn't matter. He was out. Pierre was in. Worse, Miigwan seemed to
be planning some kind of retribution, for his parting words had been
sharp with menace, and Alex wouldn't be able to defend himself even
against a fool like Pierre, to say nothing of the likes of Blake.

And so the thought arrived clearly: he'd have to tell Colonel Smyth
what he knew. He'd get his money back and furnished with those
funds he'd immediately look for a way to leave Mackinac and return
to Montréal, no matter what he had to pledge in return. He could find

work at the ports, even if it meant selling fish or newspapers the way his papa had feared, but he'd be fine, he had his brother to help him, he still felt the light in his body. Miigwan had given him that, it wasn't just a dream, and he'd cherish it always, but nevertheless Alex had no choice but to betray him, because that was what men in his position did when circumstances called upon them to do it. And anyway, Miigwan would've done the same, Namid would surely attest to that.

He entered the house and closed the door and Beaumont called out from the office. The doctor's voice was hoarse and he sat stiffly behind his desk with a tin cup of wine on one side and in the middle an open newspaper. 'Don't sit down,' he said. 'A man of your selfishness will find no rest in any parlour of mine.'

Alex stood in front of Beaumont's desk and crossed his arms as he registered the man's dark and spiteful inebriation. 'Me, I don't rest in your house, Doctor. Not even when I am sleep.'

'Be quiet, you fool. Your voice. Your accent. Your mangled phraseology. These things have winnowed the thick staff of my patience to the flimsiest of twigs.'

'Winnowed?'

'Silence!' Beaumont hammered his fist on the table with enormous force, enough to send his tin cup chattering to the edge but not quite over, and involuntarily Alex tightened his arms around his chest. 'I take it by now,' said Beaumont, 'your pathetic illiteracy notwithstanding, you've been exposed to the article in the *Free Press*. No doubt you're delighted. No doubt you feel as though you've overtaken me in some sorry contest of character, am I right? But listen closely, Alex. There's no such contest afoot. None! And your irresponsible seduction of that doddering old fool has achieved nothing more than harm to the research!'

Alex felt he might laugh. 'But it is him who ask me the questions. Me, I only answer.'

Beaumont's forehead had begun to glisten. 'Son, you would benefit from that view of yourself which is shared by those in your company. You are a weak man who cannot grow strong absent the recognition of your very—'

'No!' Alex extended one of his arms and jabbed a finger at his doctor. 'Je suis fort! You are weak!'

Beaumont's mouth fell open. He blinked rapidly and emitted a tiny croak. He shook his head and reached for his cup and brought it to his lips. He took a gulp of wine and then, with a fierce snap of his arm, threw the cup at Alex, striking him in the chest and splashing wine all over. 'Clean it up,' Beaumont muttered. 'Do it now.'

His face dripping, Alex began to crouch even before the notion of resistance reared up in his mind. He heard Beaumont chuckle and managed to stop himself from kneeling. He stood up and wiped his face with his sleeve. He opened his mouth to speak but no words came, for with remarkable speed Beaumont flew out from behind his desk and struck Alex in the temple, knocking him to the ground.

Shock travelled between them. The study was silent but for their breathing. Alex's head was throbbing and he looked up at his looming doctor and watched as the older man regarded his own fist as if attached to a different sort of person, perhaps Colonel Smyth, whose philosophy on violence Alex couldn't help but recall: there was no diplomacy more persuasive than that which followed force.

'Mais finalement et quelle surprise,' he said, trying to quell the tremor in his voice. 'You talk about your science and your history, and you talk that you are a special man. But you are not. You are a mean man, like your papa.'

Beaumont blinked and stepped forward and seemed as though he might lose himself to violence. Alex cowered, covering his head with his arms as he awaited yet another downpour of knuckles and sweat. But the blows never came, rather just Beaumont's voice, choked and distant: 'Clean it up, Alex. You have a job to do around here, and I'd hate to have to remind you again.'

45

ON THE THIRD DAY, ALEX AWOKE NOT KNOWING IF HE'D BE confronted with the finality of the Colonel's ultimatum or if the handful of days he'd been offered would extend deeper into the week or perhaps even take him into the next. He avoided the Beaumonts as he did his morning chores and kept his head down as he went to the butcher, and as usual the old man working there was spattered in blood and his fingers were thick and pale and spotted, save for the right pinky, which was missing. His lips were dry and they parted audibly as he spoke. 'You are expected presently at the gates of the fort. A man awaits and has for some time.'

Alex tucked a packet of meat under his arm. It was wrapped in a tearing from the *Free Press*, but he couldn't read the page and didn't know if it contained the article about him or not. He crossed the fort grounds slowly and fearfully, because he knew it was Miigwan who'd summoned him, and he saw his old friend dressed in a black tailored coat that hung to his bare knees. Next to him was Pierre, who'd shaved his head to the flesh and all over his scalp was a rash of pimples. Miigwan's eyes circled the new bruise around Alex's temples. He tightened his lips and nodded ever so slightly, suggesting they walk down the hill. Pierre followed a short distance behind, feet dragging through the dirt.

'Alors,' said Miigwan, once they'd moved away from the bluecoats guarding the gate. 'Your new friends have given you a fresh bruise, I see.'

Alex raised his hand and gingerly touched his temple. 'They're not my friends. And anyway, Beaumont did this, not the Colonel. It was unlike him.'

238

'You think so?'

Alex shrugged. 'Why have you called for me? To leave a fresh bruise of your own?'

Miigwan's face was inscrutable. 'Initially, I thought I might have to do something along those lines, c'est vrai, in order to encourage your silence to the Colonel. But thankfully, not long after you left the tavern yesterday evening, things changed, and positively so, for both your situation and mine. Walk with me.'

They carried on down the hill toward the village and the air was warm and the sky was clear, but Alex felt nervous and cold. Behind them Pierre coughed and spat and once he belched. Miigwan put his arm around Alex's shoulders and it was tempting for a moment to forget the immense tension between them, but of course he couldn't, rather he listened as Miigwan told him about a clap of good fortune, one surely conjured by Gitche Manitou to resolve their crisis, for Miigwan had burned much tobacco and prayed and sprinkled the shores of the island as well. And lo, his prayers had been answered. Alex's brother had arrived on the island.

Alex stopped. He scowled. His brother was inside him, he knew this, he felt it, and he said as much. 'What are you talking about?'

Miigwan tugged his wrist and they were moving again, approaching the bottom of the hill where the village rattled with its midday clamour, and standing apart from the filthy swarms was a tall man with his straight hair parted down the middle, and he wore immaculately white shirtsleeves and carried a black coat slung over his shoulder. His young, smiling face was clean-shaven and very white, and indeed his whole appearance projected a cleanliness and decency not even the filth of Mackinac could diminish.

Miigwan jerked his chin at the man. 'His name is Emmanuel. He's your brother, but distantly, his life unbeknownst to you. He's been looking for you all around the Great Lakes, and as luck would have it, he discovered your whereabouts in Detroit while reading the *Free Press*. He came as quickly as possible, and at whatever cost, because he has news of your papa. He has returned to Montréal and wants you to come and see him.'

Alex stopped again, so abruptly that Pierre bumped into him from behind, but the stench of the sailor wasn't enough to taint the revelation. A living brother? A brother in the flesh, standing there in the sunshine, drawing breath, all that *and* the return of his papa? Mais c'était impossible.

Miigwan tugged his wrist again, leading him farther down the hill. The man in the white shirt smiled and waved, and Alex imagined his papa squaring logs in a labour camp along the St. Lawrence, oui, and he pictured his arms around the waist of a woman who cooked for the men and served their rum, oui, comme c'est ça la solitude, and now he saw clearly his papa dandling a version of Emmanuel shrunken to infancy and then many years later the two of them in the fish markets of France, his papa sorting the catch with Emmanuel, more suited to that type of work, more practical for that sort of trip, but now the two of them had returned to get Alex, and they sat in a Montréal hotel, land deeds on the desk by the window, all precisely as promised, but with an added reveal: a new brother to join the spirit of the old. Finalement! Après toutes ces années!

Alex broke into a trot, his feet sliding in the loose gravel of the road, and Emmanuel extended his arms and smiled, perhaps mutely, but surely he was just tired from his journey, surely he was in fact overjoyed to have found Alex – and indeed he was! He beckoned for Alex to join him in a brotherly embrace, his grey eyes wide and warm, and the strength of Emmanuel's arms felt right in every way, and oh, how life had the power to torture and soothe, to tether and enslave and, finally, to emancipate as well.

PART IV
Au Retour

SUMMER, 1832

46

EMMANUEL HAD COME TO MACKINAC FROM DETROIT ON A
sailboat anchored off the strait. They left the island that night, pushing
off the shadow-clad shore in a rowboat loaded with victuals procured
from the village, and Emmanuel rolled his pants up to his knees and
his calves were creamy white and hairless, but muscled. He curled his
lips in distaste as he sloshed into the shallows made fetid by the men
who camped on the beach, and then he stepped gracefully over the
gunwale and sat upon the bench in the prow, crossing his legs in the
manner of a woman.

Alex understood he himself should row the boat, so he climbed
aboard and took the middle bench and put his belongings at his
feet. He'd managed to avoid the Beaumonts for the remainder of the
afternoon and spent most of his time clattering about the scullery,
forgetting what he was doing from one moment to the next, grinning with excitement, frowning with anxiety, reminding himself with
sudden starts to listen for Deborah or the doctor, lest they should
sense something awry and seek to block his escape, but his keepers
were disgusted with him and they kept their distance. He crawled
out the window of the back room just twenty minutes before meeting
Emmanuel on the beach, a potato sack over his shoulder containing
what little he'd amassed, second-hand clothes and an inkpot and a
pen, some drawing paper and a lump of coal – and his peach stones
of course – but that was all. Now in the rowboat he took up the oars
and felt the grainy wood bite into his palms, and he began to heave,
confident he'd guide the craft smoothly and directly, for clearly his

luck had improved, so why not his abilities too? Above them shone a three-quarter moon partially obscured by ragged clouds, its light reflecting off the water in the bottom of the boat. There was a slow leak in the floor, but Alex felt it too slow to mention, it posed no peril, and in silence they plowed across the vast surface of the lake toward the strait.

As they neared the sailboat a black man appeared starboard, colossal in stature and wearing a tiny leather vest and a silver earring that glinted in the moonlight, and he nodded at them and despite the slight smile he offered, there hung about his shoulders a kind of sadness that further darkened the night. Emmanuel bent over and gathered up a thick, wet rope and threw it to the giant, who pulled the rowboat against the hull of the larger vessel then disappeared from view, and Alex could tell by the sodden thrumming of the rope that he was tying it off somewhere above. When he reappeared, he threw down a ladder made of branches and bark, and Emmanuel motioned for Alex to ascend in his wake, and up he went with arachnidous limbs. As Alex waited for his turn he looked to the fires flickering on the beach and thought he heard men singing over the high notes of a fiddle, and he wondered if Miigwan was among them, looking out onto the lake. When it was his turn to climb he kept his eyes fixed on the boat's glistening hull, excitement lumping in his throat like an obstruction that might block his speech. He reached the top and saw the black man cross his arms and wait for Alex to clear the gunwale before climbing down to the rowboat and single-handedly retrieving the supplies.

The vessel was modest, maybe forty feet long with a cabin in the middle, and Emmanuel excused himself and descended therein. Alex stood in the centre of the boat with his potato sack slung over his shoulder, and he shifted his weight and cleared his throat as he watched the giant unfurl the sails. Calling out in a shaky voice, he asked after the man's name, and with a beleaguered smile the sailor said he was called Monsieur Maudit. Alex tightened his mouth in surprise, then asked if he could help set the boat to sail, and Maudit regarded him with thin brows quizzically high, then snorted with amusement and continued his work alone.

Questions swirled through Alex's head. He didn't know what to do or say and assumed Emmanuel would return above deck so the two of them could sit and talk, because he simply had to know what their papa had been doing all these years. And who was Emmanuel's maman? Had they both gone to France with his papa? If so, what did they do there? Did they remember always that Alex was waiting for them at home? Had they purchased land in the St. Lawrence Valley upon their return? Had they ever considered a peach orchard? Would Alex have a new maman, and would she be as special as his old one? Was it even right to compare them? Back on Mackinac, as he stepped away from his brother's warm embrace, he'd tried to ask these questions and more, but Emmanuel offered only his dapper smile and said their journey home would be long and there'd be plenty of time to unravel the whole story. For now, it was important they make haste to Georgian Bay and then up the river system to Montréal, because a new life awaited them in Québec.

Alex imagined the door to his room creaking open in the morning and Beaumont crossing the threshold, eager to press upon Alex the arrival of Colonel Smyth's decision hour, and eager as well to watch Alex waver, collapse, and divulge the doings of his friends, which surely he would've done, oui, as surely as the sails of Emmanuel's boat now filled with the rising wind, for what choice did he have if he wanted his hard-earned money returned? It occurred to Alex, however, that he probably would've never been made whole, not fully; it wouldn't have mattered what he confessed to the Colonel, and how naive he'd been to believe otherwise, for surely the money would've passed first through Beaumont, and the doctor would've taxed it heavily to ensure Alex's continued dependence on the status quo. Mais prenons un pot, because Alex no longer needed the money, and that morning Beaumont would open the door to an entirely different situation – a loss of control! – and likely he'd find himself the target of the Colonel's ire, and in the face of it he'd wither. Even if not, Alex was happy to withhold from Beaumont that which the doctor seemed to cherish most: the opportunity to conduct further experiments so that he might gain greater stature.

But it wasn't just a joyful thrush that flapped in his chest, rather there was sorrow as well, sorrow and grief and the slow and heavy beating of their thick black wings, which caused his heart to stumble and lurch. He'd miss Deborah, no matter the dissolution of their relationship. And the collapse of his friendship with Miigwan was a loss akin to death, to say nothing of the sudden rupture in his relations with Namid. For the first time in months, he remembered poignantly how bereaved he'd been when Serge had died in the wilderness, and now he felt the same again. He looked to the stars and asked le seigneur to spare Miigwan and Namid and Biskane any and all of Colonel Smyth's punitive machinations, and he asked forgiveness for his role in the débâcle. He hoped Miigwan would visit him in his dreams and the two would drink rum together and apologies wouldn't be necessary, love didn't require them, and anyway it wasn't words that healed such wounds, it was devotion.

Emmanuel emerged from below deck. He'd removed his shirt, and his torso like his legs was both hairless and muscled, though unlike his legs it was covered in tattoos: on his chest the snarling heads of powerful lions and the flaming hoops through which they leapt; on his left side a great brown bear standing upright and playing a fiddle; on his stomach a rope pulled taut between poles and the shadowy figure of a man in a top hat traversing the expanse; and behind all these images a pattern of red and white stripes, and these stripes didn't just cover his chest but also his shoulders and biceps as well.

Truly this was a sight to behold and Alex couldn't help but wonder how dismayed his papa must have been to discover such extensive decorations on the flesh of a son, for though it had been years since Alex had seen his papa and he sometimes had trouble recalling the man's precise nature, he knew without a doubt that so many tattoos, and of such frightening subjects, would strike his father as diabolique.

Emmanuel moved about the boat assisting Maudit with matters of sailing, and Alex grew increasingly uncomfortable when his brother didn't deign to even glance in his direction, and he wondered if he had somehow caused offence. Were these men appalled by his lack of seafaring ability? Perhaps. Or perhaps there were simply more pressing concerns than a family meeting, though as far as Alex could fathom, nothing could be more pressing, rien de tout.

When finally Emmanuel turned his attention to Alex, the anchor had been retracted and the ship's sails were swollen and the vessel now carried them away from Mackinac. Alex had barely moved from his position in the middle of the boat. He clutched his scant belongings and smiled at his brother despite an uneasy feeling that yawned wider by the moment, and Emmanuel, unsmiling, suggested Alex descend below deck, for surely he must've been tired. There was a bed down there upon which he could recline, and though Alex was dismayed to hear these words, he nevertheless took up the suggestion, and he was comforted somewhat by the image of himself in the belly of this boat, for that was much the way he imagined his little brother curled up ghostly inside his own belly. He said goodnight and descended below deck and lay in a bed as the boat rocked from side to side, and after a while he fell asleep and dreamed of Miigwan hanging by his neck from a gallows on the beach. His face was blue and his eyes bulged with accusation. A soldier cut him down and he got up, head lolling between his shoulder blades as he walked into the lake, never to return.

47

WHEN HE AWOKE THERE WAS DAYLIGHT SHINING THROUGH the cracks in the deck and something was thudding against the hull and there was also the smell of cooking pork. A dampened chill had risen off the open water and enveloped them from mast to hull. He rolled out of bed and found it difficult to stand because of the rocking of the boat, and with uncertain balance he climbed the steps and opened the hatch and heaved himself above deck, where the sun was bright and beginning to warm the day, and all about the boat was the big blue water of Lake Huron, but in no direction could he see land and still he heard this mysterious thudding against the hull.

In the stern, where there was a small galley before the helm, Maudit tended a charcoal fire burning behind a wind shield fashioned from wet wooden panels. Emmanuel sat on one of the benches, his back bent in exhaustion, and it was evident that neither of them had slept much throughout the night. For their diligence, Alex felt a flush of gratitude. He greeted them with a hearty salutation, but neither looked up in response, and the sails flapped and the boat rocked as Alex gingerly made his way to the bench and sat next to Emmanuel, who said, 'As-tu bien dormi?'

Alex said oui and Emmanuel nodded and reached into the cast-iron pan under Maudit's care, and from it he plucked a blackened strip of bacon, though strikingly he didn't wince even as the scorching meat continued to sizzle.

'Alors,' said Alex, forcing good cheer into his voice, 'we must discuss the family, n'est-ce pas? Me, I'm curious to learn about papa and get to know my new brother. I've waited so long to learn about our land along the St. Lawrence, and recently I was able to acquire peach stones, from which strong trees will surely grow, and I'd like to contribute these to our venture.'

Emmanuel examined the strip of bacon pinched between his finger and thumb as Maudit stayed focused on the cooking fire. He popped the bacon into his mouth and chewed delicately, his lips sealed tight. A crunch rang through the walls of his cheeks, but this was a gentle sound, heard in brief, for quickly the wind swept it away. 'Bon,' he said. 'Écoute. Myself, I didn't see the point in this deception, not given your situation. It was your friend, le sauvage, who insisted upon it. Moi, personellement, I find it cruel, and there's no good reason to drag it out any longer.'

These words floated eerily from Emmanuel's mouth, as though battered by the wind, and what was left of them carried devilish import, the meaning of which took slow and icy hold as Alex identified the thudding sound he'd been hearing since he awoke: it was the damaged rowboat lashed to the windward gunwale and no doubt taking on water as the waves drove it against the hull.

Alex looked from Emmanuel's inscrutable face to the bacon sizzling in Maudit's pan. 'What're you saying?'

'I think you know.'

It seemed, for a moment, that the boat would flip. 'You're saying papa isn't actually in Québec?'

A snort from Maudit, but sympathetic somehow, and Emmanuel said, 'No. That's not what I said.'

'So he is in Québec?'

'He might be. Qui sait?'

Alex forced a smile.

'But likely not. I've never met the man. I know nothing of his whereabouts. I'm not even interested. Commences-tu à comprendre?'

Maudit reached into the boiling grease and took up a charred strip of bacon and blew on it and handed it to Alex with an encouraging nod, but Alex didn't take it, just stared at Emmanuel with growing horror as the rowboat continued to buffet the hull and somewhere overhead a gull shrieked and wheeled.

'Let me put it plainly,' said the tattooed sailor. 'We're not on our way to Montréal. Rather, we're travelling to York. Serendipity has brought us together, a bolt of opportunity delivered through the pages of the *Free Press*.' He wiped his palms one off the other. 'Fascinating, the arrangement of human lives. There've been many turns in mine, many twists, all of them hinging on some form of luck. Take this sailboat, which we stole from the mouth of the Detroit simply because it was there, whereas the night before it wasn't. Without it, why, we might've been delayed in reaching Mackinac, and who knows how your situation could've developed? Perhaps we would've missed each other, quel malheur. And yet there was a boat when we needed it, just as there was another boat when first we crossed, just as there was an article in the newspaper when we needed that. I intend to complete the sequence and deliver you to Mr. Barnaby, my employer, and in so doing he shall become your employer as well, and my hope is you'll count yourself lucky, for truly, mon ami, you can be counted as nothing else.'

Alex struggled to swallow. He looked from Maudit to Emmanuel, the former completely focused on his pan of bacon, the latter sitting on the bench and smiling smugly. 'Mais… mais je comprends pas.'

Emmanuel heaved an irritated sigh and said that he and Maudit had undertaken a trip to Detroit, for Mr. Barnaby was an entertainer of the highest order, and thus he needed new performers at nearly all times, and no, true talent didn't just turn up on one's stoop, it had to be sought out. They'd gone to America in search of they weren't sure whom, and along the way, lo, they discovered Alex in the pages of a newspaper, his life story laid out in all the necessary detail. Emmanuel understood immediately that Alex would make a fine fit in Mr. Barnaby's Magical Spectacle of Marvels and Mystery, and so they travelled to Mackinac, and when they arrived, they asked around until they met Miigwan, and now the three of them sat together aboard this sailboat, headed for York. Emmanuel wiped his palms together, placed them on his knees, and arched his chest with a contented sigh. 'Et c'est comme ça, la vie.'

Alex hardly breathed throughout the whole of this recounting, as if there were something poisonous in the air that would bring truth to the events if inhaled, but a burst of fury roiled up inside him when he saw Emmanuel stretch like that, not a care in the world. Alex surged to his feet and Maudit did the same, but Emmanuel didn't budge, he sat calmly, tired but unruffled. Alex took a step forward and the sail-boat rocked and he lost his balance. Maudit reached out to steady him and with powerful hands guided him back to his seat. All he could do was sputter, and in this manner he protested: 'Bu— but what are you talking about? I want to go home!'

Emmanuel shrugged and said that was understandable but not possible, for already Alex owed a debt to the company, this because of the costs undertaken to travel to Mackinac and also to feed Alex up to this point, as well as to lodge him aboard the boat, and as they still had a significant journey ahead of them, there'd yet be more expenses incurred, and these too Alex would have to repay, which, fortunately, he could do by taking up his employment with Mr. Barnaby, for truly he had special talents in that regard, Emmanuel could tell, he had an instinct for such things, but if Alex chose instead to abscond, per-haps in that little rowboat or maybe, once they reached land, on foot through the woods, then Maudit would be dispatched to retrieve him, after which the conditions of their association would alter dramatically and, so far as Alex would be concerned, for the worse.

This was a great deal to absorb and Alex couldn't formulate any sort of response, instead he was consumed by a catastrophic disappoint-ment and a bitter disgust with himself, for once again he'd been naive and once again he'd been stupid and once again he'd handed out his trust as though it were nothing at all, pemmican at a beach camp, and so likely he deserved what was happening, whatever it might be, but just as likely he did not, for underlying these feelings was a stormy black anger, and he felt it in his jaw and the muscles of his neck and in his fingers as well, which gripped the edge of the bench as though the blade of a knife, and he threw back his head and screamed at the gull still wheeling above, and Emmanuel chuckled and Maudit looked askance and Alex vowed never again would he allow himself to be owned by the whimsy of another, and though he'd made something like this vow before, cette fois-ci, he meant it, and to prove it, he rallied his courage and turned to Emmanuel and pointed his finger and swore and said, 'You will not get away with this. I will—'

But the threat was cut short when Emmanuel slapped him. His palm cracked off Alex's cheek and the latter tasted blood, yet again, as if his face were little more than a medium through which men expressed their anger, which of course it was, from his papa to the sons of his patron, from M. Anderson to the man who attacked him while he and Serge were boarding in Montréal, and what about Rémi, who'd punched and choked him on a beach in the middle of nowhere, and then there was Beaumont, his invasive fingers wriggling deep inside, and what of all the boors who'd kicked and punched him at Miigwan's party, the bruises they'd left stinging even still, and then came Pierre, l'espèce de merde who'd hawked on his chest, and after that Beaumont again, hurling a wine cup where Pierre had only just spat, and now Emmanuel, this shameless imposter with his preternaturally tidy appearance, slapping Alex across the face as if he were a child, and was there no end to this, no end to impetuous men reaching out to strike him over and over again? He felt within himself something like retaliation and even released the bench and clenched his fists, but again Maudit's powerful grip took hold of his shoulder, and Emmanuel, standing now, yawning, told Alex to compose himself.

'I understand you're upset, and I understand why, but your quarrel isn't with me. It was le sauvage who insisted on this false reunion of your family, pas moi. What you need is time to absorb your new situation, to recognize it as an improvement over your previous circumstance. Moi, je suis fatigué. Il faut que je dorme. I will leave Monsieur Maudit to steer the ship and give you more background on Mr. Barnaby's enterprise.'

48

MAUDIT SAT BESIDE ALEX AND HIS DEMEANOUR SOFTENED
and he smiled and several of his teeth were missing and on the great
sculpted mound of his shoulder was a pattern of scarred flesh that
resembled a circle with a line through the centre. He spoke mellifluous
French and explained how Alex had come to Emmanuel's attention
purely by chance while the latter was taking breakfast with his newspaper in a Detroit hotel, for Emmanuel and Maudit had spent almost
a month roving the city and countryside in search of people who
might make interesting performers in the employ of Mr. Barnaby's
Magical Spectacle of Marvels and Mystery, which was fortifying its
operations in the Town of York, capital of Upper Canada, where for
a number of years Mr. Barnaby had offered occasional entertainment
in bars and on the grounds of the St. Lawrence Market, and now,
thanks to the success of those endeavours, he planned to offer it with
regularity, perhaps weekly, though certainly on a monthly basis, and
this in the tavern in which the troupe had taken up lodging. Greater
success was imperative, for York's population was exploding and Mr.
Barnaby's singular ambition was to entertain those pulsating masses.
Maudit said he too had been enlisted in the company by the great
recruiter of chance, for life was full of such moments, each and every
one of them attached not just to the next but to hundreds of others as
well, and skilled men such as Emmanuel and Mr. Barnaby were able
to direct this endless flow of related moments, comme c'était bizarre.

With his jaw clenched in anger and his cheek still smarting from
the blow, Alex found it difficult to listen as Maudit explained that

he'd come from Dahomey, which was in Africa, bien loin d'ici. He was one of the Fon, a powerful people who traded in slaves, and when he was a boy he played in the courtyards of the king, but then he was captured by the soldiers of a rival kingdom who made him labour in their plantations before trading him and fourteen others to a company of sunburnt whites in exchange for a Portuguese cannon. He was branded and shackled to an older man in the overcrowded hull of a rickety galleon, and on the long, wet voyage across the Atlantic to the United States, he lost the ability to commune with the spirits of his ancestors and endured harrowing experiences, the most frightening of which involved a white sailor bound to the decking and whipped to the brink of death in the pounding sun and briny winds after he'd been caught forcing relations on one of the female slaves, a girl of maybe ten years old, an indulgence that would've been overlooked had he not shared with her the crew's dwindling rations. Every morning the slavers herded their cargo to the upper deck, their tattered clothing snapping in the wind, their aching limbs shackled one to the next, and they were made to watch the bound sailor slip closer and closer to death, weeping and begging and shitting and pissing, his cheeks blistering and his lips peeling and his bouts of unconsciousness a reprieve to them all, until finally they cut him loose and threw him over, and truly this was a horrifying episode to behold not because of the man's suffering but because of what it suggested his colleagues would do to their captives should some passing reason alight. More than the disease-ridden darkness below deck, this disturbed them, and more than the corpses they sometimes awoke to after falling asleep pressed against a living person, this was something they whispered about.

When the captain announced that rations had become too few to complete the voyage with all his cargo, terror and resignation and even relief fell over those slaves who were herded to the poop deck that towered and tipped far above the sea, mostly women and children, though Maudit was among them because the man he was chained to had developed festering sores all over his legs and ankles and the bottoms of his feet, and this man was deemed unlikely to survive and not to command much at market if he did, and therefore he wasn't worth even the space he occupied below deck. The wind was powerful that morning and its buffeting gales sent the sea heaving and curling and crashing before rising anew, and Maudit watched as the slavers shoved and tossed dozens of people over the railings, their bodies limp as they tumbled through the air and vanished into the spume, and when Maudit's turn came the captain appeared and appraised him up and down, turning to a pink-eyed crewman and berating him at a holler, for Maudit was not yet jetsam, indeed such a designation applied only to the suppurating wreck of an investment he was chained to, and that man went over the side with a mumbled prayer and Maudit back to the cargo hold, where he tried not to enjoy the extra room.

After two months at sea he arrived in New Orleans, where he was sold at a slave auction to a Lower Creek Indian who'd made the trip from his farm on the west side of the Chattahoochee River. Many Creeks resisted the American way of life, but others were seduced. Like Americans they'd long valued cities and agriculture, and now progress had brought to their farms a ready supply of slave labour. The man who purchased Maudit called himself Big Bob of the Painted Rock, but his slaves called him Mr. Big, and it was Mr. Big who gave Maudit his name after he'd heard a sailor cursing in French before the auction and liked the sound of the word, never mind its meaning, that didn't concern him, rather he preferred English when it came to European languages, and of course Spanish as well. Maudit had learned the word from French settlers in his homeland and knew its meaning didn't bode well, but he accepted it nevertheless because he did not want to take up his real name in this new life across the Atlantic, at least not yet.

Mr. Big grew corn and squash, and he was a single man and every day he wore a white jacket with black stripes. He was thin and sun-burnt and most of his hair had fallen out and truly he enjoyed drinking with his friends and by himself as well, but he wasn't cruel when intoxicated, just unreliable and forgetful and not especially concerned about either. He had a number of children scattered about the Indian Territory, and sometimes they came to the farm for a visit and each time he sent them home with gifts.

Maudit was one of four slaves, but none of them were from Dahomey and they didn't know his religion. He himself hadn't learned enough of it before he was captured, so there was no way he could talk to the spirits of his family, no way to find their guidance. All he could do was work, and when Mr. Big saw how singularly focused Maudit was on squaring timbers for a loft or chopping wood for fuel or forking hay for feed or digging ditches for irrigation, le patron wanted to give him more responsibility and so trained him to look after the farm's beasts of burden, to feed them and yoke them and herd them to neighbouring farms when the money was right, and by then all the other slaves said that Maudit was the strongest man they'd ever seen, and one evening, to impress a slave girl named Pouch, he himself pulled the biggest plough across the furrowed fields, and no, he didn't break a sweat, même pas. Later, once the moon had fully risen over the stinking barn where lived the oxen, Maudit led Pouch inside and she let fall her shift so he could touch her naked breasts, and never would he forget how soft they were and also how wonderful the smell of hay and even how comforting the sound of mice scurrying through the brittle brown straw strewn about the cold dirt floor. Early the next morning, he took her to the shores of the Chattahoochee and waded to his waist then dove. With his fist he caught a largemouth bass and brought it ashore. They returned to the farm and had it for breakfast before beginning the day's labour, and many times in the proceeding months they lay together and took a breakfast of bass.

Now, aboard the stolen sailboat, Maudit smiled at the memory. He gave Alex another piece of bacon and stood and stretched and yawned. He tugged the hem of his tiny leather vest and positioned himself behind the helm of the boat and steered them onward. He spoke quietly but his voice was too strong for the breeze to scatter. After Maudit and Pouch had lain together many months, a gelding kicked Mr. Big in the head and his skull cracked and his neck snapped and he died on the ground looking up at the cloudy sky. Maudit stood over him and watched his eyes grow confused and terrified, then flat and empty, and he wondered if he'd witnessed some sort of divine justice, for wasn't Mr. Big was a slave-driver and a drunk and a traitor to his people and, indeed, to all peoples? Yes, but didn't Maudit's life on this farm include the company of Pouch, and was not her company a gift from the great being the other slaves referred to as the Goddess of Love? Yes, this was also true, and so Maudit did not concern himself with complicated notions of justice, only what made him happy.

One of Mr. Big's sons took over the farm. He called himself A Storm that Passes, and he was simple but kind, though given to explosions of rage that led him to whip the animals, and there came a night after just such an outburst that Maudit and Pouch lay together in the barn when A Storm that Passes barged in to vent his frustration on the oxen, but as the barn door swung open and the dull moonlight swept across the interior, le patron let fall his whip and asked Pouch if she wanted to join him in the house, and both she and Maudit understood this entreaty might quickly turn into something else, so she stood and pulled at the hem of her shift and walked out of the barn, leaving Maudit behind in the suddenly insufferable coarseness of the hay, and the two of them never slept next to each other again.

But he wasn't bitter. He understood Pouch would find succour in her arrangement and he was quietly glad her life had improved, but for him the farm contained no such solace, and so one night he absconded and made his way west through the forest and across the fields until he came to the banks of the Mississippi. The moon shone on the surface and revealed to him the spirit of the water, into which he dove.

At first, he swam south, hoping to return to New Orleans and maybe trace his way back to Dahomey, pourquoi pas, but conflict had come to the area as those Creek who practised the American way clashed with their brothers who didn't; the rains swept blood into the river, the taste of which filled Maudit with fear, and he came upon a young white soldier who'd been shot in the stomach and was bleeding out on the riverbank, and this man was delirious with agony and rage and he hurled insults at Maudit but posed no threat for he bore no weapon, he only spat and threw stones. Maudit went through his belongings and found some rations and ate them as the boy swatted at insects and screamed his abuse, and then with an earnest apology

Maudit left him to die, because how could he have helped and what would have been the consequences if he had?

Turning north, he swam for a few days without stopping. He concentrated on the movement of his arms and hoped A Storm that Passes would keep Pouch safe, as circumstances forbade him from doing so himself. He continued to swim, diving low to avoid merchant vessels. He fed on the great many fish he found all throughout the river's currents, and when he grew tired, which was rarely, he sloshed up the bank and hid in the tall grass so that hunters would not come across him, and he slept amid the croaking frogs and buzzing insects.

He wasn't surprised by his stamina, though he'd never put it to such a test. He was slowed only by his enduring grief for Pouch, whom he couldn't find the strength to forget, and when his imagination thrust forward unwanted images of her in rapturous congress with A Storm that Passes, Maudit found he had to stop swimming and float on his back and cry, sometimes for hours, during which time the current carried him back whence he came, and when his sadness passed he covered the distance again.

One morning he swam up the mid-river stretch and caught a largemouth bass and ate it in the usual way, underwater, raw, tendrils of blood darkening the current, except in greater abundance than usual, and with alarm he looked around and saw Pouch floating not far away. Her arm was missing and her throat had been slashed and blood stained the crotch of her shift and eddied about her thighs. Finger-shaped bruises covered her flesh, and he screamed and recoiled and thought he might inhale the river and drown as so many others since their displacement from Africa, but then he heard her voice in his head, and she apologized for her appearance, for she'd been killed in the mounting dispute between Creek factions.

Maudit swam toward her and tried to touch her, but his hand passed through her body and she explained that she was a ghost and the river spirit had allowed her to possess this small part of it in return for Maudit's dedication to swimming its currents and leaving many offerings of fish. She said the river spirit knew from other spirits that there was a body for her to inhabit in Upper Canada, and that was where she was headed so she could live again. Maudit asked where, but she didn't yet know, she was on a journey herself, there were many unknowns. To find her, he'd have to do what seemed right and go where seemed promising, and in this way they'd meet again and continue where they'd left off. Then her image grew vague and she vanished, leaving behind only her blood, which then vanished as well.

Full of hope now, Maudit swam past white settlements and Indian villages and sometimes people saw him and were either amazed or dismayed. Once a white fisherman shot at him and though he dove low he was unable to avoid the bullet, which cut through the water and grazed his shoulder but didn't cause him to tarry.

After a year, he arrived in Ohio, his clothes long since frayed and gone, and there he encountered a bear fishing along the shore, and though the animal roared and gnashed its teeth and stood on its hind legs, Maudit wasn't afraid – he kneeled before it until it calmed and continued its meal and after some minutes of watching this, he heard the footsteps of men and the cocking of rifles and then the explosion of gunpowder. Various points on the bear's body burst and bled and the animal fell into the water, displacing a large wave. These men wore military regalia, and one of them splashed into the shallows, pressed the stock of his gun against his shoulder, and stared down the barrel at Maudit, who still kneeled before the dying bear.

The men were several in number, a hunting party, and some of them went to the bear with big knives and slit its throat and set about butchering its flesh while others kept their weapons pointed at Maudit, and so it was that he spent a night in their camp, where they chained him to a tree. He could've broken these chains but found he didn't want the conflict, clearly these men were fools, it wouldn't be right for someone of his strength to wreak havoc on people so feeble, and further in a country such as this he recognized his strength as a kind of fiction, pas une vraie puissance, for even if he killed a thousand of these men his situation would never change, for the womb that bred them was out of his reach, as ever it would remain.

In the morning they brought him, still naked, to their town and handed him to a slave-herder who issued a bounty of some few dollars.

That same afternoon he was auctioned off at an illegal slave market, which was held in the woods at the base of a great oak. When he saw a tall man with a sheriff's star pinned to his chest, Maudit thought he might be set free, for long had he heard the north of this country didn't dabble in human chattel as did the south, but then the man began to bid on a fifteen-year-old girl with large white eyes, and Maudit came to understand that two opposing forces could occupy the same place without one having much influence over the other.

Emmanuel was in the crowd. He'd travelled from Lower Canada because his papa had heard of these occasional auctions and needed help on his orchard outside Trois-Rivières. They'd previously had slaves on their land, an Indian who'd run off successfully and an old African bought from a Loyalist, and that one had run off as well. Emmanuel's papa tracked him with dogs and shot him in the back three kilometres north of the property, so now he needed another.

The Canadien thought Maudit looked right for the job and bid two hundred and fifty dollars for a lifetime of service, which he was awarded. The full scope of Maudit's strength was revealed on the way home, after they'd crept across the border into Lower Canada. They were travelling down a remote road and came across a lone forester who'd felled a tree on his leg, and with barely a grunt Maudit lifted the trunk and freed the man. They took him to a nearby settlement where he could fetch a doctor, and after this Emmanuel announced they'd be changing course and heading back west, to the Town of York, where Emmanuel said they'd charge men and women money to watch Maudit perform feats of strength, and so it was that the tattooed sailor found work for Mr. Barnaby as a talent scout and the quiet giant became a performer.

As Maudit recounted his story, Alex found himself paying more and more attention to the tone of the telling, such that the sting of Emmanuel's slap and the absolute outrage that had preceded it began somewhat to fade, and in their place his mind began to circle a possible means of escaping this situation, a means perhaps rooted in a spirit of resignation that the strongman seemed to have disguised even from himself, and Alex noticed as well that Maudit's eyes darted repeatedly in the direction of the cabin hatch, beyond which Emmanuel took his repose. What would Serge have made of such an observation? Or Beaumont? What would Miigwan have done if he'd noticed such a thing? At the moment it seemed best only to note that Maudit was not fully aware of his power and so perhaps it didn't fully exist, not yet, and perhaps there'd come a time when Alex could summon it entirely and use it to his advantage, because he didn't plan to stay long with Emmanuel in York, absolument pas, there was simply no conceivable way he'd waste yet another episode of his life improving the lot of another man.

Maudit spoke only intermittently for the rest of the day, at one point telling Alex that life in Mr. Barnaby's Magical Spectacle of Marvels and Mystery wasn't so bad as at the outset it seemed, for though there was a constant disparity between the money one owed the company and that which it paid out, there was nevertheless a sort of pleasure to be found in the work. It was quelque chose de créatif, and Maudit now drew immense satisfaction from his strongman performance, which he undertook in partnership with a dwarf girl who claimed to be the disavowed daughter of a Russian royal. Her name was Natalya and together they entertained the people of York, mixing feats of strength with a romantic sub-plot, and slowly Maudit began to sense from Natalya something supernatural. He came to believe Pouch was manifesting in her body, he couldn't say why, but the knowledge was soothing and divine, and Natalya did nothing to dissuade it. Because the richness of his future was now foretold, the poverty of his present didn't bother him so.

And le voilà, the vulnerability Alex would use, the void he could fill with illusion, whatever it might be. This was a conniving ambition and Alex was dismayed to see it take such unsightly shape, however nebulous the form, and he worried his little brother might be offended by the ugliness, but when he turned his attention deeply inward he felt confident that no such umbrage had settled over the radiance of the light, for was Alex not justified in his desire to be free? Was there any man as estranged as he who didn't yearn for home? Was there any man who wouldn't bruise a few morals in his quest to get there? What was important was that he weighed these questions at all – he doubted other men bothered, non, he knew for a fact they did not.

Certainly Miigwan hadn't been troubled by such concerns, or maybe he'd considered them and judged their impacts desirable. Because Emmanuel was right, Alex's situation on Mackinac had been impossible, and it would've become only more so. He would've joined Emmanuel regardless of the terms, and besides, these terms were no different than those imposed by the American Fur Company or even the Beaumonts. So Miigwan had attacked Alex's sense of hope with the implausible pretense of family reunion, a harsh and crafty blow to a departing turncoat from a man who played even with the imagination and aspirations of his sister – to think Alex had flushed with love for l'Indien just the day before. Clearly Miigwan was endlessly skilled at this sort of fabrication, he'd done it to free himself of Rémi and likely he'd been the one who spread the story about the Dutchman and the bat cave, this to free himself of unabashed scrutiny.

But perhaps, thought Alex, twisting his fingers in his lap as he thought everything over, perhaps in his case the deception had been of sugar, not brine, for though Alex would've had little choice but to travel with Emmanuel in any event, the conditions were such that he would've done so with great trepidation, and it's even possible Alex would've tried to quit the island through some other means, and who could say what would've transpired then? Perhaps Miigwan actually resented Alex very little, actually understood something of the difficulties Alex had endured and understood as well the violence such tribulations wrought upon the soul. Perhaps he'd only wanted his battered friend far from his affairs, and the lie had filled Alex with an eagerness that was effectively strength, such that with it he took his leave of Mackinac full of spirit, a spirit that he could draw strength from even now that its source had been exposed as fraud – for what did strength owe its origins? Nothing, arrears weren't its concern, rather any debt could be decoupled and preserved, then redirected afar.

And so Alex concluded that Miigwan had been a good friend who'd helped him overcome illness and conjure new fortitude, not once but numerous times, and Alex, in a flush of desire, had betrayed his confidence. That could never be changed. He could only acknowledge the kind of person he'd been and do his best to improve whatever had made him so.

What mattered now was life had offered Alex another opportunity, or he'd recognized one in the endless interpretations of a given circumstance, and was not this sort of recognition what strong and capable men relied upon to advance their positions? Was chance not a sort of fur adventurous men rushed to market? Surely it was, and with his 'tit frère inside him, Alex knew he could find the strength to seize this very opportunity, just as he'd watched others do throughout the whole of his life – he could become a true friend to Maudit and pass on something of the gift he'd received from Miigwan.

All throughout the day Maudit didn't sleep but manned the helm and sometimes left his post to adjust the sails or pick through their supplies for dried meat or fish, which he shared with Alex, though apologetically he said he'd have to inform Emmanuel of how much food Alex chose to eat. When the star-spangled night fell at last, Maudit recommended Alex tie a rope around his waist in case he was pitched over the boat as he slept, but Alex said c'était pas nécessaire, he'd learned to swim, though he didn't explain how – not yet. It wasn't the time to tell Maudit about his 'tit frère and the manner through which Alex had come to meet him: drowning, and perhaps not far from here. Alex curled up on the creaking deck and Maudit sprawled out beside him, and every hour or two throughout the night, Alex awoke when Maudit rose to check the sails and adjust the helm, the deck creaking as he brought himself down for another spell of rest. In the morning Alex awoke to the cliffs of Georgian Bay looming all around them, and high above a hawk circled downward, gracefully and with purpose.

49

EVENTUALLY THEY EXITED THE LAKE INTO THE MOUTH OF
a river called the Severn, and they made landfall as gossamer clouds
obscured the blue skies and grew increasingly leaden. Emmanuel
told Maudit to load the rowboat with their trunks and provisions
and drag it along, and this the strongman did without complaint as
the trio travelled on foot until nightfall, during which they made to
rest, Emmanuel in a tent, Alex under a blanket, and Maudit against
the base of a tree at the perimeter of their camp. In the morning,
Emmanuel changed his clothes, taking a folded shirt from one of
the trunks and remarking to Maudit that in all the excitement of
recruiting Alex he'd forgotten to remind the strongman to do laundry
when they were on Mackinac, and why had Maudit not remembered
himself? His arms full of wood for their breakfast fire, Maudit apologized and said he'd also been excited, and at this Emmanuel simply
stared at him, his expression neutral, until Maudit again mumbled
an apology and kneeled and began arranging the wood to burn. Alex
watched as Emmanuel sat on a rock and spread a shaving kit out
before him, removing a straight razor with a handle made of brilliant
white bone from a stained wooden case and opening it with obvious
reverence, his back straight and his chin tucked and his lips pressed
lightly together. In the spindly branches of a nearby tree crows gabbled
and cawed, and when they took flight they seemed not so much to
depart the area as to be absorbed by the gloom, and Alex followed
them into the woods to empty his bowels, searching for the peach
stone he'd stowed in his fistula, but it remained inside him, which was

at first upsetting but then seemed right, his brother was holding on to it, using it for strength.

Later that day they stole two emaciated horses from a farm, one for Alex and one for Emmanuel. Alex looked at the darkened windows of the farmhouse and the empty stretches of the fields and he prayed that an incensed farmer would appear with powerful arms and calloused hands to beat Emmanuel's teeth out of his mouth, hurt him so severely that tears would spring from his eyes and his too-fine trousers darken with piss, but the place was seemingly deserted, and Emmanuel told Maudit to pilfer a wagon with peeling red paint. Maudit transferred their supplies from the rowboat to the wagon, pulling them without complaint as the trail heaved and pitched and widened and narrowed.

They pushed on for a stretch of grey days that smeared together like gruel, their specific number beyond Alex's faculties of recognition, and throughout the long hours of wordless motion, he kept his mind focused on his goal of somehow enlisting Maudit into his service, and he noticed as well that although Emmanuel shaved every morning and parted his hair down the middle before they took to their sad-dles, he'd used the last of his clean clothes, for slowly whorls of dirt distinguished them and the underarms of his shirts bore sweat stains that reached down his ribs.

In this fashion they continued south, the road gradually declining and the ground becoming wet and tempests of flies swirling about their heads. Gradually the forest gave way to deserted settlements, their cemeteries dotted with fresh mounds, and they were only occa-sionally forced to share passage with a carriage or wagon drawn by horses, and the travellers regarded one another with suspicion and seemed to shrink into their saddles or carriages. When finally they reached the northern boundary of York, they came across a barricade of militiamen in scuffed red coats, their white sashes sullied drab. They'd established themselves in front of a small tavern, and on either side of the road were barrels of flaming tar from which great columns of black smoke twisted into the heavy sky.

'Halt,' cried one of these men, advancing with his rifle at the ready, and behind him there followed a shorter man dressed in a black suit, his face like a shrivelled grape surrounded by a thick burst of curly brown hair.

'What is it?' barked Emmanuel.

The man in the suit pushed past the soldier and made a quizzical arch of his eyebrows, and Alex looked down upon him and saw something like fear hidden beneath an otherwise official bearing.

'Where have you come from?' asked the man, his gaze moving from Emmanuel to Alex and then, with a redoubled arch of his eyebrows, Maudit.

'We've been entertaining the people of the countryside.' Emmanuel's English was flawless and his accent completely natural. 'Countryfolk enjoy a performance just as merrily as the elites of York.'

'Entertaining them? Indeed. And how long have you been gone? And where?'

'Over a month now. West of here, and south. What's the meaning of this interrogation?'

'Dismount,' said the man, waving impatiently. 'Both of you. And you, away from the wagon. There's a health crisis afoot. Cholera. York is rife with it, and so are the environs. I must examine you before you can be allowed to continue.'

The man introduced himself as a health officer, though he offered no name, and he led the three of them into the tavern. Before the threshold was a mound of lime and the health officer stamped his feet in the grey dust and directed his charges to do the same. The inside of the tavern was dark and spare and a few soldiers slumped over a table and tended to their drams. The health officer nodded at the soldiers and continued to a back room with a desk and a few chairs, and he directed all to sit.

He took the chair across from them and began his examination, asking them if they'd been experiencing cramps and how much alcohol did they generally imbibe and had they been in the company of disreputable women. Emmanuel was the first to answer in the negative and then Maudit replied likewise, and after a short pause so did Alex.

The health officer frowned and turned again to Emmanuel, regarding the clothing that even though sullied perhaps suggested uncommon means. He tapped the desk with his index finger, twice, then gestured at Maudit. 'South, you said you went. Across the border, I'm made to understand? I trust you're not undertaking the importation of this fellow here?'

'Of course not, sir. His father was bequeathed by mine own, and he is here of his own accord.'

Alex was again struck by Emmanuel's English, and he imagined him practising in the dark, sitting on the edge of a bed, his back straight and his palms resting on his knees.

'Ah, I see,' said the health officer. 'So you're a Loyalist?'

'The blood pumps through my every vein. My father brought the family north after he wore red with pride during the American War.'

The health officer smiled and nodded and said, 'But pulling a wagon for God knows how long – tell me, is he beyond twenty-five? Have you papers to prove it?'

Emmanuel tilted his head and exhaled slowly. 'He is indeed, sir, as I've only just indicated. This man is no slave. He's indentured in my employ, isn't that so, Monsieur Maudit?'

Alex watched as Maudit confirmed with an enthusiastic nod.

'And papers? You know the law, sir.'

'No papers, sir. You know the practice.'

The health officer offered a smile and a nod, and he drummed his fingers on the desk once again. 'Very well. And where do you stay in York?'

'We live in a hotel.'

At this the health officer raised an eyebrow. 'Oh? Which hotel?'

'Is that important?'

'I've posed the question, haven't I? The illness has turned far too many of these squalid little water-holes into dens of rebellion. Which one are you lot calling home?'

Emmanuel sighed and with a slight lift of his chin told the health officer they were staying at a tavern called Tonight Only.

'Never heard of the place. You're sure it's a Loyalist establishment?'

A look of mild offence crossed Emmanuel's features. 'It was when I left and no doubt will remain always. I wouldn't have it any other way.'

The health officer ran a hand through his bountiful hair and regarded them suspiciously, his withered face gathered about his narrow eyes. 'Very well. You may continue, but first I must have your belongings searched. Blankets and the like will be put to the flame.'

He led them out of the room and through the tavern, where now the soldiers were all joined together in laughter. Outside, they followed the health officer to the wagon and the man snapped his fingers and pointed at their possessions and from behind arrived two militiamen. They approached the wagon with great hesitation, and one of them with wide green eyes and trembling hands unlatched their trunks and began picking through their belongings. Emmanuel's face darkened as the men emptied the trunks and brought his clothing and the blankets to one of the burning barrels, the flames briefly subdued as the soldiers fed the fire, and then they reported to the health officer with the provisions hung over their shoulders and a few assorted items loose in their hands.

'Look here, sir,' said one of them, extending Emmanuel's shaving kit to the health officer. 'Has a compelling weight, it does.'

Alex watched as Emmanuel's fingers curled and their tips sank into the shadow of his palm. The health officer took the kit and undid the buckle that held it together and whistled at the sight of its contents, removing the straight razor and turning it this way and that before tossing the rest back to his underling. 'A lovely piece,' he said, folding the metal out of the bone. 'And you won't mind making a gift of it, will you, sir? As per the aforementioned practice?'

Emmanuel nodded but said nothing.

'Very well,' said the health officer, looking them over with fading scrutiny. 'You may proceed. And we'll keep the wagon for ourselves, empty now as it is.'

The authorities went on to harass a lone man dressed in rags and leading a donkey, and Alex and Emmanuel remounted their horses and Maudit trudged alongside as they crossed the barricade and put the tavern behind them. Emmanuel wasn't angry over the loss of his clothes and shaving kit as expected, a curious observation, rather he turned his head from side to side as if the drab woods that flanked the road were somehow pleasant to behold. About a kilometre down the muddy road, they came across a toothy boy chewing a few strands of hay and hawking editions of a newspaper called the *Colonial Advocate*. Emmanuel brought his horse alongside the boy, who was damned by a cloud of flies and whose torn trousers were filthy to the knees. Tossing the boy a coin, Emmanuel asked Alex to read the headlines and articles as they continued, and when Alex was silent and regarded the paper with an ignorance he couldn't conceal, Emmanuel chuckled and asked Maudit to undertake the task instead.

The strongman took the paper with an apologetic purse of his lips. "'The mag… the magi…'" He looked up and shrugged. 'Un mot pluriel, en tout cas.'

'The magistrates,' offered Emmanuel. 'Come now. That was an easy one. Focus. And speak English, mind. No more French.'

Maudit cleared his throat and continued. "'The magistrates have failed us and now the… the quacks have come to town. Neither will help the people of York in their fight against disease.'"

Alex was disgusted with the sight of Maudit shuffling through the mud and reading aloud, not because Maudit knew letters and Alex didn't but because he saw in Maudit's relationship with Emmanuel something of what he'd undergone on Mackinac with Beaumont: oppression gilded with reward, and he wondered if this rapport might interfere somewhat with the influence he intended to extend over the strongman, and immediately he realized that it would – and yet as well it could be overcome.

Emmanuel issued a long, low whistle and clapped his hands, the reins dangling from his thumbs. He congratulated Maudit on a fine reading and said the first step was sounding out difficult words and later, when their shape had taken firm hold in Maudit's mind, Emmanuel would instruct him as to the nuances of their meaning. He motioned for Maudit to pass him the paper, and in exchange he handed over the reins of his horse so that Maudit now led the beast, and Emmanuel, in a cadence approaching song, continued to read.

Cholera had travelled from India to Europe and now to the colonies. Immigrant ships arriving in the St. Lawrence were stopped at

Grosse Île. The sick were quarantined, and survivors told harrowing stories of death and burial at sea. The disease had wriggled its way up the river, striking Québec City and also Montréal, where its victims were many, and Alex imagined M. Anderson's demise, the horrid Scot dead on the floor of his store, his face as blue as a river on a clear day, though likely M. Anderson would've been spared, for the article went on to describe the poor and their back slums as the hardest-hit areas, and in M. Anderson's place Alex saw the man who attacked him at the hotel in Montréal, recovered from the beating bestowed by Serge only to be felled by a pauper's illness, and likewise those voyageurs who'd abandoned him in the wilderness, their bodies leaking dry in the woe-benighted whorehouses along the port. He imagined all this, and he smiled.

"'Citizens of York,'" Emmanuel continued, "'the magistrates will have you believe that moral degradation is the cause of the disease, that cholera is the sad hell of the drunkard, the indigent, and the unwashed. No doubt there is a kernel of truth to this. But why are we poor? Why drunk and unwashed? Because the magistrates continue to hoard public funds. They continue to support the venal Loyalists who keep the company of John Robinson and Bishop Strachan and other members of the wretched Family Compact. These men are the true source of our pestiferous midnight, and it is up to us to resist them.'" He chuckled and folded the paper and handed it to Maudit, shaking his head. 'Imagine spending your life devoted to the tireless idiocy of this politics. What a waste when there are such better livings to be made on the side of your enemy.'

50

THE ROAD BECAME STEEPER STILL AND THE AIR STAGNANT
and warm, and as mosquitoes harried them in clouds, Alex had the
impression of entering a swamp. York was a sad place hacked out of
the marshes of the lake and disease had come to suck it back under-
ground. It contained little of the grandeur of Montréal and Alex
couldn't imagine it ever would, and yet Emmanuel said people were
settling the town in droves, who knew why, people just moved about
and suddenly they stopped, exhausted, and wherever they stopped they
tried to make money, and if they died in the effort, so be it, maybe
they'd ascend to God and in His kingdom break bread with loved ones
who'd already claimed their eternal reward.

As they approached Lot Street, they began to smell the area, and
soon enough there were houses and grocery stores and taverns, mostly
squat brick buildings rising from muddy plots. They saw an abandoned
coach with its wheels half-submerged in the muck outside a tavern,
and Emmanuel shook his head and wondered aloud why anyone would
choose to make a town in a wetland, even an Englishman. There were
stretches of milled boards underfoot, but they weren't continuous and
anyway their conditions were poor. Barrels of burning tar were positioned here and there and Alex saw at the threshold of some buildings
mounds of lime such as he'd seen during the health officer's inspection.
These smells were intense and they burned his nose and underneath
there was a heavy odour of shit – horse, cow, human – which revealed
itself fully when a lost gust of wind blew clear the fumes of tar, and
they passed a tavern outside of which people convened all dressed in

black, and the women were in tears and the men smoked their pipes with faces solemn; through the open doors, Alex saw a coffin in the centre of the room, and it was small, as though a child's.

After a time they came upon a two-storey building with one of the upper windows boarded over, and there was a sign above the door that read THE COOPER IN HIS BARREL, and the front door was open wide and inside was yet another tavern and outside were hitching posts, all of them unoccupied, and Emmanuel led his horse to one of these and dismounted. Alex's hands and neck itched fiercely from mosquito bites and he jumped off his horse and watched as Maudit smiled like a child and stepped out of the mud and onto the porch. The beaten wood groaned under his weight, and when he reached the top, he tugged his thumbs at the armholes of his leather vest and turned to no one in particular and said, 'Finalement!'

'Speak English,' replied Emmanuel, looking about the street with unmasked revulsion. 'As one does in York.'

Maudit glanced at him and nodded but was too excited to be chastened. He was about to cross the threshold but was prevented from entering the tavern when in the doorway there appeared a short man wearing a stained apron, his blond beard sparse and his bald head sweating, and in one hand he held an empty mug and in the other a filthy rag. He spat in the muddy street and with a quiet, strained voice he said, 'Where have you *been*, sir?'

Maudit giggled and said, 'Good afternoon, Mr. Mitchell.'

Mr. Mitchell tilted his head up to Maudit and narrowed his eyes, then turned back to Emmanuel. 'We've been blighted, man. Over a month of clean floors in this place. You owe me money, you do, and if you want to keep a roof over your heads, you'll settle up and get me some customers too.'

Standing quietly in the mud, Alex watched as Emmanuel climbed the stairs and looked from Mr. Mitchell to his own shoes, which were filthy, and he sighed and took stock of his clothing, soiled as well. 'Mr. Mitchell, you appear harried, sir, and indeed there's something of a shroud over the town. Don't tell me this cholera is having a negative effect on your operations?'

Alex joined them on the porch as Mr. Mitchell cleared the door to permit the strongman's entry, and the whole building shook as Maudit hurried inside.

Mr. Mitchell clenched his rag and exhaled through his nose, and Alex heard the very mud of the streets rattle in the man's nostrils. 'I've seen naught but that subversive band of labourers who buy only a dram each and a bowl of stew before scurrying off to further foment their unrest in taverns not my own. I say again: You owe me a crowd. In the absence of such a thing, it's legal tender you owe, for you and your lot.'

'Was there not entertainment in my absence?'

Mr. Mitchell's eyes landed on Alex and probed his face before returning to Emmanuel. His voice softened somewhat. 'The cholera car has been round, sir. The cemetery at St. James is full of fresh mounds, and there's talk of several bodies to a grave.'

'Tragedy visits us all.' Emmanuel gestured at Alex. 'But never fear, Mr. Mitchell. I've found a new performer out there among the hordes of the Great Lakes. This boy will draw back your guests, disease be damned.'

Mr. Mitchell turned his attention to Alex once more and they regarded each other, merely a slice of stinking air between them. A bead of sweat ran down Mr. Mitchell's temple and was absorbed by a tuft of his beard. He curled his lip and tossed his mug from one hand to the other. 'How do you propose he'll do that, then?'

'He has a gift.' Emmanuel put his hand on Alex's shoulder. 'Show him, Alex.'

Alex had sensed the moment coming. He understood his role in Emmanuel's vision and understood as well that now was not the time to resist these small humiliations but to embrace them without hesitation, for he felt there was some opportunity lurking in how little disturbed Emmanuel had been by the loss of his shaving kit, that and the clothes he'd managed to keep clean for so much of the journey — there was something there, something that could perhaps be taken. Alex pulled up his shirt and with his other hand peeled back the flap of flesh that covered his hole. His skin was scraped and dirty and the rim of the fistula slightly inflamed, and it pulsated as he drew a deep breath and exhaled.

Mr. Mitchell's mouth fell open and his breath caught audibly. He took a step back. 'What in God's name?'

Emmanuel smiled and gave Alex's shoulder a gentle shake. 'All that goes in the boy's mouth can be directed either into the dark abyss of his body or, via a secret conduit that exits through that hole, back into daylight.'

Regaining himself, Mr. Mitchell stepped forward again. 'I don't see the advantage in revolting what few customers I have remaining.'

'Ah,' said Emmanuel, 'but this sort of thing is all the rage in Europe, sir. As it will be here.'

The tavernkeeper took his rag from his shoulder and polished his mug. He looked onto the street and then at Emmanuel. He opened his mouth to speak, but before he could there came from deep inside the tavern a roar of agony so sudden Mr. Mitchell dropped his mug and it rolled off the porch and with a splash was swallowed by the mud of the street.

There came another roar, even more anguished, and Alex recognized the resonance as Maudit's. Instinctively, he moved toward the door, but Mr. Mitchell gripped his shoulder and looked to Emmanuel and said, 'As I mentioned, sir. The cholera car has been round. I'm sorry to report you've lost a performer to the sickness. We did our best to make her comfortable.'

51

THE VICTIM WAS NATALYA, THE DWARF OF MAUDIT'S FANCY. Mr. and Mrs. Mitchell had lent her a special room above the tavern and she'd passed away in the night a week before, her only company a man named Richard who performed as a clown in Mr. Barnaby's organization. It had been Richard who informed Maudit of the loss while Emmanuel negotiated with Mr. Mitchell, and with the party now convened in the scullery, it was Richard, in his thick Irish accent, who told them that Maudit had fled the tavern in a storm of grief, exiting through the back at such a speed as to displace all the mud of the alley.

Alex crossed his arms and lowered his chin and watched the clown continually apologize to Emmanuel, who offered no comfort, demanding instead to know Maudit's whereabouts. Richard described Natalya's final hours with a trembling voice, sniffling, and Alex thought him utterly foolish in checkered suspenders and a woman's floral blouse but a man's black trousers. His hands were wide as dinner plates and his chin curled away from his face like the handle of a teapot, and all he could do was point out the back entrance at the deep trench excavated by Maudit's passage and the mud drying to the alley walls.

'If ye'll give me some time,' said the clown, 'I'm sure I can find him. And again, I'm so sorry for the bother, but Mr. Maudit was keen to see the lass, you know they got on so well, and I just couldn't keep from him the horrible news – it wouldn't have been right, sir. I'm sorry for the bother, sir, truly I am.'

Alex uncrossed his arms and drew on his brother's light as he stepped in front of the stammering clown. 'Me, I will find the Mr.

Maudit. Please, Mr. Emmanuel. I know he will like to see me. I know I will like to bring him back here and we will help him to be sad and then he will be better and people will come to the tavern again.'

'Aye,' said Richard, 'but who are ye, b'y?'

'You'll come to know him soon enough,' said Emmanuel. He licked his lips and scrutinized Alex's face. 'He appears to be coming around to his new situation. Go and find Monsieur Maudit, Alex. Myself, I'll take the time to get cleaned up.'

Alex lowered himself into the alley and hurried through the mud. He had no idea what he'd say when he found Maudit, no idea what he'd do, but he felt sure his little brother would help him when the time arrived. Maudit had left his mark down the alley and through the streets: his footprints had landed so deep that the sludge could fill them but slowly; at the mouth of the alley, where evidently he'd clipped the side of the building, the brickwork was cracked and crumbling, red dust sprinkling the ground like flakes of blood. Alex slogged down the alley and rounded the tavern and stepped into Lot Street, looking left and right. A block to the east, a grocer waded through the mud to gather fallen vegetables, and Alex imagined Maudit overturning the produce stands as he tore hysterically away.

Hurrying past the grocer, Alex took up a trail dotted by signs of Maudit's passage: the deep trench in the muddy streets, the brickwork crumbling from the corners of the buildings, the men calming their horses and the women pointing and whispering. Afternoon tipped into evening and with it came a renewed onslaught of mosquitoes, and Alex slapped at his neck and arms as he continued south past a seemingly endless array of brothels and taverns. Eventually he came to Front Street and looked onto the lake and saw the peninsula curve like a crescent moon from the shore farther east, where it sheltered the harbour from the brunt of the open lake before arching west. Sailships tipped about the waves and the sun sank toward the horizon and beams of crimson light flowed through a tattered bank of clouds like streams from Heaven. Men camped on the beach, their settlement a vile mess of smouldering firepits and muddy clothing hanging from lines strung between sticks speared upright in the loose sand. Near the water, a shrieking flock of gulls tore at a fishing net tangled around what initially appeared to be a rock in the surf but then revealed itself as Maudit's hunkered form. Alex hesitated, thinking, and all at once he understood what to do, and he knew what would happen.

'Maudit!' He ran toward the strongman, and the beach gave way to mud and stank of fish and feces, sucking at his boots as he hobbled along. Maudit's face was hidden in his hands, and gulls scattered from the great and trembling slope of his back as Alex kneeled in the mud and touched the strongman's shoulder. In French the words came freely: 'Maudit! Everything is not yet lost! I've received a special gift!'

Maudit didn't lift his face from his hands but spoke into the darkness of his palms: 'I thought I might find her in the water.' He said he'd thrown himself into the harbour and was prepared to find his way back south, back to the Mississippi, where he might've met Pouch's spirit once more, for she was nowhere to be found in the mucky sink of York, but now he was tired for the first time in what felt like years, and he'd become entangled in a fishing net and thought to let himself drown as he sank to the bottom. It was dark down there and he came to rest beside a rusted ship anchor barely visible in the gloom, its short length of broken chain nudged by the current, and he thought that he'd found an ideal place to finally stop breathing, for his destiny had long been to drown, but it occurred to him that Pouch's spirit would find another vessel, as it had done once already, whereas he couldn't be sure his own spirit could do the same. What if they became separated, she wandering the Earth and he the heavens? He turned and walked along the harbour floor, headed for shore, the net twisting in the current behind him, and eventually he emerged and came to rest in the mud.

'It's good you made that decision,' said Alex, grinning, 'because the gift I mentioned is in fact the spirit of Pouch. She's inside me now.'

Maudit lifted his face from the cup of his palms. His eyes were small and glassy in the great expanse of his face, and a sodden length of netting hung from his chin as he shook his head in disbelief.

'C'est vrai,' said Alex. 'This will sound strange, it will sound impossible, and that's why I haven't yet told you – I've never told anyone – but actually my body is home to my young brother, home to his esprit. He died before I was born, died when he was just a baby, but he lives in me now and he helps me in my journey. Don't you see? I'm just like Natalya. She's not the only one. I'm like her too.'

Maudit turned his face to the setting sun. He was amenable to such a proposition, Alex knew. His life had made him such, his life and journey, and he didn't wax incredulous but rather looked to Alex with something like relief, though a good deal of exasperation as well. 'But why didn't you tell me this earlier?'

'I didn't think you'd believe me. Nobody believes such a thing.'

'And you're saying that Pouch is there too? She lives with your brother? Inside of you? How can this be that you have so much space? You must prove it.'

The sun sank farther and lit up the distant surface of the lake with slashes of violet and rouge. Maudit straightened his shoulders and Alex saw about his lips a twitch of excitement.

"Garde,' said Alex, slowly lifting his shirt to expose his fistula, and as soon he began the motion he felt the light rise from inside and spill out of his body, brighter than he'd ever imagined possible, and it was warm, he felt a soothing heat all about his chest, and as he lifted his shirt to his chin he saw that light land on Maudit's face, bathing it in a heavenly softness, and with the light there came the smell of peaches and lake weeds. The worry lines around Maudit's mouth melted away, his furrowed brow turned smooth, awe sparkled in his eyes and his lips trembled and his eyelashes fluttered and he raised one of his hands into the light and turned it this way and that and then he raised the other one and did the same. 'Oh my love,' he kept saying, his eyes brimming with tears. 'Oh my sweet love.'

They walked slowly back to Mr. Mitchell's tavern as dusk settled over York. Gaslights burned in the windows of a few upscale taverns, and torches flamed in the streets. Above them a half moon shone brightly and the stars were tiny but their numbers infinite. Alex felt the thrill of acquiring another's credulity, and he realized Serge must have felt this way when Alex invited him to stay the night in the back of M. Anderson's store, and Beaumont had been equally thrilled when

Alex left his mark on their first contract. Indeed the sensation was exhilarating. He'd become one of those men in the world who through luck and guile and timing and opportunity had been able to conduct events in his favour, or at least he'd managed to direct things that way, to get them started. Maudit's loyalty was just the beginning, now came the question of what to do with it, how to mould it, what to extract, and quickly a vision of emancipation took shape in his mind, held up to his attention by the glittering reach of his 'tit frère: Emmanuel had money – a man who brought a fancy shaving kit and multiple changes of clothes into the wilderness even as he stole from others what he needed only briefly, this was a man who had a reserve, and likely he kept it in his room above the tavern.

Alex looked at Maudit, bits of the fishing net still clinging to the giant's hulking back, trailing behind like tinsel, and on his face a smile he couldn't seem to suppress, but this visage made too clear the absence of grief, and Alex moved now to address the danger, for it was imperative that Emmanuel not discover what had transpired on the beach, and it was imperative as well that Maudit begin to think, however reluctantly, of a life beyond his performance in Mr. Barnaby's Magical Spectacle of Marvels and Mystery. 'Écoute, Maudit.' He stopped and wrapped his hand around the girth of the strongman's wrist. 'You understand that we'll have to leave York, you and me and the spirits I contain. You see this, do you not?'

Maudit looked down, his brow creased. 'Leave? But why? We're all four of us here.'

Alex let go of Maudit's wrist and strode a few paces ahead. 'I will explain later,' he said over his shoulder, 'but for now what has happened with Pouch must remain between us.'

He heard Maudit begin moving after him. 'But why, Alex? Is this not a cause for celebration? She lives on!'

'She has said she might not stay if Emmanuel and the others discover the arrangement.' Alex looked back and shrugged. 'I can't yet understand why, but for now it is critical you continue to look aggrieved, tu comprends?'

Maudit shook his head. 'Mais non. I don't understand.'

'Maybe,' said Alex, trying to conceal the pleasure of his connivance, 'she fears he will use her again, the way he does everything else, and she is too fragile to go through it even one more time, too tired after her journey within Natalya and then from Natalya to me.'

The gravity of this seemed to shake Maudit, for there was no reply, just the sounds of his heavy feet landing in the mud.

'Imagine that we are in a snowy wood,' said Alex as he turned onto Lot Street and saw a gaslight flickering above the porch of The Cooper in His Barrel. 'We'll find our way out, bien sûr, but first you must follow in my footsteps to avoid getting lost.'

52

THE FOLLOWING MORNING, EMMANUEL HELD A MEETING OF
Mr. Barnaby's surviving employees, and Alex was fully prepared, for
he'd lain awake much of the night in focused contemplation, knowing
he'd be called upon to describe just what he could contribute to the
coming performance. He slept in the same tiny room as Richard and
Maudit, a servants' quarters above the tavern and down the hall from
a few guest rooms, one of which was Emmanuel's. There was a small,
thin window such as there'd been at the back of M. Anderson's store
and there were also two bunks against the walls with barely five feet
between them, and Maudit had sheepishly asked Alex to sleep above
Richard in the event Pouch's spirit elected to drift free of Alex's body
and take up Natalya's bedding over Maudit. Alex said he'd do his best
to encourage her to roam free, and throughout the night he occasionally stole glances at Maudit spilling off his mattress in every direction,
eyes wide open and fixed on the bunk above. In the morning, Alex
checked the upper mattress to see if the thin sheet had been ruffled
or otherwise disturbed, and he couldn't be sure what Maudit had seen
there, or what he'd persuaded himself to see, but likely it favoured the
notion of a visitation from Pouch, for he looked to Alex and tried to
suppress a happy grin before going about his morning duties in service
of Emmanuel.

Now, though he hadn't much slept, Alex sat comfortably across
from Richard, who wore the same checkered suspenders over a yellow
blouse and on his face a wooden mask defined almost entirely by its
crimson twist of a grin and two wide eyes painted totally black. From

beneath his mask came his muffled voice: 'But where's the stew? And what of the liquor?'

The table was almost bare. Mrs. Mitchell had taken her breakfast there; Alex saw her nibbling a heel of bread and she left a crumpled napkin yellowed with butter at which Emmanuel now curled his lip, and with his index finger extended he knocked it into Richard's lap, but the clown pretended not to be bothered. Emmanuel wore a black coat and a red cravat and a white top hat. Gone from his person were the filth and soot of travel, and as for the mire of the town, he seemed better able to fend it off now that he'd scrubbed himself clean. The night before, Alex listened as Maudit delivered a bathing tub full of warm water to Emmanuel's quarters, the stairs creaking as Mrs. Mitchell took up after him, quietly admonishing Maudit for using precious wood to heat the stove; she trailed him all the way down the hall, whispering furiously that he must get Emmanuel to settle at least some of his account, for she was no fool, she knew he kept a reserve, that could plainly be seen, but she broke off when a door creaked slowly open and Emmanuel's voice filled the hall, telling Maudit to hurry before the water cooled. Now, seated at the head of the table, Emmanuel knuckled the hat off his forehead and scowled. 'The Mitchells will not indulge us with such perquisites at the moment, Richard. We must deliver a show this weekend, and you must draw a crowd. I shouldn't have to tell you that.'

Maudit sat to Emmanuel's right, his bare and burly arms folded on the table. Alex was increasingly concerned that the strongman wasn't exhibiting the appropriate degree of grief, and he wondered if Emmanuel had noticed as well, if his eyes were probing Maudit's face in search of a fraud or if scrutiny was merely the constant quality of his attention.

'The time has come for us to have a little meeting,' Emmanuel continued, 'in order that we might discuss the state of Mr. Barnaby's operation.'

Richard slumped in his chair, countenance eerily that of a doll, and in a chastised voice he said, 'Aye, we've all noticed the decline in audience, Mr. Emmanuel, but surely we cannot be held to fault for the

282

arrival of an epidemic, an act of God if ever one was.' He paused and could be heard to swallow beneath his disguise. 'Though if we are to be faulted, then rightly shall we shoulder the full weight of said fault, as it's not our place to deflect responsibility but rather to bear it.'

Emmanuel heaved an irritated sigh. They were among the only people gathered in the tavern, otherwise a trio of labourers in the shadowy back, but though it was lunchtime these men took no meal, instead they'd each had a pour of beer and now they sat in front of their empty glasses and carried on in whispered voices, their eyes darting sometimes to the door, and Alex assumed they were among the rebellious lot Mr. Mitchell had yesterday described.

'Save your rambling for the stage,' said Emmanuel to Richard.

'Yes, sir,' replied the clown. 'Ye might say I'm a bit disturbed over the passing of Natalya, and accordingly I've a tendency to forget myself, even at a meeting such as this, with its themes so dire.'

Maudit didn't tremble or shift as he should've at the sound of Natalya's name, for he was ever lacking in guile and Alex would need to labour steadily to conceal this from Emmanuel's suspicion, so he hurried to fill the silence: 'Me, I am confident to replace her with my own performance. I dream about it last night.'

Emmanuel turned and settled his remote eyes on Alex's face. 'You're taking to your new life with enthusiasm,' he noted, but he didn't smile, and then one of the labourers across the room gave over to a fit of coughing and all in the tavern eyed him warily, and when his eruption had subsided he looked about the room and offered an apologetic wave, bubbling in his Dutch accent that he was feeling fine, yes, fine, the tobacco had caused him to cough, that was all, a pipe in need of a cleaning, nothing more, no need to worry, he was a healthy man, a most healthy man.

All eyes made their uncertain way from the labourer to Alex, who began describing how he planned to roost among the audience, sitting at a table alone, and when the time came he'd call out to Mrs. Mitchell for a light meal, something to fill the low corners of his belly, and she'd bring him a few hunks of sausage. He'd eat one or two of these and then from his bag remove a lump of coal and a sheet of paper and

283

begin wordlessly drawing and eating hunks of meat, as if he had the room all to himself. After a few moments, a look of discomfort would cross his face and he'd leave off his drawing and with one hand clutch his side. He'd frown and groan and feign a pending sickness and then he'd reach up into his shirt and begin to remove the pieces of sausage individually from his fistula, and these he'd return to the plate and the plate he'd pass around so that the audience could see that the meat was indeed from the original serving, and once this knowledge had settled he'd pass the drawing around and explain that this hole on the page was in fact in his body, and when no one understood he'd stand and lift his shirt and show his ghastly aperture to all, and from it he'd remove another hunk of meat right before their very eyes, and here Richard groaned, the sound a low vibration rattling the centre of his mask.

Ignoring this, Alex said he wouldn't allow the audience's gaze to linger on his wound, rather he'd cover himself quickly and pass his drawing around. This would be a depiction of Alex himself, Alex au complet, curled up on a wooden floor, shot in the stomach and tended to by a man on his knees, his face in shadows. After everyone had witnessed the miracle of his anatomy, he'd exit the tavern and enter the streets, and he'd double around to the alley and re-enter the building from behind, no one the wiser. They'd have only their memories of his performance to make sense of what they'd seen, though one of them would also have the drawing, and surely this person would go forth and tell others, there could be little doubt, and those others would be drawn to the tavern despite the epidemic, so strong would their curiosity be, strong enough to suspend their certainty that they were among the next to take ill, and in the place of that horrid truth would come the notion that what they truly deserved was a night of unparalleled entertainment, why not.

It was hard to explain all this in English and he stumbled and many times had to rely on his hands to carry his meaning, but even when expression failed him he retained the attention of all those at the table, including Emmanuel, whose focus had seemed to divert from Maudit and settle almost entirely on Alex.

'Very good,' Emmanuel said, touching the brim of his hat in faint salutation. 'Very, very good. Here, friends, is a man who understands what it is to occupy the imagination of another. Take note of what young Alex has so quickly come to understand: The people who frequent a place such as this tavern have imaginations most easily occupied, for they are weak, are they not? Yes, all reducible simply to that, and so of course they strive to forget that weakness. If Mr. Barnaby were here, he'd charge each of you with the duty of briefly – only briefly – forcing your way into the imagination of your audience, for it is only briefly that you must. They themselves will offer up their thoughts once you've swayed them, their thoughts, and in time, as your influence becomes more than mere entertainment, they will offer their bodies and everything else they own as well. This is Mr. Barnaby's core teaching, this particular melody of strength and illusion.'

'Will we meet him soon?' asked Maudit, and again Alex cringed at the absence of melancholy in his voice. 'Now must be a time he wants to finally see us.'

'I'm afraid you will not,' said Emmanuel, turning his attention from Alex to Maudit, 'for he has chosen to stay on in Europe, this to continue our recruitment efforts.'

Richard and Maudit nodded in a way that suggested they'd heard this answer before, and all at once Alex understood that there was no Mr. Barnaby, Emmanuel had invented him, an authority that loomed always but could never be touched, not unlike the story of Miigwan and the Dutchman who became a bat that now lived in the damp darkness of a cave. Maybe he could convince Maudit to see through the deception, or maybe it was better to let the lie live on, he wasn't yet sure, but maybe it wouldn't matter either way, not now that he'd imparted to Maudit a contrivance of his own.

'Now,' Emmanuel continued, 'you must go and spread the word of a performance, and then you must rehearse. I suggest you give people a taste of your abilities at the St. Lawrence Market, and hurry, so you can catch the afternoon crowds.'

53

'TELL ME,' SAID ALEX, AS THEY DESCENDED THE HILL TO the market in the warm midday sun, 'Emmanuel permits you to enter his quarters each morning, non? To wait on him? To fulfil your duties?'

'Oui,' said Maudit. He cleared his throat and went to speak then wiped his mouth and took a breath. 'It's my job to bring his bathing water and other things besides, tu sais, taking down the items for our shows and making sure everything is clean. But Alex, this morning I've been thinking, and I wonder if we might tal—'

'I imagine it's nice, his room, non? It's fancy?'

On the walk over they'd sketched out the details of the little performance they'd offer, and in his excitement Richard had broken ahead of them and now reached the market gates, still wearing his black-eyed mask from the meeting and his billowing blouse pinned to his little frame by the grip of his suspenders. Beyond the gates the crowded market stalls rambled to the central building and down to the lakeshore, and barrels of tar burned here and there as they did all over town.

Though Maudit had dramatically torn his leather vest the day before, he hadn't yet thrown out the garment, and strips of it hung off his shoulders as tassels from the bit of a draft horse. 'Emmanuel has a beautiful room, it's true, I feel strange in it no matter how I often I visit, but listen, Alex, je m'excuse, but I wonder if we might talk about the necessity of leaving York, and what I want to ask you is if you are sure it's what Pouch insists we do.'

Alex had anticipated Maudit's uncertainty much as he'd anticipated Emmanuel calling on him during the meeting earlier that morning, for since their journey across Lake Huron he'd devoted the entirety of his waking moments to the luminous apparatus that circumstance was now helping him design, all his considerations pitched to the construction of its every shimmering detail, and the pleasure of this, the bursting purpose that had possessed him and enriched him and flushed out every other concern. 'I've heard her clearly,' he said, lingering such that Maudit's step faltered. 'She wants better for you, and for her. I'm sorry to say it, but she doesn't want to perform anymore. She doesn't enjoy it.'

Maudit's lips moved but he didn't speak, and his eyes were wide with credulity and concern. Alex strode ahead and led them through the market gates and they were surrounded by a din of English and German and French and Dutch, people hurrying in all directions through the acrid smoke from the barrels, some of them looking up at Maudit in surprise but most not taking the slightest notice. Though the sun had dried the mud of the streets, the market was still beset by a reeking sludge, and a man in a fine striped suit stood in the back of a hay-strewn wagon and held a tiny vial of liquid between his fingers, and merely a drop of this elixir, he told the crowd, could cure cholera in moments. In front of the wagon they saw Richard become flecked in filth as he danced and juggled wooden blocks and called out to passersby: 'It's a laugh ye crave, is it? A wind of joy to blow clear the fog of grief? Aye, sure enough it is!'

Alex and Maudit watched children point at Richard and laugh as the man selling the elixir broke off his blather and gestured to the clown with a permitting smile, and Maudit bent low to Alex's ear and said, 'But where will we go? And how? We haven't any money.'

Richard called for all to follow as he struck out deeper into the market, but the people had their own purposes to pursue and only Alex and Maudit took after him, walking slowly through the throng, the latter's eyes stuck on Richard and all around his mouth lingering the question just asked.

Alex took Maudit by the wrist and pulled until he bent low. 'We will buy land, the four of us. In the St. Lawrence Valley. Have you been, my friend? Have you seen? We will grow peaches and people will come from all around to buy them by the basket.'

Maudit seemed shocked. 'Buy land? Peaches? But how?'

'The things in Emmanuel's room, Maudit. And money. There must be a cache of money. Likely you've seen it and simply haven't understood what you're looking at. We'll take it. We'll take it all.'

'Mais comment ça? You heard him this morning. The troupe is in need. The Mitchells, they want a performance or they want money for the room and board.'

'He's lying,' said Alex simply, letting go of Maudit's wrist. 'He wants us to settle his debts for him, et tu l'sais.'

The market stank of fish and they passed a butcher in a bloody apron hanging a pig's head from a meathook, and Richard danced in circles, making his way up to the butcher's kiosk, still juggling his carvings, and he crouched until he was eye to eye with the pork all spun with flies, and hoarsely he shouted, 'Better luck next time, ye fat ole pig!' Above all this rose the central market building, atop which snapped a Union Jack, its shadow swooping across the grounds as though cast by a bird of prey.

Maudit's voice sounded with the same uncertain tone: 'Emmanuel isn't as bad as he seems. I don't want to steal from him. He's been kind to me. He freed me from labour and taught me to read.'

'Non,' said Alex. 'He's freed you from nothing. This is a man having his way with you. He uses you, if you don't mind me saying, and he uses Pouch. It's not possible to steal from someone like that. We'll just take what he owes, and he owes every one of us, don't you see?'

'But why do you feel this way when you've only just arrived?'

Alex felt a rush of anger rise to his face, but before he could respond, the butcher bellowed at Richard, and a group of women buying fish across the way giggled and pointed and clapped. Richard danced before them and announced that this weekend there'd be a show at The Cooper in His Barrel, and perhaps some of them were familiar with the establishment and had been privy to its mysteries before. One and all were invited to return, let not the woe of the day eclipse the joy of the night, and if night should bring more woe still, then at least there were entertainers to bandage the wound. He caught his whirling blocks one by one, and with a fluid gesture he directed his audience to Maudit and Alex, who he announced as The Strongman and The Aberration, and as discussed Maudit plucked Alex off his feet and held him aloft by his shoulders and his ankles as though he were reclining on a bed, and Alex lifted his shirt but didn't expose his fistula.

Richard cried out, 'Aye, but we shan't reveal all the secrets of our show right here and now. Suffice it to say, young Alex has a deformity bestowed during a vicious encounter with a shotgun-wielding bandit, aye, the literate among ye may have read about him in the newspapers, and see him now before you: he endures, alive and well, though he's experienced an anatomical change that we shall reveal two nights hence. All in attendance shall be thrilled and amazed!'

Richard juggled anew. Maudit lowered Alex to the level of his chest and the latter felt the hot, solid mass of the former before Maudit gently tipped him feet first to the muddy ground. People applauded, even the butcher, with his eyes red and glassy and the stubble of his cheeks streaked black and grey. The troupe turned now, led by Richard, and began to walk back up the gradient toward the entrance to the market.

'Maybe,' said Maudit, and he put one of his massive hands on Alex's shoulder, 'we're better off saving our money from performing. It will take longer, sans doute, but when we're ready, we can leave in peace.'

'Écoute. That will never happen. You understand, don't you? Emmanuel has arranged things so none of us will ever have enough money to leave. We'll always owe his Mr. Barnaby for our food and lodgings. Always.' Here he put his hand on Maudit's but not with affection, rather he swatted its gentle grip clean off his shoulder. 'How do you expect to commune with Pouch in such conditions? Maudit, I say again: she wants you to move on. She's right now filling my mind with the very thought.'

What they hadn't yet discussed was the likelihood of Emmanuel following them to Québec, hunting them through the farms of the

St. Lawrence Valley, a series of plots he'd know well, if that was truly where he'd been raised, and he'd creep up to their cabin one night and do them harm, for no one could amass what Emmanuel had amassed without taking a good deal from others, likely by force. And having taken it by force, would he ever release it without resorting to the same? Clearly, Emmanuel would have to be seriously injured, if not worse.

It was a strange thing to consider, the taking of a man's life. Alex felt a drag on his heart, as if he'd upset his maman; she would've never approved of such a measure, would've pointed to God and said that only He could take such action, as no man was righteous if he killed another. But his maman hadn't nearly died as he'd nearly died. She hadn't lived as he'd lived. She hadn't seen all that he'd seen and met all whom he'd met. True, she'd suffered, for there was no escaping at least some measure of fear and pain and loss, but she'd been shielded from life's most brutish and bloody cruelties, she'd been spared their unrelenting perpetuation. She had no idea the quotidian affronts to God, and she hadn't seen the way violenced men burst so easily apart, their fragility a suggestion of sorts – one that so convincingly countered their hubristic nature, it seemed divinely designed, a secret means, for those willing to seize it, of ridding bad men from the Earth. Death itself wasn't sad. Not really. It was just a thing that happened, like any other thing, and a person's soul simply carried on without their body, off to Heaven or Hell or somewhere in between. But for now there was nothing to gain by sharing this arithmetic with Maudit, not to its full extent.

'We'll have an opportunity to take what belongs to us the morning after the performance,' said Alex. 'Pouch has foreseen it. He will have money lying around, from the show and otherwise. There will be valuables and other things that belong to us. We'll take them and put them in my potato sack, and we'll leave while everyone is asleep.'

Maudit sighed and gestured at Alex with his chin. 'And you're sure she's in there? I saw only light at the beach. It was one of the most beautiful things I've ever seen, but that's not how she looked when she lived in Natalya, she was more of a suggestion in my thoughts, there was never any outward sign. How can you be sure it's her in your body and not some other soul? They're all over this town, are they not, and in the forests and everywhere else?'

The crowd had thinned out, and increasingly Richard began looking over his shoulder, peering at them through the holes of his mask and the blur of his juggled blocks, so with all the subtlety Alex could muster he responded, 'I'm sure. I felt her spirit enter me when we first got to the tavern, it came with images of the farm you told me about, the farmhouse. She was floating free, waiting for you. The light was mostly my brother's, but it was partially hers too. That's why it was so bright.'

Maudit's wide brow furrowed and he looked ahead at Richard as the clown turned onto Front Street and broke off his juggling. There were fewer people around now, and Alex reviewed their conversation and felt that he'd extracted a commitment from Maudit, however reluctant, and though the strongman now carried about him an anxious darkness, it wouldn't likely rouse suspicion, rather Emmanuel would confuse it with grief.

When they caught up to Richard, he'd lifted his mask into his hair and put his figures into the deep pockets of his trousers, and with his ruddy face peering upward at Maudit he said, 'Speaking quite a bit of the ole French, weren't ye, lads? But fear not.' He winked. 'I shan't inform the boss, I promise.'

54

THAT NIGHT, THE ROOM HOT AND HUMID, ALEX FEIGNED
sleep as he considered his options and listened to Richard snore and
Maudit shift from side to side, mumbling and sighing and clearing
his throat. The room stank of burning tar from a barrel on the street
corner, and Alex thought of all the sick people in their neighbourhood
homes, dying in their small and humid rooms while all around them
everyone else struggled to live. He went over his conversation with
Maudit at the market, evaluating all that had been said and how, looking for purchase wherever he could find it, and when he came across
a promising notion, he rose from his mattress and lowered himself
from the top bunk into the tiny space between Richard and Maudit.
Light from the moon crept through the window and dimly lit his bare
chest and the sheen of sweat on his neck and the fleshy covering of his
aperture. He kneeled and searched his potato sack of belongings hung
from the post of his bed, all this wordlessly as though a somnambulist,
and once he found his drawing paper and his lump of coal he spread
himself in a square of moonlight on the floor and began to work. As
expected Maudit sat up in bed and craned his wide shoulders out from
under the upper bunk, and he whispered a few questions at first, mais
qu'est-ce que tu fais, es-tu correct, dis donc, dis donc, but then, as the
picture took shape, he fell quiet.

Alex had to be careful to make sure he rendered Pouch as nondescript as possible, and this was more difficult than he'd anticipated. He
didn't even know the style of her hair, merely that she'd worn a shift
and removed it for Maudit in a barn in the United States of America,

a barn he'd never seen before, and the two of them had lain together in the hay. But he was determined, and so he summoned shadows, inky swirls of them, great wings of shading, and in this way he was able to avoid not just the contours of the barn but any distinguishing features of Pouch herself, rather he'd drawn a naked woman in Maudit's arms, her body concealed in darkness but for the rise of her shoulder, the small of her back, a length of her leg, and when it was finished he handed it to Maudit and returned to bed, silent all the while.

He watched as Maudit sat there staring at the drawing, the occasional tear sliding down his cheek and catching the moonlight as it fell to the floor, and he fell asleep to this sight, dreaming of what it might deliver when the sun rose over the tavern for another day. When the roosters of the neighbourhood crowed the dawn, Maudit was still sitting there, still staring at the drawing, his eyes red and wet.

'Why are ye sittin' there like that, b'y?' asked Richard, stretching and yawning and climbing out of bed in his yellowed underclothing, rubbing his tummy and loosing a belch. He shook his head and winced and pinched his nose and yawned. 'Bit dusty in here, turns out. Bit dusty indeed.'

'Leave him,' said Alex, who'd quickly righted himself and thrown his legs over the edge of the bunk such that he drove a heel into Richard's shoulder.

The clown glared up at him. 'Are ye making yerself familiar, then, young Alex?'

'You go get water from Mrs. Mitchell,' Alex said, looking the clown straight in the eye. 'Mr. Maudit, he want to clean his face.'

Richard pointed at Maudit and opened his mouth and seemed about to resist, but then he turned his head slowly between the two of them, first taking in the whole of the strongman's trembling shoulders and damp face, then turning back to Alex and seeming to ponder him, eyes moving from his face and down his neck and across his collarbone, then down to his wound. 'Aye,' he said, moving to the door. 'If it's water ye'd like, I'll go fetch some.'

He left the room and closed the door behind him, and Alex lowered himself from the top bunk, the floor creaking as his feet found purchase, and he stood in front of Maudit and extended one of his hands. 'What are you reading? Why are you sad?'

'Je lis pas,' said Maudit, licking his lips as he passed the drawing to Alex. 'And I don't believe I'm sad.'

Alex felt foolish, looking at this drawing, attempting what he was attempting, and he knew he should lift his face so that Maudit could see his features splashed with mild confusion but instead he ran a hand through his limp hair and kept his eyes on the drawing. 'Et c'est quoi, ça?'

'You drew it. Last night. You but not you.'

Alex managed to raise his face now and look into Maudit's utterly unquestioning eyes, and he couldn't help himself, couldn't keep the smile from playing across his lips, but it didn't matter now, he knew what to say, everything kept falling into place, everything kept fitting together, and how pretty it was to see it happening, how beautiful. 'Ah bon!' he exclaimed, grinning, and Maudit was also grinning, his cheeks shimmering in the soft morning light. 'Recall how I told you she showed me some of what she remembers. My brother does this sometimes too, these drawings. It's just a way they talk to us. Pouch, she just wants to tell you she loves you. She wants to say you'll be happier once we leave this place behind.'

Maudit stood and threw his arms around Alex and squeezed him close, lifting him off the floor, and all the muscles in Alex's back popped and strained and he couldn't draw a breath, as if the strongman were about to crush him, but then Maudit lowered him again and rested both hands on Alex's tiny shoulders. 'Incroyable,' he muttered, shaking his head. 'Absolument incroyable.'

'Écoute,' said Alex, placing the drawing on Maudit's mattress. 'There's one more thing we need to consider, nous deux, and it's just a little problem of Emmanuel following us.'

Maudit's smile barely faltered. 'Following us? Where?'

'Out of the tavern. Out of York. After we... after we find the things in his room, tu sais, the money and the valuables he owes us.'

'You think he will follow us?'

Alex tried to shrug but couldn't lift his shoulder under Maudit's heavy hands. 'I think he'll be angry and he won't understand that we're taking only things that are ours, so it could be that he'll follow us if you' – he raised his hands and settled them on Maudit's wrists – 'if you don't hurt him a little bit first, tu sais, just his legs, tu comprends, and just a little, c'est tout.'

Maudit stepped back heavily, his arms falling to his sides. 'Hurt Emmanuel?' For a terrifying moment it seemed as though all the progress of the morning had been lost in the lift of Maudit's eyebrows, and Alex cursed himself for being so clumsy in his persuasion, so fumbling, but then Maudit looked at the drawing on his bed and the tension drained out of his face and shoulders. He looked at Alex and tilted his head to the side and nodded. 'D'accord,' he said, still nodding, 'but only one of his legs, and only a little bit.'

55

THE TROUPE REHEARSED OVER THE NEXT TWO DAYS, AND then came the evening of the show. They spent the afternoon redecorating The Cooper in His Barrel with an array of items that came from the trunks Maudit hauled out of Emmanuel's quarters and down the stairs to the tavern. Among these were a great many paintings with frames of moulded copper painted gold, and they depicted lions and elephants and bears, each animal broken by a man with a whip and studded reins, and Maudit whispered that these were portraits of Emmanuel hard at work. There was also an oversized portrait of a glowering old man, his eyebrows grey and bushy and rising over the ridges of his sockets like a pair of thorny shrubs, and his jowls hung and his mouth was severe and he held one of his hands to his chin, where it rested pensively; that, said Maudit, was Mr. Barnaby.

It was obvious Maudit had never once doubted the existence of his patron, but that didn't much matter, there was nothing to be gained by changing his mind, not then and perhaps not ever, rather such a move could have unfurled a shroud of insecurity over the fantasies Alex himself had implanted in the soft tissues of Maudit's credulity, which would've been disastrous when those fantasies were evidently working so well, for though Maudit appeared nervous and awkward, his distress seemed appropriate given that this was his first performance without Natalya. Apart from that he went about his duties with a focus that Alex considered promising: in the morning, when the time came, Maudit would bring Emmanuel his bathing tub, and Alex would enter the room at the strongman's side, and together the two of them would fill Alex's potato sack with that which was rightfully theirs. Alex felt certain that Emmanuel's resistance would make clear the necessity of the horrid and unspeakable, and while this horrid, unspeakable necessity would no doubt disturb Maudit to his core, the ordeal wouldn't last long, and immediately after that they'd be off into the bright new morning, free to enjoy the new life Alex's 'tit frère had worked so hard to help create. For this Alex owed his little brother an eternal debt, at least part of which would be to care for Maudit in the aftermath of their scheme, because neither Alex nor his brother were elementally wicked souls, rather they yearned to be free of the greedy and the cruel and the oppressive, and they'd reward anyone who helped, no matter how unwittingly.

Mr. Mitchell poured lime all over the porch to reassure his clients that he'd taken precautions against disease, and Mrs. Mitchell hung black fabric in the windows and blocked out the evening's fading light, and now candelabras burned on most of the tables. She'd gone to the butcher and bought a side of beef for a pot of stew, and the tavern filled with its scent as Mr. Mitchell topped the lard lamps hanging from the second-floor joists, many of which he'd allowed to burn dry during the doldrums.

Their advertising endeavour at the St. Lawrence Market paid off, as a dozen people arrived in the early evening and the dinner bell clanged again and again. Mr. Mitchell brought two bowls to a table of bearded men, one of whom unfolded a napkin on his lap while the other wiped his mouth with his sleeve; he took up his spoon and dug into the stew as though excavating a ditch. Next to this table was a man in evening wear, a black cravat and a long coat, also black, and he held his wife's pale hand. Other than Mrs. Mitchell, she was the only woman in the tavern, and she and her husband exchanged a look both anxious and excited, and after a moment they stood up and resettled at another table, this one farther from the men and their stews, though before long there were few empty tables remaining.

As planned, Alex sat among the customers. The wife pointed at him and murmured to her husband: she'd seen him at the St. Lawrence Market earlier that week, and weren't these performers clever, he'd be a good one, she could already tell. Alex smiled inwardly. He had before him a dram of rum, his first since leaving Mackinac. The liquor burned a familiar passage down his throat, but unlike on Mackinac he wasn't possessed by an insatiable thirst for more, rather he drank only to blend in, for sobriety would be crucial over the course of the evening such that he could meet the morning with the fullness of his faculties, and anyway there'd be years of celebration to follow.

Within an hour there came from the top of the stairs a sorrowful melody bowed on a violin, and then Emmanuel entered the room, descending bare-chested, his skin taut and greasy and his tattoos gleaming: the teeth of the lions, the claws of the bear, the oily black length of the tightrope, and the bright red stripes with their bone-white counterparts. He wore a black top hat and played a fiddle stained brown as a horse's hide. His tune turned slow and strange, and he placed himself in the middle of the room, tapping his foot, glaring at the people eating and drinking. His audience variously stared or looked away, and the woman who'd pointed at Alex began to titter.

Emmanuel increased the tempo of his melody, and in a menacing voice he shouted, 'Enter the devil clown!' Now Richard came thumping down the stairs with speed enough to set the candles flickering all over the room. He'd carved a new mask for the occasion, one with red horns and a black spade beard beneath lips both puckered and pale, and the eyes were huge and bloodshot and pointing in opposite directions. He juggled and cackled and leapt onto a table where sat a man with tangled side whiskers, red as rust, who laughed and moved his beer and shook his head then stood and edged a few feet back from his table, not returning until Richard had leapt off again, still juggling. The devil clown danced around the bar for maybe ten minutes, his antics bordering on harassment, and when Mrs. Mitchell rang the dinner bell and her husband appeared carrying a bowl of stew, Richard approached him, throwing his blocks extra high, and in the protracted moment during which they were suspended, he rapidly dipped his finger in the stew and smeared it all over the lips of his mask, shouting, 'Too salty, my good man! Too salty by far!'

Now came Maudit's role in the performance, the slave-cum-hero wading into the fray so that he might rescue Mr. Mitchell's guests from the obnoxious doings of the devil clown. Emmanuel slowed his tempo now, producing a tumble of lower pitches as he shouted, 'Witness The Strongman!' Maudit's feet landed heavily on the stairs and Alex glanced at one of the paintings they'd hung earlier that day, an elephant with colourful blinders and its trunk hanging limply and the scar of a whip across its hide.

Meanwhile, Richard had shifted his attention to the husband and wife. He allowed his juggling blocks to tumble, freeing his hands so he could cup his crotch and thrust his hips. He hissed like a snake and howled like a wolf and the husband was spared the humiliation of failing to intervene, for Maudit arrived before his cowardice became fully apparent, plucking Richard off his feet as Emmanuel changed the tune again, now bowing a frantic run of notes that mimicked Richard's flailing limbs, and in an accent made thicker than usual Maudit cried out, 'My friends! See me as I cast this devil into blackest night! We are safe here now!' He hefted Richard over his head and held him aloft with the palm of one hand as he strode to the door of the tavern, which he opened with a light kick before tossing the devil clown over the threshold and into the dusk that stank of burning tar.

The audience applauded, a happy few, and the man with the side whiskers called for a pint of beer and some rum as well, and a group of labourers called out for more drink too, and be quick about it lest they perish of thirst. Mr. Mitchell took all this in and smiled, his patchy blond beard split by the flash of his teeth, and off he went to fill the orders.

Amid the smells of sweat and liquor and stewing meat, Emmanuel paused his playing to address the audience, thanking them for braving the spectre of cholera to behold Mr. Barnaby's Magical Spectacle of Marvels and Mystery. 'We have yet in store for you a great many marvels, though alas we're but lowly performers, paupers all, and we rely on your generosity to put food on our tables and roofs over our heads.' He doffed his hat and passed it to a man sitting near him. 'Please, if you'd be so kind, a donation so that we may continue to entertain you. The Strongman will demonstrate his remarkable abilities next, but first I beg of you to pass my hat among you, and worry not, for after The Strongman we have a very special medical marvel to show you, and I assure you that you'll not have seen anything like it before, no matter where you've travelled or what you've come across. Truly, our final performer will amaze you all. But first, let us pass the hat.'

He took up his bow again and played a gentle melody as the man to whom he'd given the hat produced a handful of coins and passed the request to his neighbours, the married couple again, and they made a donation as well. When all had taken the hat and made an offering, even the group of debauched labourers, Emmanuel introduced Maudit again, calling him a man-god from the darkest jungles of Africa, as peaceful as he was powerful, and Maudit now stepped into the centre of the tavern and grabbed his shirt and tore it off his body, throwing the shreds to the ground then bending gracefully at the waist, and again the woman tittered.

Alex watched as Maudit attempted to settle into his act. The Strongman stepped gingerly in the direction of his crates, the animal paintings looming above, and he opened one and removed from it what appeared to be a cannonball, but enormous, an object of well over a hundred pounds, according to Emmanuel, who shouted this over the song of his fiddle. And yet Maudit handled it with ease, at first gripping it with the palm of one hand, hefting it, then tossing it to the next and back again.

He approached the table of labourers now. These were men of muscled physiques, and with practised insouciance he offered the cannonball to the nearest one, who took it and even held it with one hand, but this man's face reddened and his back stooped and his balance crumbled. He snorted and seemed ready to let fall his burden, until Maudit plucked the weight from his charge. Relief washed over the man's blotchy face and he humbly took his seat while his friends jeered him and the fellow with the side whiskers hawked a mouthful of black tobacco all over the side of a spittoon, then raised his glass and hollered his joy.

Maudit walked to his crates and returned the cannonball and introduced a number of other objects, such as a ship's anchor and an anvil hammered in York by one of the town's innumerable blacksmiths. Throughout his performance he glanced at Alex and there was no mistaking his look of unsettled conspiracy. Silently, Alex urged him to collect his courage, lest his unease register to Emmanuel as something more than grief, the possibility of which concerned Alex greatly, for he understood that while some lives were studded with opportunity, his would be bereft of all but that which was under way, and Maudit's nerve was critical to his success.

The act now moved into its finale, which entailed Emmanuel standing on a chair and playing a few high notes as he looked to the audience. His gaze settled on one of the labourers and he called on the man to occupy another chair, and this drunken specimen in torn trousers took his seat in the centre of the room as Emmanuel played a busy tune. Maudit approached from behind, crouched, and placed his palms beneath the chairs. Then, still crouched, he raised them over his head. He stood to his full height, arms extended and bare chest out-thrust like a plate of armour. The labourer giggled and belched and began to kick his feet while Emmanuel played his tune and the husband and wife applauded.

All was going supremely well, but then Maudit tripped and stumbled and dropped the labourer, and the music broke off abruptly as the chair clattered to the floor. The labourer hadn't fallen from too great a height, and even though drunk he was nevertheless able to land on his feet. He wheeled around with his hands closing into fists, but in a moment of pale-faced clarity he let go the offence and returned to his friends, who snorted laughter.

Maudit then lowered Emmanuel to the ground, but clumsily, and the latter's face bulged with anger beneath the black brim of his hat and he appeared unable to speak. After a long pause, he doffed his hat and offered the audience an apologetic shrug. 'Gentlemen. My lady. Tonight, with our strongman performance, we've sought to show you something different. We've sought to remind you that no strength is unshakable, not even that which is housed in a body as savage as the one before you.'

The man with the side whiskers furrowed his brow, and Alex watched with quiet, conflicted relish, for here was a situation Emmanuel couldn't subdue, and this was perhaps a harbinger of his near future, though perhaps it threatened Alex's own enterprise in the degree of attention it conferred on Maudit. Regardless, all assembled heard the false ring of Emmanuel's words and Alex felt within himself an impulse to act. He rapped his knuckles on the table and whistled for Mr. Mitchell, and when the tavernkeeper turned to look he declaimed, 'Me, I will have some sausage.' He glanced at Emmanuel and could not suppress a slight grin. 'Parce que j'ai faim.'

Alex had hung his potato sack over the back of his chair and now he rummaged through its contents and produced his inkpot and a pen and a lump of coal and some drawing paper while Emmanuel regained himself and Maudit made his way to the staircase and slowly, thud-dingly, ascended. 'Ah,' said Emmanuel, donning his hat once more and circling Alex's table. 'But look who's been sitting among us. I wonder, has anyone ever heard tell of this man?'

It had been Alex's plan to sketch himself lying on the floor of the supply store in Mackinac, Beaumont hunkered over his fallen form and in the air above them a dark and ghostly swirl which, to Alex at least, signified his brother, and as he worked at this depiction, Emmanuel continued to circle, his fiddle pinched between his chin and shoulder, his melody slow and inquisitive: 'He's a medical marvel, this man. He was shot, you understand, by bandits while travelling the area of Lake Huron, and though he was lucky to have survived, the plain truth is his existence has been permanently altered by the incident, and in a manner most shocking. But what's he drawing? Let us observe for a time, shall we?'

The dinner bell rang and Mr. Mitchell appeared with several links of sausage arrayed across a cutting board. Emmanuel continued to circle the table, now fiddling away, and Alex took up a piece of meat and popped it in his mouth, chewing it lightly then swallowing. He maintained focus on his drawing, all the while working his insides in such a way as to direct the meat out of his stomach and up the canal of his fistula with enough force to push the flap of skin aside. For the first time he realized how truly impressive it was, his ability to exert control over a personal domain that would forever lay beyond the reach of most people – no, all people: the gift was his alone.

He lifted his chin and tilted his neck. He placed his lump of coal in the centre of the table and straightened his back, bringing his hand to his side as though a cramp were distracting him from his work. He grimaced and Emmanuel let off the fiddle while Alex reached beneath his shirt, straining, flinching, holding his breath and hunching over his drawing, and then abruptly he gasped and made himself relax; from under his shirt he removed his hand and between his thumb and forefinger he held up the slimy link of meat. The audience gasped and Emmanuel said, 'But look! He cannot hold sustenance in his body, for it escapes through the wound in his side before it can be absorbed!'

Alex studied the sausage, turning it this way and that, squinting at it in the yellow light of the lard lamps hanging above. There were barely a dozen people in the room, and perhaps a more seasoned performer would've been upset by the turnout, but Alex wasn't, he had everyone's full attention, he felt the intensity of their focus on his flesh like the heat of a fire. He exchanged his semi-digested meat for a new piece, which he tossed into his mouth, and again he picked up his lump of coal, shading some part of his fistula, and again he underwent the discomfort of pushing the food out of his body.

'But how can this be?' cried Emmanuel, fiddling evermore frantically. 'How can a man survive a situation so dedicated to his demise?'

Now the woman slapped her table hard enough to extinguish her candle and knock it over, though her husband managed to catch it before it fell to the ground, and she cried out, 'But what is going on beneath his shirt?'

Perhaps she was a little drunk, certainly unabashed, and Alex felt a surge of pride that he could compel that sort of outburst from another person. He again held his meat before him, examining it this way and that, and feigning exasperation he swallowed without bothering to chew, straining to push the meat out of his fistula, and again he reached under his shirt and now one of the labourers hoarsely shouted, 'Show us what's under his clothes! And no tricks, you hear?'

Alex stopped the meat just short of exiting his side. He stood from the table, nervous, as he'd known he'd be, but it wasn't the sort of anxiety he'd felt many times before, rather it was the result of an altogether different sort of attention: fascination, pure and simple. He'd planned to hand out his drawing first, but he now saw that part of his performance as utterly superfluous. It would only delay the revelation of the real thing, and anyway such a sight had no need of a representation by which to remember it, for it would live forever in the imagination of anyone who saw it, and he as well.

Emmanuel let off his fiddling. With both hands Alex pulled up his shirt, angling his chest to every corner of the room so that all could see as he pushed the piece of meat up through the final inches of his canal. People gasped as the little flap of flesh that covered his aperture began to shift and there was a foul smell as it permitted the passage of the meat, which clung to one of Alex's ribs before falling heavily to the floor. He'd intended now to bathe them in his brother's bliss-inspiring light, but no illumination came from within, none whatsoever, rather the flickering lanterns threw angular shadows across the shocked faces of the audience, and Alex could only stand there with his shirt wrenched up and his disfigurement in plain sight.

At first no one spoke, not even Emmanuel. The tavern was quiet but for the creaking of wood as Maudit moved about the second floor, no doubt pacing through his trepidation for the morning to come, his steps landing heavily enough to rattle the lard lamps.

Then came a shift in the room's energy. The audience was rapt, every one of them, no one looked away, and yet there was a contempt to their attention. It formed slowly, indecisively, as if it wasn't yet sure precisely what it wanted to be. Then one of the labourers swore in disgust, and as soon as he did, the woman whispered, 'Oh my God,' and her husband said, 'There, there, look away, you'll dream of it,' and the man with the side whiskers called for another glass of beer, but he wasn't rejoicing, rather he was the type who drank heavily when the horrific couldn't otherwise be understood.

Emmanuel began closing the show, but Alex couldn't focus on what he was saying; regret overtook him in waves. He couldn't understand why his brother had left him vulnerable at such a critical juncture, and it also occurred to him that he could've revealed his condition to an entirely different group of people in an entirely different context, this one back in Michigan, and whereas once it had seemed outrageous to follow Beaumont to Detroit and allow the doctor to parade him about in front of an audience of high-minded men, now, as stunned applause rang out in the tavern, there seemed in that lost option a sort of dignity, mute perhaps, but present nevertheless.

56

ALEX LAY AWAKE THROUGHOUT THE NIGHT, AND THOUGH HE knew Maudit did as well he made no effort to communicate with him, rather they both kept their silence beneath the stumbling roar of Richard's inebriated snoring. 'The judgment of others comes seldom with the verdict for which a person might hope,' Emmanuel had said to him after the performance, the two of them sitting across from Richard and watching the clown guzzle rum while Maudit brought all the crates back upstairs. 'A new performer needs time to grapple with all that this might mean.'

And grapple he did, even though he knew his energy would be better spent preparing himself and Maudit for the morning to come. He lay in bed with his shirt off, his fistula starkly vile in the pale moonlight, and he ran his fingers along the network of scars that surrounded it, a tapestry of the grotesque so repellent that he brought his hand to his chin instead, hoping to feel something more natural, but there ranged a boyish and wiry scruff that spilled down his neck greasy and soft and was passably thick only across his upper lip – for he was a boy still, wasn't he, even after all this. The audience had looked upon him as exactly that: a hideously scarred little boy, captivating, yes, but as a battlefield, not a sunset. He felt them looking still, gawking in the theatres of their minds, giddy with disgust as they lay in their beds and remembered all that he'd shown them just a few short hours before.

No doubt Maudit saw this boyishness too. This weakness. He saw it and perhaps wavered in his commitment to their plan, for Alex may have been host to the spirit of Maudit's lover, but was his earthly vessel strong enough to remain so in perpetuity? Or could Maudit risk entertaining such doubts? Would he not have to simply push them aside and go through with their plan, no matter his reluctance? Alex remembered the look on Maudit's face when he'd bathed it in his brother's light, he remembered the devotion and serenity, the grief turning to hope. When the situation in Emmanuel's room intensified as only it could, Maudit would have little choice but to do as instructed, lest his grief return. And what would it matter, come then, if he managed to recognize Alex's ugly aperture as home to his little brother alone? Surely he'd also understand that they'd gone too far to change course, that Pouch's spirit was out there somewhere and his duty now was to survive long enough to find her again. Anyway, the critical task wasn't so far beyond the horrors he'd already experienced. It was different, no doubt, to cause a man's death than to witness it or even to stand aside and let it run its course, but Maudit had only to commit himself to a few minutes of brutality, after which he could retire in succour. How Alex wished he himself were in command of such brute strength, because with it he'd have set out into his future alone and long ago, but naturally he was weak and disgusting and frail, and that would never change.

In time the moonlight vanished and the night's darkest grip took hold of the tavern, and not long after that the blue light of day leaked through the window and was shortly followed by the first of the morning's hesitant sun, which fell on the lumpy mattresses and beaten floor. Though Maudit had tossed from side to side all night, he fell suddenly still, and Alex looked down from his bunk and saw his accomplice curled into an enormous ball, his back to the room and his head concealed beyond the mount of his branded shoulder.

'Allez,' said Alex, sitting up, his shoulders near his ears as he gripped the frame of the bed. 'It's time. Go and get water for Emmanuel.'

Maudit turned, lowering his shoulder and revealing his face, a mask of despair at which Alex only nodded, his own features set in a determination he hoped to transmit throughout the room. He thought about shining his brother's light onto Maudit's bunk but worried it would fail him as it did the night before, for perhaps he'd tired his brother out with all this scheming, and it was now up to Alex himself to conclude the final steps of his plan, Alex au complet, and why not, for his resolve now seemed to emanate throughout the room and fill Maudit's frame: the strongman climbed out of bed, scraping his back against the upper bunk and knocking the whole of the structure against the wall, but as though oblivious he donned his vest and stepped into his trousers, casting his worried eyes everywhere about their tiny confines but Alex's face.

'Remember,' said Alex. 'Only his leg, and only a little. In an hour we'll be free.'

Maudit gripped his jaw between the massive expanse of his thumb and forefinger, then issued a curt nod and opened the door and stepped into the hall. It seemed to take him an eternity to prepare the water, and as Alex listened to Richard snore he imagined all the steps Maudit had to undertake: building the fire in the wood stove and lighting it with a long match and setting the stockpots on the surface, then filling the dented steel tub with cold water before turning back to the stove and standing there with a tight little frown as he watched the bubbles find their increasingly frantic way to the surface, and now pouring the hot water in with the cool, the clang of the empty pots as he set them back on the stove, all the long while the blade of Mrs. Mitchell's knife repeatedly striking a butcher's block as she chopped potatoes for hash, and then, finally, Maudit heaving the tub into his arms and moving through the scullery and across the tavern and up the stairs, careful not to make the water slop. This all seemed like a dream until Alex did in fact hear the stairs straining under Maudit's weight, and he gulped a deep breath and lowered himself from the bed and then took his potato sack from the bedpost and emptied all that it held onto the floor, all his pens and his inkpot and his drawings and his clothing and peach stones and coal, and only the stones did he return to the sack, the other items he could replace. Then he put on his shirt and took his boots from under the bed and stepped into them and laced them tight, and all throughout these ministrations Richard lay on his mattress face up, snoring, spittle cascading down the side of his puffy white face, his pillow soaked with it, and Alex noticed for the first time that Richard had freckles on his cheeks like blooms. When the hallway creaked as Maudit passed their room, Alex threw the sack over his shoulder and stepped across his old possessions and entered the hall, which smelled of cooking lard from the scullery downstairs, and he followed Maudit to Emmanuel's room and waited for yet another eternity as the strongman bent over and set down the tub and then slowly rose to his full height again, hesitating before finally raising one of his great fists slightly above his head, holding it there for a moment, and then knocking on the door. His knuckles rapped twice against the wood, the sound so loud Alex jerked both times, biting his tongue the second.

'Entre,' said Emmanuel from behind the door, voice brimming with lazy confidence.

Maudit opened the door and stepped into the room, turning to retrieve his load, and Alex lunged past him, tripping over the tub and sending water splashing onto the floor as he stumbled across the threshold and was for a moment struck by the absurd opulence of Emmanuel's quarters: the shelves of leather-bound books lining the walls and the sabre with a golden hilt hanging over the bed, the shiny bearskin on the floor in front of a mahogany nightstand draped in colourful kerchiefs and crowned by a kingly lamp of tinted glass. The window was hung with curtains of white lace, the morning's weakening sun shining on a bed wide enough for two people, non, three, and it was covered in crimson sheets and upon it was Emmanuel sitting upright with a book open in his lap and the sheets rolled down to his waist, his hair mussed and his bare, tattooed chest rising and falling as a look of frustrated astonishment curved across his face.

'But what is the mean—'

'L'argent, connard!' screamed Alex, panting. 'C'est où?'

Emmanuel blinked and glanced down into the pages of his book, almost as though he were finishing a paragraph, then he snapped the covers together and placed the volume on his nightstand, and the muscles in his chest and arms were taut as he threw back the covers and rose from his bed wearing only a pair of jet-black short pants. 'It seems you've been pushed into a bout of madness by the outcome of your performance last night.' His voice was calm, almost amused, he didn't sound surprised but rather mildly bothered, as if this were a tedium he had to endure, and he rounded the bed and stood before Alex, hands on his hips as he lifted his chin. 'You're still on the safe side of my understanding, Alex. Turn around and return to your bed. Lie down for a while and come speak to me later. We'll talk about this.'

'Non,' said Alex. 'I want to kn—'

Emmanuel slapped him, just as he had on the boat, his hand a blur between them and his lips tightening as a single furrow rippled across his brow. Without thinking Alex clenched his fist and pulled it back and swung it hard into Emmanuel's jaw. There was a pop and a gasp and a sting and Alex's knuckles went numb but still he took a step forward and made fists now of both hands and threw them with abandon.

The sounds.

The sensations.

He couldn't tell which were which or where they were coming from. He felt only the thrill of harming another person, a hated person, the swinging pleasure of skin broken against bone and the look on Emmanuel's face as it spun off his knuckles: the shock in his eyes and the tiny globe of bloodied spit moving in an arc from his lower lip, the way his hands flew up like frightened little birds then shot out to his sides as his balance gave way. He stumbled backward, tripping over the corner of his absurdly large bed, his footing gone and his back slamming into the nightstand. The lamp wobbled and crashed to the floor, the glass exploding and small specks of it hanging in the air, catching the sickly morning sun as it seeped through the window.

'L'argent!' Alex shouted again, swinging his head from side to side. 'C'est où?' He turned from Emmanuel and saw Maudit standing there in the doorway, frozen, and then he saw his potato sack rumpled on the floor in front of the tub, and as he bent to retrieve it he felt a hand on his shoulder, fingers gripping his flesh like the talons of a hawk, now spinning him around, and Emmanuel loomed with blood smeared across his chin and a bruise forming on his cheek. His voice was still eerily quiet and despite the abandon of the moment he spoke

English: 'What in God's name are you thinking?' He punched Alex in the nose and Alex's head snapped back and he felt his knees give way as he collapsed into one of the bookshelves, his legs splayed open and his eyes stinging. He moved to right himself but Emmanuel crouched and with one hand grabbed him by the scruff of his shirt and with the other began to slap him, both sides of his face, repeatedly, a smell coming off him thick and pungent, the blows sending Alex's head around his neck like a flag around a pole.

Emmanuel grabbed Alex's shirt with both hands and ripped it almost entirely in half, revealing the ribs and the scars and the wound, his face still relatively unbothered, just a slight twitching of the cheek, a single breath heavily expelled. He drew one of his hands over his shoulder and speared it forward again, jabbing two rigid fingers into Alex's fistula, shoving the little flap of flesh that covered it into the canal and twisting his fingers, spreading them, pinching the purpled lip of the aperture with his thumb and yanking downward as though trying to tear it wider. The pain was more extreme than any Beaumont had ever caused, and sweat streamed down Alex's ribs and a torrent of bile surged up his throat and foamed out his mouth and then another surge of it sprayed out of his fistula and soaked Emmanuel's chest, causing him to yank his hands away and gag and curse and punch Alex in the mouth hard enough to drive his front teeth deep into the flesh of his lip such that his tongue was awash in the taste of copper coins. Emmanuel stood and backed away, shaking drops of blood and bile off his hands and looking down at his spattered chest in revulsion.

Alex coughed and looked at Maudit, who stood there by the bathing tub, his head lowered as if he were watching something peculiar floating on the surface. 'Notr'affaire, Maudit.' It was hard to speak around the ragged swelling of his lips and the gouts of blood that slid out of his mouth. 'N'oublie pas notr'affaire.'

'What's this fool babbling about?' asked Emmanuel, wiping his chest with a towel, astonished.

'J'vais la bannir!' Alex shrieked, the tendons in his neck like the ropes of a sail. 'J't'l'jure!'

Emmanuel threw the towel over Alex's face. 'Maudit.'

Alex swatted the towel off his head and saw the strongman shrink away, his lip trembling.

'Maudit. What's he talking about?'

'I send her *out!*'

Emmanuel turned back to Alex, regarding him from what seemed like a great height. 'What're you talking about, you revolting little creature? What is it you've been planning?' He walked back over to the nightstand and opened a drawer and cleared his throat and withdrew a knife, the blade six inches long and curved like a crescent moon. 'I'll only ask you so many times.' His feet landed heavily as he returned to Alex's crumpled form. 'What is it you think you know about my money?'

Alex felt his bravery plunge through his stomach as Emmanuel crouched and gripped his shoulder and brought the blade firmly against his cheek, grey eyes moving curiously across his face. 'What is it you think you know?' He moved the blade from Alex's face to his throat and traced it from one side to the other, then settled in the middle, applying a touch of force so light that it frightened in its restraint. 'What is it you've come here to find?'

'Maudit!' Alex gasped. 'Viens! If I die I take her with me!'

Alex's flesh gave way beneath the blade and blood seeped warmly out of the wound and down his clavicle and into the sodden mess of his shirt all shredded across his chest, and he realized then that he'd miscalculated, that Maudit was too scared to intervene, too accustomed to life as it had been, and Alex would die here, finally, pressed against this bookcase, his face swollen and bloodied, his throat slick and gaping.

But then the pressure of the knife was gone and Emmanuel seemed to be sucked upward and backward, his face clenched with surprise as Maudit jerked him to his feet and spun him around, taking both his wrists in one giant hand and yanking Emmanuel's arms straight over his head such that his bare toes scurried across the floor, forward and back, forward and back. The knife fell from his grip and splashed into the tub and Maudit's hold faltered not at all as Emmanuel flexed his biceps and lifted himself so that he was parallel with Maudit's face, and he spat in Maudit's eyes and kicked his thighs and groin and even his stomach and even his chest. Maudit finally responded by swinging Emmanuel into the door jamb, once and then again, and Emmanuel went slack at the elbows and hung loose in the vise of Maudit's palm, swinging from side to side like a man hanged.

'Imbecile,' he gasped, his voice finally stripped of its composure. 'Do you know what I will do to you? If you don't release me at once?'

Alex spat blood onto the floor. 'Tu vois?' His lips had swollen against his teeth and it was hard to talk around the pulpy mass of them but still he felt the situation returning to his control. 'He will kill me now, tu comprends, if you release him? He will kill us both. And I won't let her go if that happens. I'll bring her with me even if I'm sent to Hell.'

An umbrage fell over Maudit then. His face drained of all light as deep trenches appeared in his forehead, and his eyes narrowed with what could only be recognition. He shifted Emmanuel this way and that, examining him before looking again at Alex, holding his gaze then quickly turning away, dropping his eyes once again to the tub.

'Just hold him for now,' said Alex. 'You can't put him down anymore. It's too late.'

His back hurt. His head and his chest and his wound, as if he'd been shot all over again, but this time with no one to save him. The shreds of his shirt hung to his waist, soaked through with blood. He could only see through one eye and he looked around the room and his skull pounded along with his heartbeat. It was a small room. There weren't many places to hide a cache of money. He looked under the bed, saw only dust. He walked across the room, glass crunching under his feet. He looked in the closet and saw a bag, it was leather, a copper clasp, it sat next to a rifle leaning against the corner, and Alex's gaze lingered on the weapon. Surely Emmanuel regretted not fetching it at the outset of their conflict, mais tant pis, such were the consequences of arrogance. Alex crouched and opened the bag and inside there were bundles of money, just as he suspected, a stupendous sum, more than he'd ever seen, and he laughed despite the pain in his mouth and for a moment that was the only sound he heard, as if he were now alone in the world, laughing.

Then he picked up the bag and turned back to the doorway, searching for his potato sack, and unfortunately Maudit and Emmanuel were still there, and the look on Emmanuel's face was furious, he was exhaling in gales, his lips wet with blood and saliva. 'Let me go,' he kept saying, 'after all I've done for you, let me go.'

'He will follow,' said Alex, and he tried to spit on the bed but just issued a clot of red mucus that slid down his chin. 'Wherever we go, he will follow. And you know what he'll to do us, and you know what that means for Pouch.'

'Let me go,' Emmanuel sputtered, and his voice was desperate now, uncanny in its mounting fear. 'You castrated bull. You self-forgotten chattel.'

Alex bent forward and retrieved his potato sack from the ground, felt the familiar weight of his peach stones as he sighed and sat on the bed and hung his head. The building was strangely quiet. There were only the sounds of Emmanuel's futile struggle, which Alex tried to ignore as he overturned the leather bag in his potato sack and felt the latter grow heavy with treasure. 'He'll follow us,' he said again, feeling as though he could lie back and drift off to sleep, but he had to look at Maudit and maintain eye contact at this critical juncture, for now he had to suggest a different sort of promise, not one of lost lovers found again but dire penalties evaded in the end, and he had to look at Maudit for the long moment it took this idea to fully take hold, after which he could avert his gaze forever.

There passed a second or maybe a minute, impossible to tell, and then Maudit made a tiny little sound of acquiescence and lowered Emmanuel trembling to the soles of his feet, releasing his wrists and letting him fall forward as though into an embrace. He settled a hand slackly on Emmanuel's shoulder and gently pushed him back into the door jamb before inching the hand across his clavicle toward his throat. All the while, Maudit's other arm simply hung at his side, and Alex realized it had been that way throughout the ordeal, unmoving, as if it occupied some other place.

Emmanuel made a fist and struck the heel of it into the side of Maudit's head, once, twice, and then again and again in a slow but steady rhythm, saliva bubbling in the corner of his mouth. Maudit allowed these blows as he engulfed Emmanuel's throat in his hand and began to squeeze, and it was clear when he finally committed his full strength to the endeavour, because Emmanuel jerked upright and broke off his assault and gripped Maudit's wrist with both hands, fingers blanching. He spat out a rope of foamy red saliva and made a wheezing sound and let go of Maudit's wrists to unleash another breeze of blows against the side of the strongman's head.

'C'est ça,' said Alex. 'Continue.' The sight of Emmanuel's bulging face disturbed him, so he looked beyond Maudit, farther into the hall, where he saw Richard in the doorway to their room, watching, and Alex nodded at him and he nodded in return then slipped away, down the hall and down the stairs, and all that could be heard was the thumping of Emmanuel's feet and the strained sound of his suffocation. Then this stopped as well, but Maudit continued to squeeze, until finally there was the smell of shit and piss and Maudit lowered Emmanuel's soiled body to the ground and tried to prop him upright in the door frame, but with a degrading splash he slid off the jamb and crumpled to the floor. Maudit looked down at this display and crouched as if he were about to set Emmanuel upright in the doorway, but instead he gripped the side of the tub and vomited into the water.

Alex stood from the bed. He felt light. He felt numb. He checked his hand to make sure he still had the potato sack, he did, and he looked around Emmanuel's room to make sure that was indeed where he was standing, it was, and he walked around the bed and opened the drawer of the nightstand and took whatever he found and put it in his potato sack: a timepiece, a locket, some gold coins. Then he walked toward Maudit and glanced down at Emmanuel, his neck covered in bruises, his face tinted blue and his eyes like glistening marbles, high in their sockets. Alex reached down and put his hand on Maudit's back, hoping to lend a comforting weight, but Maudit only hung his head over the edge of the tub and vomited again.

'On devrait aller,' Alex tried to say through the bloody ruin of his mouth. He let go of Maudit and stepped into the long, silent hall and waited. He listened to Maudit cough and gasp and spit, and he took another step down the hall, and then another. He felt he could leave Maudit behind, simply walk to the top of the stairs and make his way down, leave the tavern through the back door and be free, finally free. But he owed Maudit something of the aftermath he'd promised. He could continue to pretend the spirit of Pouch lived inside him, and in this way Maudit would find some semblance of happiness, so he stopped walking and leaned against the wall and waited, staring at the potato sack dangling way down there by his knee.

A few minutes passed. The hallway stank of shit. Maudit lifted his head and dabbed his eyes with the great balls of his wrists. Alex stepped toward him and patted his back again, a silly gesture, he knew it, and he tried to say that it was time for them to go, they'd done their hard work, they'd succeeded, their future was theirs, they should leave the tavern, leave York and return to Québec, where no one would own them ever again. He tried to say this but knew his words were unintelligible and knew as well that it didn't matter what he said anymore, the time for that had passed.

Maudit lifted his head and gripped the door jamb and pulled himself to his feet and sniffed and wiped his mouth with his wrist. The floor groaned under his weight as the two of them walked down the hall and down the stairs. In the tavern they saw Mr. and Mrs. Mitchell behind some tables, the former with his face pale as he stood in front of his wife, rifle across his chest, and Alex stared at them and nodded but they didn't nod back, and as Alex passed he noticed a look of revulsion in the tavernkeepers' eyes and remembered his performance the night before. He touched his side, felt his swollen wound beneath his shirt, and when they got to the scullery he heard Richard call out. He turned and saw the clown standing in the middle of the tavern, unarmed, no sign of his usual cocksure countenance, rather he was frightened, cut loose, and he said, 'Lads, I beg of ye, can ye not see yer way to leaving me a parting gift? I've nothing, ye know. Emmanuel was a bad man, I know it, but without him, I've got not a thing to me name, nothing at all.'

Richard posed no threat and Alex owed him no debt, instead saw him as the sort of person eager to endear himself to whomever loomed largest. Turning away, Alex stepped toward the back door and a moment later Maudit followed, what else could he do?

Outside the sky was cloudy and the weather was humid. It would rain soon. It would rain and the streets of York would turn once again to mud. Best they be off before that happened. They had a long road ahead of them, and the sky would soon grow dark.

ÉMANCIPATION

The years that followed

THEY BOUGHT THEIR LAND ALONG THE ST. LAWRENCE AND began their peach orchard with the two stones Alex had kept safe in the bottom of his sack as they made their cautious way from York; the one he'd stuffed into his fistula still hadn't come out, or maybe it had and he'd missed it. But it didn't matter. They started the trees inside the farmhouse Maudit built, bringing them outdoors during the summer and keeping them warm indoors throughout the winter, and after three years, they were ready to be transplanted outside, this work largely undertaken by Maudit, though Alex did occasionally take up a shovel or fetch water from the river. The two endured an anxious season while they waited for the trees to recover and bear fruit the following summer, and the winter was passed in further anxiety that sometimes tipped into hope, but the months were horrifically cold and snowy, and by the time spring came around, the tree trunks were marred with deep gashes, and their branches bore only struggling buds and certainly no fruit. It was clear to Alex, who stood before the ruins in the biting slush of early April, that the seeds he'd gotten from Pierre were of the worst quality, one final blow dealt from a past he drank regularly to forget, and he consoled himself that at least he still had the land. He knew by then that his papa would never return, and he knew that his 'tit frère had left him too, had even deserted his dreams, leaving him to a nightmare realm overseen by furious incarnations of murdered Emmanuel, but that was all right, there was nothing he could do about it, at least he had the land for himself. He'd endured a great many bruises, but in the end, he'd become a man in the fullness few thought he'd ever achieve.

Throughout these years, Maudit's strength was inexhaustible, and it was he who made their money while Alex sloped into a pattern of daily drinking and constant forgetting. Their farm was outside Montréal, and Maudit spent weekdays in the city working at the port and then came home and looked in on Alex to make sure there was sufficient food before striking out again.

It was lonely, working the port, even though he was surrounded by people every day. For the most part, they treated one another differently than him, and he watched them form bonds and laugh and sweat, and after a long day they'd head for a tavern and he to his lodgings alone. He was a glorified field hand to most of them, nothing more. Some were harsher about it than others, but the whites were wary to the last.

At the farm things were different, but not in the way he believed before they robbed Emmanuel. Rather, Alex, in the darkness of his stupors, followed Maudit around the property, a curious look on his face, and after a time he'd disappear to his room, where he spent long hours drawing, and sometimes he danced around the orchard and seemed full of joy but was actually full of rum, and the next morning he circled the dying trees with a pensive scowl. Other times he tried to swim, insisting he'd been taught, but he thrashed in the water, unable to keep himself afloat, and more than once Maudit had to leap in to rescue him from drowning.

Whether working the port or staying with Alex on the farm, Maudit was haunted by nightmares of what he'd done to Emmanuel, and he several times thought he saw his old master's spirit moving through the woods around the farm. He woke in the middle of most every night, his mattress soaked through with sweat, his soul smothered in grief and guilt and a shrieking remorse he'd never be able to express, not to anyone, or he'd be hanged for his crime.

During the first year, when the peach orchard still seemed a possibility, Alex sat with Maudit and purported to be channelling the spirit of Pouch, and though no light came from the wound, Alex said this didn't matter, that Pouch had taken up lodging in his head instead, but Maudit recognized this for the charade it was. He remembered too clearly the look on Alex's face as the situation in Emmanuel's room lurched out of control, remembered too clearly the terrible, bellowing arrival of belated comprehension: On the beach, Alex had managed to refashion a common sunset into a divine, ethereal light. Then he managed to make a nondescript drawing seem like a communication from beyond. Bit by bit, he led Maudit to a transgression so severe that it now seemed unlikely Pouch would ever want to commune with him again. If she no longer desired his company, he only hoped she'd found her way home, back across the ocean. He didn't want her to be alone. These thoughts churned and churned as the days grew large and then passed with a solitude that seemed increasingly final.

Maudit worked hard to feel some other sensation, to find some other focus, and while there was no longer any one thing that filled him with rapture, he found that after the passage of many months, there were sometimes enough little things to keep him quietly satisfied; the trick was thinking about them as often as he could. When he heard from another black port worker that black cherry trees did well in the climate and that locals liked to use the fruits in their pies, he bought first some dwarf trees and then some larger ones, a change to their operations Alex didn't even notice, so oblivious to all things had he become.

They'd had the farm for ten years and Maudit no longer had to work the port when he awoke one morning and couldn't find Alex anywhere. He looked about the house and out the window onto the orchard, but there was no sign of him, and so he went about his morning duties. When he walked to the river for his afternoon swim, he found Alex's body floating face down in the shallows, his long hair spread out like the crown of a tree. He'd fallen in, obviously drunk, and that was it. After everything, that was all.

Maudit took Alex's body into the farmhouse, stripped him naked, and cleaned him. He'd fouled himself in the moment of death, and as Maudit cleaned the mess, he came across a peach stone, the grooves of its furrowed shell misshapen and worn. He considered planting it, but only briefly, and instead he threw it in the river. It was welcome to find purchase elsewhere, if it could.

He buried Alex in the orchard and his feelings were a strange mix of sadness and satisfaction. He tried hard not to hold a grudge against Alex's spirit and this became easier and easier as the weeks went on, mainly because he saw no signs of it anywhere. The cherry trees now bore fruit in abundance, and the orchard was his. People bought his harvests with quiet contempt, but that didn't bother him, not much, and on warm summer days, when his work was done, he walked between his dozens of healthy trees toward the river, where he spent the rest of the day swimming.